Praise for

Boogaloo on 2nd Avenue

"Kurlansky is so clearly in control—and so clearly enjoying himself."
—*The New York Times Book Review*

"Funky and entertaining."—*Publishers Weekly*

"An addictive read . . . smart, funny, formidable . . . Let's hope that
Kurlansky has more deep-dish fiction on the way."
—*Los Angeles Times Book Review*

"A definitive portrait of an era."—*Kirkus Reviews*

"Teems with life from the first page . . . vivid and crackling with wit."
—*BookPage*

"Fantastically written . . . captures something lost and
shows us something eternal."—*Jewsweek*

"A dazzling portrait of a man, a time and a place. . . . Brilliantly recaptures
the hustle and bustle of the Lower East Side in the 1980s."
—*The Atlanta Journal-Constitution*

"Unusually well-stuffed."—Cleveland *Plain Dealer*

"Kurlansky has an excellent feel for time and place . . .
a talented novelist."—*Time Out*

Boogaloo on 2nd Avenue

Boogaloo on 2nd Avenue

A Novel of Pastry, Guilt, and Music

MARK KURLANSKY

RANDOM HOUSE TRADE PAPERBACKS

NEW YORK

2006 Random House Trade Paperback Edition

Copyright © 2005 by Mark Kurlansky

All rights reserved.

Published in the United States by Random House Trade Paperbacks,
an imprint of The Random House Publishing Group,
a division of Random House, Inc., New York.

RANDOM HOUSE TRADE PAPERBACKS and colophon are trademarks
of Random House, Inc.

Originally published in hardcover in the United States by Ballantine Books,
an imprint of The Random House Publishing Group,
a division of Random House, Inc., 2005.

Interior illustrations by the author

Grateful acknowledgment is made to the following for permission to reprint
previously published material:

IRVING BERLIN MUSIC COMPANY: Excerpt from "Anybody Can Write" by Irving
Berlin, copyright © 1956 by Irving Berlin, copyright renewed. Excerpt from
"(Castles in Spain) On a Roof in Manhattan" by Irving Berlin, copyright © 1931
by Irving Berlin, Inc., copyright renewed. Excerpt from "Cohen Owes Me
Ninety-Seven Dollars" by Irving Berlin, copyright © 1915 by Waterson, Berlin &
Snyder Co., copyright renewed and assigned to Irving Berlin. Excerpt from
"If That's Your Idea of a Wonderful Time (Take Me Home)" by Irving Berlin,
copyright © 1914 by Waterson, Berlin & Snyder Co., copyright renewed and
assigned to Irving Berlin. Excerpt from "If You Don't Want My Peaches (You'd
Better Stop Shaking My Tree)" by Irving Berlin, copyright © 1914 by Waterson,
Berlin & Snyder Co., copyright renewed and assigned to Irving Berlin. Excerpt
from "I'm Going on a Long Vacation" by Irving Berlin, copyright © 1910 by Ted
Snyder Co., copyright renewed and assigned to Irving Berlin. Excerpt from "My
Wife's Gone to the Country (Hurrah! Hurrah!)" by Irving Berlin, copyright ©
1909 by Ted Snyder Co., copyright renewed and assigned to Irving Berlin. Excerpt
from "Sadie Salomé (Go Home)" by Irving Berlin, copyright © 1909 by Ted Snyder
Co., copyright renewed and assigned to Irving Berlin. International copyright
secured. All rights reserved. Reprinted by permission of Irving Berlin Music
Company, administered by Williamson Music, a division of The Rodgers &
Hammerstein Organization.

WARNER BROS. PUBLICATIONS U.S. INC: Excerpt from "Shall We Dance" by George
Gershwin and Ira Gershwin, copyright © 1937 (renewed) by George Gershwin
Music and Ira Gershwin Music. All rights on behalf of George Gershwin
Music and Ira Gershwin Music. Administered by WB Music Corp.
All rights reserved. Reprinted by permission of Warner Bros. Publications
U.S. Inc., Miami, FL 33014.

LIBRARY OF CONGRESS CATALOGING-IN-PUBLICATION DATA
Kurlansky, Mark.
Boogaloo on 2nd Avenue: a novel of pastry, guilt, and music/Mark Kurlansky.
p.   cm.
ISBN 0-345-44819-7
1. Lower East Side (New York, N.Y.)—Fiction.   I. Title.
PS3561.U65B66   2005   813'.54—dc22   2004052979

Printed in the United States of America

www.atrandom.com

2 4 6 8 9 7 5 3 1

Book design by Carole Lowenstein

To the old neighborhood with love,
and to Marian, the beautiful native girl on my island paradise

We'll build a castle in Spain
On a roof in Manhattan,
And in our lofty domain
We'll pretend to be Latin.
—IRVING BERLIN, *"(Castles in Spain)*
On a Roof in Manhattan"

ACKNOWLEDGMENTS

To the great Joe Cuba, *el boogalooista número uno,* for his generosity in teaching me about boogaloo and writing the lyrics to Chow Mein Vega's "Yiddish Boogaloo"; *un millón agradecimientos para un fenomenal artista y un amigo amable,* and to David Gonzalez, my viejo mofongo mate for help con Spanglish.

To Dr. Phyllis Caroff for her insights into the disorder of claustrophobia, including the wonderfully relevant observation that the condition can be aggravated by chocolate.

To Rubye Monet for advice on Yiddish.

To Daryl Sherman for straightening me out on Gershwin and for the way she plays it.

Thanks to Nancy Miller for her support, friendship, and guidance, to Charlotte Sheedy for her backing, wisdom, and sense of fun, to Deborah Copeland for her assistance and enthusiasm, to Deirdre Lanning for all her help, and to Carolyn Kim, whose reassuring presence at the other end of the phone always brings order to seeming chaos.

And to so many friends over so many years on the Lower East Side and the Loisaida, *gracias* and *a dank.*

CONTENTS

Acknowledgments   *xi*

CHAPTER ONE **A Quick End in Four-Four Time**   *3*

CHAPTER TWO **The Natural Order of Rodents**   *7*

CHAPTER THREE **Talmudic Shortcomings**   *23*

CHAPTER FOUR **Calamity in Disguise**   *37*

CHAPTER FIVE **The Meshugaloo Himself**   *44*

CHAPTER SIX **Tribulations of a Tenth Man**   *53*

CHAPTER SEVEN **The Worn Garment**   *64*

CHAPTER EIGHT **Pink Martinis**   *79*

CHAPTER NINE **Egg Creams and *Traif***   *91*

CHAPTER TEN **Whose Bumpy Road Is It?**   *97*

CHAPTER ELEVEN **Chocolate Buttercream**   *106*

CHAPTER TWELVE **Not Easy to Be Puerto Rican**   *115*

CHAPTER THIRTEEN **No Going Back**   *127*

CHAPTER FOURTEEN **The Edge of the Planet**   *145*

CHAPTER FIFTEEN **Fireworks**   *160*

CHAPTER SIXTEEN **God-like Sparks**   *177*

CHAPTER SEVENTEEN **A Ratlike Cunning**   *197*

CHAPTER EIGHTEEN **Stimulants**   *206*

CHAPTER NINETEEN **A Plucked, Ripe Fruit**   *222*

CHAPTER TWENTY **Narrow Escapes**   *246*

CHAPTER TWENTY-ONE **Fresh Kills**   *254*

CHAPTER TWENTY-TWO **Calamity in Running Shoes**   *264*

CHAPTER TWENTY-THREE **Tears**   *273*

CHAPTER TWENTY-FOUR **The Millionaires of the Loisaida**   *282*

CHAPTER TWENTY-FIVE **The Bread of New York**   *295*

CHAPTER TWENTY-SIX **The Kishka Good-Bye**   *306*

Twelve Recipes from the Neighborhood   *309*

Boogaloo on 2nd Avenue

CHAPTER ONE

A Quick End in Four-Four Time

ELI RABBINOWITZ was shaped like a hamster, though larger and somewhat less furry. As Sonia Cohn Seltzer applied her long, skilled fingers to his rubbery white flesh, he squeaked and sighed—noises that reminded her of his rodentlike qualities.

Lying on his stomach, he reached around with his pale, stocky arm. "Touch it. Touch it," he murmured. "I'll pay extra." Grabbing her wrist, he started to turn over.

Sonia freed her hand and smacked him with a towel, a hard blow with a limp club.

"Ouch! Gawd!"

"I warned you. Get out and don't come back." She exited the small room by what looked like a closet door but actually led to the rest of her apartment. Without her, the room looked antiseptic except for a Chagall print of a couple floating over rooftops. The door was slammed and locked and Sonia went back to her desk to work on her play about Emma Goldman, the anarchist, while her husband looked after their daughter in another room.

"Aayoych," said Eli, blending several Yiddish and American expletives. Then he got dressed and left, turning down Avenue A, which was already a bit redolent as the early summer heat cooked the trash on the street. Furniture was placed neatly along the garbage-strewn edges of sidewalks—a special place where things were found and things were given away every day. The streetlamps in metallic paint were wrapped with paper flyers up to seven feet up the poles, like badly laid strudel dough, leaves dangling, advertisements for everything, some legal, including the exact time and place for demonstrations that had already been missed against every known form of repression. The trashy streets were occupied in shifts—different people at different hours of the day. The older people, such as Eli, were out first, beaten only by those who had spent the night on the sidewalk. Then the smarts, the new young people, walked quickly to the subways to their promising jobs in other neighborhoods. At eleven, shaggy young people staggered out into the blinding sunlight looking as though they had spent the night with drugs and sex and not much food or sleep. But soon the smarts would be home from their jobs and the streets filled with the entire assortment.

The tenement buildings were color-coded for age—not of the buildings, but of the last paint job. The oldest were brick red—a color designed to match the bricks, which it never quite did. Then there was forest green, that too one of the older colors, a nonbotanical attempt at greening a working-class neighborhood. More recently, buildings were painted battleship gray—paint that was said to have been left over from World War II and designed to obscure warships on a gray day at sea. Buildings painted in the sixties when the neighborhood became the East Village were in colors that escaped any rational explanation, such as orange, hot bubble-gum pink, deep purple—once brilliant but now dull as dirt. The psychedelic storefronts looked more out-of-date than the tenement buildings themselves. Then the Puerto Ricans brought cobalt, which was very big on Avenues A and B, and the Dominicans came with turquoise, and now the smarts were there with cream, peach, café au lait, and buff—colors that were so up-market, they did not even try to hide dirt.

It was raining, an unimportant warm summer drizzle that caused puddles to form in the ruts of the pockmarked asphalt streets uneven from one failed repaving over another; even a few cobblestones showed through in places. Eli saw his feet but did not bother to notice the paint-splattered sidewalks of street art that everyone gazed at and no one looked at deliberately—street artists must know that the street is the perfect spot for subliminal messages.

Walking in the fast Jewish four-beat, Eli headed toward the kosher dairy restaurant on Houston Street of which he was the unloved owner.

Chow Mein Vega, who knew more about rhythm than anyone else in the neighborhood, had a theory. He claimed that Latins and Jews walked to different beats—that Jews walked to a very fast four-beat. "You can clap your hands to it," he would say. "You can almost hear that short loud 'Hey!' between measures—dom-domdom dom—hey. Latinos have a three-beat like a cha-cha-cha. One, *du*—dat-dat-dat. It moves your body a lot more, but it doesn't get you down the street nearly as fast. Jews get there faster with less effort and don't understand that the Puerto Ricans' way is style." Chow Mein made a graceful sweep with his arm to illustrate, then added, as though he had just had the thought, "Of course, the Puerto Ricans don't understand that this is why the Jews always get there first. Dominicanos are even more slowed down by that syncopated thing. That little 'y' between the downbeat and the second beat. That's why, have you ever noticed how long it takes a Dominicano to get somewhere?"

Rabbinowitz's restaurant was closed and the Dominicanos were cleaning up. Outside, the union picketers were bundling up their angry signs and getting ready to leave. They didn't acknowledge the fast-paced, short, stocky Eli Rabbinowitz, whom they vilified in chant and by placard every evening. And he ignored them.

Since most of the neighborhood's blintz and kreplach eaters were pro-union, the picketing, in the words of Eli Rabbinowitz, "is killing me." But he would not give in. The Poles and Ukrainians had an endless supply of immigrants who worked for nothing, and they weren't picketed because their customers wouldn't care. So why should he pay union scale? "Who's going to buy a ten-dollar blintz?" he would say. "These guys are killing me. A bunch of Communists. Like my father. That's why we never had anything." And soon all the sufferings of his childhood were blamed on these ten people who had been picketing his restaurant for the last three months.

It was early Thursday evening, the evening when Eli Rabbinowitz picked up the restaurant's revenues in a canvas bag and deposited them at the bank.

"These schmucks are killing me," he said once more as he closed up the canvas bag with a few thousand dollars instead of the tens of thousands he had deposited on Thursday nights before he was singled out.

"Killing me," he muttered as he made his way up First Avenue to the deposit box on Fifth Street. In the fast Jewish four-beat, Rabbinowitz and his money were getting to Fifth Street quickly, charting a determined course around the amblers and street hustlers brought out by the first heat of summer and the halfhearted cooling rain, which had already stopped. One two-three four—hey!

A man was waiting for him, a large, dark-skinned man with eyes that seemed unable to focus. The pupils looked wide enough to take in all the night light on Fifth Street. He blinked continually as his shaking hands lifted an automatic pistol of a dull-finished metal, the first bullet already in the chamber, to the back of Eli Rabbinowitz's head. The steady finger of his shaking hand squeezed the trigger, jerking Eli forward and exploding most of his face onto the brass fittings of the night deposit box. The police would observe that the assailant must have been much taller than the victim. This was deduced by the downward angle from the entry wound at the top of the head and the low height of the place where the pieces that had been Eli Rabbinowitz's face hit the wall and the box. A pool of dark blood marked the spot on the sidewalk where Eli's body fell without the canvas bag. Rabbinowitz probably died instantly, but had he lived another minute, he might have laughed at the thought that because of the picketing, the thief had lost out on more than $10,000.

CHAPTER TWO

The Natural Order of Rodents

DADDY, why did you kill him?" Sarah, with a pencil in one hand and small notebook in the other, wanted to know.

As Nathan Seltzer looked down at the dead body stretched across the kitchen floor, no good explanations were coming to him.

"You didn't have to kill him. Why did you do it?" his daughter insisted.

How to explain such things to a three-year-old. He had been warned about the poison. It caused the victim to bleed internally and die in agony. And the body was left behind to confront the killer.

The mouse was lying belly-up, and it was a soft, white belly. It had been an almost cuddly little animal, if you overlooked the tail, a naked white worm that trailed behind. Sarah had a favorite book, a gift from Nathan's mother, about furry animals. Each page had an animal with a different kind of fur, a little fluffy patch that the reader was invited to rub. The mouse's white belly looked like such a patch. "I am a mouse. Would you like to rub my white belly?"

The mouse had stretched its body with its last breath—forepaws straining up and the hind ones back, the tail dragged straight behind. It had not been a peaceful death. They probably don't bother to make a gentle poison, something that will just put it to sleep. They could do that. It doesn't have to be some sharp, unbearable pain, a soul-splitting convulsion. How long do they struggle? Long enough to drag themselves halfway across the kitchen floor. A mousetrap breaks the neck instantly. People prefer the pet cat method, though, because it is the most natural. It is not coincidence that the most natural is the cruelest of all. Of course, Nathan had none of these thoughts when putting out the poison; only now did he, faced with the insistent questioning of the little inquisitor. But now, he had to admit, the line of questioning had an inescapable validity.

"Why did you kill him, Daddy?" she asked, pen poised over note-book as though ready to write down his answer.

"Because he can't live here, and you cannot just ask a mouse to leave."

Sarah drew three irregular but concentric circles on a page in the notebook. "How did you kill him?" She was growing bolder, poking the white belly with a small, pale index finger.

"Don't touch him. I killed him with poison."

They could hear police on Avenue A with loudspeakers. It took Nathan only a strange half second to realize that the police were not looking for mouse killers.

"Uncle Mordy said that we are all being poisoned. That the general electorate is poisoning us. Is that right?"

"What?"

"Is it true that the general electorate is putting poison in the water and it gets in the food because the food is wet?"

"No, it's General Electric. But Uncle Mordy gets a little nutty."

"Then why did you use poison? Are you a little nutty?"

"Maybe. I poisoned him because I thought it would be quick. Kinder than Pepe Le Moko."

Sarah's eyes opened round and cartoon expressive. "Does Pepe Le Moko kill?"

"Yes, he does."

Sarah put several exciting vertical lines through the circles. "Why?"

"It's nature. Everything kills in nature. Cats kill mice."

"Am I going to kill?"

"No. Of course not."

She turned the page in her notebook and drew a long, wavy line. "Does Pepe kill as much as General Electric?"

"He only kills mice."

"I like mice. Why do we have to kill them?"

Nathan listened to the sounds of Avenue A as though there were answers to her questions out there in the horns, the sirens, the clanging of some makeshift construction project, cars thudding over steel plates in the street, someone shouting, "Hey!," the police loudspeaker: "Any-one on First Avenue and Fifth Street between ten and eleven last night . . ." He thought he could even hear his father on the floor above whistling Irving Berlin.

"Daddy, why does Uncle Mordy have little nuts?"

"What? Listen, do you want to come with me to the shop? We can feed Pepe Le Moko."

"Are we going to feed him the mouse?"

Nathan thought about it for a second and decided against it. Instead he swept it up into a dustpan. The sight of the rubbery little stiff was a little sickening. She didn't seem to mind. Was the idea of death upsetting to her? She didn't look upset, but she didn't always show these things. The sight of a dead animal was a great curiosity to her, but she seemed to be troubled only by moral, not aesthetic, implications. As he dumped the dustpan into the plastic trash bag, she said, "Shouldn't he be buried?"

Ritual, too. Moral conundrums and the law. She was Jewish, after all. For as long as he could remember, his parents had worried that he would "marry a shiksa and your children won't be Jewish." Why had they always talked about this? Nathan wondered. He had rarely even conversed with a non-Jew. In high school he went out on two dates with Luisa, the beautiful Puerto Rican from Avenue C. That alone was enough for Nathan's father to say to his own brother, Nathan's uncle Nusan, "Nathan's children will not be Jewish."

Was that why he stopped going out with Luisa? Was it pressure from his parents? He couldn't remember. In fact, he couldn't really remember Luisa—only that she was Puerto Rican and that at the time he thought she was very beautiful and that when his father told Uncle Nusan that their children would not be Jewish, Nusan had responded, "*Baruch hashem,*" and let slip an ironic smile. God willing. Uncle Nusan's invocation of God's will was always intended as the darkest of ironies, his curse at God. Nusan seemed to have a close but troubled relationship with God, the same kind of relationship that he had with his brother.

Nathan was named after Nusan. At the time, no one foresaw the burden, because Nusan was supposed to be dead. As Ashkenazic Jews, they named babies only after the dead. Nusan, like the rest of the family, had vanished during the war. But unlike the others, Nusan reappeared years later with a bitter voice, a number tattooed on his forearm, and dark eyes that could see through everything. According to Nathan's father, Nusan used to have light blue eyes and they had changed color during the war. This was hard to believe, but Nusan did have the kind of broad, Slavic looks that seemed intended for light blue eyes.

Nathan was Nusan's favorite, a position that no one envied him. The family supposed that it was because Nathan was named after him, even though he was given the name only in the belief that Nusan was dead. Nusan often said to Nathan, "You are the living proof that I am dead." And with that he would reach up to put his arm fondly on Nathan's shoulder.

"Daddy," came the sweet, high-pitched, insistent voice. "Why did you kill him?"

"You can't have mice in the house."

She drew several little ovals and gave them squiggly tails that made them almost look as though she were about to explain "the facts of life" to her father. "Why not? We have Ralph."

This, Nathan thought, was a very good point. Ralph was the pet hamster, and it always seemed to Nathan that having a pet hamster made as much sense as having a mouse or a rat.

"Well, Ralph is a pet."

"Why couldn't the mouse be a pet?"

Nathan didn't know. In fact, these white-bellied, gray little creatures were more pleasant looking than Ralph. Why did you always kill mice? Why are some animals our friends, others our meals, and others simply pests to be exterminated? How were these things decided? Did we have the right to willfully extinguish life? Was this an important question to get right? Did young Eichmann ask a similar question and his father told him it didn't matter and so it began? Probably not. Most people don't become mass murderers no matter what their parents tell them. But you cannot take this kind of question lightly. She was asking for some moral definition. God, thought Nathan, it was just a goddamn mouse. "Mice are unhealthy. They carry diseases."

"Diseases?"

"They make you sick."

"So we make them sick first!" She smiled. She liked this idea, and she drew wild dark spirals all over the page.

He took his daughter's small hand, and her little fingers curled tightly around his smallest fingers—a sensation that briefly overcame him with a small inexpressible joy as they walked past his wife's workroom, where he heard the pleasing thud of flesh being pounded. It was a woman client. Tan pointed slender shoes had been left by the door. There was something vaguely erotic about the thought of it, some unknown woman lying naked on a table at the mercy of his wife's long and powerful fingers. He liked the way their shoes were left in his hallway. He would have liked them to leave all of their clothes in the hallway. But sometimes they were men's shoes.

It had been a hard year for Sarah. New people were moving into the neighborhood, and she had befriended one—a girl born on the same day in the same year and named Maya. She had awarded Maya with that most important title children are empowered to bestow—"best friend." To Nathan, Maya and her parents were new people in the neighborhood, they were smarts. But for Sarah, they had lived there all her life. They had moved in about the time the girls were born, buying an entire three-story house on Tompkins Square. Buying property in the neighborhood was a startling new concept to the Seltzers, who had owned neighborhood property since the 1920s and for a very long time had regarded their holdings as a burden. Maya's parents were undeterred by the squatters' camp in Tompkins Square, a little tent city of scraggly suburban kids having an East Village experience. They were certain that the police would soon drive the squatters out, whereas the Seltzers feared that the police would drive all of them out.

Maya's parents were not like the neighborhood people, and last year Maya had surprised her best friend, Sarah, by starting school, and though it was only a few hours a day, it came between them. Maya awarded best friend status to a different girl who went to her school.

When Sarah had asked why she didn't go to school also, Nathan had said, "But you are only three years old." Nathan and almost everyone he knew had started school at age five. But his wife, Sonia, who had gone not through the New York City public school system but instead to private schools in Mexico City and Guadalajara, was more sympathetic. Then they discovered that the "preschool" would cost them $10,000 for the year.

"What do they teach?" Nathan had asked, and Sarah relayed the question to Maya, and the answer came back, "Things."

But it was summer now, and Sarah was happy because there was no school and soon she would have her best friend back.

· · ·

Nathan took his little girl's hand on the old, streamlined art deco elevator and through the polished black-and-white art deco lobby and out into a less polished world, where Sarah took her seat on his shoulders, grabbing his curly mane with her tiny fingers.

It was a sunny day early in the summer of the Michael Dukakis presidency. That summer, Michael Dukakis and the New York Mets both looked undefeatable. The Mets had untouchable starting pitching and powerful hitters. And Dukakis had a recent poll showing that he would beat Vice President George Bush by a margin of 52 to 38 percent. The long nightmare of the monster with the Disney smile was about to be over. Michael Dukakis, whoever he was, had the simple task of being better than Ronald Reagan.

The era of Ronald Reagan had been an isolating experience for the neighborhood, watching Reagan go from national joke to popular leader in the rest of the country, while here in the neighborhood his joke status remained. No one in the neighborhood had ever actually met anyone who voted for Reagan, but statistically he was very popular, and the only ones in the country who seemed to still know that he was a joke—except for Reagan himself, who always had a silly smile suggesting the ridiculousness of it all—lived in this part of New York City. But now it was finally over and George Bush was too silly even for the people out in America. To people in the neighborhood, the fact that Dukakis was popular and not Bush was a signal that the madness had passed and it was once again safe to leave the neighborhood. The new, short, dark-eyed president, a Greek, was practically a landsman. Well, that was an exaggeration, but he looked like someone who could have been from the neighborhood. George Bush looked like one of those people who were increasingly venturing down for a quick "Friday night in the East Village," whose children might buy apartments in the neighborhood, the smarts.

When the votes were counted, it always showed that a few people in the neighborhood had voted Republican. They had voted for Reagan, and now, no doubt, they would vote for Bush. It was a frightening thought that somewhere in these dark-colored brick tenement buildings a few Republicans lived in silence. Though Nathan had spent his entire life in the neighborhood, he had never met any of them.

The closest Nathan had ever come to meeting a Republican was Mrs. Kleinman, who lived in his building. Mrs. Kleinman had voted for Ronald Reagan because she believed Jimmy Carter had mismanaged the postal service. But it was no better under Reagan, and this year she was back to Dukakis.

Mrs. Kleinman had met a man, a Yiddish-speaking man, at the social agency on Second Street where she worked. He left New York, moved to Boston, and when she received no letters from him, she was convinced that something was wrong with her mail. She would complain regularly to the landlord, who was Nathan's father. "Oh, Mr. Seltzer, have you seen anyone tampering with the mailboxes?"

"No, everything looks normal," Harry Seltzer would say.

"I can't understand it. Something must be wrong."

"Are you missing all of your mail?"

"Yes, I have not received one piece of mail in weeks. Something is wrong."

"I'll look into it," Harry would say, and walk away knowing he would receive no rent from Kleinman again this month. Harry owned a lot of property. It had belonged to his wife's family and it made very little money.

"Harry," Ruth would say, "I don't want to knock Socialism, but it would be helpful if we collected rent from the tenants from time to time."

"We're doing all right," Harry argued.

"Oboyoboy," Ruth muttered with a sigh.

"Anyone who heard or saw anything last night on Fifth Street . . . ," announced the police bullhorn. At the corner was Arnie, at home on his wooden pallet, cuddled up with old blankets he was storing for next winter. He wore a woolen beret, which may have been an homage to either Che Guevara or the international brigades of the Spanish Civil War. But the way he wore it combined with his gaunt appearance made it look more like an homage to Field Marshal Montgomery, except that on it he wore a black-and-white pin that said, VIVA LA HUELGA! from a farmworkers' strike twenty years before on the other side of the continent that he had supported by refusing to eat grapes. Technically, Arnie had been boycotting grapes for two decades, though in recent

times he would have had few opportunities to eat grapes unless someone threw some in the garbage. Arnie was in a total boycott these days.
He bought nothing. *Viva la huelga,* the meaning lost in time, had become
his greeting.

"*Viva la huelga,* friends," Arnie greeted.

"*Viva la huelga* to you, Arnie. What are you reading?" Nathan asked
with Sarah above him, leaning forward to view the steep drop down to
Arnie.

Arnie turned the thick, curled old paperback to reveal the cover,
Dostoyevsky's *The Idiot.* Sitting up on one arm, he explained to Nathan,
"I found it on Avenue B," as though Dostoyevsky had a special, different meaning when it came from Avenue B. "Do you think there is such
a thing as a purely good man?"

"Partially good would be a find, wouldn't it? Here's a question for
you, Arnie: Why do we kill mice?"

Arnie looked up with the smile of a man who had just won a con-
test. "Because we think it is a threat to our property. It is all about own-
ing property." He gestured sweepingly around his small wooden pallet
stacked with blankets, books, yellowed and wilted copies of the *Times,*
the *News,* the *Post,* a few magazines, and a few cans. "I own no property,
I have no home to protect, and I kill nothing," he declared triumphantly.

"But what do you do on Saturdays?" Sarah shouted down from
above Nathan's head, instantly erasing the victory grin from Arnie's
face. Nathan was pleased. He sometimes called Sarah "the Silencer."

"Why Saturdays, sweetie?" Arnie asked.

"Because you can watch television on Saturdays. It's allowed. So
what do you do?"

"Hey," said Arnie, "you hear about that guy Rabbinowitz?"

"Eli? The blintzes guy on Houston?"

"They just found him." Arnie stopped and looked awkwardly at
Sarah. "On the street. From last night."

"Heart attack?"

"No, somebody did him."

"Geez," said Nathan. "Who?"

"They don't know."

"Geez."

"Geez," Sarah repeated. "How did he get lost?"

Nathan handed a $1 bill down to Arnie. "You ought to lay low today or you will end up questioned by the police."

"They've already stopped by. That one over there."

He pointed at a plainclothes officer, thickset and powerfully built. Why did they have plainclothes policemen? The gray suits they wore were as identifiable as uniforms and too hot for summer weather. At least uniformed patrolmen got a lightweight blue uniform, but there was no summer-weight suit for plainclothesmen. It was the time of year that plainclothesmen were beginning to sweat. But this one was different. He had a summer suit, a vanilla-colored linen. And despite this fine summer wear, he still looked like a cop. Maybe that was why most of them didn't bother about their clothes.

The officer was across the street, questioning the man everyone called Sal A. There were three Sals. They all sold homemade mozzarella and opinions. Sal A was on Avenue A, and he had the smallest shop, furnished with a counter, a cash register, a tub of unsalted mozzarella, a tub of salted mozzarella, a rack of long seeded bread, and a few trays of delicacies he had prepared for the day. Every morning he baked *sfogliatella,* and Nathan, who loved *sfogliatella,* could smell them from his apartment the instant they came out of the oven, the fine leaves of the pastry turned amber and the hot ricotta cheese inside heaving like lungs. But Nathan, now that he was entering his late thirties, had started noticing changes in his body, including two flabby, rounded bulges above the hips on either side. He would lift up his shirt to stare at them in the mirror, trying to push them back in with his hands. But they would balloon back into position. Sarah, noting the morning ritual, had taken to calling the bulges "Daddy's tellas," and Nathan did not need an explanation. It was short for *sfogliatella.*

Besides baking his own *sfogliatella,* Sal A was different from the other two Sals in several other ways. To begin with, his name was Guido, but he called himself Sal when he opened the store because he could see that in this neighborhood Sicilian shops were run by people named Sal. He was soft-spoken and had thick, silver gray hair. The other two Sals always shouted and were desperately and futilely trying to preserve the few remains of their youthful black hair.

But the other two Sals would have said that the important difference was that they were from Palermo, the tough, crime-ridden Sicilian capital, whereas Sal A was from Catania, the tough, crime-ridden Sicilian second city at the foot of a live volcano.

"Hey, Joey."

"Eh, Sal."

"Eh, Joey, you want some mozzarell'?"

"No, *grazie*, I'm working," Joey, the cop in linen, told Sal A as though there were a specific rule about mozzarella while on duty. In fact, he was saving his appetite for Sal First, who had a bigger shop on First Avenue and whose mother made caponata. In Sal A's caponata, the eggplant, olives, and capers were turned dark with a little unsweetened cocoa powder, bitter and intoxicating, like coffee. Sal A always sprinkled chopped almonds on top because their whiteness glowed against the dark vegetables. Sal First said that this way of doing caponata was "Spanish" and would not be acceptable in Palermo. That might have been true because the use of chocolate was from Spain, but Sal First's use of the "S" word as a curse seemed to be implying a distasteful Puerto Ricanness, and that was what tilted Joey Parma toward the First Avenue version. But he did dip two thick fingers into an oily tray of Sal A's olives.

"Try one," Sal A said politely as Joey placed the olive in his mouth. "They're oil cured."

"Aw, shit!" A topaz teardrop of olive oil had landed on the lapel of Joey's linen suit.

"Don't worry about it," said Sal.

"Give me a wet towel."

"Don't touch." Sal produced a bottle of talcum powder and dusted the lapel. "Wait five minutes and just dust it off."

"You sure?"

Sal nodded.

"Thank God I didn't wear my Armani."

"You should be careful."

"Sal, did you hear any gunshots or anything last night between ten and eleven?"

"What, are you kidding? Just about every night. It's like Palermo here. But I didn't hear anything special."

Joey, whose family was from Naples so he could ignore the slight against Palermo, wondered what Sal would consider special.

"Sometimes I think it's just firecrackers. But I don't know. You can kill people with firecrackers, too, you know. It's gunpowder."

"Yeah," said Joey. "Give me just a slice of that mozzarell'."

"Sure, Joey." He cut a fat white piece. Joey tilted his head back and lowered it carefully into his mouth. "Yeah, it's good, Sal. But you ought to get some buffalo."

"Yeah, I'll keep them in Tompkins Park. With the hippie dippies."

"Yeah, take care. Ciao."

"Ciao," said Sal A, and even Nathan across the street could see Sal A salute the backside of Officer Joey Parma with his middle finger. "Buffalo," Sal muttered with an expressively quick bend of his elbow.

As Nathan and Sarah approached Tenth Street from the west side of the avenue and Joey Parma was coming up the other side, sweet-faced Ruben was waiting on the corner. He looked down Avenue A and then shouted across Tenth Street, "¡Bajando!" More than a dozen young men along the curbs of Tenth Street suddenly sat down casually on stoops and car fenders.

But Joey turned east and Ruben waved everybody up.

"Whaz up," Ruben said to Nathan with a smile. Nathan did not smile back. "Oh, the stock market's down?" It was some idea the local drug dealers had that if you did not deal drugs, you had investments on Wall Street instead. Those were the two games in New York in the 1980s, and everybody, they reasoned, must be playing one or the other—and some people were playing both.

It was important to Nathan that Ruben smiled and made an effort, because that was showing respect. That was all you needed to get along in the neighborhood.

Walking down this block of Tenth Street—in four-four or cha-cha-cha—a dozen times dealers whispered the word "Smoke?" There might be other reasons for walking down the block, but anyone on Tenth Street who was not a cop was worth a try.

The dealers had been there since the neighborhood became famous in the 1960s. People from all over the city came down by subway, in expensive polished cars that were always parked in garages, and in long white limousines, to do business with the merchants who stood on the street stupidly repeating one word—"Smoke?"

Many of the people on the block were cops—federal agents, city police, special task forces. They hid out in unmarked delivery trucks or delivery trucks with uninspired logos—a printed name such as BOB'S BREAD with no picture or slogan.

Somehow Nathan had gotten to the age of fourteen without ever trying drugs. This was not a principled position. He had wanted to try them, but he was afraid of the lean, vicious-looking men who sold them. It was exactly like the way he had longed to have the corrupt worldly experience of one of those plump, oddly dressed women on Eleventh Street. But he was afraid of the men who sold them, too. And at any moment he might run into his father, who did not seem to completely approve of him and was forever wandering the streets, singing Irving Berlin songs. As a child, Nathan thought Harry was checking up on him. Only as an adult did he understand that this local wandering was simply what Harry did. Harry had come to New York not so much to seek his fortune; he came to be lucky. He was the lucky New York son of a luckless European family, and he wandered the streets of his neighborhood singing, not checking up on anyone but just waiting for luck to meet him in the street.

Mordy, a year younger than Nathan, was not afraid of running into his father, getting caught, being wrong, or anything else. It was not that he was particularly courageous. He simply lacked the valuable sense of danger. He tried a woman on Eleventh Street when Nathan had still not tried anyone. Of course, Mordy, in what was to become a pattern for life, had no money to pay her. At the time Nathan did not appreciate this accomplishment, because he did not know that you always had to pay first. But Mordy, at fourteen, had talked a prostitute into a gift, a moment of whimsy or perhaps a yearning for innocence that earned her a beating that chipped a tooth. And then Nathan, full of envy and resentment, had to get the money and pay it to a fat man with a broken nose—you could almost make out the outline of someone's knuckle in the dent in his nose—so that he would spare Mordy.

Nathan's urge for those women passed without his ever having sampled. He did soon taste the smoke at a party on Rivington Street where they played Motown music—"Sugar Pie, Honeybun," over and over again. The other thing Nathan remembered about that party was that it was the first time he ever heard the term "East Village." Nathan had grown up in a neighborhood called "the Lower East Side." His mother, Ruth, had grown up there when it was just the East Side. Manhattan was getting more and more labels. At this party, as time stood still from his first inhalation of marijuana, he heard someone say, "You know, they are going to start calling this neighborhood 'the East Village.' " The term took hold as predicted, except that it never did include Rivington Street.

For some years after that, Nathan bought his smoke on this block of Tenth Street. A fast $5 bill for a "nickel bag." Mordy was still buying nickel bags. A nickel bag wasn't as big as it used to be. But it didn't need to be. The bags got smaller and smaller, but the smoke got stronger and stronger, and after so many years of smoking, it seemed to take Mordy only an occasional puff or two to maintain himself in a distant and timeless state.

In the 1960s, Nathan, Mordy, and everyone they knew bought smoke on the block. People liked marijuana because time stumbles by goofily—a minute, an hour, an evening—and they all stood on the street letting time escape them. Nathan started wondering what was happening to that time. In fact, he was worrying more and more about time. So he stopped. And now he didn't smile at the pushers. Everyone agreed that if you didn't smoke in the sixties something was wrong with you, but if you still did in the eighties you were just as wrong. The window for drug correctness was small and narrow.

The street pushers also changed. The Puerto Ricans from the other side of First Avenue moved in. Now Dominicans were starting to push out the Puerto Ricans. The Dominicans, not welcomed by the Puerto Ricans, had built their own neighborhood, turning dying Rivington Street into a boulevard of restaurants and grocery stores. The Puerto Ricans complained that these stores kept the entire neighborhood up all night with loud merengue music and that they were all selling crack down there, the new drug that seemed to make people crazy. Some Dominicans may have been selling crack, but there were also a lot selling bananas, cane juice, and coconut ices. The logic-defying Puerto Rican response was that Dominicans wore no socks. Dominicans, they insisted, were uncivilized because they ate bananas and wore no socks.

Crack was showing up near the East River where the Puerto Ricans lived in tall building projects and also in the old tenements where the Jews had left mezuzahs behind. All over the neighborhood, tiny vials with bright plastic covers turned up wedged in the pavement cracks the way until a few years before, syringes and needles used to be found. Neighborhood people, and the police as well, preferred heroin addicts dozing off in St. Mark's or Tompkins Square to wild-eyed, crazed crack-heads. If the drug pushers had kept anesthetizing everyone with marijuana and heroin, their trade might have lasted in the neighborhood indefinitely. But crack was causing trouble. Where these tiny colored caps were found, there were crazy people, robberies, muggings, break-ins.

On Tenth Street they sold only smoke. If they had sold crack on Tenth Street, Nathan would have had to move his shop, and he did not want to move because his parents owned the building, and the only way a photocopy shop could keep open charging as little as he did, which was all his clientele could afford, was to have a rent-free office space.

Young, well-dressed uptowners came down to buy smoke on Tenth Street in the same well-waxed, expensive cars as were used by the aging Jews who drove in from Long Island and New Jersey to shop in the delis and fish shops. The smoke crowd drove down on Friday night, the smoked fish crowd drove in on Sunday. The neighborhood was a respectable drug-trafficking area, although it's true, the pushers did not always look too good. There was one huge man with a big mop of black hair and furious eyes who would hobble down the street looking as if his head were about to explode and he was struggling to keep it on.

And none of this bothered Nathan. It was his neighborhood, and he liked the way the street was lined with people who made a distinction between him and outsiders. Nobody said, "Smoke?" to him, because he belonged. Sometimes a new pusher would be working the evening and he would say to Nathan, "Smoke?" because he didn't know. One of the regulars would lightly punch the new man in the biceps and say, "¿Qué hace', maricón? He don't fucking want you."

The pushers made Nathan feel safe. No one was going to do anything to him, his family, or his photocopy shop as long as the pushers were out there. Nobody came onto this block to rob or bother children or steal cars. And the pushers tried hard to keep people like Nathan appreciative of them. They seemed to know that at any time, the people of the neighborhood could rise up and push them out.

Nathan knew how to be just cold enough so that they knew to respect him, but not so cold that they would single him out if things went wrong some night. Because he knew, though you never saw it, that they had guns. At least the lookouts did. The ones nonchalantly passing their evenings on the corners. Ruben probably had a gun.

Recently, Nathan's attitude had begun to shift. The change had started with Sarah's birth. He could not forget those hours of holding Sonia's hands while she writhed in pain that he could not even imagine, struggling through what was termed "an easy labor." The pushing, the struggling, the tearing. Sarah came out in a gracefully arced little swan dive into the doctor's hands. It was the only graceful motion in the entire ordeal. He held her, looked into her curious eyes. She was already preparing questions.

As he turned to look at Sonia, his eyes had swept through the room like the panning camera of a documentary filmmaker, and he was astounded by the sight. The room looked like the scene of a massacre. Blood was splattered on the walls, clotted on sheets, puddled on the floor, under the table. Why was it like this? What had nature intended? This, then, was life, a violent and dangerous struggle.

And that had made him start looking differently at the streets of his home. They were full of garbage and disease and drug dealers with loaded guns. Probably one of them had shot Eli Rabbinowitz, a nice man who never hurt anyone, thought Nathan, who had never tried to give him a massage. Nathan was having these thoughts now as he walked down his street, hoping Sarah

was not hearing the discussions of Eli Rabbinowitz's remains. One dealer insisted that "the fucking cops spent all fucking mañana fitting pieces together so they could put together his face to see who the fucking *pendejo* was." Fortunately, the one who insisted that the body was headless and that the police were still searching the neighborhood for the missing part was imparting this news in Spanish.

Should he be like the new smarts? Nathan wondered. Like Maya's parents? Did he need to start earning money for types of schools he had never heard of? What did he have to do to make life safe for her?

When Sarah was riding on his shoulders, he felt an unreasonable hostility stir at the sight of the pushers. He didn't want Ruben's sweet-faced, friendly nod when Sarah was up on his shoulders, waving and laughing at the funny world. But there it was. Sarah looked down from Nathan's shoulders at the sweet-faced man and drew his portrait in her notebook, which she balanced on her father's head—two zigzags across the page.

CHAPTER THREE

Talmudic Shortcomings

NATHAN WOKE UP on a Friday morning with the unshakable sense that during this day he would commit a catastrophic error in judgment. Something had been written by the gods, and as he walked to the Meshugaloo Copy Center, Nathan Seltzer knew this was one Friday that he would regret.

He pulled open the gate of his store, rolling up a dozen indecipherable spray-painted names. "Seltzer!" shouted out Carmela, a name that means "Candy." Carmela was already living above the shop when he first opened it, one of his father's old tenants who paid a few dollars rent. She spent the entire summer sitting half out her window on the fire escape. There used to be many more on the other fire escapes, and they all shouted to one another. But in recent summers almost everyone had bought air conditioners, which hummed and dripped, and they had all gone inside and closed their windows, leaving Carmela with no one to shout at but Nathan and his customers. She planted her spacious denim-covered posterior—a nice posterior, though a bit overstated for white people, as she herself once observed—on the window ledge and twisted to see the street traffic below. "What's the *problema*? Slow down. *Quiere* me to take you to Cristofina to read *tu fortuna*?"

Nathan had never seen a reason to believe that Cristofina could read fortunes. But Carmela, on the other hand, had uncanny abilities.

People often sense that they are about to encounter fate, but usually once they do, they don't recognize it. That is why they go to fortune-tellers. At first Nathan thought his fateful moment would be the meeting. It was a slow summer Friday, and as Nathan decided to close his shop a few minutes early to get to his meeting, turning off a Beethoven quartet before its urgency had quite mounted and putting out water and dried food for the always hungry Pepe Le Moko—wasn't he finding enough mice to eat?—he had a sense of some misfortune *beshirt*—fated. It was even possible that the entire reason for this doomed feeling he had awakened with was that he knew he had this meeting. He had been contacted by a growing chain of photocopy stores called Copy Katz. Nathan thought it was a clever name. The man's name was Ira Katz.

Nathan took a subway, the F train from Houston, to their offices west of Fifth Avenue in the Fifties. Immediately he could see that Ira was not the owner of Copy Katz in the way that he, Nathan, was the owner of Meshugaloo Copy Center. It was more complicated for this fast-growing company that already had fifteen copy stores in Manhattan alone.

Their office was in a building so perfectly air-conditioned that it was climateless, odorless, temperatureless—an experiment in total sensory deprivation. Nathan tried to remember from his childhood if this was one of the tests given to qualify as an astronaut. Could you withstand several hours in a climateless environment? The chairs were all very large, which may have been intended to make the people in them feel very small, the same way Sarah sat in chairs dreaming of the day when her legs could reach the floor.

"What is Meshugaloo Copy?" Ira Katz wanted to know, probably noting that his name wasn't Nathan Meshugaloo.

"It comes from a song. From the sixties?"

He could see that they were worried about the mere mention of the sixties. Their offer had been simple—or at least that was how they'd put it. Five hundred thousand dollars for his business on Tenth Street.

"Why do you want it?"

"We like the location."

"Tenth Street?" Katz could be a drug dealer. You could never tell.

"We believe in the future of the neighborhood."

Five hundred thousand dollars. Nathan was not good with large numbers, but it seemed that this was a lot of money. But there was a problem with the Copy Katz offer. They required that he sign an agreement not to open another copy store in the neighborhood.

He did not have to be in this business. He had gotten into it by chance. In college he had studied music history without ever asking how he would earn a living from that. He wasn't even a musician, as his father always pointed out: "He studies music, but he doesn't play."

So much seemed fated. There was a cosmic string that started with Nathan's fascination with the life of Beethoven and carried for more than twenty years to his big mistake. Would the one have happened without the other? Growing up, Nathan had never heard anything good about anything German except apple strudel, which was said to be Jewish. German was the pariah culture and the ugly language. But then there was the music. What did the words of Schiller mean in the last movement of the Ninth? And for that matter, what wondrously beautiful things were Adam and Eve saying in Haydn's "The Creation"? Nathan wanted to read letters and criticism by Beethoven's contemporaries. Soon he was learning the ugly language to understand beautiful music, learning it with surprising ease, since the German language, like apple strudel, tasted a bit like something Jewish. Not only was it not that ugly, but it bore a surprising similarity to Yiddish, which he had been listening to, though not really understanding, all his life.

As he left the meeting on this Friday, Nathan could not yet see how the German language would direct his destiny, but it was probably the beginning, the first opening without which the mistake probably couldn't have happened two decades later. Life moves in tiny increments, with hidden causes and effects. Beethoven's symphonies had taught him that no note or phrase is without later consequence. The gentle role of an oboe leads to a bellyful of strings, which opens the way for the rampage of a full orchestra. And the oboe had started so quietly. Nothing in life happens suddenly. There were always hidden events that created an opening, started a pathway, like invisible advance men who cannot be controlled because their work is never seen.

Nathan's only instrument was a harmonica, which Harry insisted was not a real instrument. What was worse, he played a classical harmonica. He could play Beethoven violin sonatas on the harmonica. Harry, who not only didn't like harmonicas but disdained classical music, shook his head in despair. His other son, Mordy, also had musical interest, but, even less comprehensible to Harry than a classical harmonica, Mordy composed music on a computer that was played without any musical instruments at all. In fact, since Mordy did not have the equipment, his music was never played. But certainly to Harry it would not have been music.

When Harry complained to his wife about their sons' music, she would burst into an ironic laugh and say, "Oboy, *meshugene gens, meshugene gribbenes.*" Crazy parents have crazy children.

Maybe life was entirely *beshirt.* Nathan recalled from college that Kant had said this in his infelicitously titled *Idee zu einer allgemeinen Geschichte in der weltbürgerlichen Absicht:* "What appears to be complicated and accidental in individuals, may yet be understood as a steady, progressive, though slow, evolution of the original endowments of the entire species." Aside from the fact that Nathan's parents hated the way their son could quote Kant and had squandered his education on mastering words such as *weltbürgerlichen,* it was possible that a life was completely shaped by parents who in turn were shaped by grandparents so that a life in the East Village was shaped two hundred years ago by some forgotten incident on the Polish banks of the Vistula River.

Harry, another musician who could not play an instrument, could not see this. He managed the real estate holdings Ruth had inherited from her father. Her father, like Harry, had been a visionary down on his luck. Ruth's father had realized that the children of the Jews in the shops in the Lower East Side were one day going to have money, and when they did, they would move north because in Manhattan history, people had always headed north for better spaces. So he invested everything he had on Avenues A and B, the area just north of the slum. He bought buildings and lots. The building in which the family now lived, large by neighborhood standards, was built by Ruth's father, who had hired a noted 1920s architect. But the father had underestimated his neighbors; they did move north, but much farther than he had imagined—to the Bronx. Once the market crashed in 1929, he was ruined. Most of the Jews in the neighborhood had heard that after the market crash, he had leapt from his fine new building's art deco roof onto the pavement of Avenue A. The story was not true; he had died of illness in 1932, leaving his family with a great deal of unwanted real estate.

Ruth married Harry, an immigrant who always insisted that he had been a music impresario in Warsaw. Even when he spoke very little English, he used the word "impresario" with great dexterity, though no one was sure what he meant by it. In New York he tried to produce concerts with stars from the Yiddish theaters on Second Avenue, but no one came. He moved on to jazz and even befriended Charlie Parker, who lived on the other side of Tompkins Square. He never questioned, though many did, how Harry Seltzer was able to mount a Charlie Parker concert. "He's a friend," Harry would explain irritably. Harry helped other people and assumed that other people wanted to help him. But his friend died of a drug overdose only weeks before the concert date, and Harry had to pay back the ticket holders, incurring a debt that took him years to settle. Seeking release from these obligations, he formed the real estate holdings into a corporation for the purpose of declaring bankruptcy. But Ruth would not let him declare bankruptcy, which she insisted was dishonorable.

Harry tried to produce concerts with Chow Mein Vega, but so few people came that it didn't pay for the rental of the hall on Second Avenue and Harry slid further into debt. But Chow Mein had been a big star in the sixties when boogaloo was popular, and Harry never lost faith that boogaloo would one day be big again and when that happened he would be well positioned as an impresario.

In the meantime, Harry managed his wife's real estate inheritance. Many of the lots and buildings were left unoccupied. Nonpaying tenants, squatters, had moved in. In most cases the squatters improved the properties, and since Harry did not have any other customers, he was happy to have them stay. He could not have forced them out in any event because he thought of them as his friends. The only really paying building was the one he lived in. Except for his apartment and Nathan's, they were all rented. Of course, Mrs. Kleinman did not always pay because of her postal problems. Birdie Nagel in 2H, whose name wasn't really Birdie but was always referred to that way because she spent most of her time feeding birds, had not paid since her husband died in the late 1960s. "What am I going to do, evict a nice lady like that?" Harry argued. And it was a good argument. Everyone in the neighborhood had seen evictions—burly men roughly carrying possessions to the street, the door sealed with tape. In this neighborhood, evicted tenants ended up squatting in a building down the block, which chances were Harry owned, or they ended up living on the street in front of the building, like Arnie, who had been evicted ten years earlier from the building around the corner from the pallet on which he now lived.

Harry had offered an apartment to his other son, Mordy. But Mordy, who took home a considerable array of women, did not want them scrutinized for ethnic origin by his parents. He settled into an abandoned building on Second Street that he had decorated with trees and vines that he made of papier-mâché and was festooned with sardonic graffiti in dripping letters, most of which he had scrawled himself. He had written his favorite message, "Rehab Is for Quitters," on several other buildings, some of which were owned by his parents.

Mordy was the family nogoodnik. Parents always make this mistake. In every family that has two children of the same gender, one is always marked the nogoodnik and the other the allrightnik. The parents so label them at such an early age that they invariably grow up to live out their designated labels.

That was why Mordy had assumed his role as the third generation of failed entrepreneurs but Nathan, feeling the pressure of being the allrightnik, had opened a photocopy store. Nathan was no more capable of charging neighborhood people for photocopies than Harry had been able to charge them rent. But he did manage to charge enough to cover his operating expenses, which were not much because his family owned the building. Artists from the neighborhood—poets, painters, musicians—would come to Nathan because he would not only charge very little, but he could spend an hour or more working with the artist on just the right layout and size for the poster or flyer.

Nathan felt that he should take the half million dollars from Katz, but he also knew that the store that would replace his would not help East Village artists and so it would not contribute to the neighborhood. Instead, it was part of an attempt to drive all of them out and replace them with people like the parents of Sarah's inconstant best friend, Maya.

These were the issues being juggled—several balls too many—in his mind while seated on a contour-molded bench on a downtown F train burrowing under Greenwich Village to a clearly un-Latin beat. It was a fox-trot. Chow Mein would have called it a Jewish beat. One-two, three and four. One-two, three and four. Suddenly the rhythm changed. Somewhere under Manhattan in a dark and barely lit tunnel of rock, the train slowed and then stopped. Nathan felt the oxygen steadily depleting, as though movement had created the oxygen, the same way fish have to keep water moving through their gills to breathe. His heart was throbbing, reverberating through the thick cavities of his frail body, shaking him, thudding loudly enough for the other passengers to hear.

He realized that he was having a heart attack. His body was chilling and heating up at the same time, feeling cold inside while his skin was burning and sweat was pumping out of him at a startling rate. He had to get out of this train before his heart exploded. But the heart attack was only part of the problem. He was suffocating. Drowning. Or he was about to drown, and he could not get to the surface. He had to get out! Yet he could not do anything but remain motionless and pretend that he was perfectly all right—just riding on the subway. Could he scream for help? The act of screaming might save him. Or pounding the conductor's cabin, telling the son of a bitch to move the train *now*! But he could not let people see that he was panicking, because then they might try to restrain him—hold him down. He had to control himself. If he seemed in control, he would gain control. He wished he could talk to someone. Normal conversation could bring him back, occupy him until the train started moving.

"When do you think they will move this thing?" he said to a heavy-set woman with a square jaw standing in front of him.

He knew he had sounded a little too desperate, but if he could just talk to her until the train moved, he would be all right. She shrugged and inched herself to a barely perceptible but safer distance.

"I'm sorry," said Nathan, springing to his feet, realizing that his own movement could relieve the anxiety of the train not moving. "Do you want this seat?" She didn't, but Nathan gave it up anyway and began pacing the car. Why didn't they move the train while there was still oxygen left? Not much was left. Could he talk to someone? Not the thin man in leather with gold oval dark glasses that made him look like an insect. Not the gaunt man with an African face in the powder blue suit and black silk shirt with tan-and-black patent-leather shoes that he tapped to a religious song that engrossed him. It was a hymn. Like on the deck of a sinking ship. Was he praying?

Of course, Nathan was being completely irrational, and he only had to gain control until the train moved. If he didn't, he would have a heart attack! It could start at any minute. The heart attack. Or the train. Maybe it wasn't going to move at all. It could be stuck for hours. Or even a half hour. He couldn't make it! If only it could get into the West

Fourth Street station, probably not far away at all, he would get out and never take a subway again. It was a solemn pledge. A bargain he was offering.

The difference between swimming and drowning was just state of mind. Swimming! It had all started with swimming. Sarah wanted swimming lessons. But he couldn't think about that now. No. He needed to think of something. Think about swimming lessons. Of the $500,000 offer. Money for swimming lessons. It didn't matter. What mattered? Breathing mattered! No, something else. Sex. Sex could always clear everything else out of the way. What would sex be like with someone on this train? He looked frantically through the car. Not good. He could have sex with Sonia. This was no time for sex with his wife. You can never distract yourself by sex with your wife. He found this thought funny. He may even have been distracted by it for a second. If only the train had moved. The German pastry maker's daughter. What would it be like to remove her clothes article by article?

The train lurched. They were gliding into West Fourth Street. He could get out and walk across Fourth Street. But the door didn't open. They were going to keep going without letting anyone off!

The train stopped. The doors opened. Slowly the air came back. His skin cooled off. The sweat was cooling on him. It was over.

This had never happened to him before. Had he contracted a case of claustrophobia? Could it happen like that? Was it a disease that was picked up somewhere? Was it curable? Could he never again take subways or elevators? That would be possible if he stayed in his neighborhood, the way his father did because he feared rivers, Nathan didn't know why. Something had happened as a child and now his father feared the East River, even got uncomfortable as he got closer to Avenue D. Nothing was ever mentioned about the Hudson on the other side. Was Nathan, too, now trapped in his neighborhood by his fears? Was he afraid of all confinement or just subways? Maybe it was just the F train. Maybe it would never happen again.

This could be a turning point in his life, just like the $500,000 Katz deal. But Nathan knew that neither of these conflicts was what he had woken up dreading. Something would make this a bad day. A worse day. On this Friday he was meeting with an ill-fated destiny.

. . .

On Friday night, bakeries on Second Avenue sold challah. The one on Fourth Street was still kosher but sold out by three in the afternoon, not because that many Jews had to have their challah kosher, but because the kosher bakery did not make many, on the assumption that few kosher people were left. Since all the kosher people knew this, they bought early. By three o'clock the action shifted to the bakery on Seventh Street, which was not kosher but at least was Jewish. Once that bakery had sold its last loaf of braided egg bread, anyone who wanted challah had to resort to Chaim's. Chaim's was one of the oldest bakeries in the neighborhood, but several years earlier Chaim, having decided to spend his remaining years pondering a blue sea he never wanted to step into, had moved to Boca Raton and sold his bakery to an industrious Korean family.

The Koreans carefully learned the recipes and continued all the traditions, even though they found many of the foods unpronounceable. Halvah was a particularly daunting oral challenge. They never ran out of challah, baking it fresh every day because they did not understand that it was for Friday night. This destroyed the Edelweiss challah business. The Edelweiss too had tried selling challah on Friday night, but most Jews would rather get their challah from a Korean than a German, even if most of the Jews in the neighborhood regarded the Edelweiss as the best bakery. The store had been there since the 1940s, the late 1940s—that was the problem. No one knew where Mr. and Mrs. Edelweiss came from. They had posters of Heidelberg and Munich's Oktoberfest on their walls. But Nathan happened to know that their real name was Moellen and they came from Berlin. Actually, he wasn't sure that Moellen was their real name. There was no reason to be suspicious of them, and even Nathan's mother bought their strudel. In fact, she loved their apple strudel.

Ruth served the same meal every Friday night: pickled herring in sour cream, brisket with boiled vegetables, and Edelweiss's apple strudel. Ruth Seltzer was not a great or imaginative cook. She had never wanted to be a good homemaker. She would have liked to go to college and thought she would have liked being in business. But her parents saw no point in that and were relieved when their only daughter found a man to marry. They accepted Harry's claim of impresarioship without question, turning over the family business affairs to him. Ruth understood that Harry's important credential to her parents was being male. She was angry but remained silent. She had an idea that she could manage the holdings much better, but if she had questioned Harry's business skills to her father, he would have said, "So why are you marrying this bum?" Besides, everyone loved Harry, and if she ever criticized him to anyone, the response would have been that she was unappreciative for "all Harry was doing." Harry, it was said, had kept their holdings solvent in the 1960s and 1970s, when crime and poverty drove down the little value neighborhood property had once had.

"Thank God for Harry," Ruth's oldest friend, Esther, who had moved to the Bronx decades ago but still visited, would say. "He keeps this neighborhood alive on charm alone. You're lucky to have a charmer."

"Oboyoboy," was Ruth's only answer.

Ruth knew that for all Harry's charm, the family was not as solvent as everyone imagined. She could have managed the properties and made money. Even in "the bad times" you could charge rent and make people pay the way other landlords did. But she would be hated for it, because everyone loved Harry.

Her revenge was to refuse domesticity. She said, "A woman who cooks too well is asking for trouble." It can never be certain that she would have been capable of cooking well if she had chosen to.

"What kind of trouble?" Esther would ask. Ruth would shrug and point at Harry. Esther would think that Ruth was difficult and she was lucky she had a man like Harry.

No one thought of Harry as trouble. Added to Ruth's frustration, he did not care if their house was orderly and he far preferred going out to dining in. But Friday night was Ruth's weekly bout with domesticity.

Nathan, the family allrightnik, avoided his mother on Fridays because she would ask him to "stop off and buy a little strudel from Mr. Edelweiss." It was not Mr. Edelweiss he dreaded. It was his daughter, Karoline. For the past twenty years, Nathan had dreamed of tearing the clothes off of Karoline's fleshy body and devouring her nakedness like an apple strudel. He didn't know why he felt this way. She was an ordinary-looking woman. He was certain that most men barely noticed her short brown hair, her porcelain blue eyes, or the fact that when you were close to her body, she had the scent of fresh butter. Was it because of all the butter in the pastry shop? Had her body somehow absorbed butter fumes?

Nathan would watch other men not look at her and feel reassured that she was not a particularly attractive woman. But he could not look at her without imagining. Would her entire body smell of butter? He once came very close to finding out.

He had planned to take her to dinner, only the second non-Jewish date of his life, but thank God his mother never learned about this. Karoline lived in an apartment in the building with the pastry shop. Her parents lived on the upper floors. And of course, that entire building smelled of butter.

But once they were alone and she got close to him, his dairy-driven libido went wild. He grabbed her, squeezed her, pulled her toward him, ran his nose along the soft line of her flesh—but, for some reason that he would ever after regret, he decided that they should have dinner first, as planned.

At dinner, over an appetizer of mussels at an Italian seafood place on Seventh Street, they somehow blundered onto the subject of Germany. Maybe they both thought it would have been too unnatural not to. She knew he was Jewish. He knew she was German. She said that her father came from Berlin and that he arrived in New York in 1949. Nathan couldn't resist pointing out that this was the same year that his uncle Nusan was found with numbers on his arm. She said that there "was a lot of confusion in Europe in those years" and volunteered that Moellen wasn't her father's real name.

"Really," said Nathan, failing at disinterest. "What was his real name?" He wanted to suggest Eichmann as a little joke, but he used restraint. She didn't know what his real name was. He grew more curious, asked more questions, grew less polite about it. She grew suspiciously defensive and finally accused him of suggesting that her father was a Nazi. He, misquoting Shakespeare, said that she "doth protest a bit much."

Later he had to admit that you couldn't really protest too much about your own father being accused of being a mass murderer, but at the time he thought it was very significant that she took such exception to his questions. They both went home full of anger. But he never got the scent of her from his nostrils—more than butter, maybe butter and sugar? Even after he was married, he sometimes lay in bed at night imagining Karoline Moellen naked in his bed.

For several years, while he was having these thoughts, they didn't speak. He denied himself those wonderful, thin layered tortes that he desired almost as much as their confectioner. For a time he even refused to get the strudel for his mother, suggesting that they might be Nazis, which Ruth then passed on to Harry's brother, Nusan. Nusan had ways of finding out such things, but he never said anything more about it. Ruth kept buying the strudel. Nathan would sometimes buy it for her. He did not bring up the subject of the Moellens' past again because he thought that perhaps *he* was protesting too much and would give himself away.

One day on Tenth Street Karoline kissed him hello, a light touch of her lips on his cheek, close enough for the scent—not butter and sugar: buttered flesh. Buttered sex. He quickly moved down the street. After that he would sometimes see her and feel so overcome with lust that he thought it showed. He would never go to the Edelweiss with his wife for fear she would see his yearning.

As Nathan entered his apartment on this fated Friday, his destiny had already been set in motion. He had planned to talk to Sonia about Ira Katz and his offer, but when Sonia told him that his mother had asked him to pick up the strudel, panic erased all thoughts of Copy Katz. Fearing his wife would want to come with him, and having already acquired the too quick false voice of an adulterer, he agreed and, taking Sarah with him for protection, mounted her on his shoulders.

She liked riding up there. She liked playing with his hair, and he liked it, too—tiny fingers stroking, and curling, and gathering up his hair. But now he could feel her recalcitrance above his shoulders. She was not playing with his hair, was not happy. They rode to First Avenue, avoiding Sixth Street, where aging men were always in search of Jewish men for their Friday night minyan—one of the things his small daughter on his shoulder could shield him from.

On Tenth Street the pushers, still discussing the remains of Eli Rabbinowitz, knew to avoid Nathan and his daughter. There was only that fat little boy—a sturdily built little cube of a boy with black curly hair. He reminded Nathan of Fat Finkelstein, who was the meanest kid when he went to school. Finkelstein was the only boy in Nathan's class who had not successfully avoided the draft. He went to Vietnam, and it was an unverified rumor that Fat Finkelstein had died in a place called Khe Sanh. Nathan kept a horror of that name Khe Sanh, the cruel place that had finally given Fat Finkelstein much more than he deserved.

Now Nathan recognized that this boy was the ill-fated Fat Finkelstein of his generation. It was his belief that, like a Talmudic legend, every generation had its mean but luckless Fat Finkelstein.

The chubby eight-year-old looked up at Sarah and stuck out his tongue. He always did this, trying to catch her at a moment when she was looking and Nathan wasn't. On cue, Sarah began crying. He was a mean kid, but Nathan had to be sympathetic because the Fat Finkelsteins are all fated to meet a bad end. Nathan had tried to convince Sarah that the boy stuck his tongue out only because she cried and that if she wouldn't cry, it would ruin it for him. But it always made her cry. The Fat Finkelstein of his generation thought that he might have made a mistake in timing. Nathan might have seen him. He waddled up the stoop of his brownstone as fast as he could hoist his pudgy cubic body and then hid in the entrance to his building. The door remained opened a crack, through which he still watched.

Nathan took Sarah off his shoulders, but she was inconsolable. This was about more than the Fat Finkelstein of her generation. Finally she told him, still sobbing, "They're going to Punim County!"

"Who is?" asked Nathan, struggling not to laugh because *punim* is Yiddish for "face," and the county was named Putnam.

"My best friend, Maya, is going to Punim County."

"Punim County," Nathan repeated, but Sarah saw nothing funny. Her best friend was hardly ever going to be around this summer.

"And Daddy," she added pointedly, "she is taking swimming lessons."

Swimming lessons. There, she was asking again. The Gemorah, the midrash, somewhere in the Talmud, the obligations of a Jewish father are listed. Teaching the Torah, teaching a craft, finding a mate. And one is to teach the child to swim "because his life may depend on it." Nathan asked Rabbi Litvak to explain the significance of learning swimming. "It refers to the Egyptians who drowned when the sea parted. Why? We are our enemies and we must be ready. This raises the questions How can we be our enemy? and Ready for what? It is interesting that in most languages both the enemy and the enemy's enemy are called enemy. A killer or a robber has a victim, but an enemy has only an enemy. . . ." In time Nathan excused himself, still not knowing why he had an obligation to teach his child swimming.

Of course, these obligations were only toward a son and included circumcision. Nathan's father had not taught him to swim, because Harry was afraid of water. But he had to do better than his father. That was the point. Was he supposed to have a summer home in Putnam County? There was no doubt in his mind that he did not want one, but was this something contemporary fathers were supposed to offer? After a couple of millennia, was it time to revise the list of a father's obligations? Preschool, summer home in Putnam County, sell your business and take the money. A modern Talmud might read differently.

Nathan turned up Eleventh Street, walking toward this Friday's nameless fate. So far, he had learned that he was a financially insolvent claustrophobe who harbored adulterous lust and had not taught his daughter to swim. And it was only four o'clock.

CHAPTER FOUR

Calamity in Disguise

W AS THAT ALL? Was today the Friday he realized all his short-comings? Or was there some other fate, some unforeseen defining moment still waiting for him? Had he avoided a mistake on the Copy Katz deal by deciding to put off a decision? "I need some time," he had pleaded at the meeting.

"Sure," said Ira Katz. "Take a couple minutes." Then he laughed and said he was joking.

Nathan turned up to Eleventh Street with his daughter back on his shoulder, moving away from the drug pushers that Maya's parents probably didn't expose their daughter to. He stopped in to see Sal Eleven, who had the best mozzarella and bread, although Nathan's mother would have neither for *Shabbas*—though any other day it was a welcome alternative to cooking. Both Ruth and her family welcomed alternatives to her cooking.

Sal Eleven was short—none of the Sals was tall—with thick dark hair, one bushy eyebrow across his face like a thick black hyphen between his two large ears. He wore disdain the way most people wear simple indifference. He had a television mounted on the wall at exactly his eye level, which was an awkward height for most people. He kept it on a news station, which he greeted with dismissive waves of his hand and disgusted, disbelieving nods of his head.

"Hey, how ya *dew*-in," he said, and handed up an olive to Sarah without ever removing his gaze from the television. He always gave her an olive, which resulted in olive oil being rubbed into Nathan's hair, which the anointed father reasoned was a positive thing, though he never understood what became of the pit. At home her mother was still cutting up grapes so she wouldn't choke on the seeds.

"Terrible about Rabbinowitz, isn't it? He was a nice man."

Sal brushed away Rabbinowitz's claim to niceness with his usual sweep of the right hand. "So what do you think of the block committee?"

"The block committee?"

"Yeah, these cockamamies with the meetings want to push the pushers off." He said this while staring at the television, as though this were the subject of the news program.

"Well, I guess that's a good idea."

Sal smiled cynically and dismissed everything with a wave of his hand. "So you got a few Puerto Ricans selling smoke in the neighborhood. As long as they don't let those Dominicans in with the crack. And they won't. Puerto Ricans hate the Dominicans. It's dumb guys and dumber guys. But it's good for the neighborhood. You know why?"

Nathan knew Sal would wait until he asked, "Why?"

Then he continued, "Because it keeps the fucking Japanese out."

Nathan had learned to amuse himself by pursuing logic in these conversations that he knew logic would deftly elude. Sarah, who probably looked as though she were not listening from her lofty perch, would absorb it all and later reinterpret it for Nathan in a way that made even less sense than the original. Sal reached up with another olive, more oil for Nathan's hair.

"How do they keep the Japanese out?"

"Are you really that naïve?" Sal Eleven asked, his brow furrowed in feigned concern. "The Japanese? The Japanese take over everything. First they move in with their sushi, then sesame, then sezayou—before long, it's a Japanese neighborhood. And the Koreans work for them. They worked this all out ahead of time over there in their old country. The Japanese send in the Koreans to work for them. You see all these Korean stores with the soy sauce and the little dried peas. The Japanese put them in business. Yuppies and Japanese. Why do you think that German is pushing this?"

"German?"

Sal looked impatient. "That German, Herr Achtung Swinebraten."

"Mr. Edelweiss?"

"Mr. Edelweiss. Whatever. I'll tell you something. Nobody knows his real name, but it's not Edelweiss."

"I know. I just always called him that. It's Moellen."

"Yeah, nobody knows his name," Sal reasserted as though Nathan had not really spoken. "The Germans, the Japanese." He held out his hands as though comparing the weight of the two nationalities. "They are always in it together, remember that. The Germans. The Japanese."

"And the Italians."

"Get out of here. You want a mozarrell'?"

From Sal's they turned the corner to First Avenue, which had its own Friday competition. Rosa's Pizzeria made *bacala pomidora* for the weekend. Rosa was from Naples, and her shining long hair, the color of chrome, and deep-set chocolate eyes and carefully placed cheekbones gave her a beauty that stayed with age. There were still people left in Naples who ate salt cod and tomato sauce on Fridays, but none on First Avenue, where the dish was remembered as one of the reasons for leaving. Joey Parma, who grew up eating it, would not sample Rosa's, even though she offered him a taste for free.

Yet she went all the way to New Jersey, to a Portuguese neighborhood, to buy the best salt cod she could find, fish dried stiff as a quarter-inch plank of plywood. She soaked it in her apartment because customers complained of the smell in her shop. At home, where her husband claimed to like the smell and their children had left years ago "for reasons such as this," according to her oldest son, the fish occupied a basin in her bathtub until Friday morning, when it was thick and soft as a flaky fresh fish. It was fried in olive oil, and a sauce made from summer tomatoes and oregano grown on her windowsills was added. She made only a small amount and by Sunday afternoon managed to sell most of it. This caught the attention of Sal First, who felt that his mother's *bacala* in the Sicilian way with olives and capers would sell better than Rosa's Neapolitana salt fish and tomatoes. But it didn't until he started adding hot pepper to entice the Puerto Ricans. Now he was living in fear that his mother would come into the store on a weekend and find out what he had done to her *bacala*.

Nathan liked to try out Sal First with his Sal Eleven information. And today of all days, he wanted many opinions before he decided on anything. Sal First was short and dark like the soon-to-be-elected President Dukakis. Sal First's hair stuck up and pointed the wrong way, as though it were misdirected by static electricity. For a few years, Sal's hair had been vanishing, and then one day he added rows of dark tufts so that his head took on the appearance of a freshly planted rice paddy.

Soon his hair was growing back, but some mistake had been made and it was growing in the wrong direction, making him permanently appear as though he had just gotten out of bed.

"So what do you think of the block committee, Sal?"

"What do I think?" Sal said, seemingly outraged. He looked around the store to see who was listening and then leaned forward furtively. "I think I don't give a good flying shit. Oh, sorry," he apologized, looking up at Sarah and covering his mouth. "Here," and he delicately handed her a half artichoke bottom. More olive oil for Nathan's hair.

"I hope they arrest that man," declared Mrs. Skolnik, who had worn white pearl rhinestone-studded 1950s pixie glasses, the kind that came to a sharp point at both temples, for so long that they had come back into fashion. Mordy called her "the shoelace patrol," because every time she had seen him in the last forty years, she had followed him down the street, calling, "Mordy, Mordy," and when she got his attention, which was always difficult, she would point at his shoes and say, "You are going to trip." And he would smile pleasantly and continue walking.

"What man?" said Sal at the meat slicer, curling off paper-thin prosciutto.

"The one who shot Mr. Rabbinowitz."

"Forget about it. They're still trying to piece together his face." Nathan pointed at Sarah above him with his eyeballs, trying to get Sal to stop. But he continued, "It's like a broken teacup or something. You can stand there all day with the fucking glue, but there's always a few pieces missing."

"I gave the police a description," Mrs. Skolnik confessed nervously.

"Who knows where the missing pieces are. You never find them."

"I very carefully described the man to them."

"You saw him?" said Nathan.

"Who?" asked Sal.

"Yes. I heard the gunshot and I saw a man running up First Avenue."

"How do you know it was the man who shot him? Did he have a gun?" Nathan probed.

"You see, the police said the exact same thing. But you could see he was a killer. You could see he had just killed."

"Did he kill him because he didn't want him in his house?" asked Sarah.

The woman looked over Nathan's head in confusion. "He just looked like a killer."

"Daddy," said Sarah, "where is my notebook?"

"What did he look like?" Sal asked.

"Daddy," Sarah half whined and half shouted, "I need my notebook!"

"He was very large and had a lot of black hair and wild crazy eyes like a killer."

"Daddy, I need it now!" Her mood was starting to turn, and Nathan knew he had to leave.

"The police said they needed more details, but what more do you need? They should arrest him. He was from the neighborhood."

"Daddy, I want to take notes. Now! I want to!"

Nathan was running out of time and drifting dangerously close to Sixth Street, where the minyan grabbers were waiting. He gingerly walked up to the Edelweiss window and looked past the rows of wondrously layered tortes. Moellen and his wife were behind the counter under a poster of Heidelberg, a city with which they had no connection. Karoline was not in. It was a better day than he had thought. He did not want to see her today. He had almost had sex with her in his mind on the F train earlier.

Not wanting to add cookie crumbs to his oily hair, he lowered Sarah off his shoulders and walked in.

He baked and she sold. When caught together, they smiled. They smiled much more than either of them ever did separately—as though it were a competition between them. He was lean and tall and seemed stern, except that he had an unpredictable sense of humor that functioned better in the unpredictably dark world of children. Without warning, he would be on the floor pumping off five push-ups, then standing up with arms raised, flexing his biceps. Sarah looked dutifully frightened when his lips protruded and he put on his stern Teutonic face. She understood that this was the game and that soon he would do something funny.

His wife was not robust like him, and she never did anything funny. She was thin and fragile looking. Her hair fell straight down and was gray. She had never colored it. Her face was delicately but not unpleasantly lined with age. Oddly, there was a slight crease vertically down her right cheek, almost as though tears had left a scar. Nathan didn't remember ever noticing this line before, but surely it had been there for a very long time. He thought back on all the years he had known her and was horrified to realize that since boyhood he had always found something very desirable about her, and though she was now quite old, it was still there. She looked as though she desperately wanted to be held. Was that what drew him to her daughter also? He could not remember.

"Why do you come in here with your big eyes?" Moellen snapped. Sarah, taking her cue, looked worried. There was always a treat to eat at the end of the game. "Ven big-eyed children kom in hier, you know vat I do. No? I show you." And with his lanky stride he went to the kitchen doorway. "Look! You see? *Jah.* An oven. Into de oven mit dem all. Und den, vait, I show you."

Nathan was frozen to his place, filled with horror, though a smile of feigned delight was painted too broadly on his face. Moellen quickly returned from the kitchen with a baking sheet. Now Sarah smiled.

"Take one!" he ordered. "It may be one of your friends." Sarah squealed and gurgled laughter as she looked at the tray of gingerbread men, chose one, and started to nibble on a foot.

"Yes," commanded Moellen. "Start mit a leg—one of your friend's legs. Und den—den, vat do you eat next?"

Sarah only laughed. Mrs. Moellen smiled distantly until the door opened. Nathan did not have to turn to know who it was, and no, her appeal was entirely different from that of her mother.

"Come on, Sarah, let's get the strudel. An apple strudel, please."

"Achh!" said Moellen. "Now dat you have eaten the legs of your fwiend, you must eat"—he looked around his shop—"a head!" He presented a plate of garish pink marzipan heads with kelly green hats. "You better eat one."

Sarah hesitated and looked at her father. "I think you've had enough," he said. "It will make you sick."

"No, it won't."

"And your mom will blame me."

"Let's not tell her!"

That sounded like an enormously good idea. Sarah ate one of the bright little heads, sadistically nibbling a feature at a time, the nose, the chin. Nathan tried not to think of Eli Rabbinowitz's face. How well this German understood children, and they loved him. Nathan too as a child had loved going to the Edelweiss to be teased by the funny German. Was that where this interest in things German began? Nathan wondered.

After the strudel was wrapped and paid for, Nathan turned around. She was there waiting, her hip cocked in a casual pose, her lips moist and soft. Did it show? Did it show?

"Hello, Karoline, nice to see you."

"Hello, Nathan." She gave him that slight touch of lip on the cheek, just close enough to fill his head with her buttery perfume and then retreat. "You could call me," she whispered.

Nathan smiled politely and walked out with his apple strudel and daughter. When they got home, Sarah ran to Sonia and said, "Mommy, Mommy, guess what? I had three olives, an alphachoke, and somebody's head."

Some co-conspirator, that Sarah. He should remember that. Still, he was home, it was *Shabbas,* and whatever he was dreading had not happened. Unless it had, and he couldn't see it. Calamity sometimes wears disguises.

CHAPTER FIVE

The Meshugaloo Himself

SWEET-FACED RUBEN had given the block an all-clear wave because the linen-suited Joey Parma had turned east, away from their block toward the Casita Meshugaloo, a vacant lot on which a Puerto Rican country house had been built. The house had been covered with enough red and turquoise paint to conceal the questionable carpentry and in places skilled carpentry with questionable materials. A railing across the front porch was made out of dismantled wooden chairs. On top of this little one-story building dwarfed by six-floor tenements on three sides flew the red, white, and blue flag of Puerto Rico and the blue-and-white flag of Israel.

The remaining lot space was used to grow tomatoes, beans, and corn. They had even planted two banana bushes. It was an uncertain agricultural society, New Yorkers trying to grow food with the memories of their parents. Aside from five brilliant amber sunflowers, the crops were not doing well. But it was still early summer. Already, prospering weeds had grown into high bushes that gave the lot the illusion of lushness, much the way thick tropical vegetation had hidden the poverty in their parents' island. New York in the summertime is tropical, too, and any patch of soil left alone will turn uselessly bushy and green. It must have been a jungle each summer before Europeans started building here.

But in Manhattan, buildings had their own natural law the way plants do in other places. Vacant lots where tenements had been removed by real estate speculators stood like gaps from missing teeth, waiting for the right time to build. The right time would be soon. In the meantime, the holes had been overgrown by gardens, parks, casitas. In Manhattan's natural law, space does not go unused. The squatters who had moved into Harry's buildings followed this natural law, too. Real estate abhors a vacuum even more than does nature.

Most of the time, Chow Mein Vega, the Meshugaloo himself, could be found seated inside the casita at a round table made from a huge spool that had once held cable.

Chow Mein Vega had invented the word "meshugaloo," perhaps the only word of a language called "Spiddish" that was a cross of Nuyorican Spanish and Lower East Side Yiddish and thus a purely New York idiom. For the contribution of the word "meshugaloo," Chow Mein Vega was the only gentile to have had his name in the sidewalk of Saul Grossman's Deli on Second Avenue, where the greats of Yiddish theater were meticulously inscribed in concrete. The *Forward* interviewed him on the occasion of his name being installed and asked him what "meshugaloo" meant.

"It's a cross between meshugenah and boogaloo. If you think about it, it is a meshugenah boogaloo."

"But what does that mean?"

"Meshugenah, you know, means meshugenah."

"Yes."

"You know, crazy. And boogaloo . . . boogaloo means everything. It is a fusion. A rhythm-and-blues beat with a Latin twist. It is very elusive, you know. A cha-cha-cha has that three-beat, and a salsa—let's face it, you have to have form for salsa and mambo. But with boogaloo you can do anything. Wave your arms. You can wiggle your hips. You are in tempo. Boogaloo means everything and yet it means nothing. *Es gornisht pero todo.* You know what I'm saying. That's its appeal. It's very heavy-duty. Boogaloo—ahhh! Forget it!"

This answer was then translated into Yiddish for the Yiddish-language edition. Chow Mein Vega spoke Spanish and English the same way, offering rhythms, not clarity. Nor was his name really Chow Mein Vega. It was Carlos Rodriguez. According to his promoter, Howard Gold, another Spiddish speaker, "The name Carlos Rodriguez would be excellent for baseball, but for boogaloo *eso no dice bupkiss.*" It says nothing.

New York Latinos did not remember the Chicago act Tom and Jerrio, which recorded the first boogaloo in 1965. Its most enduring innovation was the line "Sock it to me," which became a mantra, repeated for all occasions in the late sixties. In Detroit, Chicago, and Philadelphia, boogaloo was black music. But in New York, Puerto Ricans fused it with salsa and made "the Latin boogaloo." Latin boogaloo was invented not by Carlos Rodriguez, but by friends of his with whom he had grown up playing baseball in East Harlem, such as Joe Cuba, whose real name, Gilberto Calderón, had also been changed because it was deemed to have said nothing. They had all made money playing together at Jewish clubs in the Catskills in the 1950s. Back in New York in the sixties, playing to Latin and black crowds, with new names invented by Jewish promoters, they had accidentally developed a Latin boogaloo without knowing what the word meant. No one could even remember how it came about.

Many of these Nuyorican boogalooistas carried with them the memories of Jewish clubs in the mountains, though their Jewish fans did not remember them because they now had new names. At first, Carlos did not want to be called Chow Mein. But after his biggest hit, "The Yiddish Boogaloo," people all over the world knew him as Chow Mein Vega and the name to him became synonymous with money and success. "It's funny," he said. "You become somebody and that's it. *Es fartík.* It's done." After "The Yiddish Boogaloo," he knew that he would always be Chow Mein Vega, even though he suspected that he was trapped in a half-truth.

Most boogalooistas had a defining boogaloo, such as Ricardo Ray's "Danzon Boogaloo" or Pete Rodriguez's "Pete's Boogaloo." It was New York music. The idea for "The Yiddish Boogaloo" came from the neighborhood. Joe Cuba's 1967 "Bang Bang" described the cultural tension between blacks and Latinos in Harlem, between cornbread and *lechón.* But "The Yiddish Boogaloo" was about a different neighborhood:

> *Eh! Yiddisha bugaloo*
> *Meshugaloo—ahhh!*
> *Meshugaloo—ahh!*
> *Second Avenue—ahhhh!*
> *Go to the deli,*
> *And you will find,*
> *Corned beef, pasteles,*
> *And pastrami on rye.*
> *And for dessert—mofongo pie!*

And as you leave
They'll give you
A kishka good-bye.

Thousands of people would raise their arms and shout in a slow crescendo, "Meshugaloo—ahhhh!" It became a spontaneous cry whenever Chow Mein Vega and his six-piece band appeared on a stage—in New York; San Juan; São Paulo; Paris; Juneau, Alaska; Tel Aviv; Tokyo— "Meshugaloo—ahhhh!"

For a moment, it transformed the neighborhood. It was the late sixties, and the yippies had moved in, buying their smoke on Tenth Street. Yiddish theaters on Second Avenue were being turned into rock concert halls. But after Chow Mein Vega's "Yiddish Boogaloo," hundreds came downtown to eat at Saul Grossman's Deli. He even added *pasteles* to the menu. Chow Mein's mother came down to show his cooks—most of whom were uptown blacks—how to make her *pasteles,* while Rabbi Chaim Litvak from the little synagogue on Sixth Street observed, making certain that these *pasteles* were in accordance with the book of Deuteronomy, certifiably kosher *pasteles.* Rabbi Litvak worked with Mrs. Rodriguez on a recipe with ground beef instead of pork, mixed with a hamless tomato *sofrito,* which is a sautéed sauce base. Problems came with the masa, the grated green banana dough, on the outside. Mrs. Rodriguez almost gave up when Rabbi Litvak told her she could not add cream to the masa because the filling had meat. She had always regarded the cream as the hidden touch that made her *pasteles* special and had even hesitated to reveal her secret. She did not care that her snobbish neighbor from the island always claimed that the cream was "a completely Nuyorican thing." There is a great difference of opinion on whether Nuyorican is a pejorative adjective. It depended on the speaker. Sal First could make "Spanish" sound pejorative.

With great reluctance, Mrs. Rodriguez backed off from her Nuyorican cream recipe. Still, it took considerable research to find a supplier who was able to assure that their banana leaves, the outer wrapper of *pasteles,* were acceptable to rabbinic standards.

Saul liked the *pasteles* and tried to get the team of Rodriguez and Litvak working on a *mofongo* pie, Saul not realizing that *mofongo* was never served in a pie. But Mrs. Rodriguez was not difficult. She accepted the idea of putting *mofongo* in a piecrust. But what to her was not negotiable was mashing the green bananas in pork fat. Everyone knows that it is pork fat that makes *mofongo* good. They tried numerous alternative fats, but they could never find one that both Mrs. Rodriguez and Rabbi Litvak could approve. Rabbi Litvak thought mashed plantains in garlic and soy oil—"a good pareve oil," he argued—was a great dish. "You could even boil them like dumplings and put them in soup," he suggested. *Plátano knadlech.*

No, Mrs. Rodriguez shook her head insistently, raising her arm and waving her outstretched fingers. "This *mofongo* tastes of nada. *Na-da!*"

Rabbi Litvak, a connoisseur of didactic hand movements, admired the gesture. A stubborn man, he profited from the entire encounter. Though Saul Grossman could not find an acceptable *mofongo* for *mofongo* pie, Litvak started using mashed green bananas, garlic, and soy oil as a snack along with the herring for Friday night kiddushes. Litvak's *mofongo* was also perfect for the rabbi's Sunday morning breakfasts, which by tradition emphasized fats and carbohydrates. Every Sunday morning, a handful of aging followers sat with the rabbi and debated on Jewish writings and the events of the day while being served Scotch, bourbon, noodle kugel, Yankel Fink's knishes—arguably the densest material ever made by man—and the rabbi's kosher *mofongo*. Sometimes Eli Rabbinowitz would come, and then he would contribute blintzes laid out in disposable aluminum pans that got misshapened as Litvak's followers hungrily grabbed for them because Rabbinowitz never brought enough, and the polite and the slow would be left with *mofongo*. Thank God for the noodle kugel. Thank God for the bourbon.

With the shooting of Rabbinowitz, there would be no more blintzes for the rabbi's breakfast. From a gastronomic point of view, they would have preferred that Yankel Fink had been shot.

When Joey Parma arrived at the casita, his linen wilted in mid-morning heat, he admired the neat rows of struggling crops, pastel flowering peas, drooping tomato vines with small, misshapen yellow fruit, and lush weed patches. Chow Mein was standing in front of a four-foot fruitless banana plant, stroking a broad, limp leaf. He had gained almost one hundred pounds since the boogaloo days, and with his often incomprehensible pronouncements and his rounding size, he was becoming more suggestive of Buddha than boogaloo. The banana bush looked very small next to him.

"Joey, did you ever see a banana grow?"

"I'm Italian."

"Me either. I'm Puerto Rican. I should be able to grow bananas. I wonder how they do it," Chow Mein said, thoughtfully stroking his gnarled and stumpy ponytail, which was not doing much better than the bananas.

"Well, I'm Italian and I cannot make a good espresso. Not like they make in Italy. Some say it's the water. But there are Italian restaurants here that do it. What are you going to do with the bananas? Did you see the article in the *Times*? Enrico Petruchi uses them with sea bass and endive."

Chow Mein was silent for a minute. He was not going to give this white guy the satisfaction of showing that he didn't know who Enrique Petuque was. "I just want to see them grow. A casita should have bananas," he finally said.

"Were you here last night?"

"The Hamptons are so crowded this time of year."

Joey showed no sign of appreciating the joke.

"Is it true you couldn't find his head?"

"We got his head. We even got the angle of the firing, so we know the height of the killer."

"Unless he shoots from a weird angle," said Chow Mein, knowing that the cops had already decided that whatever height they came up with was the height of Latino people. He stood up, as though daring Joey to make a note of his height, and said, "You know we shouldn't talk here. Cops in a casita is a very bad gestalt, *tu sabe'.*"

"Let's go eat something."

Chow Mein knew he would say that. He tried to cooperate with the police because he, too, had loved drugs in the sixties but hated them in the eighties. He had lost too many friends. Also he liked to eat with Joey Parma, because if you ate with Joey, it was always "on the house."

"You know," said Chow Mein, "I'd like to go to Rabbinowitz's. I loved his blintzes. With the sour cream." He snapped his fingers.

"Well, closed today."

"It was the last good blintzes in the neighborhood. What are we going to do?"

"There's a new little French place."

"If I can't have blintzes," said Chow Mein, gently dusting some kind of white powder off Joey Parma's linen jacket, "let's go *cuchifrito*."

As they walked around the corner to the *cuchifrito*, Chow Mein nodded thoughtfully while Joey explained what he had just learned: how to use talcum powder to remove a grease stain. They stood at a counter and ate fried bananas and beans and fat slices of pork roasted with garlic and coriander seeds, served with a pepper sauce that immediately produced intense pain. When Joey was able to speak again, he looked at Chow Mein through the tears in his own eyes, shook his head, and said, "Good, huh?" And Chow Mein laughed.

"It's the endorms," Joey opined.

"No, it's Consuela. She makes it like that. It's murder. Forget it."

"But we like it because of the endorms. It causes pain and makes your brain send out endorms to kill the pain."

"Why is that good?"

"Makes you feel good."

Chow Mein pulled on his ponytail. "Couldn't you just stub your toe or hit your thumb with a hammer or something?"

"Wouldn't be the same. So, were you up late last night?"

Chow Mein shrugged. "You know, the Meshugaloo never sleeps."

Joey did know. Chow Mein Vega did not sleep at night. He spent his nights at the casita, his Buddha-like body by the cable spool table, working on an autobiography in which he had not yet reached the age of fifteen. While Chow Mein Vega sat at this makeshift table, in his fake farmhouse, with his fake name, pondering the myths and minutiae of his life, he often heard a lot. But he heard nothing the night Eli Rabbinowitz was killed.

Consuela had given huge quantities to please Officer Parma, but she knew the pepper sauce would assure that most of the food went to the Meshugaloo. If she had to give a free meal, she would rather give it to Chow Mein. The Puerto Ricans in the neighborhood knew that the Meshugaloo was not getting many concert bookings anymore and, ignoring the compelling visual evidence, worried that he was not getting enough to eat.

Finally, Joey's endorms getting the best of him, he went to the washroom to put cold water on paper towels and wipe his face, his reddened eyes—he even tried to soothe his burning lips and tongue by patting them with the cool wet paper.

"Chucho," Consuela called out to Chow Mein in a low, conspiratorial voice, using the name only a few in the neighborhood knew him by.

"*Sí, amor,*" Chow Mein said with his show business smile.

"Chucho, we have *problemas* for the fiesta." She was talking about the Avenue D street fair, which was far enough east to be purely for the Puerto Ricans and was in two weeks.

"*Por qué,* what's wrong?"

The problem was that they had no one to play "El Dominicano." Every year Jimmy Colon, who ran the food market on Avenue C, took on El Dominicano in a wrestling match. Jimmy had blond curly hair, blue eyes, and a friendly manner. El Dominicano was large and dark and wore a cape that was the checkered Dominican flag. Always, the good-humored Jimmy Colon appeared to be no match for the ferocious Dominican, El Dominicano. But in the end, El Dominicano found himself pinned to the blue canvas by the friendly and agile Puerto Rican. The problem was that the large and dark El Dominicano, whose name was Joaquin Morel, had perhaps gone too far in playing his national stereotype and was now on what was known on Avenue D as "an island vacation." El Dominicano had sold a little vial of crack cocaine, small and easy to palm with its little red cap with the rose on it, to a fleshy, falsely blond, dark-skinned woman. Not only the hair color was false: She was an undercover agent, and when it was time for the summer street fair, El Dominicano was locked up on Rikers Island prison—an island vacation.

So the neighborhood needed someone else to play El Dominicano. Chow Mein Vega immediately suggested Ruben, the son of his former conga player.

"Ruben is Puerto Rican," argued Consuela.

Chow Mein did not want to point this out with Joey Parma about to come out of the washroom with reconstituted endorms, but Ruben had been spending a lot of time around certain Dominicans, and with what he had been doing, a lot of people in the neighborhood were starting to think he was Dominican. Chow Mein was worried about him and looking for ways to get him involved in the casita. But all he said was, "Ruben has dark skin."

"That boy has such a sweet face. Nobody will believe he is a Dominican," said Consuela. "People will root for him instead of Jimmy."

"He is a big boy, very heavy-duty body. He will look like he can kill Jimmy. He can grow a beard and we can take him to Cristofina for some tattoos and other stuff and . . ."

Joey came out, his face looking patted and pale. "I've got to go," he said. "*Gracias,* Consuela."

"*Por nada.*" Consuela smiled sweetly as Joey went off to Sal First in his continuing investigation of the death of Eli Rabbinowitz. Consuela began wrapping up the leftover food for Chow Mein, adding to the *pernil* two choice pieces of *cuerito,* crisped fatty pork skin—the best part.

"I think Officer Parma didn't like my food," Consuela said with a smile.

"*Eso es como la kikhl tsebrokhn,*" said Chow Mein, staring out at the street.

"*¿Qué?*"

"The way the cookie crumbles," said Chow Mein, already thinking of other matters.

CHAPTER SIX

Tribulations of a Tenth Man

RABBI LITVAK had long ago given up on women. It wasn't sexism, merely pragmatism. The synagogue on Sixth Street had been founded in the 1880s and, it seemed, had slowly lost members ever since. It was down to eight, and it needed ten. Jewish law said so—ten men, a minyan to hold a service. When all else failed—it seemed to be happening more and more—Nathan was nearly kidnapped. Since women did not count for a minyan, they were of no help; they simply did not address the primary problem, which was trying to hold a service. They were welcome but unnecessary, and since no one tried to get women to come, no women came. The horseshoe-shaped balcony where women used to pray had been empty for years. No one ever went up there. It was rumored that squatters lived there.

When the small congregation stood and faced the east for the silent prayer, the *amidah,* taking three steps forward and three back, and began furiously bowing and jerking their heads in impassioned reverence, reciting in their minds the silent prayers, Nathan stood there politely, staring at the eastern balcony.

Suddenly, on more than one Friday, he would see a graying bush of hair appear above the balcony's dark velvet curtain. Slowly his brother Mordy's head would become visible. Mordy would be staring out with sleepy, unfocused eyes, trying to see who had disturbed his rest. Nathan would be looking on in horror as the other men recited the *amidah,* bowing and bobbing their heads, seeing only the Hebrew letters in the book in front of them. A minute later, a woman's head would appear on the balcony, and—though she would always be conspicuously unkosher, black or Chinese or large and blond, and always beautiful and a bit naked—Mordy would shrug and smile weakly at his brother and mouth the words, "She's Jewish," as his bushy head and the silken mane of the Chinese woman slowly disappeared below the dusty balcony velour.

It never really happened, but ever since Nathan had heard that there were squatters living in the balcony, he had been expecting it. He would close his eyes and take three steps backward, and the hallucination would vanish.

The men would gather early. They all wore hats. They even had extra hats for the people they took off the street. If one asked for a yarmulke, Rabbi Litvak would say, "What are you, an Israeli?" Only once the answer came back "Yes."

They wore old gray fedoras that they had been wearing since fedoras had been fashionable. They paced with their hands in their pockets. Some read Hebrew passages from the siddur. They waited anxiously— three of them, five, then seven, then eight. When they got to eight, they wandered the street looking for a ninth man. They tried to get someone from the neighborhood. This was a skill almost everyone in the neighborhood had, recognizing who was from the neighborhood. When Joey Parma found a witness to identify a suspect, one of the first questions, even before the physical description, was, "Did he come from the neighborhood?"

They only needed a ninth man because the tenth man they knew would come eventually, though always a little late, teasing the deadline of official sundown. The tenth man was Nusan, whose lateness was intended to make clear his stand on religion. The older he got, the more Nusan, who no longer believed in God, resembled a Talmudic scholar. He was devout about not believing in God.

But he did keep his head covered with the same dusty brown felt hat all year. Added to that was a maroon scarf that almost passed for a prayer shawl. It was strange to wear such a scarf in the summertime, except that Nusan wore the same clothes all year. He refused to acknowledge the seasons, as though even this would be too much homage to God. He always wore the same dark gray wool suit. It was certainly wool because he had never cut the white embroidered label off the sleeve that asserted "100% pure wool."

In the spring of 1985, Nusan had had a heart attack, which had left him with the habit of rocking back and forth impatiently. Was it a problem of balance or some inner impatience with his weakened state? He had collapsed during a Passover seder, which he had explained he was "going to but not attending." Taken to Beth Israel Hospital, he was told that he had suffered a heart attack. In fact, the doctors discovered that there had been others. Just one more thing that he had suffered alone and would not talk about. And he began this rocking.

Whatever the reason, Nusan the atheist was frequently seen with his head covered, a scarf around his neck, rocking back and forth in the manner of a devout Jewish prayer—davening. He, of course, insisted that he was not davening. "Davening," he often sneered, "is God's one truth. You should be ready to duck at all times."

All he was missing was the beard, which was the subject of the longest-running family joke. Ruth used to say *"Beser a yid on a bord, vi a bord on a yid,"* which literally meant "Better a Jew without a beard than a beard without a Jew." But Nathan and Mordy liked saying, "A Jew without a board is better than a board without a Jew," and eventually, "A Jew without a board is better than a bored Jew," which became the family motto on religious practice.

It was possible that Nusan truly had no religious feelings, that he completed the minyan out of friendship with Rabbi Litvak, who was his age and had a similar tattoo on his arm, though he had never explained it. Actually, not much was known about Nusan's tattoo, either. He never talked about what had happened or which camps he had been in. He rarely showed his forearm. There was no day too hot for a jacket. Sometimes he would have bad days, angry days, and on those days his forearm was made visible. When Nusan showed his tattoo, the family knew to be careful with him.

On this Friday, only seven men arrived; they found the eighth buying a Korean challah, and when Nusan arrived it made nine. This was the consequence of the killing of Eli Rabbinowitz. They couldn't even say kaddish for him without one more. "They are killing us, one by one," Yankel Fink said glumly, and Nusan snickered for reasons known only to him. Jack Bialy—whose real name was Jack Kimmelman but whom everyone called Jack Bialy because he made them in his factory on Grand Street and his black shoes always had a fine dusting of flour— protested, "What do you mean by 'they'?"

"They, *they*! The ones that killed poor Rabbinowitz, may there be no unions where he now rests in peace," said Yankel Fink.

"Who killed him? What do you mean by *they*?" Jack Bialy insisted.

Yankel reached his hand up to heaven for assistance in his argument. "Rabbinowitz is dead, we have no minyan, and big deal Mr. Socialist wants to lecture."

"What does Socialism have to do with this?" Jack Bialy argued.

Though it might not seem apparent to an outsider, Nathan, blocks away, would have known where this argument would lead. Nusan said, "We can get my nephew."

Yonah Kirchbaum, who sold Judaica on Avenue B in a little store full of mezuzahs and menorahs from Israel that stayed in business because Harry Seltzer owned the building and did not charge much rent, knew that it would be his job to find Nathan, because at the age of sixty-seven, he was the youngest in the group. Actually, the youngest in the group by five years was Jack Bialy. But they could not send Jack Bialy for Nathan because he might run into Nathan's father, and Jack was not speaking to Harry since Harry had lost his $200 on the canceled Charlie Parker concert. Harry had long since paid it back, but it was the principle, the mismanagement, that angered Jack. "You think this is nothing," Jack said when Harry gave him the money. "This is three hundred and twenty bialies." Jack Bialy measured his life in increments of sixty cents.

So it was Yonah Kirchbaum who walked to the shop on Tenth Street, but it was closed. He was surprised by Nathan's observance of the Sabbath. At the end of the street he asked sweet-faced Ruben, who said that he thought he had gone home.

And there was Nathan, captured and brought back for services. At the end, the rabbi would raise a large silver goblet, so tarnished and black that no one remembered that it was a mid-nineteenth-century German masterpiece, filled to the brim with wine so that it always spilled on Litvak's hand, and said the blessing. The cup was passed from man to man, and Rabbi Litvak would pat the challah they had reserved from the kosher Fourth Street bakery with all ten fingers, as though it were a chicken whose plumpness he was measuring, and say the *motzi* and tear off ten pieces, dipping them in a bowl of salt and distributing them with precise and complicated movements.

Nusan would not eat his piece but would put it in his pocket. Then Rabbi Litvak would serve the herring and *mofongo*. The herring would go first. But Nusan would eat huge quantities of both.

"We have dinner waiting," Nathan would plead.

"Maybe, maybe," said Nusan. "But we know we have this."

. . .

By the time Nusan had his fill of kosher *mofongo* and herring, it was considerably past sunset. Ruth had already lit the two *Shabbas* candles, covered her eyes with her hands, and said the blessing. At the last words of the blessing, "*shel Shabbat*," the entire family turned their heads to the door for Nusan's imminent arrival. They would wait for him before blessing the wine and bread. *Shabbas* was a night in which he made everyone wait for him twice.

Even Mordy was already there. To Mordy, *Shabbas* dinner was a chance to take a girl to dinner without having to pay. Otherwise he would take her to dinner and order only a salad, arguing the environmental abuses that had befallen everything else on the menu. He used to take women to Saul Grossman's Deli because Saul gave him credit. But he never paid, and in time Saul canceled his credit. Even then, Mordy could sometimes talk a waiter into two dinners, until Saul had a sign made:

Do not take checks or orders from

MORDY SELTZER

He placed the sign by the telephone behind the counter where customers got their carryout orders, so that everyone in the neighborhood would see it. Harry paid his son's debt to get the sign taken down.

An alternative was to invite someone home for a Friday night dinner. Whenever possible, he would find someone Jewish. This *Shabbas*, the chosen Jew was about twenty years old. Ruth and Harry were not disturbed by this. She wore a flimsy top with bare shoulders and enough skin exposed to get the general idea of the tattoo covering most of her upper body—and maybe more—in three colors that resembled a Blake illustration of *Paradise Lost*. Ruth was prepared to overlook this, though Nathan and Sonia worried that their daughter was absorbing the notion of piercing and tattooing by living in the neighborhood around such girls.

Nathan professed a horror of tattoos. Harry, though he didn't approve, thought it was well done, probably Cristofina's work. Secretly, he understood what Mordy liked about her multicolored torso. But he would never want to kiss a woman with rings through her lips.

Can you kiss like that? Harry wondered.

Are they real silver? Ruth wondered.

Sarah, notebook in hand, moved in for a closer look, but the young woman let out a barely audible shriek and recoiled. She was afraid of children because she had been told that they like to pull on the rings and sometimes even yank them out.

For Harry, the most difficult part was the leather dog collar with silver studs. But her name was Naomi, so apparently she was Jewish.

"Naomi," Harry repeated cautiously. He had made mistakes before. When Nathan started dating Sonia, Harry was distressed to learn that his son was dating a Mexican. Sonia was from Mexico, though her parents were from Poland. But Harry didn't hear about her parents. He did not even notice her curly, ginger-colored hair or that her name was Sonia Cohn. The first time Nathan brought her to a Friday night dinner, while Ruth served the brisket, Harry nervously talked to her about tacos and enchiladas, food her family never ate in Guadalajara. The brisket was all too familiar, but Harry hadn't noticed. "Ruth, maybe Sonia would like some of that hot sauce Chow Mein's mother gave us."

"Who is Chow Mein?" Sonia had asked, looking at Nathan for help.

Nathan followed Ruth into the kitchen. "I don't know why Dad is acting like this. She's Jewish. Her grandparents were born in shtetls."

Ruth's face warmed to a smile. "She's not Mexican?"

"She's Mexican, but she's Jewish. I told you. Her name is Sonia Cohn!"

"Sonia Cohn," Ruth repeated, savoring the words. "Oboyoboy."

Nathan smiled back and gave his mother a kiss on the forehead. "Okay?"

"Okay," said Ruth. "But don't tell your father. Make him earn it."

And they did, and so now Harry graciously offered to let Naomi say the blessing over the bread. Naomi moved toward the bread but retreated slightly because Sarah was there. Mordy stood between them and Naomi touched the bread, her fingernails painted a pearly green that made her skin look white, her right hand with a blue spiderweb tattoo, her left one with a spider, and said, "*Baruch ata adonai elochenu melech ho'olom chomethi lechum minh'areth,*" and proceeded to break up the challah, dip pieces in the salt bowl, and distribute them while Mordy stared at her with the look of a man who had been defrauded and wanted his money back. Her Hebrew, like her English, was perfect except for a slight "th" sound on some words, which may have been caused by the small silver balls that were riveted to her tongue.

Nusan took his piece of challah and slipped it into his jacket pocket.

During herring, the conversation turned to the death of Eli Rabbinowitz.

"That was the last real dairy restaurant in the neighborhood," said Harry. "And he was a nice man."

"Yes," Nathan quickly agreed, but the rest of the diners were silent.

"I love dairy footh," said Naomi.

"What difference does it make," said Mordy, "if you get your hormones and chemicals from the dairy industry or the meat industry?"

"But it was kosher," said Ruth. Nusan laughed, but no one turned to him because Nusan was not a merry man and they had all learned to fear his laughter.

"There are still good dairy restaurants in Brooklyn," said Sonia. This observation met with silence. Neither Harry nor Ruth could go to Brooklyn. In a perfect marriage to a man who feared rivers, Ruth feared bridges. She would take the Midtown Tunnel to Queens or the two tunnels to New Jersey, but Brooklyn, she feared, required a bridge. Subways went through tunnels but some went over bridges, and she could never remember which trains, and not wanting to ever find herself suspended on a bridge in a subway car, she avoided Brooklyn.

Impressive amounts of herring were consumed, probably because everyone knew the brisket was next. Mordy, however, didn't eat fish. In fact, between political convictions, economic restrictions, and a general belief that most food had been poisoned by someone, Mordy ate almost no food at all. To Nathan, who had seen how much herring Nusan had already eaten on Sixth Street, it was striking to see how much more herring he ate now. And Harry loved herring.

But soon the dreaded moment arrived, and Ruth carried out the large chunk of meat, jagged as though it were a handful yanked from the side of a stringy animal, cooked for hours until it was reduced to a bundle of fibers languishing in mawkish brown liquid.

"I'm a vethetarian," Naomi announced in a rapid preemptive strike. "So ith Mordy."

"The strings would get caught in your rings," suggested Sarah, who herself refused to eat brisket.

"That's not nice, Sarah," said Sonia.

But Sarah reached toward a silver ring that was looping an eyebrow. Naomi let out a breathy shriek and Sarah pulled back. "I just wanted to see what it is for." Naomi put up her forearm defensively.

But since Sarah had innocently raised this interesting issue, Harry decided to pursue it. "Isn't it a problem for eating? And for . . ." He decided not to ask her about kissing.

"Just a small slice," said Nathan, who also hated brisket. In fact, they all did. Ruth hated it, too. But her mother always made brisket on Friday nights. She vaguely remembered it being better. The packaged onion soup mix might be a mistake. Ruth always made enough for several families, and after a small amount was eaten the rest was wrapped up and given to Nusan, who rarely spoke during the meal.

"Not only have we lost the last dairy restaurant," said Harry, "but Moishe Apfel is closing."

Everyone looked down at their plates, not daring to look at one another, especially not daring to look at Ruth. Moishe Apfel owned a kosher butcher on the ground floor of their building. He was the source of the hated brisket.

"And that's the last kosher butcher in the neighborhood," Harry pronounced gravely.

Thank God, thank God, they were all thinking. Ruth had lost her source for brisket.

"What are you going to do?" Nathan asked his mother, trying not to sound cheerful.

"Now I'll have to go all the way to Elizabeth Street," said Ruth, crushing all the hope in the room.

"I couldn't find another butcher. I ended up renting to the Japanese. Carryout sushi."

"Ohh," squealed Naomi, "I love thuthi. Mordy won't eat it."

"The Japanese are cleaning out the oceans," said Mordy. "Besides, the fish is all full of mercury."

"Well," said Harry, "I am ashamed of renting a Jewish store to the Japanese."

"You don't mind eating German pastry," said Mordy, and Nusan smiled malevolently.

"I have known Bernhardt Moellen for forty years," Harry said defensively.

"Fifty would be better," Nusan muttered in a barely audible voice.

"He is a good man. I like him. All the kids like him. You kids used to love going over there, remember?"

"You still like going over there, don't you, Nathan," said Ruth.

Nathan wondered why she had said that.

At last the shredding carcass was removed. As the apple strudel, which had been placed on a long, ornate silver tray and redusted with powdered sugar, was brought out, Nusan hurled the look at Nathan that he always gave him at this point. It was a reminder that Nathan suspected the pastry maker of being a Nazi. Nathan wished he would forget. Nothing was found. There was nothing to it. Just racial stereotyping because he happened to be German. It would be like suspecting the three Sals of being connected to the Mafia—which, actually, he did suspect. "You could call me," she had whispered. Call me for what? What had she meant by that?

Harry cut the strudel, dividing it carefully into equal pieces so there would be no leftovers. Nusan refused to take the German's strudel home.

"One thing is certain," Harry began his pronouncement while slicing into the strudel, and everyone knew what would follow, "whoever killed Eli Rabbinowitz is an anti-Semite." It was usually at this point in the meal that Harry would review his list of anti-Semites. Recently added to the list were Vice President George Bush, Ronald Reagan, the Republican National Committee, the black mayor of New York, the Jewish ex-mayor of New York, Woody Allen, and Fidel Castro. Jews and non-Jews alike were subject to Harry's list.

"Who's Eli Rabbinowitz?" asked Mordy, who was only now recuperating from the knowledge that Naomi knew how to say the *motzi*.

"How do you know the killer was anti-Semitic, Dad?" said Nathan.

"Yes," said Ruth. "How do you know who killed Rabbinowitz? If you don't know who, how do you know why?"

Sonia picked up a notebook and pen that she kept on the table in front of her and wrote something down. Sarah then picked up her notebook and drew several lines. Sonia was writing a play, and she kept a notebook with her to record snippets of dialogue that she thought might be useful. She was particularly interested in the way Ruth spoke. "There could be a lot of other reasons for shooting Eli Rabbinowitz," Sonia cautioned.

"Someone could have killed him because they didn't want him living in their house," suggested Sarah. This was beginning to worry Nathan. He should try again to explain about the mouse.

"Why would someone bring down the last dairy restaurant? Who is that attacking?" Harry argued.

"And where did they put his head?" Sarah offered, notebook at the ready.

But no one responded because they had all given up the argument, knowing that Sonia was about to say what she always said at this point: "Some people accused Emma Goldman of being an anti-Semite." That always ended the conversation, because nobody understood what it meant and they had all learned to avoid letting Sonia stay too long on the subject of Emma Goldman. Instead they all stood up and began clearing the dishes off the table.

"Who wath Emma Goldberth?" asked Naomi.

Mordy, a head taller than Naomi and half her width, led her to the door. They said good-bye. Naomi dutifully thanked Ruth for the wonderful meal, though she had eaten only the herring. As she spoke, Ruth studied the movement of the silver rings in her lips.

As soon as they left, Harry said in a quiet voice, "What a nogood-nik." Everyone shrugged. "You know, it's a *shanda*. A Jewish girl like that."

"What?" said Nathan. "I thought it was a *shanda* if it wasn't a Jewish girl."

"No, I mean the rings and the tattoos. It's against Jewish law. Mutilation of the flesh. Any time you see a Jew with a tattoo it's an offense to God."

Nusan laughed an unkind, quiet chuckle.

Nathan held Sonia that night. He was safe. Everything was all right. Nothing had happened and the day was over. Unless it was something that he couldn't see. Some little thing that would reach far into the future. The police said that the killer was waiting for Eli Rabbinowitz because he always made his deposit at the same time. It was a decision he had made years ago based on some forgotten calculation that yesterday had caused the end of his life. Kant was right.

Nathan shuddered slightly and then held his wife, her long fingers reshaping his muscles, and soon they were making love, quickly, quietly, gently, with Sarah sleeping in the next room and a vague rhythm from overhead that might be Harry singing Irving Berlin. When it was over, Nathan was feeling peaceful. But then he thought, Am I a claustrophobe? And Sonia sat up on one arm, her curly hair running wild, still looking a little sexy, and said in a soft but stern voice, "Why didn't you use a condom?" And they went to sleep without another word and barely spoke when they woke up.

CHAPTER SEVEN

The Worn Garment

Birdie Nagel preyed on single men. If Harry had left his apartment with Ruth, she would not have approached him. But he flew out of his apartment on a song, waving a salutation to the mezuzah on his door, and as he descended in the elevator, his song—really Berlin's—filled each floor:

> *Cohen owes me ninety-seven dollars*
> *And it's up to you to see that Cohen pays,*
> *I sold a lot of goods*
> *To Rosenstein and Sons*
> *On an IOU for ninety days.*

Birdie Nagel, a small woman whose rust-colored, wiry hair was teased straight up, as though trying to make her taller, heard him from her apartment. She ran out, stopping only to blow a kiss to the mezuzah on her doorway, which was a bird with the Hebrew letter *shin* on its breast, and flew down the stairs. "Mr. Seltzer?"

" 'Levi brothers don't get any credit.' . . . Yes, how are you?" He lightly held her right hand and continued, " 'They owe me for a hundred yards of lace.' "

"Mr. Seltzer, can you help me?"

> *If you promise me, my son,*
> *You'll collect from everyone,*
> *I can die with a smile upon my face.*

"I want to feed the birds on Eleventh Street, and I don't want to be alone with that killer out there. Will you come with me?"

"Eleventh Street? I have to go get some money on Fifth Street. I'll come back and get you on my way back."

"Oh, Mr. Seltzer, you should live to a hundred." She fumbled in a small leather handbag and produced three crumpled $1 bills. "Could you stop at Third Street and get me some birdseed? The mixed seeds. They like that."

"Sure, Mrs. Nagel," said Harry, as though Third Street were on the way.

"And you should be careful at the bank. Remember Mr. Rabbinowitz, not such a nice man, really, may he be in heaven, though I doubt it."

"I'll be back in a few minutes," said Harry, escaping back into song for the moment:

> Old man Rosenthal is better now,
> He just simply wouldn't die somehow. . . .

And he was out the door. He stopped in at the newspaper shop, which he had rented to a man named Mohammed. The shop was next to the butcher, soon to be carryout sushi.

"Salaam, Mohammed," Harry said.

"Shalom, Harry, my friend," said Mohammed, taking his hand. It was one of Harry's caprices, like Sonia's enchiladas. He did not understand that Mohammed, being from Pakistan, was not an Arabic speaker. It had begun one Yom Kippur. Mohammed had seen Harry on the street with a white yarmulke, and knowing it was a holiday and wanting to say something, Mohammed said his one word of Hebrew. Harry, wanting to respond in kind but having no idea what language Mohammed spoke, replied in his one word of Arabic. And then it was set. No changing it now. He bought a *Times,* realized he had no money, and used one of Birdie Nagel's dollars.

"Harry, my friend, the new *Foreign Affairs* has an article on Israel." Mohammed always looked for articles of Jewish interest for Harry. Harry thought Mohammed tried too hard. "A philo-Semite. He probably hates us."

At the bank on Fifth Street, the deposit box had been cleaned and the police crime scene tape and chalk had already been removed. But there were flyers on the wall giving a number to call if anyone had information about the killing of Rabbinowitz.

Poor Rabbinowitz, Harry was thinking when a large man with an unruly tangle of thick black hair and a sleepy, friendly face, a face that reminded him somehow of his son Mordy, opened the door for him. Harry thanked him and went to the bank machine, withdrawing $100—five $20 bills.

The large, dark-haired man held the door for him again. "Can you spare a little change?"

"Look," Harry said gently, "this isn't any kind of business. People come here because they are out of money and they leave with nothing but twenty-dollar bills. So why do you think this is the place to get change from people?"

"I—I don't know. Because they stop here."

He handed the man Birdie Nagel's remaining crumpled bills. "Here, but I think you ought to look for a better idea."

After Harry walked away, the large man shoved the bills in his pocket and, realizing that he had enough, quickly left the bank.

José the fish man, who had been selling fish for so long that everyone in the neighborhood called him José Fishman or even Mr. Fishman, ran by Harry, pushing his slightly misshapen shopping cart full of fish and melted ice. José walked to the Fulton Fish Market every morning and, by plan, was the last one there. He bought what was left over for bargain prices, covered it with ice, and pushed it back up to his shop on Fourth Street. It was not difficult in the winter, but in the summer he had to run to get the fish out of the morning heat, the melting ice leaving a zigzag trail behind him. "Good morning, Seltzer-san," he shouted to Harry, not stopping or even turning to look. "Have to hurry, sayonara, Seltzer-san."

It seemed to Harry that José was trying to speak Japanese, and he wondered why. Harry returned with the seeds to the lobby, where Birdie Nagel was waiting patiently for him on the original black leather couch placed there by his father-in-law in the 1920s and chained to the wall by Harry in the 1970s. They walked to Eleventh Street, and Birdie began spreading seed with extravagant sweeps of her arms, bringing more than a hundred oily-necked cooing and fluttering pigeons to the sidewalk. Harry would have rather left poison.

"Hello, Harry Seltzer."

He turned and saw the black woman who was usually in this part of the neighborhood. She was as tall as he was, and her dark flesh was bursting out of the edges of a very small, shiny, black lace dress as though she had been inflated after being placed in the dress. She had once walked up to him and said, "Hi, my name is Florence," and he had reflexively responded, "How do you do? Harry Seltzer."

Then she said, "You look lonely," and he realized he had made a mistake. But it was too late. She had his name, and now, three years later, she still remembered it. It was embarrassing having her always call him by name. He could see that Birdie Nagel was giving him an odd look. Who was Birdie Nagel to give other people an odd look? Florence was a nice woman, always pleasant and friendly.

"Hello, Florence, how are you today?"

"Not today, Harry Seltzer?"

"No, not today, Florence."

"You wouldn't be sorry," she said, and she walked past him, wiggling the bright red polish on the nails of her right hand to say good-bye. Harry couldn't help watching her walk away, the direction that showed off Florence's best side. Harry wondered how anything that large and that soft could keep its shape.

Nathan looked down at Eli Rabbinowitz, who had muttered as he often did something that was not quite audible. Nathan leaned closer and Rabbinowitz repeated the words, "You could call me." Funny, the words were not that significant after all. Then there was an explosion and Rabbinowitz's head, bloodlessly, vanished.

The side of Nathan's head was being swatted by an awkward and loving little hand.

"Daddy?" said Sarah. "Daddy?"

"Yes," Nathan answered, trying to shake off the dream.

"You are very, very bad," Sarah said in a scolding voice.

"I am? What did I do?" Nathan asked, almost afraid of the answer.

"It is a game. You are a bad boy and I am going to put you in your house."

"Okay."

Sarah had collected pillows and couch cushions from throughout the apartment and was distributing this cache on top of her father, one pillow at a time, until Nathan saw no more daylight, and then he felt a forty-pound creature pounce on the pillows, pushing them into him until there was no more air. "Accidental suffocation" was the phrase that came to Nathan, and he realized that he was about to die. He sat up, sending the creature and the pillows rolling off the bed. As Nathan heaved his chest, struggling for air, a worried Sarah looked up. "What's wrong, Daddy?"

Nathan smiled, though Sarah could tell he didn't mean it. "Nothing. What are you doing down there?"

Sarah could see that there was something wrong and concluded that he really had been bad and couldn't talk about it. She understood. She had often been caught in the same situation. She patted Nathan's hand sympathetically.

On Saturday mornings Sonia gave Nathan a massage, and this Saturday would not be an exception just because Sonia was barely speaking to him. Sonia had, according to Nathan, "the world's greatest hands." This morning he could feel some anger in those great hands, an urge to cause pain. She lingered disapprovingly along his sides where they were becoming a little pudgy. "You should give up pastry," she said. Her fingers were long and slender and had great strength. They could search out the imperfections in muscle fiber and knead them out like . . . like a skilled pastry maker working a dough until it was silken. What had she meant, "You could call me"? Her scent was still in his nose. But he should not be thinking these things, because his wife's fingers felt as if they could penetrate his thoughts. It was possible that it was her hands with which he had first fallen in love. Even the first afternoon on Thirteenth Street. Now, only four years and a daughter later, he was lying on her table analyzing someone else's phrase, "You could call me."

Sonia was explaining progress on her play about Emma Goldman, the Lithuanian-born, early-twentieth-century American anarchist, and Margarita Maza, wife of the nineteenth-century Mexican leader Benito Juárez. Emma is completely opposed to property. Margarita does not oppose it. She just thinks it is wrong that she has it and most Mexicans don't. "But that was exactly Emma's point, you see? That was why she called property *robbery*. Because it was the product of all the people who had none, you see?"

Only one person she had met really saw it. Her brother-in-law, Mordy, would eagerly talk to her about it. But he told her, "I think they are from different latitudes but similar longitudes, which is always what happens to relationships. Margarita needs to get on Emma's longitude. You need the commonality of longitudes." And thus far, she was thrilled to have such an insight. But from there he went for a very long time into his theory of "longitudinal separation," and Sonia had to admit that whatever it was that Mordy was trying to say, they were on different plays.

Mordy, after spending his undergraduate years on electronic music, earned two graduate degrees: one in Western philosophy and one in biochemistry. He thought the biochemistry work would lead to skills in designer drugs. But that degree proved disappointing. The Western philosophy degree, on the other hand, he felt had paid off.

The only other person who liked to talk to Sonia about her play was Arnie. Arnie loved Emma Goldman and, though he knew nothing of Juárez or his wife, could talk for hours about what Emma thought. And miraculously, one afternoon as she walked up Avenue A, Arnie presented Sonia with a copy of *Living My Life,* Emma Goldman's autobiography. It was a hardback edition published by an anarchist press in the 1930s and found by Arnie on a curb of Essex Street along with an electric fan that no longer worked. The frontispiece was a black-and-white photo of a severe-looking, short-haired woman with black, round glasses frames holding thick lenses behind which two magnified, worried eyes appeared to stare out at two different angles. For a second, Sonia was surprised that this woman looked nothing like Ruth, whose eyes were glowing with passion and whose face was soft and feminine. Only the thick black eyebrows looked similar. Sonia read the opening:

It was the 15th of August 1889, the day of my arrival in New York City. I was twenty years old. All that had happened in my life until that time was now left behind me, cast off like a worn out garment.

A worn out garment. Sonia pondered the phrase. She, too, only a few years earlier, not quite one hundred years after Emma, and on an August day as well, maybe even the fifteenth, had arrived in New York with the exact same feelings. Not twenty but over thirty, she too was casting off her past and beginning a new life—as a playwright. But then she did something Emma wouldn't. "Marriage and love have nothing in common," Emma once wrote. Emma had been married but did not make the mistake of prolonging it, and the divorce was the occasion for her moving to New York to begin anew. Sonia had not divorced but had left behind a confining relationship. And then in her new life, she got married! Then Sonia thought of Sarah, and like a plant wilting in heat, her resolve was gone. She thought about Nathan's seriousness. Whenever she thought of her love for her husband, that was what came to mind. She loved him for his moral conundrums. She smiled as she thought: Who else could spend six months debating about someone trying to give him half a million dollars for nothing?

Sonia pointed out to Arnie that the book was probably worth something and she should pay him, but Arnie looked up from the sidewalk, his beret defiantly askew, and said, "Emma wouldn't approve."

Sonia smiled and added that Margarita wouldn't have, either.

As she kneaded Nathan's shoulders, she was talking about the dress. Not the "worn out garment"; Sonia was fascinated by a dress Benito Juárez gave to his wife that she took into exile and wore to meet Abraham Lincoln. "But she apologized to him in a letter for dressing in expensive clothes while Mexicans were suffering. Do you think Sarah can learn these things? Will she ever apologize for having too much?"

"Will she ever have too much?" Nathan replied, but he was really thinking about the words "You could call me."

It was still early for Mordy to be outside, and he was walking on his toes, unconsciously sneaking down the street, hoping to find strong coffee before someone ran into him and forced him to speak. Too late.

"You're Mordy Seltzer, aren't you?"

"Owww," he slowly groaned in a nonresponse.

"I am Naomi's father."

"Ohhh." Why was this happening?

As Mordy deciphered the words in vibrato echoing from a distance, he gathered that the father was worried because Naomi was not married and she was twenty-four. "Every year she will be less and less desirable."

"Yes," Mordy groaned in a soft voice barely audible to the father.

"Because every year she gets more holes and tattoos. You should marry her off while she still has unused portions of skin."

"And you?"

"And me?" Why was this happening? It was starting to feel as though someone were slapping him over and over again.

"You are not married. Isn't it time?"

"Oh yes, I would love to be married. And Naomi is such a treasure." In precious metals alone, he thought to himself. "But Naomi is interested in somebody else."

"Somebody else? She is marrying him?"

"You'll have to talk to them. The—ah—what's-his-name. The bookseller."

"A bookseller? She's found herself a bookseller! He's Jewish, of course."

Mordy nodded. "I think so. He's right over there. You know, that guy over there with the pink hair."

"With the pink—"

"Yeah, right there." Mordy pointed across the avenue near Sixth Street, and there was a tall, skinny man standing by a table of used books. And though his spiky hair was bright pink, he somehow looked Jewish. He sold books that he found, and it was true that he went out with Naomi, and it was on that very corner that Mordy had met her talking to the bookseller about a paperback on the work of Hegel with an essay that had begun, "World history is not the verdict of mere might, i.e., the abstract and nonrational inevitability of a blind destiny." Mordy, like his brother, had a perverse and irrepressible fascination with Germans.

After his massage, Nathan left and Sonia was freed for paying customers. Ruth looked after Sarah, which was how Sonia could keep her business. She could hear Ruth in another room, teaching Sarah songs.

"*Bay dem schtetl schteyt a schtibl*," Ruth would sing.

"*By da stubble, spit a stibble*," Sarah would try to repeat.

"*Mit a grinem dach*," Ruth would continue.

Ruth admired Sonia and especially admired the way she ran her little business. She had select clientele, and she charged good prices. "You make copies all day to make what Sonia gets in an hour," she would say to Nathan, who she thought, like Harry, had a habit of undercharging. Sonia charged full prices to everyone, except the family. Even then, Ruth admired the way she would not extend her free family service to Mordy because, as Ruth put it, "she could see what a schnorrer he was." She did not want to charge full price to Ruth's friend Esther, who visited from the Bronx on Saturdays. But Ruth wanted Sonia to charge her. "Otherwise you'll end up operating like a Seltzer." Sonia wrote the observation in her notebook.

Sonia and Esther would trade neighborhood crime reports while Sonia's skilled fingers reshaped Esther's soft body.

"We had a shooting down here."

"It's everywhere now. Who did they shoot?"

From the next room came the insistent Sarah: "*By da stupple, struk a stibble.*"

"Let's go back to *feygele,*" said Ruth, laughing.

"Rabbinowitz. Do you remember him?"

"The dairy place!"

"Yes," said Sonia, and braced herself for the standard eulogy she had been hearing. But all Esther said, her face framed by an oval cushion at the head of the table, her voice trailing off underneath, was, "Not such a pearl, that one." Sonia would give her a good rub.

"*Feygele, feygele, pi-pi-pi,*" Ruth and Sarah sang.

Nathan bought a *Times* from Mohammed and walked to his shop. What was this sense of predestination, the fatal error? Was it somehow tied to Rabbinowitz? He resolved not to do anything because of the Rabbinowitz shooting. He must be alert not to let that event alter his course. That decision of a decade ago on when to make the deposit would not be part of his destiny.

But then again, might not the decision to ignore the shooting be in itself a fatal error? Could he both not respond to and not ignore the shooting? Was this possible?

Pepe Le Moko curled his soft black fur around Nathan's leg, always glad to see him. The name came from Nathan's favorite movie, *Algiers,* which he had seen exactly fourteen times.

He first saw it at the St. Mark's in a triple feature for a dollar along with the French original. He could no longer remember the third film. Pepe Le Moko, the cat, really did resemble Charles Boyer in his black suits and black shirts. Pepe Le Moko was king of the Casbah in Algiers, a maze of garbage-strewn alleys, stairways, bridges, and tunnels too complex for outsiders, including the police, to find their way through. But if he ever set foot outside the Casbah, the police would grab him instantly. Sometimes he went to a gate and looked out at clean streets and cars and the world outside. But he stayed in his slum kingdom and lived almost regally—until he met Hedy Lamarr. In pursuit of Lamarr, he was lured out and handcuffed by the police right at the port with the whole Mediterranean just out of reach. He sees her, a tiny figure on the stern of an ocean liner leaving for Marseilles, and he runs uselessly toward the ship. He is shot by the police, who think he is escaping, and dies on the dock as the ship sails away.

Nathan thought about the movie, rerunning it in his memory, imagining Boyer's chocolatey baritone while he stroked Pepe Le Moko's black fur. Thinking of the movie always gave him a strange, melancholy, almost frightened feeling. He realized now that it was a milder version of the same feeling he had experienced on the F train. So that was not the first time. And there were the pillows that morning. When else had this feeling come to him?

Nathan sank into the pivoting chair in his copy shop and, as he began most days, picked up his newspaper and, to the lively tintinnabulation of a Beethoven piano concerto, turned to the obituary page and began counting. An unusually bad day: Of six obituaries, four had been younger than him. AIDS, cancer, heart attack, and one didn't say. One thing Nathan hated was an obit that failed to give the cause of death. Why did they think people read obituaries? Nathan railed in silence. Not to read about lives. We want to know about the deaths. Life is easy. It's death we are trying to learn about.

Thoughts of death were abruptly shoved aside in the second movement of the Beethoven when Jasha Sternberg walked through the door and, as though it were contraband, nervously placed on the counter a flyer to be copied. Jasha owned the Bukovina Baths on the next block. On Thursday evenings, so many religious people used to line up to use the baths in preparation for *Shabbas* that Nathan could see the crowd from his shop. But the *mikve* business had almost disappeared, and Jasha was in a desperate search for new business. His "A Place to Bathe in Peace" campaign had not gotten a response. Nathan examined the new flyer, "A Place to Meet Boys," and Jasha could see the skepticism in Nathan's face. "So how do you attract gays?"

As though to answer that, Gecko came through the door in his black leather pants and matching sleeveless top. The lack of sleeves on the heavy leather outfit was the only concession to the warm weather. But more likely it was only to expose his tattoos—snakes that slithered intricately up a fruit tree.

"Gecko, do you attract gay customers?"

"All kinds, man," and he sifted through his latest tattoo designs that he had drawn with pen and ink—scenes from Dante's descent into hell, strange, winged creatures. "Have you noticed, it's getting harder all the time to be an artist in this neighborhood. I sell my designs framed. Then this guy comes in and he wants a flag. I mean an American flag. And he wants it on his arm. Right on his fucking bicep. . . ."

Jasha was eagerly following the story, hoping it had an insight for him. "He was gay, right?"

Gecko ignored him. "I mean, there are interesting places for a flag, but that is not one. So I am thinking, what can I do to make this special? So this is what I come up with. Look at this."

He placed on top of the pile a drawing of an unfurling red, white, and blue American flag. The tall, straight mast from which the flag is flying is a bright red penis.

"That is a masterpiece," Jasha declared in feigned awe.

"Well, yes, it is," Gecko condescended to state the obvious, "but he says, 'I can't have *that* on my arm.' Why not? 'It's a penis,' he says. What is it with these people? Is he afraid of penises? I told him, 'Are you sure you want a flag? Because flags are for people who are into penises'—the guy walks out. If he wants schlock, he can go to Eighth Street. I was offering something original. Art."

"He just wasn't gay," suggested Jasha.

José the fish seller came in. "Seltzer-san! *O-high-yoh. O-genki des-ka!*"

"Ohio to you," said a confused Nathan. "What's going on?" He picked up the pages José had put on the counter. It was a sushi menu.

"What's making *dinero in este barrio,* Seltzer-san? Japanese. Japanese everything. Why should I sell fish when I can cut it up in little pieces and get *tres veces* the *dinero*. Ee-yo!" The Japanese words were said with great grunts and sudden breathy shouts, sounds that he had learned from rented samurai films. His phrases were entirely from the *Japanese for Business* phrase book. Some of his most impressive declarations made little sense, such as when he shouted angrily, "*Futari-yoh-no tehburu-o onegigh shimas!*" which meant "I would like a table for two." But it sounded impressive, and who knew, anyway? Not Jasha, who stared with appreciation.

"Maybe I'm making a mistake with the gay thing. Maybe I should be going for a geisha thing. Or maybe"—he held his temples for a second while the idea was forming—"gay geishas! Why not?"

A day's work had begun at the Meshugaloo Copy Center. Nathan had a new act of *Emma and Margarita* to copy, flyers for a party on Second Street that involved reducing a newspaper montage, and the posters for the Avenue D street fair, which featured Chow Mein Vega and the Yiddish Boogaloo and a three-round "grudge match" between Jimmy Colon and El Dominicano.

The day was already warming up on the streets. Young girls with rings through their noses were facing the heat in flimsy lace or swaths of thin cotton that showed the tattoos on their bodies. A young woman rode a bicycle once every morning down Avenue A, leaning forward on the handlebars, always in a thin cotton summer dress translucent in the sunlight. A tiny part of Harry's busy heart belonged to this woman, whoever she was, and he would try to be on Avenue A at the right time every morning to have this moment. Harry wondered if people noticed how much he was looking. Mordy, who walked a slow, very un-Jewish four-step with his untied shoelaces clicking like taps on the rim of a snare drum, certainly looked. But his eyes never seemed focused on anything, and he just smiled. Was it that aloofness that was so irresistible? The thing most people seemed to notice about Mordy was that his shoes were untied. It fascinated Mordy how many people in the course of a day would tell him that his shoes were not tied. He walked down the street with a faint smile, undressing women with his eyes, and periodically he was told that his shoes were not tied.

Harry, in his role as producer, had to meet Chow Mein and Ruben at Cristofina's and somehow make Ruben into El Dominicano. Cristofina—odd for a Dominican woman—looked a little like Emma Goldman. Of course, no one realized this until Sonia pointed it out, presenting a photo of Emma as evidence. They were both heavyset with broad features, angry eyes, and thick, round glasses. They both had the same vertical crease between their eyes. Cristofina had taped the photo of Emma to the shelf that housed a delicate blue statue of Yemayá, the Yoruba spirit of womanhood, and several manifestations of the Holy Virgin, and Emma seemed to glare from the shelf, angry about the company she was keeping these days.

The botanica was lined with shelves of bottles, mostly old perfume bottles with potions that could do many things, especially make people fall in love. Cristofina said, "All anybody really wants is for someone to love them. Whether I make someone fall in love with them, or I make them look younger so that someone will fall in love with them, or I make them a better lover so that they will be loved, or they want someone punished for not loving them—*eso es todo.*" There were also statues, some very small, some large, like a five-foot palm tree with the face of Changó, a spirit of power, passion, and thunder, in the top with a bolt of lightning. Some were Indian warriors, some were sailors, some were dark-skinned dolls in white or bright blue dresses. No one's life was so perfect that at some time they didn't go to Cristofina for a few drops of magic.

When the door was open to the back room, it revealed walls covered with fanciful designs from devils to paisley to devils in paisley. Originally this had been part of her botanica business. A santo, spirit, or orisha or its sign could be tattooed on the body. But the dark, complex themes of her tattoos became popular with many young people who had no interest in the orishas but simply liked the designs, her African mythology giving fierce competition to Gecko's artistry.

Ruth, although appalled by the product, would have admired Cristofina's business acumen. Her approach was simple: One way or another, anyone who walked through her red door on Avenue C left money there.

In walked Chow Mein, Harry, and sweet-faced Ruben. After Chow

Mein explained the problem in Spanish, telling about the fair, the match, the role of El Dominicano, why the old El Dominicano was in jail, Harry, not knowing what Chow Mein had said, explained it again in English while Cristofina waited patiently and finally said, "*Entiendo, amor,* I've got it," which made Harry instantly certain that Cristofina could be depended on.

She reached up and rubbed Ruben's sweet face with her thick fingers, rubbing the surfaces, examining the planes, as though she were a plastic surgeon. Ruben, large and awkward, withdrew a half step in embarrassment, then helplessly endured the study from his only slightly safer distance.

"*Venga, amorcita,* you think this is going to be easy?" Which Chow Mein but not Harry understood to mean, *You think this is going to be cheap?* She continued, "I could make him Dominicano. He would make a nice Dominicano. But El Dominicano, who must strike fear into all your timid little Puerto Rican hearts, Chucho?"

"He's a big boy," argued Chow Mein.

"Maybe you can do something with the hair," Harry suggested.

"*Verdad,* it's nice hair. I can give you something to make it really black and stick straight up. And I can give you a powder. An orange powder to blow on Jimmy."

"What will the powder do?" asked Harry.

"*E'cucha,* it will get orange powder all over Jimmy. *¿Qué piensa' tu?* I've got ethics. *Exactamente* like Emma," she said, pointing at

the photograph proudly while glaring at Harry. "You leave this boy *conmigo*. We can fix him up."

Harry agreed to pay later for whatever they decided, and he and Chow Mein left to talk to Nathan about the flyers. Cristofina led sweet-faced Ruben to the back room. "*Dígame, cara dulce*, have you ever gotten a tattoo?"

Ruben, who was very tired of all this sweet-faced *cara dulce*, studied the designs on the wall with wide-eyed wonder.

"What do you say, Harry?" asked Chow Mein Vega. "*Cuchifrito* and beer? Consuela makes *gandules* on Saturdays."

"*Shabbas*, you know. I have a lot of eating to do with my family. I've just recovered from the brisket, and it's almost kreplach time."

"Just have a *lek* and a *shmek*, Harry, *tu sabe'*, just have a little bit," said Chow Mein as he led him to Consuela's for pigeon peas and pork fat.

CHAPTER EIGHT

Pink Martinis

LIFE UNFOLDS THIS WAY—one bad decision can unravel everything. The more Nathan thought about it, the more convinced he became that the mistake he was looking for was called "cocktails." Sonia and he had agreed to meet Maya's parents "for cocktails." Nathan and Sonia never met people for cocktails. This would be a mistake. He was certain of that as he thumbed not quite absentmindedly through the telephone book and confirmed that there was a listed number for a Karoline Moellen.

Xabe walked in with a new ad, interrupting Casals's poetic but flawlessly restrained rendition of a Beethoven trio. Beethoven was aflame in the hands of a man who made even Bach impassioned. Nathan put down the obituary page and looked up at Xabe, who was at most five feet tall, his face barely higher than the counter, so that the paper he was showing Nathan was only inches from his face, as though he were about to eat it. Now the leading East Village artist, he had lost his outlaw standing. Xabe had always had an irrepressible urge to write on buildings. He was even arrested once for writing "Free Transport" on subway cars, accompanied by an illustration of someone hopping a turnstile. The illustrations gradually overtook the messages until they became elaborate spray-paint murals that were mentioned in enough fashionable magazines that it seemed almost everyone who opened a new business in the East Village wanted a Xabe mural on their wall. Xabe promoted this business with flyers that included photographs of his work. These flyers were carefully reproduced at the Meshugaloo Copy Center by Nathan under Xabe's demanding instruction. "Can we be a little less contrasty?" Try again. "The shadows should gray out. Let's try enlarging ten percent." Nathan was known for this kind of patient work. He was also known for not charging much for it.

Patience was the one rule at the Meshugaloo Copy Center. The

Nuyorican poet Gilberto Banza, tall and lean with his long hair wrapped up in a red, white, and blue scarf that was the Puerto Rican flag, waited patiently to have three hundred copies of his new poem, "Chingada on Second Street," for immediate distribution. "Nathan, *tu* heard about Rabbinowitz?"

"Yes," said Nathan, struggling with the control buttons on the copier. "Terrible. He was a nice man."

The shop fell silent.

"He still owes me for *un trabajo,*" said Xabe.

"That *cabrón* owes everyone *por aquí,*" said Gilberto Banza.

Nathan thought these were harsh words for a man who had been so unfairly and brutally undone by his destiny.

He had to close early for cocktails, and since Chucho and Harry had been delayed by *gandules* at Consuela's, they missed him. The cocktails had been set in motion by the news of the house in Punim County and the swimming lessons and the preschool, which was all connected to the issue of money, which came back to the $500,000 sellout. No single event stands by itself.

First came the preschool that Maya went to but Sarah didn't. This caused discussions about other schools. Suppose Sarah didn't want to go to the public schools in the neighborhood that Nathan had gone to. The high school he had gone to on Fifteenth Street was famous, said to be the best in New York, but suppose she didn't get in. "She needs options," Sonia kept saying. "And colleges. NYU costs a lot more than when you went there," Sonia said. "And suppose she doesn't want NYU. Suppose she wants to go to Columbia. That's even more expensive." Sonia had gone to Columbia, but Nathan acted as though he had never heard of it.

"Columbia? On a Hundred and Sixteenth Street? It's so far away."

"She might want to go even farther. We are supposed to be offering her options in her life."

Nathan knew she was right. Each generation had its obligation. Harry had offered Nathan more than Harry's childhood in Poland had offered, and because of that it was Nathan's responsibility to offer Sarah more than he had.

Much of this would not have come up if the police hadn't insisted on cleaning up the neighborhood. They were slowly driving the squat-

ters out of Tompkins Square Park, attacking in waves like a military assault and tearing down their tent city, only to have the squatters rebuild
it in the night among the thick, leafy trees. The one small triumph of
the police was in reclaiming a playground area where Sarah played. And
that was where she had met her best friend. It was all connected.

"*Mira,* Seltzer is going to his *destino,*" Carmela said with a smile warm
as a kiss from the fire escape above as Nathan walked out of his shop.
Nathan continued to close up his shop. Why was she suddenly talking
about *destinos?* Nathan asked himself.

"No," he shouted up, loving his own ridiculousness, "I am going for
cocktails." He gave the exact same special emphasis to the word "cocktails" that Carmela had given to "*destino.*" Carmela laughed a crude, lov-
able cackle, and Nathan waved good-bye as he walked away.

Walking up Avenue A, Nathan, Sonia, and Sarah passed several police officers who looked familiar enough to nod at. "Hello," Sarah insisted on saying, and most of them smiled and waved at her. But when
they got closer to the park there were hundreds of them, and hard as
Sarah tried, there was no smiling or waving.

"You notice something?" Sonia said in a low voice.

"Everyone's dressing like cops this year?" said Nathan.

"Jerk," she said, slapping him playfully in the chest. "No badges."

It was true. None of the police had badges on their shirts.

Nathan had never noticed before, but some of the houses on the
north side of Tompkins Square Park, unusual for the neighborhood,
were more like houses of the wealthy than tenements. The outside
walls had been cleaned on the house that Maya and her parents lived in,
and the wooden door frame and windowsills had been refinished. The
three stories had tall windows that let in light, mottled by the swaying
leaves of the park. Dozens of police were on the sidewalk, preparing for
the attack on the park squatters that was a part of summer evenings in
the neighborhood. They clubbed everyone in sight, so it was not a good
idea to watch. But Maya's family could see everything from their window, like a more refined class that stood above society's frays.

Nathan, Sonia, and Sarah were ushered into the house by Maya's
father, a young man with thick red hair and amber glasses frames care-

fully selected to match, and it was quickly apparent that everything in the house—the clean-lined, dark oak furniture, the brass and copper lamps, the deep colored rugs—was carefully selected to match.

"Arts and Crafts," Maya's father explained.

Sarah, the only Seltzer who looked happy to be there, noted the father's assertion in her notebook with a series of dashes. Sonia did not write in hers.

"And Mission," explained Maya's mother, a tall woman in a flowing dress of tissuelike thinness, and Sonia wondered if this was a rebuke for her failure to take notes.

"Ted got us unbelievable prices on these things."

"I'm an architect," he explained shyly, "so I knew where to get the deals."

Nathan nodded, while contemplating this new concept that architects necessarily know where to get deals. He had always been told that people in garments knew where to get deals, and he had never before thought about architects or what they knew. He kept trying to see what the cops were doing in the park without getting caught peeking out the window. Maya, a merry little spirit of the same size as Sarah, came running out, followed by a dark-skinned Puerto Rican woman in a bright purple dress. Nathan and Sonia both knew her, Rosita, the daughter of Consuela, who owned the *cuchifrito*. Nathan greeted her eagerly, relieved to see someone he knew from the neighborhood. But she was quickly sent away by Maya's mother, who wanted her to take Maya and Sarah off to some nether room of the house to play.

"She was a find," asserted Maya's father. "She is so good with Maya."

At first Nathan thought he was talking about Sarah.

"She's like a member of the family," said Maya's mother. "We wanted her to come to Putnam County with us this summer, but she didn't want to."

"She helps in her mother's restaurant," said Nathan.

"Yes," said Maya's startled father, "that's what she said!" Sonia thought that they were only a few years older than their young babysitter. "Come on, we'll give you the tour," said Maya's father with a gracious, sweeping arm gesture. Nathan stole a last glimpse of the park, which hundreds of uniformed police, clubs in hand, had surrounded, looking like a swarm of blue insects crawling over one another.

Maya's parents took Nathan and Sonia through every room in the house, and they could not find one trace of the normal disorder of life—except through the tall windows of the front rooms, where Nathan noticed the attack in progress. They had been in a back room when the assault began, and a great collective shriek could be heard. Nathan wanted to run to the front to see. He looked at Sonia. She had heard it, too, but had a look that said "Don't you dare move." Maya's parents did not seem to hear anything.

Maya's father showed them their workout room full of bright white and shiny chrome machines. "How do you stay so nice and trim?" Maya's trim young father asked Sonia.

"I don't like his mother's cooking," Sonia quipped, and Nathan laughed, while worrying that his own tellas were showing. Maya's parents looked at them quizzically.

"Let's have some drinks," said Maya's father, steering them back to the oaken living room. "What would you like?"

"A beer would be great," said Nathan. Sonia asked for white wine. People were running on the sidewalks with wet, fresh blood dripping from their heads, and police, clubs high, were chasing them. The sound was muffled under the rumble of air conditioners and behind the newly installed, tightly closed windows.

"Let's have martinis," said Maya's father as though they had not answered.

"Do you know Sagittarius, the new place on Third and First? Ted knows the owner. They make *colored* martinis. And they taught Ted."

"What color do you want? What holiday is coming up? Fourth of July. Red, white, and blue! You want a blue martini or a pink one?"

"Pink," Nathan said ambiguously, all the while wondering if these people were Jewish. Their name was Kaplan. He had assumed they were, but there didn't seem to be anything Jewish about them. Sonia also reluctantly agreed to a pink martini.

A woman on her knees on the sidewalk—had she fallen, or had she been clubbed into that position?—looked up at a police officer who was about to hit her again and let out a wail so loud that it could not be ignored even in the living room.

"My God," said Sonia, "what are they doing?"

"It's just the East Village," said Maya's father. "It's pretty noisy down here now. But that will change." He closed the oak shutters so that his guests would not be further disturbed and turned to his mixology with a glass shaker and a stirrer.

"Linda can't have one," Ted asserted happily.

Is she too young? Nathan asked himself, but Sonia immediately knew the real reason. She was pregnant. Sonia politely congratulated her and noted that she was not showing. But she suspected that she was the type who didn't show until labor, which would be painless. She could have two children, even more, and still do the things she wanted in life because she had money. Money for preschool. Emma often said that women who wanted children but did not want to spend all their time in child rearing should send them off to schools to be cared for by women who wanted to do that. But Emma Goldman did not know what preschool would cost. Sonia was not going to give this woman the satisfaction of asking what month she was in. But of course, Nathan, genuinely excited by the news, did. "When are you due?"

"November," she said. "Are you going to make a playmate for Sarah?"

A playmate for Sarah was an uncomfortable subject.

Ted produced three drinks, one blue and two pink, in long-stemmed glasses looking enough like designer crystal to make Nathan afraid to hold one.

There was a house, now an apartment building, on Thirteenth Street, whose brick facade with brownstone trim was like that of many other buildings in the neighborhood. From 1864 to 1867, while her husband, Benito Juárez, was freeing Mexico from the French, the highborn Margarita Maza lived alone in this house. From 1903 to 1913, Emma Goldman, the Russian-born anarchist, lived there. Margarita had been devoted to her husband, and they wrote letters to each other about how deeply they missed each other. Emma had a long relationship with Alexander Berkman, with whom she had unsuccessfully plotted the murder of an industrialist before they renounced violence. But Emma did not believe in marriage, was politically opposed to it. Also, Emma was at home in New York and later driven into political exile in Russia, whereas Margarita was in exile in New York and later went home to

Mexico. They never met each other. Emma was born two years after Margarita moved back to Mexico.

It is probably for these reasons that the house had never attracted much attention, in spite of the fact that it is marked with plaques. Nathan had walked by the house his entire life without reflection until the day he saw a lean woman with curly, ginger hair standing in front of the fluted stone pillars that framed the steps and doorway, seemingly transfixed. What was she looking at? He read the plaques.

"Remarkable, isn't it?" she said.

Nathan turned and looked at her. She unfurled her left hand. "Emma," and then her right, "and Margarita. Emma Goldman and Margarita Maza de Juárez." When she said Emma Goldman she sounded American, but she said Juárez—Hwaah-rdace—like a Latina. He failed to see the significance of these two women. But what struck him most was the two unfurling hands. He thought that the most graceful gesture he had ever seen. What beautiful hands. He was in love with this woman's hands before he even knew her name.

And she looked Jewish! Except for when she said Bay-needo Hwaah-rdace. "Two very different women with different ideas about the same problem."

"What's the problem?"

"Being a woman and a lover. Living a life and living with love. Doing both well." She knew that he did not understand her but that he would pretend he did because he was attracted to her. A good Emma observation. "The question is, who had the better life? Of course, it seems clear who had a better life in the house. Margarita was alone pining away for her husband and writing him letters, while Emma had one and sometimes several lovers. I think that somehow, in addition to the two women, I have to have Emma's lovers in the house. There was no demeaning cheating or sneaking around. It was all in the open."

"Is that what you would like?"

"No, I want to be alone writing letters," she said with a smile. "Actually, I want to be alone writing plays."

He had little reaction to the fact that she was a playwright. He knew several playwrights, but he was thrilled to hear that she earned her living as a masseuse.

"I knew it."

"That I was a playwright."

"That you are a masseuse. I could see it in your fingers."

She studied the telltale digits that were wriggling in front of her like the tentacles of an octopus. "I suppose playwrights have fewer physical manifestations." She had never had a play produced. In fact, she had never completed a play. She had moved to this neighborhood to write her first play, *Emma and Margarita.*

"But if they never met each other . . ."

"It isn't a documentary. It's not realism. You have to imagine Margarita Juárez, the exiled wife of Mexico's democratic president, and Emma Goldman, an anarchist immigrant. Both radical women of their day. You put these two together and what have you got?"

"A Mexican Jew?" he said, trying to be clever.

But she smiled as though she had just won a prize and said, "That's me!" She, too, was quietly thinking, He must be Jewish.

Nathan had thought it was a fine thing for her to be writing a play. Most people he knew had some project or other. Sooner or later they all had him photocopy their pages. Even Chow Mein Vega was working on his memoirs. He too would someday write something. But after Sarah was born, which Nathan remembered as "the plan" and Sonia remembered as "an accident," Sonia argued that she did not want another child until she had finished *Emma and Margarita.* Sonia was now thirty-eight years old and still working on the play, and the more she talked about her work, the more irritable Nathan became. She would talk about it just to annoy him, if she was angry with him. Few of the people whose pages he copied had ever finished their projects. He too had his life of Ludwig van Beethoven, known only to him and a handful of music history faculty at NYU. Nathan did not believe projects such as *Emma and Margarita* were destined to be completed. Nathan was a great believer in destiny.

Nathan could still hear some shouting beyond the shutters.

"You know," said Ted, the expectant father of Maya's future sibling, accidentally stumbling over Nathan's secret thought, "got to look out for that biological clock."

"But *you* don't have to worry about that!" said Sonia with a touch too much mirth. "Having just made it through puberty!" And she laughed.

Nathan looked at her. In her discomposure she was drinking her pink martini in regular, quick gulps. A pink martini is a serious mistake in judgment. He, in fact, was drinking his at about the same rate.

"We have a wonderful place up in Putnam County. You should take Sarah and come visit us this summer."

"Yes, that would be lovely," said Sonia in a peculiar accent. "Just lovely," she repeated, showing her front teeth, Queen of England–like, on the word "Loveleh."

Nathan, trying to carry the conversation, said, "I had to laugh. You know what Sarah said? She said you had a house in Punim County."

Maya's parents looked at Nathan without finding a response. "*Punim*," said Nathan, and he laughed, but no one followed his lead. "You know, *punim*, like what a *punim*, a *punim* like that." And then, seeing that his point was not clear, he said a bit too loudly, "*Punim!*" And he reached over and grabbed a handful of Ted's left cheek with a pinch— his face, in truth, was a bit jowly. "As in 'Look at this *punim.*'" First the cheek and then the face turned pinker than what was left of their martinis. Nathan quickly withdrew, realizing he had transgressed.

"What work do you do?" said the expecting Linda, trying to turn the conversation away from the embarrassing men. By now, Nathan was only praying that they got through the entire event without breaking any crystal.

Sonia, pleased by the question, answered warmly, "I'm a playwright," as Nathan sank deeply into his chair and watched the light playing with the antique crystal stem of his oddly colored and almost finished drink. Beyond the shutters was silence, as though everyone had been beaten unconscious.

"Have you done anything we might have seen?" asked the still redfaced Ted.

"Not yet," Sonia said without the least embarrassment. "But I am working on a play about Emma Goldman and Benito Juárez's wife, Margarita, in New York."

"Were they friends?" Linda asked.

"No, actually Emma Goldman was not even born when Margarita was here."

"Oh," said Ted, turning his recovering *punim* toward Sonia. "Emma Goldman was a Mexican painter?"

"I don't understand," said Linda. "They never knew each other?"

"They lived at different times."

"Then how can they be together?"

"You see, you ask that because you are obsessed with the dimension of time. They had all other dimensions aligned. Two radical women who could understand each other. How important is it that they were in different times? They were in the same place and the same plane. People can be in the same room at the exact same time, but they cannot talk because their worlds are so different, but no one questions the logic of them being together because it is assumed anyone can share time and space. But when they have everything putting them together except time, people say, Oh, that's impossible. In reality, this is what is impossible."

"What is?" asked Linda, and there were worried expressions on the faces of both of Maya's parents. But Nathan rescued the moment with a huge belly laugh.

"These are impossible," he said. "You can't drink pink martinis. What makes them pink, anyway, nitroglycerin? I can't even talk."

"I'm sorry, can I get you something else?"

"Oh no, no, thank you. This was very nice. We just aren't used to it." He was thinking, They are Jewish, right? Kaplan? Why don't they know what a *punim* is? And suddenly he had a terrible thought: Maybe they are Republicans. Maybe these are the hidden Republicans in the back recesses of the neighborhood who cast their clandestine vote. "What do you think of the election?" he blurted out.

"I think Dukakis is going to walk away with it," said Ted. "Thank God."

"And that will be it for Bush and company," said Linda. "Thank God is right."

"Linda was going to work for Dukakis until she found out her due date would be too close," said Ted.

"I don't want my baby born under a Bush," said Linda, and she laughed. They all laughed, relieved to find something they could share besides time and space. And they all started feeling much better about one another. The Kaplans brought up the Seltzers' visit to Putnam County again and even tried to get them to commit to a date. But the Seltzers demurred.

"And they teach swimming up there?" Nathan asked.

"Yes, they have a whole summer camp. Sarah would love it."

By the time they left, their pink martinis were beginning to wear off. Nathan had insisted on opening the shutters to make sure it was safe. The park was empty, and as far as he could tell, so were the streets. It was as though the stadium had been cleared and the game was over.

"What nice people," said Nathan after walking down the front steps and seeing no one on the sidewalk in either direction. He noticed a dark blood spot on the sidewalk where the woman had screamed.

"They are very nice," Sarah confirmed. "She is my best friend in the world."

"That's nice, sweetie," Sonia said with encouragement in her voice.

"Yes, and they have boxes in every room. You push it and you can hear everybody in the other room." Sarah started to laugh. "We heard you!"

"They are just the nicest people," said Sonia.

"And such a nice house," said Nathan.

"Arts and Crafts," said Sonia.

"Mission," said Nathan. "Really nice people."

"They have a television the size of a whole wall," Sarah said.

"And they probably have a nice house in the country," said Sonia.

"Yes," said Nathan. "We'll have to go there this summer. It will be very nice."

Both Nathan and Sonia were hoping they could get through the summer without this subject ever coming up again.

"Maya has a music computer," said Sarah, as though this proved the niceness of it all.

"Oh, Uncle Mordy will be jealous," said Nathan.

"Me too!" said Sarah.

The police had wagons into which they were jamming young people who seemed prepared to be taken quietly.

"They have a lot of stuff, Sarah," said Sonia. "But you will learn that this is not important."

"I know," said Sarah, sulking only a little. "But we could use a little more stuff, too," she added, looking up at her mother with a smile successfully calculated to be irresistible.

"Well," said Nathan, rubbing his head, "we are not going to get pink martinis."

"Until I grow up," Sarah added.

"Not even then," Nathan insisted.

"Okay," said Sarah. "Let's just get stuff!"

On Ninth Street, a police officer put his badge back on his shirt and rounded the corner to Avenue A, where he interrupted Harry Seltzer in midphrase of an Irving Berlin song. "Hello, Daniel, how are you?" said Harry, who prided himself on knowing everyone's name.

"Not bad," the officer said pleasantly, fingers tapping the billy club holstered to his belt. "And yourself?"

CHAPTER NINE

Egg Creams and *Traif*

RUTH AND HARRY had passed essentially the same Saturday night together on Second Avenue for the last fifty years. They had dinner together at Saul Grossman's, then they went to the Yiddish theater, then they walked down to Chaim's for an egg cream, then they walked home. Over the years, certain compromises became necessary.

They still went to Saul's. But it was no longer filled with their friends from the neighborhood—Esther and the others had moved away or died. In the old days, they didn't have to watch the time. The waiters would make sure they got across the street to the theater before curtain. Sometimes even some of the actors were there. They often saw Menasha Skulnik, and he would greet them in Yiddish.

Nobody in the restaurant—neither customers nor waiters—spoke Yiddish anymore. Most of the staff weren't even Jewish now, and they were polite, even obsequious. Who could have imagined polite waiters at Saul Grossman's? In the old days, if you ordered pastrami and they had run out of it, the waiter would shout, "Take the corned beef. It's better!" and make the customer feel like the village idiot for having ordered pastrami. Now if they were out of pastrami, they apologized. "I'm terribly sorry, we just ran out of pastrami." The first time a waiter apologized to Ruth, she shook her head and said, "Oh boy." One waiter even introduced himself by name—and his name was Wallace. Soon Saul told him to stop doing that. "You could do us all a big favor, Wallace, and serve the food incognito," said Saul unkindly. At least Saul had not become polite.

The Yiddish theater had closed and the building was converted to a multiplex cinema with almost a dozen theaters. Harry and Ruth always went to the one that had been the actual theater. There could be a children's movie, or ferocious Asians chopping their way through cities with acrobatic kicks and thrusts, or muscular men winning wars with a dazzling array of firepower. They didn't care. They dressed, and Harry's suit was always perfectly pressed even on the hottest day of the summer. He wore it with a hat, a well-made Italian sisal one in the summer. They took their seats in the balcony, and he took his hat off and rested it on a knee until the lights dimmed. They caressed the ornate walls with their eyes, working slowly up the intricate gilded patterns to the ceiling and finally to the Star of David in the center of the ceiling. Ruth clutched Harry's arm through the movie. This Saturday they saw the big hit of the summer. The posters had been everywhere, featuring a double high-rise tower with smoke pouring from the upper floors and a plane flying into the smoke. There were international terrorists and a smart and determined cop acting courageously and all alone. It didn't matter. They were just there together. All week they fought and belittled each other, but every Saturday night they were in love.

After the film, walking down Second Avenue, they rarely talked about the movie they had seen, though Harry did ask Ruth what she thought the title, *Die Hard,* meant. Ruth shrugged and they moved on to better subjects. They talked about the people they had known, some dead, some living somewhere else, many fallen to that horrible Jewish fate, Florida.

Egg creams were essential. The drink had been in its first bloom of popularity when Harry first moved to New York and they began dating. To Harry, who never knew New York before egg creams, no neighborhood was a true New York neighborhood without them. Since he rarely left the Lower East Side, he didn't realize that this was one of the few neighborhoods where it was still made. Egg creams can survive only as long as there are soda fountains, because bottled soda does not have enough gas to produce the foam on top from which the name is derived. Harry and Ruth always got their Saturday night egg cream at Chaim's, and tried to stick with Chaim's without Chaim. The Koreans still made fairly good egg creams—and a good one is not easy to make. The milk has to be slightly frozen. The milk and chocolate syrup had to be mixed by hand, not machine, and then the jet of soda had to be ricocheted off a spoon to get sufficient foam.

When Harry finished his chocolate egg cream, he always asked for a little shot of seltzer for the chocolate syrup that remained at the bottom of his cup. But the Koreans wanted to charge twenty-five cents for the extra shot of soda at the end.

"It's the whole reason I get chocolate. I'd rather have vanilla but there's no syrup at the bottom."

This was just something he was saying to the Koreans. Harry was a purist and never would have dreamed of any other flavor, because the original egg cream, the real egg cream, was chocolate. Chaim had offered four different flavors and the Koreans had expanded to eight, including blackberry, but drinking a blackberry egg cream was like a blueberry or a raisin bagel—not right.

Harry missed his extra shot of seltzer and chocolate syrup, which may have been why he called his granddaughter Syrup Cone Seltzer—also because her real name was Sarah Cohn Seltzer. But when Harry complained about having to pay for the extra shot, the Korean smiled, hoping this was some kind of Jewish joke. So they retreated to the only other place that still made egg creams on Avenue A, where they suffered other indignities, being served by Poles who put the egg cream in red paper Coca-Cola cups.

Nathan and Sonia had their own Saturday night ritual, which they called *traif* night. Still recovering from Ruth's brisket from the night before, they indulged in oysters, lobster, and a favorite, the prosciutto bread, which was made by all three Sals—a loaf of bread infused with small cubes of *traif.* On Saturdays they would eat almost any *traif*—food forbidden by Jewish law. Sometimes they would just get ribs from Bob's Greasy Hands. They loved ribs. Saturday night *traif* was usually carryout food, because if they cooked, they imagined the smells drifting up to Harry and Ruth's apartment above. They thought about this even though they knew Harry and Ruth were always out on Saturday night. They didn't know that Harry had spent the afternoon eating pork fat and *gandules* with Chow Mein Vega.

There was no Bob at Bob's Greasy Hands. There was a Pakistani man with a name he always insisted was too difficult. "Call me Bob." He had dark skin and large, soft black eyes, and his smile tripped off so easily that withholding it would have been a disappointment for anyone who knew him. He had a grill on which he cooked ribs, and he offered almost nothing else except corn, which was a later addition when a salesman showed him a machine that steamed the corn and kept it permanently warm—also permanently soggy, but no one cared because

Bob's had the best ribs in the neighborhood. In truth there was only one other rib place in the neighborhood, a strange chain restaurant that had settled on Second Avenue with the arrival of tourists who wanted to go to the East Village. But Bob's had good ribs to go. No one actually ate there. Nighttime and Cuquemango draped themselves in the two aluminum chairs that were too small to attract diners, drinking Cokes out of cans, taking a short break from selling smoke on a Saturday night.

Sarah was already asleep—with visions of "stuff" no doubt dancing in her head—and Nathan was getting the ribs and renting a movie. He and Sonia had had a fight, which may have been the last traces of the pink martini. He wanted to rent *Algiers,* and Sonia said she could not watch it again, and Nathan pointed out that they had seen the documentary on Emma Goldman five times. Sonia insisted that was for work. When there was a fight they rented *The Red Desert* and watched fleshy Italians roll on the floor with too much air pollution to have sex. There was something oddly appealing about this, and they had seen it more times than the Goldman documentary and *Algiers* combined.

As Nathan walked into Bob's, Nighttime, who had ten gold rings in his left ear, dark gold to match the ring on his finger and the cap on one front tooth, was talking to Bob, while Cuquemango was staring at the ceiling fan as though thinking of hanging himself. "Cabezucha got some money and he's fucked up again. *Mira,* the man is out of it. *Sabe',* he just asks anybody. Cops, neighbors. He doesn't care, *tu sabe'. Una ve'—vi* this fucking cop coming down First. *Puñeta,* I shout the alarm. *Y no' vamo'.* I look up First, you know, then I turn back and the street is *vacío,* empty, man, *se fueron todo',* the only motherfucker on Tenth Street is stupid Cabezucha, man, standing there in the *medio bloque, sabe',* with his big *cabeza,* saying, 'Smoke?' "

"Ah," said the man who was not Bob. "You should be very careful. This neighborhood is getting difficult." He smiled. Nathan ordered his ribs. Nighttime did not seem to want to continue talking, but the man who was not Bob did not appear to care about Nathan and just went ahead. "You have to be more careful. There is trouble coming," he said with an even bigger smile. "It is that German. You know the German?"

he said to Nathan as he took his ribs order. Nathan nodded. "He is a real Nazi."

"How do you know that?" Nathan asked.

"He does not like people of color. He is out to get us each and every one. A typical Nazi."

"You're just saying that because he's German."

The man who was not Bob smiled. "No. He is SS. A colonel in the SS. Ask him."

Nathan took his ribs and on the way home pondered what it would be like to be German, how he had mishandled that evening with Karoline years ago, how he wished it had gone differently . . .

Nathan and Sonia ate the ribs and watched the fleshy Italians rolling around. Just as the actors were about to not have sex, there was a knock on the door. It was Harry. "We got you some liver knishes," he said.

Did he intentionally intrude on *traif* night?

"They're good," Harry pleaded. "Not from Yankel Fink."

"Dad, what am I going to do with all these liver knishes?"

"Give them to Syrup Cone for a treat."

"Sarah hates liver."

"Even chopped liver?"

"Any liver."

Harry threw up his hands in despair and bobbed his head in that "I told you so" nod to God. "See that? She's not Jewish. Sonia, you are raising a Mexican."

"I've got good news for you, Harry," said Sonia. "I tried to give her an enchilada. We had carryout Mexican. You know what she said? She looked at the enchiladas and said, 'Blintzes, yuck.' "

"I'm going to bed," said Harry.

"She likes German chocolate and Italian olives. No chopped liver," said Nathan.

"She's four years old and already exhibits a soft spot for Fascist cultures."

"Three years old, Dad."

"That's better? To be pro-Fascist at three? So why don't you bring her by and we can play. I want some fun in my old age. Listen, it is supposed to be a hundred degrees tomorrow. Go see Uncle Nusan."

"All right. Did you hear any more about Rabbinowitz?"

"Something, isn't it. Guy walks up to someone right on the street and shoots them and nobody knows who did it."

Nathan heard Harry muttering on his way up the stairs, "How can anyone not like chopped liver?" and he wondered if Harry knew they had been eating ribs.

CHAPTER TEN

Whose Bumpy Road Is It?

H ARRY HAD A SNAPSHOT of Nusan slipped into the frame of a mirror over his dresser. It was not the mirror he shaved in every morning, but it was almost that. It was the mirror he inspected his shave in, the mirror he straightened his shirt in. Even though he had no office, nowhere to go, really, Harry dressed every morning in a fresh starched shirt. He loved the stiffness of them, the way they looked like an unstarted day, a fresh skin. He had always imagined that when he got married his wife would iron and starch shirts for him. But long before they got near a chuppah, Ruth had announced, "I am not doing shirts," and said it in a way that was non-negotiable. She had noticed Harry's shirt habit, and it was not going to be her life's work. So he got them done at a 20 percent discount from the Chinese man in exchange for a rent deal on a storefront in his Tenth Street building.

As Harry put on his stiff, crisp shirt and straightened it in the mirror, he would always see the snapshot of his brother, Nusan, weighing about eighty pounds in a baggy suit on a street in Paris, wearing a smile without the least hint of humor in it.

Nathan was sure that Nusan had come to New York because his brother was there. Nusan always referred to Harry as "my brother," and if he was angry, if he was having a bad day, he would add the phrase "my only living relative," which always perplexed Nathan, since he was Nusan's blood nephew.

Since both brothers grew up speaking Yiddish, it would have been logical that they still spoke Yiddish to each other. But they didn't. They didn't speak very much to each other at all. When they did, it was usually in English. When Nusan did speak Yiddish, it was only to mutter a phrase, some idiom that was more a riddle than a statement.

He frequently grumbled to his brother, "*Aach, tokhes oyfn tish.*" Literally, this means "ass on the table," and if it had any meaning beyond that, Nathan never learned it. When Nusan said it to him, Nathan would nod in response as though it were irrefutable.

Nusan made clear that he thought Harry lived a comfortable life of which he disapproved. But this was more an expression of Nusan's resentment than the cause of it. It seemed as though Nusan wanted to be poor to upset his brother. And it did upset Harry that Nusan was living in a sixth-floor walk-up studio apartment on Rivington Street on the air shaft, a cluttered little cave that he had settled into when he arrived in New York. His rent was now up to less than $60 a month, which probably made it one of the cheapest apartments in Manhattan.

Harry kept trying to give Nusan a better apartment. Harry told him it was an investment. "You'll be doing me a favor," he argued. "With the tax break I'll be making money."

But Nusan always had the same strange answer: "I do not take blood money." If Harry knew what he meant by this, no one else did. When Nathan was younger, he assumed that his father was looking after Nusan. But as he got older, it became apparent to Nathan when he went to see his uncle how alone he was, how grateful he was for the company, for someone to go out with. Gradually Nathan realized that Nusan was *his* responsibility. Harry never complained, never said anything about it, but he probably did not enjoy Nusan's company, the blood money references, the other hostile statements. Yet Nusan's photograph was tucked in his mirror.

There was a lot Nathan and Mordy didn't know. Almost nothing had been explained to them. Nathan was not even sure how he knew that Nusan was a camp survivor. It seemed as if he'd been born knowing it. Can knowledge become coded in DNA? Will knowledge of the Holocaust become genetically encoded? Worse, will the experience? Will Jews genetically know the Holocaust the way salmon know the river of their birth?

The building on Rivington Street where Nusan lived had a smell of fried food and sweat and sometimes cats. The Dominicans had brightened the neighborhood with the blue and red squares of their flag, enlivened it with restaurants serving hot island food, made it bounce with their brassy merengue music splashing out of windows. Gang insignias were sprayed on the walls of Nusan's building and the walls of the Portuguese grocer across the street who had been there before the Spanish people. An unreadable swirling design in spray paint blocked the view from the wire-reinforced glass entrance to Nusan's building. Once the door to Nusan's apartment was opened, a different, overpowering, unidentified smell took over. It may have been just sour air. Even on the hottest summer days, when the old air conditioners in the other apartments were all rumbling and coughing like the distant sound of a busy small-craft airstrip, Nusan had his windows shut, Brahms swelling and the Mets striking out.

Nusan saw a synchronism between the dark, somber, Germanic tones of Brahms and the lineup of the New York Mets as they loaded the bases and failed to drive in a run or lost a winning game by an error through the legs. As summer began, they were still in first place in the National League East, but Nusan, with a connoisseur's eye for tragedy, could see the flaws that would doom them. The tall and goofy Darryl Strawberry would lope to the plate and pound the ball out of the park. But Nusan noticed that he hit like that only when the bases were empty. With runners in scoring positions he tended to strike out, revealing a hidden will to fail in spite of his enormous ability. Sportswriters said that he felt the weight of carrying the entire ball club. But Nusan knew this was simply a built-in desire to fail, just as Nusan saw Dwight Gooden's fate awaiting him, even while he pitched shutout innings, in interviews in which he denied using drugs.

The Mets were ill-fated champions. The Yankees had less talent and of late fewer victories, and for the moment the championship was eluding them. But they would be back because they thought like champions, walked with the blessing of winners. Nusan could never be a Yankees fan.

A few years back he discovered the Red Sox, a team so determinedly ill-fated that they had allowed the Mets to beat them in a World Series. How else could the Mets have won? There they were, converging on the infield, leaping on top of one another victoriously and improbably, while Nusan watched to the deep-voiced chorus of Ein Deutsches Requiem. Nusan was fascinated by the sight of the somber Red Sox slouching toward their dugout, not even looking surprised. More cursed than even the Mets. Nusan would have switched instantly, except that the Red Sox were not available on New York television.

Brahms and the Mets were Nusan's summer Saturdays as he sat in the dark in his studio on Rivington, deep notes billowing as the innings went by and the wins and losses accumulated. Still in first place, yes. But Nusan could see the demons waiting. He knew their disguises. He knew a lot about demons.

That was how Nathan found his uncle when he checked in on Sundays. Sometimes he brought Sarah, who had the only really open relationship with Nusan. Nathan wondered if Nusan ever had children. He had heard somewhere that he had had an entire family before the war. But no one would ever ask something like that—except Sarah, who might say anything. She called him Nussy.

"Nussy, you're smelly," she said one day.

And then the rarest of occurrences, a large smile spread Nusan's mustache wide, and his teeth—good teeth—showed. "You're smelly, too, little girl." They both looked delighted with the exchange.

Visiting Nusan was an opportunity for Nathan. He had not been on a subway since the incident on the F train. Was his condition still there, ready to attack him unexpectedly? He hadn't told anyone about it. Maybe it would never happen again. A brief test was available. The F train again, one stop from Houston to Delancey. The ride passed quickly and uneventfully; he had been lost in thought and had forgotten to monitor any signs of impending anxiety.

Nathan always let himself in to Nusan's apartment. Nusan had given him a key, supposedly so that Nusan would not have to get up to let him in, but Nathan knew what he was really thinking. He wanted Nathan, his namesake, the proof he was dead, to find the body. And every time Nathan opened the door he braced himself, first for the smell and second for the sight of Nusan dead.

Nusan was always in his chair with his scarf on. If the Mets were playing, an old scratchy record, usually a great classic recording played too many times, would be on and Nusan's pale face would be absolutely blue in the light of the television, possibly one of the last large black-and-white sets in Manhattan. If there was no afternoon Mets game, Nathan would find Nusan in the same chair with a hat on, holding a book inches from his face in the dim lighting.

Sometimes, if he saw Nusan in the neighborhood, Nathan would hurry over to his empty apartment to clean it up a little bit, in the hope it would attract fewer mice and cockroaches. He had filled the apartment with poison—poison for rodents and poison for insects. But Nusan had entire drawers of stale food. He had a desk drawer crammed with stale chunks of challah from a hundred *motzi*.

After his heart attack, his first documented attack, he refused to change his diet, which alternated between the neighborhood's heavy, fatty Jewish food, heavy, fatty Ukrainian food, and heavy, fatty Polish food. Also someone occasionally left him a bag of bialies. Nor would he move from his six-story walk-up. Moving was Harry's idea. Even the doctors said the stairs were healthy for Nusan.

"Better people than me have had heart attacks. Why should I have special treatment?" he said. But it seemed the six floors were getting difficult, and he went out less and less frequently. He was getting lonely. He was also shrinking back to the weight in the photograph. For the first time since he had moved to America, someone would be able to recognize him from the snapshot in Harry's bedroom.

As Nathan approached Nusan's door, he noted as he always did that Nusan didn't have a mezuzah. But he had often seen Nusan as he entered the apartment give an almost imperceptible tap on the right doorpost as though touching one. No mezuzah, just this unconscious tap on the blank doorpost where it might have been.

Nathan braced himself for the smell as he opened the door. It came over him like a bag dropping over his head to smother him, blocking out air and light as he forced himself into the dark room.

And yet—he could breathe. He was not having an attack. He was just in Nusan's small, dark, foul-smelling apartment. There was a desk and a foldout couch and little more, yet the room seemed full. Nusan had given up unfolding the couch to sleep. A blanket and pillow were crushed in opposite corners. The floor, the couch, the desk, and the windowsills were stacked with newspaper clippings. Nusan was in his chair hunched over a paper, rocking back and forth, his gray hat on his head, looking every bit like a davening Talmudist lovingly reciting a favorite passage.

But Nathan knew that his head was covered not out of respect, but rather from a strange habit in old age of leaving his hat on. Nathan wondered if Nusan's father, his grandfather whom he had never met and who was one of many relatives who was never spoken of, really did cover his head and read passages while davening back and forth. All that was left was a vague notion of wearing a hat while reading.

Nor was Nusan's reading material Talmudic. Every scrap of writing in the apartment was on the same subject—Nazis. No one in the family ever took this very seriously until the case in which Nusan had played an important role. It seemed to be his revelation that the factory worker who had been exposed and deported was only one of three Treblinka guards who had been let into the United States.

Nusan had extensive information on all three. Once the case became known, Nusan retreated and let other, better-known figures do the interviews, but he had been the one who followed the trails. In his dark and stinking cave, he was more than a madman. He was a hunter.

Nusan looked up from his papers, stopping his davening motion as Nathan walked in the door. "You are late."

"It's three o'clock. I said I would be over in the afternoon."

"What time is the game?"

"They're playing the Astros in Texas. It's a late game. Gooden is starting," said Nathan, ready for the question.

They left the apartment and slowly made their way to a small Ukrainian place where they ate pirogis that were very much like the kreplach they used to eat at Rabbinowitz's—the same tart cheese filling, the same buttery soft noodle covering, and the same feeling in the stomach, as though small rocks were being placed there.

"Uncle Nusan, do you remember the German pastry shop up in our neighborhood?"

"I should eat German pastry?"

Nusan approached the topic with the same feigned indifference with which Pepe Le Moko approached rodents. But Nathan knew he hadn't forgotten. Nusan was cursed with a perfect memory. At least from 1940 on. He never talked about before the war. This was one of the problems between him and Harry. When Nusan arrived in New York, they had only prewar memories in common and Nusan wouldn't talk about those things. Nathan wondered if Nusan's problem with Harry was that Harry *was* a prewar memory.

"Remember, I mentioned the shop one time, the Edelweiss. We used to go there when I was little."

"With your father. I don't go to German shops."

"Did you learn anything about the owner?" Nathan asked, almost wincing as he asked it.

"Of the Edelweiss?"

"Yes."

"Why don't you order applesauce with the kreplach."

"Pirogi. This isn't Jewish. I don't want applesauce. Ever heard about him?"

"You get sour cream no matter what you say. So it's a waste to order sour cream."

"It's a waste to order applesauce if you don't eat it."

"A philosopher *klug vi der velt.*" Wise as the world.

"Do you think it would be possible for an SS colonel to be living all these years in the neighborhood?"

"You have no idea what is possible. You don't want to know. Now you're not eating all your sour cream, either?"

"Look, Uncle Nusan, this is not an expensive place. I can get you whatever you want. I think people just say these things because he's German."

"Because he's German. That's not a good enough reason for you?"

"No. It isn't. How could an SS colonel get in here? Is it even possible?"

"How? How? So there's no NCWC?"

"NCWC?"

"Aach. What are you asking for? You want to know. *Aach, tokhes oyfn tish.*"

There it was again. Ass on the table. "What does that mean, Nusan, *tokhes oyfn tish?*"

"It means hurry up before the Mets lose without me."

Nusan would never admit it, but he was grateful for company. But he wanted to watch the Mets game alone, which to Nathan meant being spared nine innings in that apartment. He closed the door behind him, and before he had finished descending the stairwell he could hear the slow, soft moan of the first few bars of the Brahms First Cello Sonata and knew that Dwight Gooden was warmed up and ready to throw.

As he turned down the last set of cracked marble stairs, hand on the red banister, its ornate designs turned into shapeless blobs from more than a century of regular repainting, it occurred to Nathan that Nusan had left him with a free afternoon—and that he could, if he wanted to, call *her*.

He walked out of the dark building to a blinding white heat and carefully approached a pay phone in a little metal box. Since most pay phones on Rivington Street had been beaten to death for their coins, it was not likely that this phone would work. That would be the test. If the phone worked, he would call her. The metal box was covered in the same indecipherable graffiti that marked Nusan's building. Someone had pasted a sticker on the black receiver handle that said, "Eat the Rich." He put the phone to his ear and heard a long steady tone.

At this same instant, Harry Seltzer was going home, looking forward to his air-conditioning, passing Mohammed's newsstand, singing, "We may never, never meet again, on the bumpy road to love." It felt good to dip down to a baritone voice for the word "love." Chow Mein Vega had insisted the song was Gershwin.

"No," Harry assured him with good-humored tolerance. "Irving Berlin."

"Gershwin," Chow Mein insisted.

"I'm sorry, Chucho, it happens to be Berlin."

Chow Mein shook his head with enough emphasis to wag his stumpy ponytail. "Gershwin, man. In fact, it's both Gershwins. Words by Ira. From a show called *Shall We Dance*. It was a movie with Fred Astaire." And Chow Mein started to float his tonnage across the sidewalk in surprisingly graceful Astaire-like steps.

"You better stick to boogaloo."

"How about some action, bro'? Loser buys *bacalao* lunch for two at Rosa's?"

They shook on it, but the lunch would never take place because Harry would never look it up, fearing that he might be wrong. He wanted to keep the song in his Berlin repertoire just for that dip. He did it again: "On the bumpy road to"—now the dip—"love."

What was that? He saw something. It was in Mohammed's window.

Florence! Florence from Eleventh Street was on the cover of a magazine called *Big Black Booty*. Harry wondered what that meant, but the cover photo helped clarify. Florence was in a very small, very short red dress, and she was leaning over and looking back over her shoulder. Her booty, if that was the term, was exposed and impressive. He looked carefully at the face. It was Florence.

He stepped gingerly into the shop, hoping Mohammed would be busy, but he was waiting behind the counter with a toothsome smile. "Shalom, my friend!"

"Salaam," said Harry, trying to match Mohammed's cheerfulness.

Harry made his selection quickly: *The New Yorker, Foreign Affairs, Big Black Booty,* and the *Forward.* He placed them on the counter.

Mohammed offered him a bag, and Harry, a little too casually, said, "No thanks, no. . . . Well, okay. Put them in a bag."

"Enjoy them, my friend," said Mohammed, and though Harry searched the notes of Mohammed's voice, he could not find the least shading of a connotation to the simple statement.

Harry never saw the pages displaying Florence's magnificent, dimpled, big black booty. He took the entire bag of magazines, contraband too hot to examine, immediately into his office room in their apartment and buried them in a file cabinet where he kept tax records. He could never remember exactly where. But he never forgot that it was in there somewhere and that someday a man from the IRS whose every feature, even his socks, would announce that he was "not from the neighborhood" would arrive for an audit and there, in between forms and receipts, Florence's glorious big black booty would flop across the table.

CHAPTER ELEVEN

Chocolate Buttercream

"COME OVER," she had said, "I'll show you all my secrets."

There was something about Karoline's manner that made Nathan feel that she was toying with him, that everything she did was calculated to manipulate him for her amusement. It was a demeanor that promised abuse and disaster, and he was hurrying up Second Avenue toward it. Even in this heat he could have run. The thought of her gave him limitless energy.

"*Viva la huelga,* Nathan," Arnie shouted cheerfully from his sidewalk perch. Arnie in his wool beret on a shadeless block of Avenue A was not noticing the heat this day. Arnie never seemed affected by temperature, though his skin was starting to resemble the weathered bricks of tenement buildings.

Nathan realized that he was acting suspiciously. He slowed down and said hello to Arnie. Then he realized that to act normally, he would have to stroll over and chat.

Why? Acting suspiciously? Did he think this would end up in a court of law? He picked up his pace again and soon was at the Edelweiss. The shop entrance was on the Avenue A side, but the doorway for the building was conveniently around the corner on the quiet side street. He pressed the button. What should he say? "Hi, it's me," or "Hi, it's Nathan," or . . . A loud buzz unlocked the door without the need to say anything. Inside, she was waiting at the top of the stairs barefoot, in a clean white apron, and—Nathan was quickly debating this in his mind—possibly wearing nothing else.

As though reading his thoughts, she said, "It's a hot day for baking," and she gave him a very light kiss on the cheek that seemed shy—almost embarrassed.

But surely her naked arms and legs and shoulders and back were a calculated effect. When a woman coifs for a man, no matter how casually she coifs, to the intended target she always looks coiffed—planned, calculated. Otherwise the effort has failed. Women know magic, and their willingness to use it excites. Was she barefoot by chance with perfectly painted toes? If her hair was falling down, why was only one beautiful dark strand draped over a bright blue eye? On the lower back was the beginning of a tattoo, as though to say "If you want to see the whole tattoo, you have to untie the apron." Did she know how the inelegant white muslin of her apron made her skin look that much softer and more elegant?

She knew. She knew. She knew exactly what he was aching to do as she led him into her apartment with seeming disinterest—and yet still with a touch of a shyness that he was sure was not intended.

Her apartment was one room, a large studio with a king-size bed in lacy linens on one side. On the other side was a kitchen: professional baker's ovens—five of them, long, deep, and wide and arranged floor to ceiling; a stainless-steel stove, gleaming and spotless; metal racks; a large mixing machine; crock canisters with whisks—some balloon shaped, some elongated. Other canisters had plastic scrapers and spatulas. A wall rack contained knives with gleaming blades. There was a large industrial refrigerator. And there were huge sacks of flour and sugar.

By her bed were five cardboard cases and a number of wooden boxes.

"It's the cool side of the room."

"What is?"

"Where the boxes are. It's wine. It all belongs to Joey Parma."

"Joey Parma the cop?"

She nodded her head in delight. "Look." She sat on the edge of the bed and started pulling bottles out of boxes. She held up a thick green bottle with a vanilla-colored label with maroon lettering—CHASSAGNE-MONTRACHET—and then a white-labeled Aloxe-Corton. "Prefer Bordeaux?" she asked, holding up a bottle with a yellow label that said BOYD CANTENAC. "Try a Margaux. Now let's see," she said, sifting through other boxes. "Now here's something," she announced, hoisting a long thin bottle. "From Erbach in the Rheingau. My father would kill for this wine. Oh, it's a Trockenbeerenauslese. My father would kill for much less than this." She looked up at Nathan with a pleasant smile.

Was she laughing at him? Teasing him? Could she see how much he wanted to have her on that bed at this very moment? "Why does Joey Parma keep his wine here?" asked Nathan, realizing that he might sound a bit jealous.

"You can keep your wine here, too, if you like."

How he would have enjoyed walking out on her at this moment, leaving her alone by the bed with Joey Parma's wine. But he knew he wouldn't do that. Worse, she knew he wouldn't.

"Joey Parma, like you," she said with a small but almost sad chuckle, "has a wife. And his wife would kill him if she knew what he spent on wine. So he keeps it here and comes over and fondles the bottles and every now and then takes one home for a special event, and the wife always agrees that it is a nice wine and has no idea how nice."

"And you make the pastry here?"

"No, my father makes it in the back downstairs. I just make special orders up here. Let's get started."

"Started?"

"I told you I was going to show you all my secrets. We'll start with a genoise. I love genoise because it seems rich and buttery and solid, but it's light as cotton. Everything is about paradoxes. That's what good baking is. Making paradoxes."

She put a pot of water on the stove to boil and then took a large tray of eggs from the refrigerator and with fluid and efficient motion, two eggs at a time, one in each hand, opened six eggs, cracking them on the side of a mixing bowl, dumping in the contents, and flipping the shells into a nearby trash barrel. "A little more than two-thirds cup," she said as she jammed a metal scoop in a bin of sugar and tossed some, unmeasured, into the bowl. She grabbed a wire whisk as she carried the bowl to the stove and beat the mixture over the boiling water. Nathan tried to get closer to her and widened his nostrils to detect her scent of butter, but butter was everywhere in the room—or was it she? As she pounded the metal of the bowl with the whisk wires in a circular manner, he watched her entire body moving—and longed for it. "Make it thick and creamy," she said, briefly looking up at him.

Then she put the mixture in an electric mixing bowl at high speed and busied herself brushing butter in cake molds and dusting them with flour, taking out utensils and ingredients like a nurse preparing an operating theater. "You have to be ready, because there is no time to waste," she nearly whispered as she lowered the speed in the mixer. Finally, the mixture was a pastel yellow and had quadrupled in volume.

"Now," she announced in a low and hungry voice. "Now we fold." She sifted a light layer of flour onto the mixture by barely tapping the sifting hoop three times. "Folding is everything. If you don't have the hands for folding, you can't do anything. You are not mixing, not stirring. You caress the mixture with the spatula." She held his hand in hers and rubbed the palm gently and then placed a rubber spatula in it. "I'll show you," she said as she guided his hand. "Gently," she whispered. "Oh, that's nice. Mmm. You have to get rid of all the pockets of flour, but don't let the air out. Yes . . . that's good. Turn the bowl slowly. You keep doing the same slow motion with your right hand and you slowly turn the bowl with your left.

"Now," she ordered as she brought over a pot of melted butter, "I'll pour and you fold."

It was true. Nathan was astounded to realize that as she poured the cooled liquid butter, it released the same perfume that came off her warm body, slightly moistened by sweat in the hot afternoon. Her skin shone as though it were buttered. His hands trying not to tremble, he gently folded as she poured. She carefully emptied the light, fluffy mixture into cake molds and slid them in an oven.

"Now," she said, and she untied her apron and dropped it to the ground. It was true. She was naked. She had coiffed.

Nathan caressed her breasts, gently, like folding a woman's genoise batter. Then they went to the bed and fell on each other hungrily—for precisely thirty minutes.

"Cake's ready," she announced, and jumped out of bed, went to the sink and washed, put on her apron, and handed another to the now naked Nathan. She pulled out a cake, put it on the counter, and put her ear next to it. "Come here," she said, and Nathan, still recovering from the last exactly thirty minutes, staggered over. "Listen," she said, holding her ear close to the cake and tapping it. "Hear that?"

Nathan brought his ear close and heard a slight rustling, almost hissing noise as she tapped the cake.

"It's perfect," she said. "Next we are making a *dobos torta*. Hungarian. Hungarian is the best. My father doesn't admit this, but it's true. In

1962 they celebrated the seventy-fifth anniversary of Dobos's invention of the cake. My father doesn't like this story because they were Communist. He thinks people only suffer under Communism. But in 1962 they made a *dobos torta* that was six feet in diameter. Hungarians attach a lot of importance to size. But this one that we are making is twelve inches, which is a profitable-size cake. Smaller—too much labor per slice. Larger—too hard to cut a reasonable serving."

As she leaned over, working, Nathan looked at her moist and shining back. Above the apron string was the beginning of the tattoo. He had seen the rest now. It was a spoon with something dripping out of it arching gracefully down one buttock. When had she gotten that? Why?

"Hungarians make nine or sixteen of these for layers. They also do a slightly different cake, folding the beaten whites into the beaten yolks, but this is better. I take these four and split them in fourths." She began sawing a thin layer off the first cake. "And I'll have sixteen."

"We have to start on the buttercream," she declared while crumbling chocolate in a double boiler.

Had he not been entangled in this woman's body three minutes ago in the most impassioned embrace of his life? Nathan wondered. Is she just playing with me? And what have I done? Betrayed Sonia and Sarah for—for a twelve-inch *dobos torta*? Why?

"The chocolate buttercream. That's what you do it for," Karoline said in wild-eyed excitement. "The whole cake is just an excuse to eat chocolate buttercream." She was boiling sugar and water. "You can test this with a sugar thermometer. But there is a better way." She poured a glass of cold water from the faucet and with a wooden spoon deposited one drop of syrup in the water. Then she reached in with her fingers. Taking her free hand, she pushed aside Nathan's apron, exposing his chest, and pressed on him the small, gummy, clear drop of sugar she had rolled in her wet fingers. It fell off and she kissed the spot on his chest. "If it stuck, the sugar hadn't been heated enough. It can't be sticky when it cools." She turned to the electric mixer, where egg yolks were being slowly beaten. Nathan was rubbing his chest and looking at her, looking troubled. "The kiss was free," she said. "Not part of the test."

"The test."

"For the sugar," she asserted, slowly adding the syrup to the eggs. Then she added little cubes of butter. Why did the butter always excite him? He knew what would be next. He put his arms around her, but she pushed them off. "Not yet. It's not chocolate yet." She started to add the melted chocolate. By the time the buttercream was chocolate, Nathan was struggling to resist the temptation to pounce on her like a famished predator. He didn't care about the *dobos torta.* But she did.

"Now, let's see about your hands," she said, going to the refrigerator and taking out a mixing bowl filled with white, fluffy, unbaked meringue. "Fold this into the buttercream. Very gently. With nice hands."

He obeyed, and after she built the *torta* into thin, alternating layers of cake and buttercream and put it in the refrigerator to set, he used his now well-trained hands on her.

They were outlaws, outside the law, far beyond the rules, so they were free to do anything. She entered him with her fingers. He spanked her with a rubber spatula, which made her squeal in delight. She decorated between his legs, applying French meringue with a pastry tube until he had a huge baroque ornament of white swirls and little stars. Then she licked it like an ice-cream cone.

"I'll show you what I like," Nathan said, taking another pastry bag, filling it with chocolate buttercream, placing swirls around her breasts, decorating the nipples with little stars the way she had shown him to do, giving the bag a little twist before lifting up. And then he feasted.

She rolled over resplendently across the bed, and, eyeing her tattoo, he started at the spoon and followed the drip with his tongue across her buttock. It had already become a favorite route.

"You like my tattoo," he heard her say from the other end of the bed.

"Yes," he answered obediently. Yes, he did. Nothing mattered anymore. She had made him like her tattoo. A victory for her—defeat for him. He loved the way she defeated him. He could feel it pulling him deeper into a desire that offered the ultimate pleasure—complete and total destruction. He was not even disturbed by these thoughts. He was excited by them.

Then she showed him how to make the caramel wedge and pipe buttercream with the pastry bag—with which he had already had sufficient practice to finish the cake, making neat rows on the top so the caramel wedges could be placed at jaunty angles, making the top of the cake look like a broken plane of some cubist portrait.

When it was finished—tall cylinder in a purple tan chocolate with amber wedges of tilted carmel crowning the top—they briefly admired it.

"Wait one minute," she said, and slipped it into the refrigerator. Then they went back to the bed. Nathan was amazed. She had turned him into some extraordinary male force, tireless, athletic, insatiable. And then they collapsed.

He looked at his watch: 8:10. He jumped out of bed.

"Wife and child waiting?" she jabbed.

He was ashamed. But it was an inescapable truth.

"Not so fast," she said as he struggled to slip on his clothes. "Sit over there." She pointed to a chair by a table. He sat there, and she carefully cut a wedge of *dobos torta*. It was striped—thin stripes of yellow cake alternating with taupe-colored buttercream, the airy, textured cake suspended in layers of dense buttercream, the caramel sharp, sweet, and crunchy. Just when he thought his senses had been exhausted.

You have to love a woman who can do this for you, thought Nathan, and he lied to himself and pretended he meant the pastry. Did he love her? Oh God, don't let me love her.

He had to go. She saw him to the landing of the stairway.

"Don't ever come back," he heard her say. In the dark stairwell, a certain shine on her eyes told him she was crying. "Damn it, why do I do this?" she muttered.

"Do what?" he protested.

"Do what?" she repeated mockingly. "Just don't come back. A great afternoon. We enjoyed it. I'll give you the *torta* if you want. Bring it home to your little girl."

He realized that she was right and walked silently down the steps. Four steps down, and then he turned. "I am going to have to come back. We both know that."

"Yes, and then you'll have to come back again and again and again. And then finally do you know what you will do? The same stupid thing that men always do. You will decide to confess. You will tell your wife everything and beg absolution."

"Jews don't beg for absolution."

"Yes, they do. From their wives. And then she will hate me. And here in my neighborhood will be this probably very nice woman with a beautiful little girl, and they will know everything about me. And they

will hate me. Good-bye, Nathan Seltzer." And she turned and started
to slam the door shut.

"Wait, Karoline!" he cried out, and she stopped.

"What?"

Perhaps he just couldn't think of anything else to say, something to
break the finality of the door swinging shut. She was waiting.

"When you were a child, did your parents send you to swimming
lessons?"

"What?"

"You know, did they send you somewhere to learn how to swim?"

"Yes."

"They did?"

"Yes."

"Where?"

"The Y."

"The Y?"

"You know, YMCA or YWCA."

Nathan nodded.

"See ya." And she closed the door.

When the Talmud lists the obligation of a father, it lists a few very
precise things. It says nothing about being faithful to the mother of his
children or—and this was certainly not Nathan's own fault—child. Just
a few things. Studying Torah, teaching a craft, going to the YMCA.

Nathan came home fearing he smelled of chocolate buttercream, of
butter, of Karoline Moellen. But all Sonia said was, "How is Nusan?"
He almost had to recall who Nusan was.

Sonia was very excited. She had had what she regarded as a major
breakthrough on her play. "You said it when we first met, remember?"

"What?"

"They never met. They lived in different times. Now I realize how
to do it. Emma Goldman moves into this house on Thirteenth Street
with her lovers. She realizes that the house is haunted—haunted by—a
Mexican woman—named Margarita. Do you see?"

"That could work," said Nathan, realizing there would be new
pages to photocopy. He looked at her, at her fleshy, generous body and

her long, beautiful fingers. Had he ever noticed how long they were? He must have, but suddenly it seemed he was once again seeing her for the first time. It seemed he had never loved her as much as at this moment—her and their daughter—and he wrapped his long arms around his wife, thinking of everything he was in danger of losing. And to his astonishment, he made love to her. He may have made love to her better than he had ever done before. Would it make her suspicious?

Now he understood that the more sex a man had, the more he wanted. That was why monks refused sex. He used to wonder how they could bear it. When he was a teenager, this was an important topic with his Italian schoolmates. But now he knew that only through abstinence could the sex drive be diminished. Which was a sensible goal, because there was absolutely nothing in human nature as self-destructive as sexual desire.

Nathan got out of bed and looked at his naked body in the mirror. He felt *fit*. Sex would keep him trim. He had been thinking of taking up running to burn off his tellas. But now he had a much better idea. "Do you think I am gaining weight?" he asked Sonia only now because for the first time in months he was confident that he wasn't. Sonia only moaned in response. She was asleep. Nathan returned to the bed and held her, and they slept that way, holding each other.

CHAPTER TWELVE

Not Easy to Be Puerto Rican

FELIX, EL CUQUEMANGO, had been a Puerto Rican for more than ten years. He noted with a sense of accomplishment that when Chow Mein needed an El Dominicano, he completely passed him over and recruited a real Puerto Rican. He was passing in this neighborhood where they didn't like Dominicans. A Dominican selling grass was a link to Colombian cartels. A Puerto Rican selling the same stuff on the same street was a friendly neighborhood dealer. Cuquemango had heard that in the old days even the white people used to deal. Now white people got less excited about Puerto Ricans, not that they knew a Dominican from a Puerto Rican. Lots of people were dealing. There was even a Panamanian working Tenth Street. The job was good money and required no green card. Cuquemango didn't need a green card, nor did he live down on Rivington. He was passing for an East Village Puerto Rican.

But on warm Sundays, Cuquemango liked merengue and he didn't like *plenas*. The Puerto Ricans always complained that merengue was too loud. The casita was theirs, and in the summer it was the best place in New York. It was supposed to remind them of those places in western Puerto Rico where they had never been. But Cuquemango had actually been to them. He landed in western Puerto Rico and had even picked coffee in the mountains and lived briefly with a family in a two-room farmhouse that looked like the casita.

He came from a richer place—richer land but poorer people—in the green fertile valley of the Cibao in the northern Dominican Republic. He often thought of those tough, balding mountains and the green valley floor where the soil underneath was as dark as blood and the turquoise wooden-shingled towns where people cared about one another. That was how he remembered it, anyway. Why was it that the richer the land, the poorer the people? The land in Manhattan was not good. But the people here did well nevertheless, a lot better than in the rich-soiled Cibao.

His family raised eggs. They were the only ones for many miles to raise them, so it was a good business. But not good enough to support twelve children. A Haitian woman once told him, "Always have eggs around you because eggs are life. They have power." It must have been true, because his family had a great number of eggs around them and they kept having babies.

He did always keep a hard-boiled egg on him, which he had the habit of rolling one-handed between the fingers of his right hand. Even hard-boiled, an egg is fragile, and he might have hoped that the delicate egg's presence would force his life to be more gentle. He held it in his hand as he crossed a choppy, foaming sea in a small boat from the Dominican Republic with two dozen other people, scrambling to shore near Aguadilla. Most of the others were sick as they dragged themselves quickly across the night beach to the bush. But Felix was hungry, and he ate his egg. They were all put into a van and taken to the coffee slopes in the Puerto Rican mountains. All for the five hundred pesos he had prepaid in the Dominican Republic. He hated picking coffee and understood that to do anything else, he would have to learn how to be Puerto Rican.

Immigration officers were Puerto Rican, and they could always spot a Dominican. In Santo Domingo, before crossing over, they were schooled in the trip-up words used by the INS. When they hold up the little olive-size green fruits, do not say "*limoncita.*" It is a *gnipa.* And *lechosas* are papayas. One day, at a lunch counter ordering pigeon peas and rice, he heard himself say "*guandules*" instead of "*gandules.*" No one caught it, but he resolved to learn how to be completely Puerto Rican—not just the words, but the accent, the haircut, the clothing, the walk. People from the Cibao did not have those giveaway traces of Haitian blood, and with his hair, nose, and lips he could pass. Once he looked and walked and sounded like a Puerto Rican, he moved to San Juan, where the only job he could find was washing dishes in a restaurant owned by Cubans, which clearly marked him as an illegal alien. It took him another four months before he found a job in a Puerto Rican restaurant, a little fish place in Santurce, and successfully passed.

Once his Puerto Rican was good enough, he just got on a plane. It was Christmastime. Puerto Ricans create chaos at Christmastime, filling all the San Juan flights, carrying bags full of pork-filled *pasteles* and bottles of boozy *coquita* and other Christmas things, making noise and traffic on their way to New York to visit their relatives, who then told them that life was good in New York except for the *hijo de puta* Dominicanos who were moving into the neighborhood wearing no socks, eating bananas, and making too much noise.

As long as he was a Puerto Rican, there was no immigration and no passport. He was just another American, a spic in New York, an American spic in the Loisaida. "American Spic" was the title of one of the most famous poems by the neighborhood laureate, Gilberto Banza.

No one in New York was looking for a Puerto Rican dishwasher. Unskilled jobs would mark him as an "illegal alien"—it was not enough to be alien, you were an illegal alien. Everyone was hiring illegal aliens. But Felix had to get a U.S. citizen job, and he had no skills. He found a part-time job as the assistant to a super of a building on Avenue B. Then he met Chow Mein Vega. He started going over to the casita and playing congas for Chow Mein. He had heard that Chow Mein was a big star, and he thought playing congas would earn him. But no one ever seemed to pay Chow Mein Vega anymore.

Felix wanted to go back to the Cibao someday, but only when he had all the money he needed for the rest of his life, because he knew that once he was there, he could not make any more. In the meantime, he had a mother in the Dominican who was waiting for money from her son in America.

In those days, there were two Dominican things Felix did not want to do: sell grass on Tenth Street and live on Rivington with the rest of the Dominicans. In time he did both.

Desperate for a job, he wandered down to Rivington Street and on the way, on Grand Street, saw a HELP WANTED sign in Jack Bialy's. He took little domes of dough and twirled them with his powdered fingers on a flour-dusted board to make the well, and then he tossed onions into the indentation. The bakery had no wall to hide behind. Customers, owners, and salesclerks could all see him, and he was expected to move fast. No one ever moved faster. Felix could make seventy-five bialies a minute. People would come just to watch him do it. Jack Bialy would pat him on the back admiringly, shake his head, and say, "You are

a real *kuchen macher.*" Felix didn't like the name because he did not want
to be a *kuchen macher,* a bialy maker. This was like the jobs in the Dominican Republic. He earned barely enough money to survive, and he
had no possibilities for a better future. He asked for more money, but
Jack Bialy just looked sadly at his flour-dusted black shoes and said,
"There is no margin, Kuchenmacher. It's sixty cents a bialy. What can I
do? But you can eat as many bialies as you want. Take them home." And
Felix did, making whole meals of nothing but bialy and hard-boiled egg
or sometimes bialy, hard-boiled eggs, and chorizo. Jack asked that on his
way home he bring a bag of leftover bialies to his friend Nusan, close by
on Rivington Street. Felix would warily climb the stairs and brace himself for the sour smell when Nusan opened the door. Sometimes, especially if he tapped lightly enough on the door, there would be no answer,
and he would leave the bag in front of the door and quickly descend the
stairs.

Felix came to hate the puffy cushions of chewy bread that Jack Bialy
reverently called *bialystock kuchen.* He was not even making money to
send to his mother, so he began selling "smoke" on Tenth Street, and
then he could send impressive quantities of dollars home. He explained
to his mother that he was doing well, doing business in New York with
the Jews, a plausible story.

The amount Felix made on Grand Street was minuscule next to
what he could make on Tenth Street, and it was likely to remain that
way—unless the government suddenly legalized marijuana and outlawed bialies. So Felix, according to Jack Bialy, broke Jack's heart and
left. Jack told him that he could have his job back anytime he wanted.
And to tempt him, he would go up to Tenth Street where Felix was
dealing, arriving in shirtsleeves and suspenders with his flour-dusted
shoes, and hand Felix a bag of the loathed bialies. "So you remember
your friends," Jack would say. Not knowing what to do with the bialies
while he was dealing, he would hide them behind the stoop where he
kept his stash of marijuana and a hard-boiled egg. Even Joey Parma had
noticed that Jack Bialy was "involved in something."

People continued to call Felix "Kuchenmacher," which inevitably
became Cuquemango, or even El Cuquemango. Felix felt that he had
not learned how to be a Puerto Rican and moved to America just to be
Cuquemango. When he heard someone call him El Cuquemango, he
would say angrily, "Felix, *solo Felix.* Okay?" Just Felix.

It was hard to break in on Tenth Street, but the dealers paid good percentages to lookouts. He worked about five hours a night and made more money than he had ever made in his life. This is more than five thousand bialies, he said to himself one night, counting his money and thinking of his old boss. All he had to do was warn when a plainclothes cop came, and they were so obvious that they might as well have worn uniforms. Soon he too was a dealer, and he even helped Ruben take over his spot as lookout. Helping a young Puerto Rican break in on Tenth Street helped to establish Felix as a Puerto Rican. Felix was sending money to his mother, who could see from the amounts that her son was doing well in New York. New York was turning out to be exactly what everyone in the Cibao said it was.

Felix didn't want to be in drugs. Whenever anyone questioned him about it, which was not often because most people preferred not to talk about it, he said, "I know people in the barrio on welfare that eat dog food. That canned shit. I'm not eating no fucking Ken-L Ration, bro'."

But Felix understood that the drug business had no future in this neighborhood. That was why white people were not dealing anymore. The Nazi or the cops or somebody would shut them down. He had to become a real American businessman. He was looking for his chance to prosper the way other immigrants had—like the Italians on First Avenue. He thought opportunities might be found at the casita, if not from music, then farming. Felix was the only one at the casita who knew how to grow crops. When he first came to the neighborhood, he could see that these Puerto Ricans were not like the ones in the island. An island Puerto Rican could grow a whole crop in a back alley—anywhere there was soil. They grew things all over San Juan.

But these Nuyoricans couldn't grow weeds in a sunny lot. Well, they could. In fact, that is mostly what they did. But he showed them how to plant a second crop in between rows, to find crops that helped each other out, that some places were better than others, that wind direction mattered, that creepers and vines could be trained upward to get more space, that growing onions enriched the soil, that laying a mulch of straw saved the low-hanging vegetables, that some crops were grown from seeds and others from planting seedlings. The reality that he did not want to tell anyone was that the one crop that was well suited for this vacant lot in the city would be marijuana.

The tomatoes were coming in—late, but they would ripen into real tomatoes that would be juicy with crisp flesh and the flavor of tomato that had been forgotten by gringos. And the peppers burned hot and were ready for pepper sauce. The corn was growing because corn always grows, but the beans between the rows were not getting enough shoots. The pigeon peas would prosper because they are easy to grow, if he could only convince the Nuyoricans to stop watering them. The banana was not growing and probably couldn't because the roots could not survive winter. He had finally convinced them of the folly of planting coffee at sea level. The flowers—gladiolas and snapdragons, magenta, white, and yellow—were going to do well this year if the heat didn't burn them down.

He could sell these things. Share the profit with the casita. Then he could be a neighborhood businessman instead of just a spic or, to use the longer version favored by Vice President Bush's campaign, a "Hispanic." There were several empty storefronts on Tenth Street. The neighborhood had many new businesses, but most did not last long—a used-furniture shop, an art gallery—East Village–type businesses that were now struggling, with fewer and fewer East Village–type people around. But even though there were always storefronts available, many of the landlords would not rent to Felix because they knew El Cuquemango was involved in drugs. They would rather leave their storefronts empty a few more years until they got a Japanese restaurant or a boutique selling things that no one had ever wanted before.

But the Weinberger brothers didn't care. They lived in New Jersey and didn't know who was dealing drugs in the neighborhood. They had let shops and apartments go empty for years because the fewer tenants they had, the more valuable the property would be when the money came in to level the blocks, bulldoze them, and build tall luxury apartment buildings with low ceilings. Six floors of tenement held eight floors of luxury. But so far that hadn't happened, and they had given up and started renting again. So they rented Felix a store where he sold flowers and vegetables.

The casita didn't produce very much, and the store was mostly empty. He filled several buckets with gladiolas and snapdragons, which made Joe the florist regularly walk down the block for reconnaissance. Many of Felix's early customers were plainclothes policemen and Drug Enforcement Agency agents who assumed the shop was nothing more than a front for drug traffic and wanted to figure out how it worked. This was unnerving to Felix, who could recognize a federal agent when he saw one.

Jack Bialy came to Felix's store. He brought bialies, which he said were "on consignment." Jack Bialy defined consignment as "Pay me when business picks up." So every day a young Puerto Rican would show up with one dozen bialies for Felix to sell. Nusan, who hadn't been getting bialies since Felix left Grand Street, started appearing at the end of the day, and Felix gave him what he didn't sell, which at first was a dozen. But soon word spread that they were really good bialies, and Felix had to hold one or two back so that he would have something for Nusan. When Joey Parma came in, Felix would not give him a free bialy. If Joey reached for one, Felix would defiantly say, "Sixty cents!" Joey started to get the idea that somehow El Cuquemango, Jack Bialy, and Nusan were involved in some kind of drug ring. He reasoned that "the old tough one," Nusan, was probably the leader.

The others at the casita were pleased that Felix had come up with a use for the things that they grew. Most wanted only a few vegetables or flowers to bring home. Panista, a drummer who always tapped nervously, gave snapdragons and tomatoes to Consuela's daughter, Rosita, while he stared irresistibly into her eyes, saying nothing. He knew he did not have a good voice. His strength, he reasoned, was his look. But it made Rosita nervous the way Panista always tapped his fingers. Felix was sure Rosita would be happier with him. They danced well together. Though of course he could not say this, he thought that she danced like a Dominican. She loved the way he danced and told him so.

"Baile' ta' bueno, Cuquemango."

He was glad she liked it, but first she had to get his name right. "Felix, por favor. Solo Felix."

Panista, a tall, thin stick of a man called Palo, Chow Mein, and the others at the casita didn't like drug dealers. It was a complicated point of view, because the younger ones like Palo spent the afternoons around the casita listening to plenas and smoking what they had bought from Felix. They all believed that the future was not in drugs, but in sushi, for which the price per ounce seemed almost as good. They called José Fishman "the only smart dealer on the Loisaida."

The Japanese were coming in. Many kinds of new people were

slowly appearing. Property was going to become valuable, and one day
some white guy was going to come strolling through the fence gate and
the garden and up the wooden steps of the casita to announce that he
owned this lot and was selling it to some real estate development corporation. Then they would have no place. Already most Latin people
were gone from First and Second avenues. The only *pasteles* on Second
Avenue now were sold at Saul Grossman's. Chow Mein insisted that
the one hope was that boogaloo would get hot again and he would buy
the lot.

"Sushi, sashimi," Panista repeated, tapping out the rhythm of the
words.

"Chow Mein could do a Japanese boogaloo," said Felix, "except no
one wants boogaloo."

"What's the difference *entre* sushi and sashimi?" asked Panista.

"What difference. No difference *pa' nosotros*," said Palo.

"No, bro', these guys are smart," said Felix. "*Sabe'* how much they
charge for a *pedacito de pe' cao*."

"*Y* they don't even have to cook it."

"Sashimi you don't even have to give rice and they charge the same."

"*Solo un pedacito de* tuna, *nada ma'*."

"*Toro.* I remember that. And wasabi. What's wasabi?"

"Wasabi's not a fish."

"Yeah, it means 'friend' in Indian," said Panista.

Felix charged just enough at his store to make a small profit after
the rent. With little overhead, his produce was good and the prices
cheap. But he had few customers. It was getting tougher in the neighborhood. He couldn't even open on Tuesdays because there was a
farmer's market in front of St. Mark's with good prices for the same
things. It was a hot, sunny summer after a good rainy spring, and everyone was going to have nice tomatoes.

For now, Felix could accept that he was not making money the way
he had when he was in drugs; although he was barely getting by and
didn't want to move down to Rivington Street with the Dominicans,
the most painful part was thinking about his mother in their village in
the Cibao. When he was dealing, he used to transfer her money every
week. She was becoming one of the richest people in the village, and she
would just smile coyly and tell the neighbors, "My son Felix is doing
very well with the Jews in America." Now he had nothing to send to his

mother, and it was not difficult for him to imagine the villagers coming up to her from time to time and asking, "*¿Y cómo van las cosas con tu hijo Felix en Nueba York?*" What's going on with your son Felix in America?

And his mother would answer with a long, solemn sigh of sympathy, "*Nueba York, qué lucha.*" What a struggle it is.

But Felix had a plan, to be an American, like the Italians. That was why almost no one in the neighborhood, possibly not even the Chino, was as angry at Cabezucha as Felix.

Cabezucha had gone crazy. He did that. Too much crack and his head became a bomb. He got $200 from the Chino with the laundry. Who would expect to get more from a shop like that? And the Chino saw him, of course, since he stuck the gun in his face and demanded money.

The other dealers didn't like what Cabezucha had done, either. You weren't supposed to remind people that there were guns. You weren't supposed to have any action at all in the territory, you weren't supposed to, as it was always put, "piss in your own bed." It always seemed a strange expression to Felix since he had never heard of anyone pissing in someone else's bed. In the Dominican, you weren't supposed to piss on your own door, which made only slightly more sense.

According to the story that was circulating the neighborhood, Cabezucha was so "ripped" that he did not remember to speak English. But the Chino could guess and handed over what he had in the wooden drawer—$214.37. The Chino was one of several people who saw him try to run into Felix's store. Then the Cuquemango hit him hard in the groin, an easy shot with their height difference, and pushed him out.

Nothing was clear. Maybe he had run there because Felix was involved, but maybe Felix was a hero who had tried to apprehend the thief, or maybe he was involved but then turned against him. But no one even asked Felix what had happened, which proved that the neighborhood saw him as on the other side. Only the cops would talk to him, spreading his legs and slamming him against their car hood, cracking the hard-boiled egg in his hand.

Five blocks to the east, Cabezucha was hiding in the old amphitheater in the park by the river, cooling off, calming down, watching the red tugboats pass under the bridge and the ships tie up at the Domino sugar dock in Brooklyn. He strained to see if they were Dominican boats, but he never spotted a Dominican flag except for the small one he stuck in the broken end of a rusted railing by the steps where he slept. He counted the folded bills in his pocket. Of the $200, there was only $25 left.

"*Acht und Zwanzig,*" she heard him puff out as she drew another sip of good sour mash.

"*Neun und Zwanzig.*" Down he went again, his body straight as a board.

She began to clap. "Bravo, Bernsie. *Dreissig.* The new world record."

Bernhardt Moellen collapsed on the floor of their apartment two floors above the Edelweiss Pastry Shop. "You must admit—" Bernhardt wheezed and coughed and then continued. "Thirty push-ups is not bad for a man of eighty-two."

"*Ja,* Bernsie, I will just sit here and sip and not correct you."

"All right, eighty-one." He stood up and walked over to her and kissed her on the forehead. "But it was thirty push-ups." She smiled and took his hand. He studied her face. "You know, I wish you would not let that woman upset you."

"What woman," she said. It was a response—not a question.

"She is completely crazy. From the times. Those times made crazy people. We were the lucky few who could get out with our bodies and minds and—and our honor intact."

"But you know that Viktor will visit us one day."

"Viktor Stein is dead!" Moellen whispered.

"The one really good thing about this country," she said, and she stared into the darker pools of the amber liquid in her glass.

"Yes, good bourbon."

She smiled and shook her head.

"All right, sour something."

"Sour mash, Bernsie."

"I am taking a shower. I have a meeting tonight. That angry man who came in the shop today . . ."

"I didn't ask."

He clasped her two delicate hands in his large ones. "Hanna, it's about the block."

"I didn't ask what it was about."

"The Chinaman around the corner. He was robbed."

"That's terrible."

"Yes, some of these drug pushers. With a gun. He is very angry. He is right. So we are going to the police again. Get them to do something. What is the name of that man who comes in the shop?"

"Which man?"

"The one with the daughter."

"The one who wanted all the cookies?"

"No, the one who used to be a boy—from the neighborhood. I think Karoline knows him."

"The Jew with the little girl."

"Yes, what's his name? He's always been here. He has a little girl. This is the kind of people who should fight for this neighborhood so it will be decent and safe for children, like it was when we came here with our daughter."

"I don't know his name."

Bernhardt stepped into the shower and Hanna poured some more Jack Daniel's, which is sour mash.

Only a few blocks away, Tom Rosen, a thirty-year-old from the Upper West Side, was having a night in the East Village. He did this more and more often and was thinking of looking for an apartment in the neighborhood. On this evening he decided to try some of the old "ethnic" restaurants that had been featured in that day's *Times*. But it seemed most of them did not take credit cards. Fortunately, he found a cash machine and got $200 out of his bank account in $20 bills that fit inconspicuously in his wallet. You had to be careful down here. He looked around and saw no one who was particularly menacing. But when he turned the corner off the busy avenue onto the quiet street, a very large man with a thick shock of black hair was staring at him wild-eyed, almost as though he had known Tom Rosen was about to turn that corner and he was waiting for him. Rosen, who was athletic and had fast reflexes, pushed the man away, which felt like shoving a wall. The man did not move. Rosen turned to run but realized he was being held by the right arm. The giant looked so confused; he did not seem to realize he was holding him and did not understand why Rosen did not run away. Half in anger, half in panic, the large man took out a small handgun, which Rosen could neither reach nor run away from. Rosen struggled. He tried to at least hide his head from the pistol. The more he fought, the angrier the giant became that this man refused to back off. The giant's black-and-red eyes showed a kind of panicky desperation. He fired twice at Rosen's infuriating, bobbing head.

Chow Mein Vega was wide awake in his empty casita, working on his memoirs. On page 583, the boogaloo had still not been invented. Outside were tomatoes and snapdragons, and beyond the fence was the East Village with sirens, and rumbling cars, and people shouting, sometimes in Spanish, and in the distance—a popping noise that caught Chow Mein's attention. He heard it again. Knowing he would be asked, he looked at his watch: 11:53 P.M.

CHAPTER THIRTEEN

No Going Back

"MIT LIGN KUMT MEN VAYT, OBER NIT TSURIK," Ruth would say with a pointed index finger and the other hand on her hip, which had gotten a little wide but not too wide for swinging to emphasize the point. With lies you can go far, but there is no going back. Nathan remembered these words as Pepe Le Moko stared at him, the two seated waiting for business in the Meshugaloo Copy Center.

This day, in which Nathan traveled to the edge of madness, began quietly. He walked to Tenth Street, and as he opened the loud metal gate of his shop, the little Fat Finkelstein of his generation scurried for the cover of his brownstone. Reasoning that Nathan would seek revenge for the wanton thrust of his tongue at Sarah, the round little boy always hid when he saw Nathan on the block.

Sitting in his shop, Nathan checked the *Times* as the speakers were swooning. The voluptuous strings of the early movements of Beethoven's Ninth were gathering. Five obituaries had been published. All but one, a singer who was hit by a bus—that was what it said, he read it again—were older than him. Good to know.

Nit tsurik, no going back. The lie was there. It needed no words. Karoline had offered a way back. They would end it and go back to their lives. But he knew that he would be in her bed again. There was no way back. How could this end?

A health columnist in the *Daily News* said that birds carried diseases and that dead bird carcasses could be dangerous to children. Nathan kept Sarah in the neighborhood, which seemed free of bird carcasses, leaving the ancient question Where do birds go when they die? Not to the Lower East Side, in any event. The neighborhood was safe. Pepe rubbed against his ankle in agreement. He could sell out, turn his neighborhood over to some corporation, and get $500,000. Nathan gazed out his window on a busy summer day on Tenth Street. If it were not for his air conditioner allowing him to keep his windows shut, he would not have been able to hear Beethoven over the nervous vendors not only of "smoke," but of dubious watches and rings, a baby crying in fifteen-second blasts with barely a break between, men with carts sifting through trash cans in search of bottles and cans to sell at machines on Fourth Street, some looking for food. A small, bony man kept shouting as he sifted through garbage cans, "I pay my taxes! Goddamn it. I pay!" Even he was careful to stay out of certain garbage cans.

"¡Paga! ¡No paga! Who needs you!" Carmela was shouting. "Good morning, Nathan," she added, as though she could see him looking through his closed windows. Nathan had to open his door, walk outside, and crane his neck to look up and see her, her fleshy base pushing through the spaces in the fire escape steel.

"Buenos, Carmela."

"Ay carajo, Nathan," she said, staring down. "What kind of trouble are you getting yourself into?" Nathan quickly retreated into his shop, as though to avoid getting caught at something. How did she do that?

Nathan watched the way one dealer would signal Ruben on the corner of First or he would signal one of them. The way at a certain moment one might go to a certain trash can—the garbage can that all the drifters knew not to look for bottles in—or another would reach into the fender of a certain parked car. One even groped under the roots of a thin, struggling tree.

Could he give all this up for half a million dollars? Oh, yes.

Sal First's mother had made *minni di vírgini,* which means "virgin breasts" in Sicilian and are little round almond cookies. Sal Eleven, to show that he made them better, also made his own *minni di vírgini* and adorned his virgin breasts with candied cherries that made bright red nipples in the center of each cookie. Sal First sneered at this, pointing out that no one in Palermo did such a crude thing. "In Catania, maybe, but not in Palermo." Sal Eleven, who was from Palermo, was told what Sal First had said and, being from Palermo himself, understood the slight of being called Catanian. He dismissed the insult with a wave of his hand. "Can I help it if his virgins don't have nipples?" Sal A, who was from Catania and did not make virgin breasts but recalled that in Catania they did have cherry nipples, laughed at all of this.

But Joey Parma, who was a Neapolitano and did not care about these differences, had noticed that Sal First's mother made a better *minni di vírgini* because it was filled with candied squash from Sicily, the long and twisted *cucuzzata* that had been soaked in jasmine petals and water, whereas Sal Eleven had used American yellow summer squash and soaked it in rose petals and water. Later, after he sampled both virgin breasts, Mrs. Moellen at the Edelweiss offered Officer Parma another almond cookie, this time an *Ischler krapferln,* from the Austrian town of Ischl, which was two round, sweet almond cookies filled with raspberry jam and covered with chocolate. Joey thought that while not Italian, this was not bad, either. "Thanks for the *krapferln,*" Officer Parma shouted back to the kitchen as he left.

A police car came down Tenth Street announcing that they were looking for anybody who had seen anything about midnight near Fifth Street.

According to Sal Eleven, a tourist had been shot. "Tourist" meant someone who was not from the neighborhood. Someone had shot him in the head as he left the automatic teller and taken his money. "Just blew up his head and left a mess on the sidewalk. You can still see it!" Sal was telling every customer all day each time with the same shudder of disgust. It was enough of a mess so that it took weeks of summer rain to remove the stain where what was left of Tom Rosen's head had landed on the sidewalk. Everyone in the neighborhood sooner or later found an excuse to walk by Fifth Street and look at the spot.

They all knew that this could have been their blood. The automatic teller, the blown-up head, could anyone doubt that this had been done by the same man who had killed Eli Rabbinowitz? Did he have a motive? Whose head would be shattered next? Without any evidence, most neighborhood people blamed the killing on the drug dealers and were demanding that the police do something. Why was it that drug dealers were never arrested?

Sal First, who saw most things philosophically, explained to Joey Parma, while the officer was crunching his mother's nippleless virgin breasts, "The problem with New Yorkers is that they don't know how to defend themselves anymore. They let themselves get talked out of the right to bore arms. Boring arms is constitutional. I am keeping my handgun. They come, they get it. I'm not prejudiced, you understand. To me it don't make a difference your race, the figmentation of your skin, your credence or religious indoctrination—whatever, I'll blow your fucking head off." Twenty minutes later, he repeated his philosophy almost word for word to Nathan. Nathan gave an ambiguous nod that might pass for agreement. He realized that he had memorized Karoline's phone number and was repeating it in his mind: 674 . . .

The neighborhood committee was meeting with the police at the Boys Club. Who would represent the police? Joey Parma? "Officer Parma," Nathan would say in midmeeting, "do you want to tell us about the wine?" He didn't trust this cop with his wine collection. He did not completely believe Karoline's story. Like Nusan's stories, it seemed to have missing parts.

Nathan could not see from the angle of his shop that Joey Parma at that moment was across the street talking to Felix in his shop. Joey wanted a name. "You've got to give up someone."

"This is an honest store. I sell vegetables," said Felix, methodically massaging a hard-boiled egg with the fingers of his right hand.

"Really?" said Joey, sadistically biting into one of his best tomatoes. But a look of surprise came over his face. "Where do you get these tomatoes?"

"I grow them."

"You're kidding. These are really good. My wife makes bolognese this time of year. How many of these tomatoes can you get me?"

"I don't have much. You've got to pay."

"These tomatoes are so good, I'd even pay for them."

"Okay. I can get you some."

"Aw, shit!" Tomato seeds on the linen lapel. Felix started to rub it off with a wet cloth.

"Don't touch! I'm going to use talcum powder. You have any talcum powder?"

"Talcum powder," said Felix. "That's for grease. Cold water for tomatoes."

"You sure?"

"Trust me, it's my business."

Joey tugged the lapel in Felix's direction, and Felix scrubbed it with the cloth. "I must be nuts. Okay. After the holiday I'll come for the tomatoes. And a name. Come on. Give up somebody. Just one name. And all the tomatoes you've got." He started for the door and then stopped and picked up another tomato and left with it.

It was a customer, a steady client. Felix could see that his store would succeed. And he could show Rosita that it would succeed. Rosita, who would not go out with him because she thought he was a drug dealer—Rosita, who in her purple dress set the whole neighborhood aflame on a summer afternoon, the most beautiful woman in the Loisaida—a competitive title to hold.

But Felix was also worried. He couldn't give anybody up to the police and still stay in the neighborhood. And he had a store now.

Nathan saw Linda Kaplan, mother of Maya. Why wasn't she in Punim County? She was working for Dukakis on Tenth Street. She carried a sign that said DUKAKIS FOR PRESIDENT and was passing out buttons that said DUKAKIS. After she left the block, every drug dealer on Tenth Street was sporting, on tank tops, on blue jeans, a DUKAKIS button. Was this good for the campaign? Nathan wondered.

Sal Eleven, staring at his TV and not looking at Nathan, told him to try one. "It's called virgin titty." Looking at the bright red cherry, more a stripper's pastie than a virgin's nipple, Nathan would have agreed with the bakers of Palermo. While Nathan sampled, Sal told him about the meeting with the police in the Boys Club. "If you want to know what I think"—there was never a pause after this phrase for a response—"it's bullshit. It's that German guy. I don't know what he's up to."

That was what caught Nathan's interest. What was the German guy up to? In his heart, he agreed with Sal Eleven that the pushers kept away the people who would really destroy the neighborhood, such as the ones who wanted to buy his business. Though to Sal, it was always "the fucking Japanese." Of course, not all the Japanese were Japanese. Some were French and wanted to open little pastry shops. Some, like Ira Katz, were Jewish. They all wanted to buy the neighborhood, to own it, which would destroy everything about it worth having. If the pushers were gone, they would all come in. Only the pushers were stopping them.

But it wasn't going to be Nathan's problem. He was selling. One of them had to leave, him or Karoline.

Nathan had made an appointment with a financial adviser in midtown, someone who was eager to tell him how to invest $500,000. He could have taken a bus. But he had to know if this disease was still with him, this curse that sucked the breath out of him. He felt confident that it had been only a single claustrophobic incident and was not a permanent condition. But he had to know.

He walked to Astor Place and descended a recently restored subway entrance with its steel-and-glass hood resembling the mouth of a dragon. As he stared down into the darkness, he could feel a vague nervousness, a warning, the early stages of an attack.

He went back up the stairs and walked to Cristofina's botanica.

"I see. A sense of being trapped. Of no way back."

"Yes," said Nathan, "no way back. *Nit tsurik.*" Was that it, then? No. The attack had happened before the lie.

"This is psychological," said Cristofina. "It is not a curse. I can't cure it with a powder. I have to give you a sense of a way out. As long as you think there is no way back, no escape, you will feel doomed."

The logic of Cristofina always surprised Nathan. She would be able to solve this.

"*¡Siéntete!*" She ordered him to sit on a stool, which she first dusted off with the smack of a newspaper, producing a choking cloud of tan dust. "Yes, I can do it!" she declared.

"Are you sure?"

"Yes, *sin duda. Es obvio, mi amor.*"

Nathan started feeling better just knowing that there were solutions to problems. He would sell, get money, move uptown where they cleaned the streets and even removed snow in the winter instead of waiting for it to melt—uptown, where bony women looked as though they thought about nothing but clothing, while tired men in careful haircuts thought only about the equation converting energy to money. Nathan's optimism had lasted only an instant.

"What should I do?"

Cristofina stroked her square jaw with her thick fingers as she examined the figures and bottles on her shelves. "First, you must get a tattoo."

"A tattoo!"

"*Sí*, a little *tattolita*."

"Where? I hate tattoos." He thought of Karoline's buttock and realized that this was no longer completely true.

"*Escucha', mi amor,* I can only help those who want to be helped. This is very important. A tattoo of an open doorway on your body. You put it somewhere where you can find it when you need it. It will be your doorway."

"No, I can't do that. I don't believe in tattoos."

"Don't believe in them? This isn't about belief. This is about practical solutions."

"I'm opposed to them. I don't like them, and they are against my religion."

"Because you are Hebrew."

"I'm a Jew."

"A Jew with a tattoo is better than a tattoo with no Jew."

"Where did you learn that?!"

"It's logic. It is the way the orisha teach."

"Them and my mother."

"Has your mother been cut?"

"Cut?"

"Is she a santera?"

"Just Ashkenazi."

Cristofina took a figure off the shelf, a dull, dark, cast-metal figure of a muscular man pounding an anvil with a hammer. It was a blacksmith, but in a defiant pose, as though he dared commit the outrage of being a blacksmith. Cristofina placed the heavy figure on the counter and began removing a thick layer of gray dust with a duster made of chicken feathers, which had a certain poignancy because Cristofina was known to have killed a considerable quantity of chickens. She looked at the duster. "I should come to your house and kill pigeons in your doorway. It will give you flight."

"No. I don't think I can do that."

She backed up to the rear of her store and motioned for him to follow. Knowing that she tattooed back there, he said, "No, let's stay here."

"Come here!" she ordered in a voice that was both a whisper and a shout. He stepped carefully behind the counter and down the back hall lined with cone-shaped concrete heads, cowrie shells, palm trees, bolts of lightning . . .

She was muttering about the Jews while shaking her head. "They are so smart, but so *difficult*. Argumentative." Then, jerking her head as though she just realized that a Jew was listening, she said in a full voice, "*Mira*, we could kill a . . ." Realizing the strength of her voice, she returned to a whisper: "Kill a dog."

"Why?"

"For Oggún. Oggún loves dogs."

"Why kill the dog, then? Most dog lovers wouldn't like that."

"Oggún is different."

"How so?"

"Why do you argue about everything? You do this and he is your orisha. But it is dangerous and very expensive."

"How expensive?"

"I don't know. You would be better to get the tattoo."

"I couldn't even explain to my daughter why I killed a mouse. What would I say about this?"

Cristofina looked very agitated. "You can't ever tell anyone. *Anyone, ever!*"

"How much for the statue?"

"Forty dollars. It's Oggún."

"Who is the orisha of discounts?"

She did not answer but went to the front counter and wrapped the statue in newspaper. "*Mira*, he is a powerful orisha of war. Also of employment, if that helps. He also knows love. He has hopelessly fallen for Oshún. In Nigeria, Oggún is always placed near the Oshún River to be near his love." Then, looking around her small, dark shop, she handed him a string of green and black beads. "*Mira*, wear this on your wrist. Oggún will protect you," she said. "It's only three dollars."

After Nathan walked out, Cristofina looked up on the shelf and pointed an accusing finger at a small concrete dome with three cowrie shells forming eyes and a mouth. "It is you, Ellegguá, who sends me these Jews, to test me."

Ellegguá was silent.

. . .

Nathan had bought an attaché case—a whimsical purchase to put him in the proper frame of mind. It was one of those hard, cordovan leather–covered rectangular cases with brass fittings that, it seemed to him, a man investing half a million dollars ought to have. He put Oggún, still in his *El Vocero* newspaper wrapping, in the case, closed the latches, and left for his meeting about investments. Walking toward the subway stop at Astor Place, with his dark shaggy hair, his untrimmed mustache, blue jeans, knit shirt, and a string of beads on one wrist, he looked as if he had stolen the case.

Armed with the fierce but hopelessly in love Oggún, he entered the mouth, descended to the subway platform as easily as the descent to hell. Hot air was rising up the stairs, and the platform below was twenty degrees hotter than the sweltering air on the streets. Waiting on the platform, he felt that he was cooking slowly, the way Karoline had explained to bake a meringue, the only relief being a rush of cooler air pushed out of the dark, underground tunnel by the oncoming number 6 train. Nathan's only thought was the relief of air-conditioning, and he rushed in the opened doors and took a seat, feeling that he would have enjoyed spending the rest of the day in this cool gray metal box. Then the doors closed.

The train left the station, beating out its rhythm in little bumps as it slid into the dark tunnel where the oxygen got thinner and thinner and thinner. Maybe this was a mistake. There was no way back. The train slowed, was barely moving. Please, don't let it stop. Nathan, feeling panic surging up from his belly, opened his attaché case. Just the physical task of unwrapping the statue would distract him. The train stopped. The lights dimmed. The air conditioner was cut off, along with the rest of the air. That was when Nathan realized that he was going to lose control, grab someone, break a window, and get out of this train. Suddenly, the lights and air-conditioning came back. But the train did not move. A voice was heard: "We are being temporarily delayed. We will be moving as soon as possible."

"As soon as possible"—that could be days. Nathan wasn't going to stay here for days. He could smash a window with the metal statue of Oggún, show the transit company the power of his orisha, and then be out in the tunnel. Out in the tunnel. He could never get back walking through the tunnel. *Nit tsurik*. There was no way back!

It was important that he look normal, that people could not see what was happening to him. He was not sure why, but he had a vague notion that if he was identified as a claustrophobic, apprehended having an attack, he would be confined in some way and never be free again. He stood up and walked to the other end of the car. He walked up to a woman with bright green hair and a ring through her left nostril. He could see on her chest above her cotton top the beginning of a butterfly tattoo. She was probably from the neighborhood. "Don't you just hate getting stuck like this?" he said to her in a strained imitation of a conversational tone. The woman looked at Nathan, who was clutching a strange doll half-wrapped in shredded newspaper. "They say 'as soon as possible,'" he continued, a smile pressed on his sweaty face. "When is that supposed to be?"

"Exactly," she finally answered. "Probably three years."

"Really?"

Perhaps he had been too earnest. People were noticing. If people see that you have completely lost control, they take you and put you in a straitjacket. Can you imagine how a straitjacket feels? You can't even move your own arms. Why would they do that? That would be the worst thing they could do. Can you imagine what a straitjacket feels like when you are trapped in a tunnel with no air? Then they lock you up somewhere in a small room. You never can get back your life once you've been caught like that. *Nit tsurik*.

He had to talk to someone to establish his normalcy—an imitation of inner calm from which real inner calm could be derived. If he were forced into a normal conversation, he wouldn't be free to lose his sanity.

He walked up to a man in a light-colored suit, shoving his right hand in his pocket so that his beads wouldn't show. "Some service," Nathan said, and then, trying to smile, he added, "You pay your taxes and . . ."

The man nodded nervously. Nathan realized that he sounded like the man who was picking through the garbage in front of his shop. "I pay my taxes! I pay my taxes!" He had probably been a normal person at one time. Now he picked through garbage and shouted about paying his taxes and thought he was being conversational.

He had to get off of this train!

The train lurched. It rolled slowly. It stopped. And then it was speeding toward Union Square, where the doors opened and Nathan again experienced almost instant recovery, like a jackhammer that suddenly stopped. He walked the four blocks back to Tenth Street and went to his shop.

"Good to see you made it," said Carmela with an engaging smile. Nathan was thinking he would kill a dog, a pigeon, wear a tattoo, whatever he needed to do.

A shrub of dark curly hair and the bubble-gum good cheer of hot pink French glasses frames, looking almost like a gum bubble had burst on her face and was still stuck at the top, were all that was visible of Dr. Simone Kucher from the softly upholstered chair on the other side of her desk. Her twelve o'clock patient had finally left and her lunch had arrived: a salad of mixed field greens; chicken salad with low-fat mayonnaise, bean curd, and broccoli; mixed fruit and low-fat yogurt; two fat-free blueberry muffins; and a low-cholesterol chocolate bar. Dr. Kucher was dieting.

Barely over five feet, round, and soft looking, as though she were made of some fluffy low-cal pudding, she had cheeks so fleshy that it was hard to see if her eyes were open or shut behind her glasses. But when her interest was caught, the glow of slate-colored almonds showed through the lenses so distinctly that it seemed there had been no eyes there before. When listening to a patient, she nestled catlike into a black overstuffed leather chair and held a yellow pencil like the needle on a barometer over a yellow pad, where she occasionally scribbled notes. Sometimes the pen would just slide slowly out of her thick little fingers and make the dull sound of a bubble bursting in oatmeal as it plopped on the empty sheet. This had happened during the previous session. But now she had her diet lunch and one more patient and then home on time for the Mets game.

Dr. Kucher was not a lifelong baseball fan. She had discovered baseball only two seasons earlier with the excitement of the Mets winning the World Series. She became enthralled with the champion Mets, failing to understand that this was an aberration. True Mets fans, such as Nusan, tested themselves against the frustration of untimely losses.

But Dr. Kucher expected the Mets to win, which they were doing again this summer. In time, she would probably realize that she was not cut out to be a Mets fan and switch to the Yankees. For now, if work kept her away from a game, she set the timer and recorded the game. Then she had to get home without hearing anything about the game so that it would be new when she played her tape.

"Nyahn, nyah, nyah, nyah, nyah, nyah . . . ," she said over and over with her fingers in her ears as she made her way out of her office and out of the building.

"Have a good evening, Dr. Kucher."

"Nyahn, nyah, nyah, nyah, nyah, nyah . . ."

Then she had to find a taxi that was not playing a radio. Then past the doorman and into her building. "Welcome home, Dr. Kucher."

"Nyahn, nyah, nyah, nyah, nyah, nyah . . ." She hobbled in with the furious waddle of an angry duck.

Don't talk to anyone in the elevator. "Nyahn, nyah, nyah, nyah, nyah, nyah . . ."

Into her apartment. Safe!

She was taking few new patients over the summer. But if they pronounced her name right—*Kooker*—she would meet with them. Anyone calling her *Kootcher* was out.

This Nathan Seltzer, referred by NYU, had unhesitatingly said Dr. *Kooker*. Nathan found Dr. Simone Kucher through New York University on the mistaken theory that NYU could provide a reliable therapist in the neighborhood. Kucher's office was on the Upper East Side.

Dr. Kucher did not want this new patient. She was bored with her patients. They kept her from baseball. She had a patient who wanted help having orgasms with men other than her husband. The patient's husband saw other women, so she wanted to see other men but was unable to achieve an orgasm with them. She insisted that her husband was somehow causing her to fail. A twenty-three-year-old man was convinced that he could manage his stock portfolio more profitably with the aid of therapy. Another man in his twenties was convinced that he was "not cool" and he wanted to be. First, Dr. Kucher pointed out, they would have to come up with a definition of cool. But to herself, Kucher noted that anyone who went to therapy to become cool never would be. She had three different women who complained that they "loved too much," though the claim seemed to Kucher somewhat exaggerated.

The most interesting recent case she had was a man who was sexually aroused by women in waitress uniforms. He had decided that he needed to come to terms with this fetish because Schrafft's had closed, Horn & Hardart was gone, and there were very few uniformed waitresses left in New York anymore.

So when she asked Nathan what he hoped to achieve with therapy and Nathan answered, "I wanted to keep from losing my mind in the subway," Dr. Kucher's pencil was already at forty-five degrees and due to plop on the yellow pad.

"What do you mean by 'losing your mind'?"

"Bonkers, insane, can't breathe, about to explode and die . . . what else? I think I am becoming a claustrophobic, I guess. I'm becoming some kind of nutcase."

Kucher wrote something on a pad. Nathan wondered if she was writing the word "nutcase."

"Tell me about it."

"I never felt claustrophobia until last week." He described the attacks, and Kucher took notes in a light hand.

"Well, first, Nathan, I have to ask you some questions, just to learn something about you. Are you ready?"

"Sure."

"Have you ever had any kind of phobia before?"

"No. Nothing."

"And your family. Any phobias in your family?"

"Phobias?"

"Irrational fears."

"You know. Typical Jewish family. Fear of paying full retail prices." Kucher wasn't smiling. "My parents had an irrational fear that I would marry a shiksa."

The patient was afraid of the question. Who cares? What is wrong with Gooden, anyway? He has good stuff. Why does he blow the game in a late inning? She wondered if this patient was a Yankees fan. Most of her patients were. Wealthy neurotics root for the Yankees. "Did you marry a shiksa?" said Dr. Kucher, still taking notes but the pen slipping almost parallel with the paper.

"No."

"Where is your wife from?"

"Guadalajara, Mexico."

"Did you find it difficult to separate from your mother?"

"I'll let you know."

"How do you mean?"

"We haven't separated. She lives upstairs from me, and I see her every day. I think she can tell what kind of food we eat through the floorboards."

Dr. Kucher was still writing notes. "Can you tell what food the people below you eat through the floorboards?"

"Below us? No. Why?"

"So why would your parents be able to? Same kind of floor, right?"

"Right. . . . It's not a big thing."

"You brought it up."

"I just meant we are close."

"I am hearing too close."

"Really? No. It's—it's good."

Dr. Kucher heaved a sigh . . . and a slight burp. Probably from the salad. "And no phobias of any kind in your family."

"None."

"No fears of any kind?"

"Fears? I mean, my uncle Nusan has this fear of starving. He hoards food. But he is a Holocaust survivor. So that's not very surprising, is it? My brother, Mordy, is afraid that most food has been poisoned by multinational corporations. But he may be right. Maybe he goes a little overboard. But that's because he has been stoned for the last thirty years. It makes you paranoid."

Dr. Kucher's yellow pencil was now vertical as she feverishly wrote notes.

"And my mother is afraid of bridges. She thinks they may fall down. And maybe they will. The Williamsburg Bridge doesn't look too good to me, either." Nathan thought for a moment and then laughed lightly. "Once the bridge falls down, the problem is my father's."

"Why is that?"

"My father is afraid of water."

"All water?"

"I don't know. He's afraid of the East River. It's something that happened to him in Poland when he was a child. But I never found out what it was. I know I am making everybody sound crazy, but they are perfectly normal people. Why? Do you think any of this stuff is hereditary?"

Dr. Kucher did not answer. She was writing notes, bearing hard on the blunting pencil point, turning pages in fast jerks, filling the long pages of a yellow paper pad. "Just a minute." She straightened her pink glasses. Nathan, on the other side of the desk, could not see enough of her face. "What was that? Heredity. Yes, it's possible. Tendencies, anyway."

"So you think I can inherit what Hitler did to my uncle?"

"Not exactly. But Hitler didn't make your mother afraid of bridges."

"No."

"Anything else? Grandparents?"

"Didn't know them. I always hear that my mother's father killed himself. Jumped. I guess he wasn't afraid of heights, anyway." Nathan could see that everything he said impressed Dr. Kucher, though nothing made her smile.

"Is there anything new in your life?"

"New?"

"Upsetting changes?"

"No, not really." A staged sigh of boredom.

"Are you feeling guilty about anything?"

"What kind of anything?"

"Anything at all."

"No."

"Really? It's hard to imagine a guiltless person."

"I guess I could come up with something if I had to."

"Like what?"

"I haven't taught my daughter how to swim. The Talmud says you have to teach your son to swim, and I wonder if I am not teaching her because she is a girl."

Kucher's writing fingers were exhausted, but she pushed on as fast as she could. "Were you disappointed that she was a girl?"

"No," Nathan insisted in a defensive tone of voice.

"Do you think you are passive-aggressive?"

"How do you mean?"

"Some people cannot face their own anger and so they repress it but find other ways of getting back at the person toward whom they feel the anger." (Like that bitch on the co-op board, Kucher was thinking.) "Perhaps without even realizing that they are doing this."

"And you think I do that?"

"I don't know. I am just here to help you discover yourself," Dr. Kucher explained. "It is sometimes very difficult for someone to know themselves. Claustrophobia is a type of anxiety attack. You could get it in a number of situations or possibly only in subways. It could even be only in certain subway lines. We have to work on this step by step. It could be the result of something in your present life, but it could also be some suppressed childhood experience. Try to remember your dreams. Dreams can hold clues. A person with a phobia may experience the world as a dangerous and hostile place."

Nathan thought. "I can't think of any dreams right now, and I don't know that the world is a hostile place. . . ."

"But . . ."

"But dangerous, yes. Do you have any children?"

She didn't answer, though she was thinking, You don't need kids to see how bad it is out there!

"Well, when you have children, you suddenly realize that there is danger everywhere."

She looked at her watch. The session was over. They would schedule another one. "In the meantime, try to remember your dreams."

"All right."

Dr. Kucher was not standing up. She never stood up in front of the patient, never revealed her height. "Are you a Mets fan?"

"Yes!" said Nathan, for the first time truly impressed.

"So what's wrong with Gooden?"

Nathan took the subway downtown, without incident. Even when it slowed down in the tunnel approaching Grand Central, he felt nothing. With great pride he imitated the boredom of the other passengers. The therapy, apparently, was working.

Nathan did not always remember his dreams. But in the early

evening, while listening to the pleasant, splashing, squeaky sounds of Sarah taking a bath, no doubt dreaming of swimming lessons in a real pool, he suddenly recalled a dream. It might have been from the night before:

He is lying on Sonia's massage table and she is working him with her long fingers. But she is massaging too hard. He realizes that her fingers are penetrating his skin. She reaches into his body and pulls out—an iron cross, an SS insignia, a swastika. Nathan feels mortified, not only that he has these things inside his body, but also that she has found them.

Then he realizes that someone else is in the room. It is Uncle Nusan, and he has seen Sonia pull these things out of him. Maybe he hasn't seen. But he is right there. Then Nusan says to him, "Get your *tokhes* off the table." Suddenly Nathan understands what he means. He is starting to understand Yiddish. He feels very excited about finally mastering the language. He wakes up.

Should he tell Kucher about the dream? Then he would have to explain a lot of things. Cristofina asked fewer questions.

In the next room, Sonia was reading a large, colorful book to Sarah, Sarah looking so small against Sonia, her little hands and big eyes. The two of them looked safe and happy and absolutely perfect. He had never seen anything more perfect. And he was sick with fear.

(*Emma walks into the room and finds a tall, thin woman with long fingers and curly hair.*)

EMMA: Who are you?

MARGARITA: I am Margarita Maza Juárez. (*She waits for a moment but gets no response from Emma.*) Wife of Don Benito Juárez, the exiled president of Mexico.

EMMA: Boyoboy.

MARGARITA: This is absolutely true.

EMMA: The exiled pres... Exiled my *tokh* ... You know, you can get pretty far with a lie. (*She raises an index finger and swings her hips for emphasis.*) But there is no getting back.

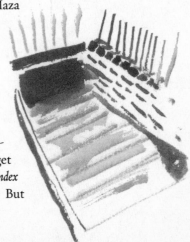

MARGARITA: But it is not a lie; I am Benito Juárez's wife.
EMMA: . . .
EMMA: . . .

"Oh, hell," said Sonia. She looked at her little girl, asleep and completely at peace. "What does Emma say to that?" If she could only figure that out, she was certain the entire play would fall into place. But she could never get past this moment.

CHAPTER FOURTEEN

The Edge of the Planet

IT WAS ONLY MIDDAY and a few bombs had already gone off. An occasional burst of small fire in the distance made the women wince as they arranged chairs and tables on the roof. The air was already sulfurous with the smoke of gunpowder. It was like this every year. Worse every year. It was the Fourth of July.

For people living uptown, July Fourth was a day to leave town. To people downtown, it was a day to attempt to have picnics among the bombs and explosions and then to top it off with the big bombs—the fireworks display over the East River.

The grassy patches in the East River park filled with picnickers from the projects—the tall, uniform rows of brick buildings on Avenue D. They would leave their picnics for the street fair and then return to their picnic spots to see the fireworks. Most of the locals still there in the neighborhood—drug dealers, family people, shopkeepers, observant Jews, secular Jews, all three Sals, and boogalooistas alike—imperceptibly tensed their muscles with each detonation, trying to assess if it was the blast of a firecracker to celebrate the nation's birth or the flatter, popping sound of a handgun blasting the face off someone else at an automatic teller. Chow Mein Vega sometimes looked at his watch to mentally record the time of a particularly suspect pop. The children didn't seem upset by the explosions. In fact, they were causing a lot of them, and every year a few people were hurt. Two years before, a man on Third Street was killed because he did not understand that a bunch of explosives sealed in a metal trash can constituted a large and lethal bomb. Successful guerrilla armies have been armed with less gunpowder. But these people were not trying to overthrow anything. They just wanted to make very loud noises.

Every year, the Seltzers hosted a Fourth of July party on the roof that culminated with a perfect view of the fireworks over the East

River. Fortunately, they were close enough that Harry, unless he looked straight down, could avoid seeing the river so that only the Brooklyn skyline would be visible. If he stayed on the opposite side of the roof, there was no view of the river at all.

Ruth, Sonia, and Sarah were setting up chairs on the roof of their building. The armchair for Harry was set up in its place near the Avenue A side.

"Ruth," said Sonia, "why do men always have midlife crises and not women?"

"It's probably our fault. We keep telling them they are cute and then one day they start to suspect that they aren't that cute. They start suspecting that they are just foolish and they will die and it will have all been foolishness."

"So they act more foolishly than ever?"

"Sometimes. Harry is still in the phase where he thinks he is cute."

"Harry *is* cute."

"That's the problem. Harry is like Mordy. Oboy, those two will never have a crisis. That's why they never earn any money. Harry thinks that if he actually collected rent, the tenants would realize he is the landlord and they wouldn't like him anymore. Why?" Ruth suddenly looked worried. "What's wrong with Nathan?"

"Nothing. He's just acting a little funny. Haven't you noticed?"

"You mean the bracelet?"

"What is that bracelet? Who gave it to him? That's a midlife crisis bracelet."

Sarah was staring with her large, perfectly round, molasses-colored eyes. Ruth smiled. "Believe me. Just don't ask. If you ask, you will hear something truly ridiculous. And you never will find out the real story."

"Come with us to Avenue D," said Sonia, taking hold of one of Sarah's small hands.

"My husband the impresario. I guess I should."

Ruth, as a lifetime habit, avoided Avenue D, not because it had become another neighborhood belonging to Puerto Ricans, but because of her memories of it when it was Jewish. When she was a child, the Lower East Side was her country and Manhattan her planet. Avenue D was the edge of the planet. If you swept Manhattan and pushed the waste to the edge, that was Avenue D. The closer to the river, the worse it got. Buildings turned into shacks, shacks into junk piles, junk piles into garbage. When she was small there were still stables there and sweaty, rank-smelling horses. Since then, the garbage heaps were cleared and the highway was built. The shacks were torn down for groupings of brick housing projects. The streets became lined with *cuchifritos,* grocery stores with boxes of roots and tropical fruit, and botanicas such as Cristofina's. But Ruth had not noticed the change. She continued to think of Avenue D as a place that you didn't go—the garbage heap at the edge of her world.

"It's always great," argued Sonia. "Chucho Vega is unbelievable. I think he really will bring boogaloo back."

"Boogaloo. I didn't listen to boogaloo when I was supposed to. Why should I listen to it now? Well, it makes Harry happy. See, everybody wants to make Harry happy because he makes such a good happy person."

"That's a talent, too."

"*Sí, señora,*" said Ruth.

Nathan couldn't go to Avenue D because it was his assignment, every July Fourth, to check on Nusan, who would be hunkered down on Rivington Street, dug in as though trying to survive a bombing raid that was blowing apart the city, which may very well have been what was happening in Nusan's mind.

Nusan was always the same on the Fourth of July. He wrapped his maroon scarf tightly around his neck, clutching it with both hands, and stared at his door as though expecting someone. It wasn't Nathan he was waiting for, because he would always continue staring at the door after Nathan arrived. The gray, bushy eyebrows over his deep-set black eyes flinched with each explosion, but the rest of him did not move.

As Nathan climbed the stairs on Rivington Street, he could already hear muffled bursts in the neighborhood. As expected, Nusan was in his chair, motionless except for the barely perceptible shudder around the eyes, staring through Nathan at the door. He said nothing.

Together they listened to the explosions. There was no place for Nathan to sit, so he stood by the door, just out of line of Nusan's stare, trying not to notice the overbearing and undefinable sour smell of the apartment, while trying to guess what nightmare Nusan was reliving. Did he hear the Gestapo climbing the stairs, the Wehrmacht coming to get him, or the Red Army coming to free him? What Polish town was under siege in his mind? In which camp was he dying while waiting for the gates to be smashed? His eyes said nothing—not fear, not anger, only fatalism.

Nathan tried to engage him by talking about anything he could think of, about the Avenue D fair, Chow Mein Vega's concert, the boogaloo, the Mets and Dwight Gooden's six-inning no-hitter against the Astros the day before, comparing Gooden to Nolan Ryan, another shooting at the cash machine, the drug dealers, the police, people in the neighborhood getting angry. "They have been having meetings with the police at the Boys Club."

He still had made no eye contact with Nusan, who did not move his gaze from the door, on which dark coats and hats had been hung, obscuring the tiny, tarnished brass peephole. If the door were to move at all, the coats, clothing Nusan never wore, would move first. Nusan had only to wait for the telltale swing of a sleeve.

"They have meetings all the time now. I think some of these new Japanese are involved. Not that all the new people are Japanese. I think they are getting organized. Shop owners. Like the people at the Edelweiss."

Why did he say that? He did not want to bring up the Edelweiss. And this, of course, was what finally caught Nusan's attention. His eyes focused on Nathan, and in a quiet voice he said, "SS Standartenführer Rheinhardt Müller."

A string of little Chinese crackers went off, sounding like a prolonged trigger squeeze on an automatic weapon. It was hotter than one hundred degrees in the apartment. The air was stale and rotten. Nathan wanted to open a window, but that would have brought the explosions and the gunpowder that much closer. "SS Standartenführer who?"

Nusan looked at his desk and held his spread fingers over the stacks and hills of papers the way a pianist paused over the keyboard before playing. "Müller. SS Standartenführer Müller. Owner of the Edelweiss Bäckerei." Something went off in a single burst with an echo like a rifle shot, but Nusan did not flinch.

For Nathan, the worst of it was that when he thought of the Edel-weiss he was suddenly overcome with desire—desire to get out of this fetid cell, find Karoline, tear off her clothes . . . "No. He's not SS, Uncle Nusan. It's just the German man who owns the Edelweiss. He's not a Nazi. He's just a pastry maker."

"Just a pastry maker, a businessman, a doctor. Just a German."

He was expected to spend the day here—with the windows shut. A day in which Nusan would not go outside. It was a perfect day to slip over to the little bakery above the Edelweiss. What was she baking today? "Being a German doesn't make him guilty of something."

"How old is he? If he was there and he was German, he is guilty of something. You can be sure of that. He is guilty of doing something or not doing anything—while Leah was hanged by her feet and beaten to death."

A loud bomb went off, and Nusan jerked his head and stared at the door.

Leah? Nathan thought. Who was Leah? He had never mentioned anything like this before. In a soft voice that he tried to make sound soothing, he asked, "Who was Leah, Nusan?"

Nusan turned to him and, with an equally soft voice designed to mimic him, said, "Who was Moellen, Nathan?"

Nathan had planted this idea years ago. He wished he could open a window and the thought, the idea, the air, the smell—it could all rush out. He was standing in the center of this stinking room. He could have cleared a place to sit. Maybe on the couch where Nusan slept. Had he ever washed that pillowcase? The real reason he was standing was that his body, independent of his mind, was expressing its desire to leave.

"Look, Uncle Nusan, it was a mistake. I made a mistake. I even talked to him. He was just in the army. . . ."

"I vas just in the Wehrmacht, like everyone else." A wicked smile came over Nusan's face as he looked at Nathan. He could see in Nathan's eyes that he was right, the baker had actually uttered the cliché, "I was just in the Wehrmacht, like everyone else." That was what he had said. Actually, Nathan had never talked to him about it, but Karoline had said, "He was just in the Wehrmacht, like everyone else."

"They always say that, Nathan. They all say the same things. They were following orders, they had no choice. I never did anything against the Jews. I never knew about that until later. What a terrible thing. And I always liked the Jews." He studied Nathan's face and was disappointed. "No?"

"No. He never said that."

"Talk to him some more."

"I have to go now. Will you be all right?"

"Yes, yes. I will be fine."

It was easy. All Nathan had to do was ask if he would be all right and he would tell him how fine he would be and Nathan could ignore the disappointed look on his face and be away, free of the decaying remnants of the Holocaust, free to enjoy the eroticism of his own destruction. "Is there a Mets game this afternoon?"

Nusan nodded but did not move. Nathan put on the television and picked up an old, scratched record in a torn cover by the phonograph—Eugene Ormandy and the Philadelphia Orchestra, Brahms Symphony No. 1. He put the record on the turntable, placed the needle on the record.

He looked at the television and said to Nusan with false cheer, "Look, Cone is pitching. Against the Reds. Who knows, maybe Strawberry will save them." He exited to the dark and throbbing strings, a steadily encroaching force, that open the first movement.

Nathan did not feel good about leaving him, but he had to. What was worse? Where was he going? "To *schtup* the *Standartenführer*'s daughter." Why did Nusan say that? He wasn't a *Standartenführer*. He was a pastry maker.

Harry Seltzer was wearing a freshly pressed white linen suit, his summer Latin impresario suit, walking up Avenue A singing:

> *Don't do that dance, I tell you, Sadie*
> *That's not a business for a lady.*
> *Most everybody kn—*

"Harry!"

It was Cristofina in a very tight red dress—silk that glistened like liquid running over her plump body. Harry had always thought of her as fat. But it was very nice fat. There was something appealing about a woman making the effort, just trying—that was all Harry wanted.

While he admired Cristofina, she handed him a piece of paper. "Oh, what's this?" he said, unfolding it as though unwrapping a surprise gift. It was a bill for $987.45—itemized. It was a very long list. "This is a thousand dollars! All this for Ruben?"

"Do you think it is easy to make a Dominican with nothing to work with but a Puerto Rican? Wait until you see him," said Cristofina, rolling her eyes dreamily. "El Dominicano." She walked on toward Avenue D while Harry examined the bill. He could not decipher any of the items. But he did not mention anything about this when he went over to the casita to check on the band. He was the producer. Chow Mein Vega was the star.

When Harry arrived at the casita, his suit already wilted and sagging, the band was struggling into turquoise-colored shirts with ruffled and ballooned sleeves. Felix was practicing on the congas, his eyes closed, his head back, bringing his hands up high over his head, beating them with such irresistible waves of rhythm that everyone swayed at least a little. Sonia was there with Sarah, swaying slightly. Sarah was hopping from foot to foot, wearing a toothy smile.

For Sonia, the casita was a chance to speak Spanish, but more important, for Sarah to speak Spanish—though she barely accepted that the Nuyorican spoken there was Spanish. But it was better than no Spanish at all. "I can always add the consonants later," she said teasingly. Sarah had taken to saying, "Whazup wi dat?" When Sonia asked her why she was talking like that, she would explain with tutorial condescension, "I am speaking Spanish."

Felix played with his eyes shut, hoping to be lost in rhythm and beyond thought, like having sex. But, also like having sex, thoughts sometimes intruded. At the moment, he could not help thinking of how ridiculous he was in his ruffled shirt—a Dominican, posing as a Puerto Rican, dressed like a Cuban.

But to Harry, it was all "Hispanics"—Sonia, Felix, Chow Mein—"a wonderful culture." Someone had put up a sign on the casita—"No Hispanics Here"—in response to candidate George Bush's recent assertion that he intended to give a cabinet post to "one Hispanic."

Inside the casita, Chow Mein Vega was having a crisis. He had

popped the buttons on his turquoise shirt. Cristofina had hurried back
to her shop for a needle and thread—yes, she assured him, she had
turquoise thread. But she could not run very fast on the tall, thin heels
of her red shoes with her legs tightly bound in a silk dress.

"I've got some news," said Harry.

"You've found a bigger shirt?" said Chow Mein.

"Better than that. I talked to Tommy Drapper. He's coming to hear
you."

"From Tommy's Bar?"

"That's the one. He will book you in the Village. From there you
will get a tour. We're bringing boogaloo back."

Harry and Chow Mein slapped hands. "That's great, man. And it
will be just in time for my biography. We can get a movie contract. And
we can do the sound track." Then, changing voice, he said, "Listen to
Felix. That is the stuff. In 1962 I worked with a guy from Bayamón who
played congas like that. Drugs got him, though."

The crowd was gathering on Avenue D. Firecrackers exploded in
the street, sending dogs whelping under the bandstand while people
looked around anxiously, as though making sure everyone still had their
face on. Grossman's Deli had a stand selling kosher *pasteles.* And at the
cuchifrito stand, Consuela, with a Puerto Rican flag painted in sparkles
on her soft and ample upper arm, sold *lechón* and garlicky *bacalaitos,* the
batter thin and watery so that it would spread out and stay thin and
crisp when poured in the hot oil, then served in a paper napkin that
turned translucent as it absorbed the grease.

Dolby rode by and everything stopped. No one seemed to know
Dolby's real name. He was just Dolby, an angry-looking man with
long, receding hair and a beard, all of which stuck out around his head
like a lion's mane. Dolby rode around the neighborhood on a bicycle
with a sound system taped to the back that was so large, it made his
bike look like an ice-cream cart. He played pounding, throbbing
disco music through speakers so powerful that the sound was felt in
the stomachs of passersby. When he rode down a block, everyone
stopped what they were doing or saying until the throbbing sound
had passed.

When Dolby reached Avenue B, Tommy Drapper, even though he
was late, stopped his Mercedes and waited for Dolby to pass. Drapper,
whose name wasn't Drapper when he had been growing up an Italian in

Brooklyn, would have been on time if he had known where to park his Mercedes. He went to many bad neighborhoods looking for talent, and the problem always was finding a place for the car. He didn't know the neighborhood, and the more he drove around looking for a garage, the more convinced he was that he could not leave his car on the street over here.

While Tommy Drapper was looking for a garage, more and more people were pouring into narrow Avenue D, eating Grossman's *pasteles,* milling around among the little bursts of firecrackers lit by children, waiting for Chow Mein Vega. Finally, Harry stepped out on the bandstand, his suit as rumpled and edgeless as well-worn jungle fatigues, the pant legs gathering in rolls at his ankles.

Yet Harry glowed on the bandstand. It was only in front of an audience that he was at last able to forget how close he was to the dreaded East River—just across the highway and a little strip of lawn. But this was his moment, unmarred by the hoots and shouts of "*En Español, Harry,*" and "*¡Baila, Harry, baila!*" But he was not going to dance. To him, their calls meant no more than the pop of firecrackers that also peppered the moment—part of the festivities.

Out came Chow Mein Vega, near bursting in his ruffled turquoise skin, and Felix and the others—a six-piece band. Felix slapped the congas and Chow Mein said in a slowly mounting crescendo, "Ahhhhh*hhh*!"

The crowd swayed in unison from left to right and threw up their hands, shouting back, "Ahhh!"

"Yiddish boogaloo! Ahhhh!"

The crowd swayed again.

"Meshugaloo!"

"Ahhh!"

"Meshugaloo!"

"Ahhhh!

"Second Avenue!"

"Ahhhhh!"

"*Avenida D!*"

"*Ahhhhhhh!*"

The vibes chimed in, followed by keyboard. The Avenue D crowd screamed and threw lit firecrackers. People shrieked and jumped as the little bombs exploded around them. Over all this came the voice of Chow Mein Vega:

> *Go to the deli,*
> *And you will find,*
> *Corned beef, pasteles,*
> *And pastrami on rye.*
> *And for dessert—*mofongo *pie!*
> *And as you leave*
> *They'll give you*
> *A kishka good-bye.*

And then he screamed in a strained falsetto, "A *kishka good-bye!*" and the crowd screamed more, set off more little blue-and-white cardboard bombs, as the musicians played on.

Chow Mein introduced a new work, "The Squatter's Boogaloo," which contained the lines

> *The landlord thinks*
> *The place is cleanah*
> Cuando *gives a light*
> *To* la gasolina.

Whoops loud as firecrackers exploded into the sapphire-clear summer sky that glowed over the dark brick buildings. Behind the silliness of Chow Mein's boogaloo lyrics was his irresistible phrasing and rhythm as he rolled over the keyboard and Felix bounced a conga beat and the vibes tiptoed through it with timbales and a double bass in counterpoint. Chow Mein could do anything—from rhythm and blues, he could move to jazz. His lyrical voice was haunting when he sang slow ballads in Spanish. It was physically impossible for anyone within ear range to keep his or her body from moving. Most of the crowd was dancing. Sonia held Sarah and danced and wished that Nathan didn't have to be with Nusan.

Ruth shrugged and squeezed up her face and said, "Boyoboy. It just doesn't speak to me." But Sonia could see that even she had a slight sway to her hips as she said it.

Cristofina danced with anyone she could find—most of Avenue D were customers. She slid from partner to partner, and her soft and abundant flesh, sealed in tight, shimmied like liquid mercury.

"It's surprising," said Harry. "I never thought of Cristofina like that."

"She's hot," said Chow Mein. "She could be Puerto Rican." Then he went back to his microphone and sang some more. He said to Harry, "You are going to be famous. The man who brought back boogaloo." And Harry smiled like a cat in sunshine.

Karoline looked at the great, gaseous ball of buttery dough blown huge with yeast and, with an impatient gesture, smacked it. The dough deflated with a sigh. She added rum-soaked raisins and chopped almonds, working the dough quickly in twisting motions like rapid strangulations. Then she put the bowl back in the refrigerator to let the dough slowly rise once more. While brushing melted butter into the brown crock *kugelhopf* mold, she caught herself daring to think that her life might work out after all.

For the first time, she could see a future. She could be safe. She had never been safe. No one ever trusted her parents because they were immigrants. Because they were Germans. She grew up with an ambiguous sense that something was about to happen, that someone would come to the shop and their life would be turned into chaos.

And then this man came into her life, so American that his name was actually Dickie, from another part of New York where they had people with names like Dickie. Dickie wanted to marry her, and he wanted to take her away from this neighborhood and help her to have a pastry shop on Madison Avenue, the kind of place that is always mentioned in *The New York Times,* the kind of place that does wedding cakes for the daughters of politicians and movie stars. It would all work out. If only *he* didn't call. If only the phone didn't ring.

She looked at the phone with dread, but instead the doorbell rang. "It's me, Joey Parma." And Karoline laughed quietly alone in her room with her rising *kugelhopf* dough.

Tommy Drapper walked to Avenue D, sweat beading on his shaved head, the parking garage ticket in his sweating left hand, which stayed in his pocket guarding his wallet. By the time he arrived, the crowd had

left the bandstand and was gathered around a raised and roped platform, a wrestling ring, draped in bright blue, red, and white Puerto
Rican flags.

Harry, in the wilted cloth that was his summer suit, went to Tommy
and assured him that Chow Mein Vega had the whole crowd moving
and would do it again after the match.

Tommy looked skeptical. "Just watch this match," Harry said. "We
do it every year. Then he plays some more sets."

Tommy looked around the crowd nervously and kept clutching his
wallet while Chow Mein leapt up to the wrestling ring and popped a
button. "Ah, shit," he said, barely picked up by the microphone, and he
introduced "the Borinquén bomber, the big *cojón* de Carolina, the boy-
chik from the barrio, the pride of Bodega Borinquina, the *alter kake
amoroso* of Avenida C—Jimmy Colon!"

Jimmy leapt up to the ring and vaulted over the ropes in his blue
tights and red, white, and blue tank top of the Puerto Rican flag, the
star over his chest. He was tall and broad shouldered and only a little
out of shape—a modest distortion of bulges pushing against the red and
white stripes running up his shirt. His curly blond hair betrayed only a
suggestion of dark roots. As he walked around the ring smiling and
waving, just as nice as he could be, the crowd applauded.

After a few merry minutes of Jimmy Colon, Chow Mein took the
microphone again. All he said was, "And now..." and his voice was
drowned out by a wave of bass boos and hisses. "*Por favor, mis amigos,*" said
Chow Mein, "we have to show respect to our amigo from"—he paused
to give the audience an extra second to prepare its protest—"*la otra isla.*"

Like the deep roar of a jet, the crowd responded to mention of "the
other island" with a loud boo that swept over Avenue D, punctuated by
firecrackers thrown in the air and José Fishman shouting, "*Bonzai. Bonzai,* get him, Jimmy-san!"

Blue, white, and red paper was thrown into the ring. "Please, show
some respect or we will have to call the fight," said Chow Mein, and the
crowd quieted down as they did every year at this point. "And now, the
champion of the *Republica Dominicana, El Diablito Dominicano,* the Slammer
of the Cibao, the Santiago Crusher, the *mamzer mamarucha* from the
Malecón—El Dominicano!"

The crowd booed and jeered and threw more paper, and out of a side street emerged Ruben—the former sweet-faced Ruben. He was draped in a huge cape showing the red and blue squares of the Dominican flag. He had a black goatee that came to a sharp point. The black lines of hair that connected his mustache to his goatee formed an unpleasant sneer. His head was shaven on the sides, and on this whitish bald border a red-and-blue Dominican flag had been tattooed. This was the only part to which Ruben had objected, but Cristofina convinced him that it would not show after his hair grew back, and to compensate she gave him a free tattoo of a Puerto Rican flag on his stomach where it would not show in his costume. The Puerto Rican stomach tattoo had hurt and was still a little sore, whereas, unjustly, the Dominican one around the border of his head had been painless. The dark hair on the top of his head had been waxed so that it stood up in black spikes. He had several gold rings on his left ear, and his eyebrows had been shaven off and replaced with demonically arched blue tattoo eyebrows. He leapt from the street over the ropes and into the ring in one startling, needlessly aggressive—just like a Dominican, the audience was supposed to think—vault. Then, with the grace and fanfare of a bullfighter, he removed his cape and swirled it across the ring, taunting poor Jimmy Colon with it, a Dominican flag that Jimmy politely shoved away from his face. The more people booed, the more El Dominicano swirled the Dominican flag in front of Jimmy. Jimmy smiled good-naturedly and winked at the audience as though to say "Don't worry, El Dominicano will get his."

Once his cape was off, the audience not only could see the curves of Ruben's muscles, they could see a steel blue chain with red background tattooed around his neck and the metal rings that had been placed in his nipples like undersized door knockers gleaming white in the sun. His fists were the faces of two growling tigers, and tiger stripes tattooed up his arms accentuated his thick forearms and large biceps.

El Dominicano was frightening, and clearly Jimmy was in trouble. The crowd was silent. This was not last year's El Dominicano. They had never seen an El Dominicano who looked like this.

"Man, he looks like a million," said Chow Mein.

"Well, not quite that bad," said Harry, remembering the bill in his pocket.

Felix pounded the congas and Chow Mein Vega rang a brass gong that they borrowed every year from a restaurant in Chinatown. El Dominicano stalked Jimmy, making the ring smaller and smaller, until Jimmy, who tried to go inside but kept slipping out before El Dominicano could grab a hold on him, was trapped in the corner. As El Dominicano was closing in, Jimmy suddenly jumped at him and wrapped his legs around El Dominicano's waist, knocking them both to the ground. El Dominicano slammed the mat helplessly with his powerful arms as Jimmy applied some painful pressure, and the crowd cheered joyfully.

Then, without warning, El Dominicano managed to stand up and slam Jimmy into the mat so hard that he lost his grip. He slammed him again. And again. Jimmy seemed barely conscious, and El Dominicano was throwing him at will. He was killing him. Women shrieked. Men cried, "¡Falta! ¡Falta!" Foul!

"Damay yo," No good, shouted José Fishman. "F-kay, f-kay," he yelled, mistakenly but effectively evoking the Japanese word for dandruff, as events worsened for Jimmy.

The referee, Sam Lipman, a small, balding man who drove the Mister Custard ice-cream truck and, worse, was wearing his white Mister Custard uniform, attempted to intercede. But El Dominicano slammed Mister Custard to the mat, too. Clearly he knew no limits. And then he picked him up and slammed him again. This was terrible. El Dominicano was killing Mister Custard.

But while he was distracted with this new victim, Jimmy Colon managed to get up, tried to shake off his grogginess, threw a lock on El Dominicano's head, and—and flipped him to the mat! Then he picked him up and flipped him again. The crowd cheered. Firecrackers were exploding. "Bonzai! Bonzai!" shouted José.

Suddenly, from somewhere in his costume, El Dominicano pulled out a handful of something and flung it in the direction of Jimmy Colon. The entire ring was consumed with bilious, bright orange clouds. Jimmy was covered in orange. He started coughing. Then choking. Then he fell to the mat and clutched his throat. His legs twitched violently. El Dominicano, the former sweet-faced Ruben, stood over him smiling demonically while angry fans shouted, "¡Brujería! Haitiano!"

Sam the referee, in his now orange-stained Mister Custard uniform, investigating the fans' charge of Haitian witchcraft, attempted to approach El Dominicano to examine what he had in his right hand. El Dominicano reached out with his menacing, tiger-striped arms and the referee backed off. But Jimmy Colon, in another miraculous resurrection, leapt to his feet again, hurled El Dominicano into a corner, threw him to the edge of the mat, crashed onto him feetfirst, lifted him by the head, and slammed him to the mat several more times until El Dominicano went limp, barely conscious, while Jimmy rolled him over, pinned him on his back, and stood up, raising his arms triumphantly. Not only was Jimmy victorious, he had saved Mister Custard for the neighborhood.

Slowly, El Dominicano, the black spikes of his waxed hair knocked askew, raised his tattooed head slightly to look for Rosita in the audience—just one wink for Rosita. But all he saw was the nacreous sheen of a woman's rhinestone-studded, white pearl pixie glasses. Her shriek was so loud that it silenced the rest of the crowd, and the uniformed policemen started moving toward the ring. She pointed at the vanquished El Dominicano and shouted, "That's him. That's him!"

Mrs. Skolnik was hopping up and down with one hand extended like a bayonet, pointing at tattooed Ruben on the mat. "That's him! He killed Eli Rabbinowitz. I saw him!"

As the police moved in, Tommy Drapper quickly made his way back to the parking garage.

CHAPTER FIFTEEN

Fireworks

T HE MORE HE THOUGHT about Nusan, the guiltier he felt.
But the worse he felt, the more he wanted Karoline. He could not understand this, did not want to understand it. He just wanted to turn his
back on his life and beliefs and have sex over and over again with this
woman.

She answered the phone as though she were expecting his call. He
had prepared his arguments, but she wasn't interested. She sounded re-
signed.

"What are we going to bake?" Nathan asked.

"Kugelhopf."

"What kind of kugel?"

"Kugel*hopf.* Just get over here and I'll show you."

"Kugelhopf."

"Yes. It was Hitler's favorite dessert."

He hung up. He hated the way she did that. Teasing him, which was
an understated form of laughing at him. She knew he hated it, but she
also knew that it made him want her more. She knew everything about
his soul, could hold it in her hand like *kugelhopf* dough, and he had to
have her to get it back—or that was what he reasoned walking up from
Rivington Street through the explosions.

Farther east on Rivington, some people had broken into an abandoned building. It had been a high school; by family legend, it was
where Harry had learned English. Rumored to have been bought by a
developer who planned to turn it into luxury apartments but must have
been waiting for a better moment, the building was deserted and most
of the windows were broken, the walls claimed by competing gangs in
colorful spray paint on the dark walls. Rockets were being fired out of
some of the windows, balls lobbed out rhythmically like orchestrated
meteors. It lacked only a "star-spangled banner" to look like Fort
McHenry under siege by the British. Smoke rose above the buildings,

and the ornamental metal edges of the roofs were revealed in sudden flashes of light.

Nathan had to choose streets carefully. A few little crackers went off near his face on Houston. He stamped out a fuse on First Street just before it exploded and was glared at by three disappointed boys. The wide avenues seemed safer than the streets, where the explosions echoed against the stone of the tenements and where Eli Rabbinowitz's hunted killer probably stalked. It drifted across Nathan's thoughts that a killer with a handgun could fire unnoticed this night.

Even this warm, smoky air seemed almost cool and clean after Nusan's. Nusan would be fine. Why worry about an octogenarian with a heart condition in a permanent depression who would spend the Fourth of July locked in a small room, jumping every time he heard a firecracker? Nathan tried to talk himself into going back. Instead, he went up First Avenue, heading toward the home of a possible Nazi. To accuse Mr. Moellen of being a Nazi, Nathan told himself, was completely unfair, a kind of racial stereotyping that was in itself Nazi-like. It would be like suspecting his family of greedy business practices because they were Jewish. Well, maybe that was going too far. But certainly Nusan's assertion that all Germans were Nazis was extremely unfair.

The instant he pressed the button for the second floor, the issue of Moellen's past, the firecrackers, the killer, Nusan's heart condition, and all other thoughts vanished from Nathan's mind. A loud buzz released the lock. She was anxious, Nathan could not help noting. Or maybe she was just anxious to get him away from her door. When he got to the top of the stairs, the door was opened wide and there she was, in her apron, the entire apartment smelling of butter. But then, seated by the table was Joey Parma, his gray blue, silk-blend pant legs spread wide, balancing as he tipped back his chair, rotating clockwise a glass of wine in his hand. Staring at the glass, he swirled the wine in that manner that all the new people in the neighborhood had. It was as though the smarts went to wine school before moving to the East Village, and so had Joey Parma.

"You know each other?" asked Karoline.

Nathan noted with relief that Karoline was dressed under her apron.

"Here, have a glass," said Joey, straightening the chair on the floor and pouring another glass from a tall, thin, green bottle. "It's eiswein, from Riesling in the Rheingau. They can only make it certain years when there is an early frost. The berries freeze and it becomes concentrated and forget about it!" He handed Nathan the glass. They sipped the richly fruited wine, like cold, pungent syrup. Karoline and Joey discussed the Rheingau. Nathan tried not to look at his watch but knew that he had only two hours at most and this cop was sitting there talking frozen berries.

But then Joey looked at his own watch. "Oh! Got to go." He grabbed three bottles on the table, thanked Karoline, wished everyone a good holiday, and galloped noisily down the stairs.

Alone, Karoline shrugged at Nathan. "He wanted to come by."

"To get wine," said Nathan, finishing the sentence.

"Yes. I wonder why he thinks you came." They were both quiet a minute. "He just took about two hundred dollars' worth of wine, including an Alsatian Gewürztraminer, a Château—"

Nathan cut her off irritably. "I don't care."

"But it's funny. He is going to a picnic in Queens. He tells me that they all smack their lips and say, 'Nice wine, Joey.' Sometimes he can't bear it and he puts the wine in decanters so that he can slip his guests cheaper wine. They don't know. And he can't tell anyone. If his wife knew what he spent on wine, she would kill him."

Nathan pulled the tie string on her apron, but she grabbed it. "No."

He looked at her for that brief instant, but then she lowered her eyes and said, "The *kugelhopf*." She instructed him to brush melted butter into the still unbuttered molds on the table.

"I lied, you know, it wasn't the Führer's favorite," she said, deliberately pronouncing the German word with the perfect Prussian accent she had learned from her parents. "This is the French way. The Austrian one has less butter. This is better."

"Hitler had bad taste?"

"He was Austrian."

Hefting the large mixing bowl of dough from the refrigerator, she said, "It's like a brioche. Or a challah. My father used to make the most wonderful challah. But no one bought it, because he is German." She said the word "challah" with the appropriate Hebrew *ch* sound from the back of the roof of her mouth.

Suddenly she slapped the rounded edge of the dough rising out of the bowl—slapped it three times, forehand, backhand, forehand—like a good boxing combination—until it went limp, sinking in the bowl.

She showed Nathan how to make rolls of dough and fill each mold only about two-thirds full. "Now," she said, unbuckling Nathan's belt, "we have to wait for it to rise. Very slowly." She smiled at him.

"How slowly?"

"About two hours."

Nathan smiled, too, and they undressed each other with ritual care, folding each other's clothes and draping them carefully on the chairs. When they were both naked, she pointed at his beaded bracelet. "That, too. I want you completely naked."

He carefully removed the green and black beads. He felt no panic. He could do this without Oggún. He placed the beads in the pocket of his folded pants and looked at the naked Karoline.

An idea overtook him.

He took the butter pot and began carefully brushing butter on her skin until her entire body was gleaming and golden like a Cellini Venus, and then he began meticulously to lick the butter.

Karoline knew that it was too late. That was the way it was. The first time is a mistake, but the second time means that it is "an affair," that they would keep meeting, fill their lives with lies, sink deeper and deeper, and not stop until they were destroyed.

Even without Tommy Drapper—what happened to him, anyway?—Harry thought the concert was a great success. He walked back from Avenue D with little bombs exploding around him, not loudly enough to upset his Irving Berlin:

> *If you don't want my peaches,*
> *You better stop shaking my tree.*

He thought about how he probably would be known as the man who brought back boogaloo, saved boogaloo, made boogaloo great.

> *Let me say that you're mighty slow,*
> *You're as cold as an Eskimo—*

"Hello, Harry Seltzer."

Harry turned. It was Florence in a tight black dress, the fabric pulled to its limit and shining across her "big black booty." Her hair was pulled up on her head and she was wearing a thick layer of a magenta lipstick that seemed to clash oddly with her skin color. "It's Florence," she explained with a hopeful smile.

"Yes, I know. Hello, Florence."

"This could be our time, Harry Seltzer. Just a few very good minutes."

"Oh, thank you, Florence, no time right now." She had placed a soft hand in the sag of his pants. He was surprised what a good touch she had, and while he protested that his family was waiting, she noticed that he made no effort to remove the hand.

"Come over here a minute," she said, and maneuvered him below a brownstone stoop, against the wall on the steps to a basement doorway. It seemed to Harry that she had just led him by his penis, but how could that be possible? But he now realized that his fly was open and her hand was directly on his organ.

"Ohh," she said with a note of half triumph and half feigned surprise as she felt his excitement. Her touch overtook him.

"You like me, don't you, Harry Seltzer," she purred almost in amusement. Then she knelt on the step and placed him in her mouth. In three minutes it was over, and whatever was left of the moment was instantly destroyed by Florence, her purple lips curled as though she would be ill, leaning toward the sidewalk and spitting across to the curb, then wiping her mouth with the back of her hand.

"I'm sorry," said Harry, not certain what to say. "What do I owe you? I mean, how much do you—" He took out his wallet full of crisp flat twenties newly minted from the cash machine. He tried to hand her two twenties, but three stuck together. "Is this all right?"

"Whatever you think, Harry Seltzer."

Why did she have to say his name? Harry thought, handing her another twenty. Then he heard footsteps. It could be somebody who knew him. He grabbed Florence and tried to shove her into the doorway below the stoop. At that moment a firecracker exploded, and taken by surprise, Harry jammed her head into a wrought-iron gate.

"Ohh!" Florence protested softly, and reached up to touch her temple where blood was running down her face—the wrong shade of red, the color of her lipstick, which had mostly vanished.

"I'm so sorry, Florence," said Harry. "Are you all right?"

"It's nothing," said Florence, laughing. She could see how urgently Harry wanted to leave.

"Here," said Harry, handing her what was left of the money in his wallet, three more twenties, and he ran quickly down the street, leaving Florence to nurse her wounds and marvel at her stack of $20 bills.

Nathan hurried down the stairs to the side door around the corner from the Edelweiss. Almost at the bottom, his footsteps sounding like a commotion of hooves, he saw Mrs. Moellen looking up at him, so sadly, so silently, that Nathan wanted to take her hand and say, "I'm so sorry." But instead he smiled pointlessly and sidestepped past her, saying only, "Excuse me."

Out on the hot July street as the door was closing, he thought he heard her say, "Yes."

As he turned the corner, he heard a strange Teutonic sound like marching orders in German—it sounded the way Nathan imagined a German army in training would sound. The shades of the Edelweiss were down, covering the windows with flat sepia images of steepled German villages that had been bombed and rebuilt. Nathan peeked through a corner and was able to see inside. A few unpurchased linzer tortes were still in the window. Moellen was on the floor. He was doing push-ups, snapping them up and down with his body very rigid in a martial rhythm while counting in German, "*Acht! Neuen! Zehn!*" His face was getting red and veins were beginning to stand out. Nathan noticed something odd. He had always imagined Moellen to have pale blue eyes, but in fact he had very dark eyes—like Nusan. Had the war turned his eyes, too?

The sun had not quite set, and the last amber rays were catching a haze of greenish smoke. Nathan was hurrying toward the building roof party on Avenue A when he remembered—just in time—that he would give himself away, lose his alibi, if he didn't know the final score of the Mets game.

There was a bar on First Avenue, a dark, partially belowground place with dusty Sicilian ornaments in the window. Three shadows were hunched over the bar. Nathan knew that he should order a drink first but couldn't spend the time on the ritual.

"Does anyone know the Mets score?"

"The Mets," repeated one of the shadows.

"What do we look like," said the bartender, "the sports page?"

They were treating him like one of the smarts. He ran to Avenue A. Maybe there would be something at the newsstand.

"Shalom, my friend." It was Mohammed, walking up the avenue. "Are you not going to the roof?"

"Yes, I was just on my way. Tell me ..." Nathan stopped. Another close call. It could come out that he had gotten the score from Mohammed. "Oh, nothing. I forgot something. Have to go back to my shop. I'll see you later."

"Good-bye, my friend. Shalom."

Nathan had a radio in his shop. He would go there and find out the score. But on the way, he noticed that Arnie and his pallet were missing. The spot on the sidewalk where he had been for several years had been cleared. Nathan looked down Avenue A and saw the pallet on the next block, but Arnie wasn't there. When he reached the pallet, he realized that something was moving under a pile of blankets.

"Arnie?"

The blankets, one salmon colored and another blue with cheerful snowflake patterns, slowly moved. From a corner, Arnie's gaunt face emerged, his beret undisturbed at its customary jaunty tilt. "Hey, Nathan, *viva la huelga*."

"What are you doing here?"

"They made me move. They're opening a new store. Selling running shoes. You know, hundred-dollar sneakers. They didn't want me in front of their store. Bad for business. Everything about me says, 'Why run?'"

"It's about ninety degrees. You're going to suffocate under these blankets."

"There's bombs everywhere. I had to take cover."

"Why don't you come up to our roof? My family is having a party. They do it every year. Get something to eat. Get off the street."

"No thanks, man. The street's my home."

"Just a couple of hours."

But Arnie wouldn't come. He wished Nathan a "*Viva la huelga*" and withdrew his head, turtlelike, under the blanket.

"Say, Arnie . . ." He could try, Arnie always knew everything. "Arnie, how did the Mets do?"

From under the blanket, in muffled tones, came, "Cincinnati killed them. Five–nothing. Cone fucked up."

"Did Strawberry get a hit?" The smirking, lanky Darryl Strawberry was something special to Nusan. To Nusan everything was written, life was *beshirt*. But the long-legged Strawberry sauntering up to the plate, giraffelike, always filled Nusan with the exciting idea that anything might happen. Strawberry at bat was the only time Nusan felt that way.

"Strawberry struck out with runners on base."

"Thanks, Arnie!" said Nathan, handing Arnie a $5 bill.

"*Viva la huelga,*" said the bereted tortoise head as it shrank back into its woolen shell. And Nathan strode with confidence toward his building, prepared to talk about the game. He had completely forgotten that no one in his family ever talked baseball.

As Nathan hurried home, he suddenly caught up with his father, doing the same thing.

"Hi, Dad, I'm on my way from Nusan's," he said quickly, and then realized that he was coming from the opposite direction. But fortunately Harry didn't seem to notice. Harry said, "I'm coming from Avenue D," and Nathan did not think about the fact that Avenue D was to the east and he was coming from the west.

"Yes, I'm just getting back from Avenue D."

"Yes, I'm just getting back from Nusan's."

"Yes, good, good."

Nathan did think it was odd that his father didn't ask how Nusan was. Should he volunteer the Mets score? Probably not. Wait until someone asks. But maybe nobody would. And it was such a nice detail.

Down Avenue A came Mordy in slow four-four, his untied shoelaces clicking, his arm around Rosita, who came up to his ribs— Rosita in her purple dress moving down the street, her body flowing like waves rolling and disappearing on the ocean's surface. The two walking arm in arm was a dramatization of Chow Mein Vega's theory of ethnic walking rhythms. It was impossible for them to walk together.

Mordy's four-four was slower than the usual Jewish step, though his long legs covered the distance just as quickly. Rosita, next to him in a bouncy three-beat, had twice the movement but could not keep up. Anyone with a sense of rhythm could see that these two were not going to make a couple.

"Excuse me," said an elderly man hurrying in the opposite direction with a plastic bag heavy with groceries. "Excuse me." He had to say it several times to get Mordy's attention. "Excuse me, but your shoelaces are untied."

Mordy smiled, nodded, kept walking, and saw Nathan and Harry in front of him stepping so quickly that they seemed to be racing each other. But Mordy with his long stride caught up to Nathan, which allowed Harry to take the lead.

"Mordy," said Nathan, "you are upsetting people again."

"Rosita? It's good the way she upsets people. Oh, you mean she's not Jewish."

"You know it upsets them."

"Jewish, not Jewish, different names, different ages. All arbitrary designations to try to show that we are all different, but in reality we are all identical. It's like deer. Could you tell one white-tail deer from another? A white-tail deer could not tell one person from another. Do you think a white-tail deer could tell the difference between Mom, Rosita, and Birdie Nagel?"

Mordy had always been like this, and no one ever tried to argue with him. When they were boys, they once decided to cross the Second Avenue subway tracks, and the older Nathan had cautioned Mordy not to step on the third rail. Mordy had said, "Who's to say which is the third rail? It depends where you start counting. One man's third rail is another man's first rail." Nathan had not known how to answer, and he always dated his policy of not arguing with Mordy to that statement.

By the time he and Mordy and Rosita got to the roof, Harry was already installed in his green canvas director's chair, carefully positioned away from the East River side. Ruth managed to separate Mordy from Rosita for long enough to ask, "Where's Naomi?"

"Anything for a Jew," said Mordy, laughing, "Sthe musth have been detainth." Then, as an afterthought, "By a bookseller she's going out with on Avenue B."

He walked Rosita away from Ruth. Rosita looked up at him. "Can I ask you something?"

"Anything," Mordy said expansively. "What would you like to know about me?"

"Why don't you tie your shoes?"

"Why should I?" said Mordy, as though he had hatched a great and liberating idea.

"So you don't trip and fall."

Mordy smiled. "*Escuchas,* Rosita." He trilled the R so long and loudly that Rosita thought he might be laughing at her name. "There are two great lies in this world that are always told to try to control people. The first is that you will trip and fall if you don't tie your shoelaces. I haven't tied mine in more than twenty years and I have never fallen."

"And the second?"

"The second?"

"You said there were two great lies."

"Oh yes. . . . That you can get ahead by hard work."

Rosita shyly covered her mouth and began laughing. She put her arm around Mordy's waist and began swaying happily to salsa music that was rising up to the roof from a distant window.

The Seltzers' July Fourth roof party had always been catered by Schneider's, whose specialty was a kosher Hawaiian luau. Schneider served everything, including the barbecued lamb, which he somehow displayed to look like a pig—albeit one without the unkosher hindquarters, and of course there could be no head to put the apple in—and he was on hand to personally flame the pineapple dessert, which was always lit just before the fireworks began.

But two years ago, Schneider too moved to Florida—did they all see one another down there? Would the whole neighborhood be waiting for him one day? Harry often wondered.

Last year, they got grilled chickens from Bob's Greasy Hands, and Birdie Nagel became terribly upset. This year, the new sushi maker on the ground floor had provided the food. His name sounded like Kamizaki to everyone else, though Harry insisted it was Mr. Kamikazi. It must not have been very close to either one, because he did not respond when these names were used. He had set up a table with little fingers of rice covered with perfectly manicured strips of raw fish—

rose-colored tuna, orange salmon, golden eel, sparkling salmon eggs piled up like jewels—all fanned out like the speckled wings of a butterfly.

"Fantastic," said the young man who had just moved into 3E with his English spaniel and, thus far, had been seen wearing only seersucker suits. "*Unagi.* I love *unagi.*"

"It took forever to put things away on Avenue D," Harry explained repeatedly to Ruth, though no one had asked him why he was late.

"Yes," agreed Nathan, the only one listening. "And the Mets game seemed to last forever." He was just daring someone to ask him the final score, but nobody did.

Ruth was not listening. She was watching her husband and both her sons, all three staring at the two shiny purple parts of Rosita's lower half swaying at the edge of the roof as she listened to music from below. Ruth was smiling. Sonia, who saw the same thing, was not.

"He's really very attractive," declared Mrs. Kleinman, startling Nathan.

"Who is that?"

"The Japanese gentleman who did all this lovely food." Mrs. Kleinman was wearing a red sundress that left her muscular back exposed. She stared with hatred at the purple-dressed Rosita, who did not need a bare back, then waved flirtatiously at the Japanese man, who was explaining to Harry that he had to leave and hoped they enjoyed the food. "Mr. Kamizaki," Mrs. Kleinman shouted, realizing that he was leaving. But he did not seem to hear her. "Mr. Kamikazi?" He opened the door and left the roof. Helplessly she turned back to Nathan. "Well, very attractive anyway." She tried to flare the skirt of her red sundress and move a little like Rosita. "I like the Fourth of July. There isn't any mail today, is there?"

"No. No mail. National holiday."

"Probably tomorrow our boxes will be stuffed."

"I hate this day," Birdie Nagel volunteered. "Do you know why?"

Nathan could imagine.

"Birds have very good hearing. Better than ours. It's a higher frequency. Do you know what that means?"

"More sound units per second," said Mordy.

"Yes," said Birdie Nagel, looking frightened at Mordy. "I was talking to Nathan. Nathan, did you know with all these firecrackers and bombs and everything in the sky, it's terrible for the birds. They have to migrate to Staten Island."

"That *is* terrible," said Nathan. "So then is Staten Island covered with birds today?"

"Yes, and Hoboken."

"Don't they have fireworks in Staten Island and Hoboken?"

"You know, that is a very good point. I just don't know. But I will find out."

"This is the best *ikura*," said the new tenant, who was eating more sushi than anyone else in the building. "But the *unagi* is unbelievable. Has his place been reviewed?"

"I don't know," said Harry. "I was late from Avenue D and I just got here. What is *unagi*?"

"Eel."

"Eel! Where?"

"These over here."

"Isn't that something," said Harry. "Here he knew we were Jewish and he gives us eel. And that's not anti-Semitic?"

The new tenant did not understand.

"Eel, it doesn't have scales. Jews don't eat it," said Nathan, trying to be helpful.

"Actually," said Mordy, who had been stroking Rosita's dress hungrily by the edge of the roof and giving no indication of listening, "it's all a complete misunderstanding. Eels have lots of scales. Their natural defense system is to be slippery, so they are covered with a slime and their scales are embedded in the skin. But unlike the *uni*, which has spines, eels have scales. And they are not full of industrialized crap like the *sake*, which is farmed salmon; they are not high on the food chain and loaded with heavy metals like the *toro*, which is tuna. So in fact, Jews who know their stuff"—he reached to the table and theatrically picked up an *unagi* and popped it in his mouth—"can eat eel."

Rosita, Birdie Nagel, Mrs. Kleinman, the new tenant, Sonia, and even Sarah looked at Mordy with wonder.

"Boyoboy," said Ruth with a proud smile, looking at Rosita, "*der yingl* is a lot more than a hunk of *fleysch mit oygn*."

Rosita looked at her quizzically, and Mordy, as he led her away to a different corner of the roof, explained, "I'm not just a piece of meat with eyes. Reassuring, really."

"That's what your mother calls you?"

"It's hard to translate."

"After all," Harry said to Ruth, "it's a Jewish neighborhood. It wouldn't kill him to serve a little cream cheese with the fish."

Sarah found Nathan in a dark corner by himself. "Daddy?"

"Yes?" said Nathan, his face brightening quickly.

"What's a baketion?"

"What?"

"A bacation."

"A vacation is when you stop working or whatever you are doing and go away for a week."

"Why don't we have vacations?"

"I don't know. Not everybody takes them. When you work for someone they are supposed to give you a vacation."

"Do you give Pepe Le Moko a vacation?"

"No. It's just when you go away for a while."

"Like Mr. Apple?" Mr. Apple was an elderly tenant who had died.

"No, Mr. Apple is not on vacation."

"He went away."

"But he's not coming back."

"I know. Because he's dead."

"Yes," Nathan said uncertainly. "That's right."

"I know where you go when you die."

"Really?"

"Florida."

"Well, you could go to Florida on vacation."

"No, because the people who go to Florida never come back."

"Do you need a vacation?"

Sarah nodded her head yes, and Nathan smiled and held her close to him and felt her small arms hold him with surprising strength. Then she went off to see her grandfather.

Ruth, finding Nathan alone in the dark, said to him, "Are you all right?"

"Yes, I'm fine. I was at Uncle Nusan's."

"Yes, I know."

"Let me ask you something." Nathan hesitated. "Do you think I am passive-aggressive?"

"What? What does that mean?"

"It means that I don't confront people when I am angry with them but then find little ways, maybe subconscious ways, to get back."

"Oh boy! Who have you been talking to?"

"No one, I just wondered."

"I'll have to think about it." Ruth announced that everyone should eat up because she was bringing up a special dessert before the fireworks. The family braced themselves for apple strudel. Nathan took Sonia's hand and smiled at her sadly. Sonia looked down at her hand in his and then studied his sad face and said, "You lost your bracelet."

"My bracelet?"

"The beads."

Suddenly, panic—not at all the kind of panic the beads were designed to protect against, but the panic of having stepped into a fatal trap—overtook him. Had he left them at Karoline's?

Ruth went down the stairs to her apartment on the top floor. But when she opened the door to her apartment and turned on the lights, she saw Mordy with his pants to his ankles and his hands far up Rosita's purple dress. Ruth shrieked involuntarily.

"Well," said Mordy, "better a Jew with no pants than pants with no Jew."

Back on the roof, Nathan, who had already explained to Sonia how the string had broken and he had lost his beads, reached into his pocket and felt the bracelet and in his surprise pulled it out to examine.

Sonia looked at him with a worried face, but before she could decide what to say, Ruth had come back to the roof and was coming toward him with the special dessert.

"Look, Daddy," said Sarah, who was dragging Nathan toward his mother. "I picked it."

As Nathan got closer, he recognized the tilted wedges of caramel, the violet brown chocolate buttercream. "Why did you get a *dobos torta*!" he shouted at Ruth.

"Sarah picked it out," Ruth argued. "At Edelweiss. It's Hungarian."

And although Nathan could feel many eyes, including Sonia's, pressing into him, he could not help crying, had lost the will to stop the tears. It was as though something had burst and it was a tremendous relief to have the built-up pressure give way. His shoulders heaved and water poured out of his eyes as he tried uselessly to cover his face.

"Hungarians are among the worst anti-Semites," said Harry.

Sarah, too, was staring at her father. Nathan picked her up and held her tightly, which made him sob all the more.

"The Hungarian record during the war," said Harry, "was one of the worst in Europe."

At that moment, a white rocket whistled through the sky and Brooklyn was lit up. The fireworks had begun.

"You know, Sonia," Harry said as he settled into his chair, "next year let's do Mexican. Can you get us some enchiladas and Jimmy Chongas and those things?"

"I don't know, Harry," said Sonia.

"A little guacamole," said Harry, saying the word in three syllables.

Ruth stared at her husband, and it made him uncomfortable. He whistled.

"Everyone is acting a little strange tonight," Ruth asserted with her eyes still fixed on Harry, as though he might try some sleight of hand if she looked away. He continued to whistle, trying to look innocent. He went for his favorite slide. "On the bumpy road to—love."

"Why are you singing Gershwin?" Ruth demanded. "You never sing Gershwin."

"It's Berlin."

"No, it's Gershwin."

Harry remembered his bet. "That's what Chucho Vega says. He bet me. Do you believe it?"

"He's right," Ruth muttered. Then she sighed. "How much?"

"How much what?"

"What did you bet?"

"Bacalao."

"What?"

A rocket exploded and shards of green light stretched across the sky. Harry remembered that he hated *bacalao*. It was like bad lox, he thought—either too salty or no taste at all. Herring was better. That was another reason he was in no hurry to look up the song's author.

Nathan put Sarah to bed.

"Daddy?"

"What? Go to bed."

"What's a midwife?"

"What?"

"A midwife. Mom says you are having trouble with your midwife. That's why you wear the bracelet."

"Never mind. Go to bed."

She knows, Nathan thought as he examined his thinning body in the mirror. She knew. That's why she got the *dobos torta*. She went with Sarah and let her pretend she picked it. That's a standard game. Passive-aggressive. She picked it because she knew. But how? Women know how to figure these things out. It's their genius.

"Nathan," came a soft voice.

"Yes?"

"Can we talk?"

"Okay." It was extraordinary. He could eat all the pastry he wanted and still lose weight.

Sonia sat up in bed. "Who gave you the beads? Was it a woman?"

Nathan could not help but smile. "Yes." He waited a moment. "It was Cristofina."

"The *bruja*!"

Nathan shook his head.

"You believe in those things?"

"I don't know. I am having a problem. I didn't want to talk about it. I thought I could make it go away. I went to Cristofina and also to a psychiatrist."

"Why?"

"I think it's claustrophobia. Sometimes I just can't breathe."

Sonia smiled.

"Why are you so happy?"

"That stupid thing. I didn't know what it was. It looked like you were going steady or something."

"Going steady?"

"What do you call it?"

"Sonia, do you think tattoos are sexy?"

The smile was gone from Sonia's face. Why was he asking that?

As Nathan fell asleep, he decided that Karoline was right. Women are not that clever. It is just that men panic and they tell them everything. Then they wonder how the woman found them out. Psychiatrists and fortune-tellers play the same game.

Before Harry and Ruth went to sleep, Ruth said, "I think our son is acting very strange."

"You don't have to worry about Mordy," said Harry.

"No, I mean Nathan," said Ruth.

"I'm sorry I was so late. It took a long time clearing things up at Avenue D," said Harry.

"I know, you said that," Ruth answered.

Sonia thought of something Emma Goldman once said: "The scriptures tells us, God created man in His own image, which has by no means proven a success."

CHAPTER SIXTEEN

God-like Sparks

A T 4:00 A.M., Nathan woke up from a dream. Dr. Kucher had said he should remember his dreams, and by morning it would be gone. He stumbled in the dark for a pen and paper but could find nothing until he went in the room where Sonia worked on Emma and Margarita. There at the refinished oak desk they had bought on Houston Street he wrote down his dream.

It was a meeting. A meeting about the neighborhood. It was run by Moellen, who was wearing his SS uniform, which neither surprised nor upset anyone. And Karoline was there, naked and covered in butter. And this did not draw anyone's interest, either. Felix, the drug dealer with the grocery store, was there. Joey Parma was serving wine. Mordy was lecturing on the Jewish dietary laws. But the odd thing was that every one of them had a large, evenly cut wedge of Swiss cheese on his or her head. No matter how the people shook or turned their heads while speaking, the wedges always remained perfectly balanced on their heads. After Mordy's lecture and Joey Parma's description of the wine and Moellen's call for driving Dominicans from the neighborhood, they all turned to Nathan and said, "And what do you think, Nathan?"

And Nathan replied, "I think there is merit in your arguments, but it is hard for me to take this seriously because you all have cheese on your heads."

Cabezucha awoke in center stage. Golden early morning summer light was on the East River, his front yard, making the bridges glisten. He stretched and stood and scratched the animal tattooed on his belly. He looked around the abandoned amphitheater, ruins like ancient catacombs with dark concrete passages below curving ledges where space was once sold. Someone on one of the top rows was looking for a vein, finally found one in his upper calf and stuck the syringe in, and was at peace. Scraps of paper, a beer can, squashed and burned checkered tubes of spent firecrackers—the detritus of the national holiday were strewn around the lawns of the park.

Fourth of July was over and Dukakis still had a comfortable lead in all the polls and the Mets were still in first place in the Eastern Division. Neither of these landmark reasons for hope in the world meant anything to Cabezucha as he rubbed his big black tufts of wild hair and looked at the path along the water. Beyond, across the pea green river, were the sugar docks where freighters landed from his native island.

Back on the Manhattan side, the new tenant was rounding the curve toward the Manhattan Bridge. He was not wearing his customary seersucker, but the low morning sun gave the white of his virgin running shoes from the new store on Avenue A an electric glow. A woman all in white with the same new shoes glowed next to him.

Cabezucha scratched himself as he studied these two like a bear studies movement in the bushes once hibernation is done and he is ready to forage for food. The new shoes made him smile. And the woman. He liked the way women were starting to run in his park, the way their breasts swayed rhythmically as they loped past his overgrown amphitheater. He checked his pocket. The thick bundle of dollars was still there. He tucked in his shirt and walked through the park up the steel footbridge over the FDR Drive already choked with traffic. The new tenant and his girl were right behind, deep in conversation, not the least out of breath.

"But I am a little worried," he was saying nervously to her. "I hope you don't resent my success." There was a moment of silence. "Should I have it."

She answered softly, "Why don't you just get there first."

"But I want to know how you will react."

So engrossed were they in this debate about the future that they passed the huge, disheveled, and staggering Cabezucha without noticing him. Still walking like a bear that had not entirely shaken off the winter, Cabezucha stumbled through Alphabet City—Avenue D, Avenue C. He stopped off at the casita. The gate was open, but no one was in the yard. He could hear the steady, determined, arrhythmic clicking of a typewriter inside the casita. He read the sign on the outside wall,

"No Hispanics Here!" and thought it meant that everyone was away, which seemed odd, because he could hear the typing. It was probably Chow Mein and he did not want to be bothered. Seeing a box with a sign, "The Ruben García Defense Fund," Cabezucha peeled two twenties from the wad in his pocket and, after rolling them carefully into a tube, placed them into the box.

He used another $20 bill to pay his entry to the baths in the brownstone on Tenth Street. Here he was perplexed again, because the entire outside of the brownstone had been painted pink. When he entered, he found the pink hallway decorated with photos of actresses he could not quite identify. They were Barbra Streisand, Judy Garland, Bette Midler, and Molly Picon. Jasha acknowledged that gays would not be particularly drawn to Molly Picon, but neither would she do any harm. He liked her. In any event, the new look did not seem to be working. This dark and menacing giant—Jasha did not think he was even gay—was the only customer this morning.

The shower and towel made Cabezucha's hair even wilder than usual. He examined the card in his pocket for the address of the masseuse on Avenue A—"Sonia." A nice name.

Nathan pulled up the iron gate and unlocked the door to the Meshugaloo Copy Center. "A beautiful day today," Carmela asserted.

"I think so," said Nathan, looking up both at her on the fire escape and at the slit of sky that the six-floor buildings on Tenth Street allowed. It was a good omen that Carmela had no dire predictions. But then he heard her say, "I hope no one gets shot today in the neighborhood." Nathan, unable to conjure up a reply to this, did not attempt one. He put on his recording of Herbert Von Karajan and the Berlin Philharmonic playing Beethoven's Ninth. Beethoven was the best workout. Especially the Ninth. Beethoven never stopped building, no cooldown, no letup, just squeezed more, even when you thought there was nothing left. Some mornings Nathan needed that.

It began with agitated strings, like something exciting about to happen. Pepe Le Moko strolled to the doorway and lay in the sun. How sad it must be, Nathan thought, to be German. Without meaning to, he was addressing his thoughts to Oggún. A muscular black arm holding a hammer and a black face with no particular expression were all that was showing. The rest was still covered in newspaper, swathed in *El Vocero* like a plush evening wrap.

Karoline, Nathan reasoned to the half-wrapped orisha, was born in New York—wasn't she? She did not even have an accent. She was raised here, and her father is someone I have known. . . .

The music was getting very insistent, full orchestra with kettle-drums, then strings, then woodwind, soft but driving, becoming more melodious.

Jackie, the performance artist, short for either John or Jacqueline, came into the shop. His—or her—flowing black hair was clearly a wig, and the heavy makeup could not have been intended to be convincing. He or she had the large square hands and feet of a man, but in his flimsy sundress it was clear that she had breasts and hips. In the summer, Jackie always carried a Chinese fan that he or she waved impatiently while complaining about the heat. She was preparing flyers for a new one-man—or one-woman—show. She had photos of her in both genders and worked with Nathan placing them on the page, adding the print, designing the flyer, and running off three hundred copies—forty minutes' work for which Nathan charged $5.

It was a good day—seven obituaries, all older than him.

Speaking Spanish, Cabezucha explained that he was Serrano Badigo and Chucho Vega had recommended her. It meant something that he said Chucho and not Chow Mein. "He said you were Spanish. I didn't want an Anglo masseuse."

She told him to take off his clothes. "You can leave your underwear or take it off, whatever you want." And she left the room. In the living room, where Ruth was keeping Sarah amused learning a Yiddish song about a little bird that she had been teaching her for months, Sonia called the casita to ask Chucho what he knew of Serrano Badigo. He seemed polite, but she had to be careful. But no one answered at the casita.

Upstairs, Harry was searching frantically through his files for a certain magazine he had lost. He realized that if he died, someone would go through his papers and it would be found. He didn't find it but instead found a big black water bug—like a cockroach, but five times the size—crawling from behind a cabinet. He grabbed a folder of his 1985 income tax records and smashed it on the water bug so hard that he heard it crunch. He hated water bugs. They came from the water.

At the casita, Chow Mein Vega had heard the phone, but he often didn't answer. He had turned from his typewriter and was plucking an old acoustic guitar, picking out the mountain ballads that his father had liked. Felix was in the garden, caressing his tomato crop, trying to think of something to say to Rosita, who was sitting at a table inside, slapping down domino tiles.

"Is it too much to ask—a man who is not dealing drugs?" she said to Chow Mein.

"Ah, I am yours, *Quericita*," he answered.

"I'm thinking about it. I thought Ruben was cute. Then look what he did to himself."

"Ruben is innocent."

"Maybe he killed nobody, Chucho, but he's not innocent. *Como Felix* over there."

"Felix has gotten out. He is trying to have a store."

"With *que dinero*? Where does he get the money? You know, I thought I'd go with a Jew, an older Jew. Everybody says they don't deal. They make money, but they don't deal. That's perfect, right?"

"Which Jew?"

"Seltzer."

"Harry?"

"No, Mordy."

"Well, at least you found a single one. But I have to tell you, the Seltzers don't make money. None of them. Wrong Jews. It happens sometimes. It's like Puerto Ricans that can't dance."

"Well, Mordy can't dance *tampoco*."

"That's not surprising. He's probably too stoned."

"That family is weird. Do you know what his mother called him? A piece of meat."

"With eyes?"

"What's up with that? She is a really tough woman. She didn't like me. And the father acts like he's having some kind of affair."

"Harry?"

"Yes. You can always tell a man with something to hide. That sort of nervous way. I can tell. He came home late and nervous. But the worst part is that Mordy was the biggest pothead I've ever seen. And I think he got busted today."

"Mordy Seltzer was busted?"

"I think so. The cops are really active this morning. They have all these weird baseball sombreros with initials. DEA, FBI, NYPD, JERK. They searched his *edificio y* found all kinds of shit. I didn't think Jews were like that."

Felix was in the garden, trying to look as though he were not listening.

When Sonia went back in the room, her client was stretched out on the table, a huge, powerful body. This would be work. From the next room she could hear Ruth singing about the little bird. "*Feygele, feygele,*" and Sarah responded, "*pi-pi-pi.*"

"*Vu is der tate?*" sang Ruth.

"*Nisht ahie',*" Sarah shouted. Daddy is away on a trip.

Sonia smiled as her long fingers stretched toward the large back.

A theme began as a low murmur of cello, and then lyrical violins sweetened it to a melodious song with brass and woodwind. Suddenly there was a deep voice: "*Freude.*"

Joy.

"*Freude, schöner Götterfunken,*" beautiful, God-like sparks, which sounds better in German. Then there was a moment of silence and a single note and then another and the theme came back. A pleasant, upbeat little melody "like the heavenly bodies that he set on their courses." But now something started going wrong. The beat got harsher. A rhythmic, metallic clanging intruded. It became martial music. A strong, harsh beat almost like—like goose-stepping.

Almost against his will, Nathan was tapping the ever more belligerent beat, imagining the long, rigid body of Moellen jerking push-ups—"*Eins, Zwei, Drei . . .*"—all the while laughing while the big mixer kneaded dough to this now fierce Teutonic beat. It had all gone wrong, and now the symphony itself was about conquest: *"Ein Held zum Siegen"*—a hero going to conquest.

Even Beethoven in the nineteenth century, when Germany was just an idealistic dream, understood that these beautiful themes would turn ugly, turn harsh, become goose-stepping. Or was that not what Beethoven meant at all? It didn't sound like that when Bernstein conducted. Was Bernstein closer to Beethoven? Beethoven was deaf when he wrote the Ninth. At the Ninth's premiere concert, a singer named Caroline had to tell him to stop conducting because the orchestra had finished. She pointed to the audience applauding, which he also had not heard. But maybe Beethoven had known. Nathan could spend hours on such issues, if only he didn't have customers.

Robbie Herzog, who had not had a job for as long as Nathan had been running the copy store, walked in the door.

"How's the job hunting, Robbie?"

"Things are looking up," said Robbie, cheerfully tossing several sheets of paper on the counter.

"New résumé?"

"Yup. Thirty copies, please."

Nathan ran off the copies while wondering how a man who had never worked could have a three-page résumé. He charged him $3, which Nathan calculated would more than cover the shop's cost.

Then he was back to Oggún with his thoughts. Was it such a certain fate? Had Germany been doomed from the start? Was that why so many Germans wrote about the role of fate in history? Are Germans all damned? Is Karoline damned, too?

Oggún held his hammer and stared blankly.

Was it a coincidence that she had the same name as the singer? Karoline, Caroline Ungher. That was the singer who had told Beethoven the symphony was over. Why had he remembered that name? Cristofina would want to know. Dr. Kucher would certainly want to know. Was there something wrong, something perverse, in their relationship? And had it all been hidden for almost two centuries in a symphony everyone listened to but now he was hearing for the first time?

Unexpectedly, footsteps. Pepe Le Moko vanished behind reams of paper. It was Ira Katz, his shirtsleeves rolled up for summer.

"Hi, Nathan. Nice to see you."

It was interesting. What Dr. Kucher would have called a "clue." When Katz walked into his shop, Nathan experienced, for only the briefest moment, the feeling he had on subways. Suddenly the shop seemed very small and he was reminded that it lacked a rear exit. But unlike in the subway, the feeling passed very quickly.

"I'm sorry. I'm thinking about it, but I still haven't made up my mind."

"Don't worry about it, Nathan. This is my day off. I just wanted to come down here. You know, more and more, I just love this neighborhood. I think it's going to be *the* place. You know what I'm doing here?"

"Getting something photocopied?"

Ira slapped the counter and laughed loudly. "That's good! See, I just like the whole ambience of the place." He attempted the French pronunciation on "ambience." "No, Nathan, I am looking for an apartment," Ira said with tremendous enthusiasm. "I am ready to buy!"

Nathan stared at him with no particular expression. He wished that he, too, like Pepe, could just vanish behind the shelves.

"You don't happen to have any leads in the neighborhood?"

"Not really," said Nathan. "My parents own a lot of property, but they're not selling." Why did he say that? Now his father would have Ira Katz after him, too.

"Where do I find him?"

"He's definitely not selling."

"Maybe he just hasn't had a good enough offer. How do I find him?"

"He turns down great offers all the time."

"He's in the book? Seltzer?"

"Herchl Seltzer."

"Okay. I'll see you around the 'hood."

"Tell me, if this neighborhood is such a cool, happening place to be, why should we sell?"

The question momentarily froze Ira Katz in the doorway. He turned around and stared at Nathan. He seemed to be studying his molecular composition. Then he walked up to him, putting his face directly in front of Nathan's, as though he needed a closer look, and whispered, "For the money, stupid."

. . .

If he took only buses, how would he know when he was cured? So Nathan courageously descended the staircase to the Lexington Avenue line. The subway ride to Dr. Kucher was without incident, which he announced victoriously to Dr. Kucher, who then told him that it would not work like that. To herself, Kucher resented the way people looked for a quick cure and had no interest in the "road to self-discovery." Pulling on the too tight waistband of her skirt where it was strangling her low-fat-tea-cake-bloated belly, she told Nathan that he should not look for a cure. In time he would learn how to deal with the attacks. But she did think that testing himself was a good idea.

"Work with someone you trust."

"Trust to do what?"

"Trust to save you. Isn't that what trust is?"

Yes, Sarah would have understood immediately. If you trust someone, it means they can be depended on to catch you when you fall or pull you back when you start to go over.

"Why don't you try your wife?"

"How do you know that I trust my wife?" It was a short-lived victory, coming back at Kucher with a Kucher-like question. The moment was ruined by the eager way Kucher reached for her notebook.

"I was just joking," Nathan protested.

"Why do you find that funny?"

"I don't."

"You work with someone you trust. You allow yourself to give up control, go down in the subway, or other things, and he or she will be there to help you if it doesn't work out."

Nathan took out a small package and put it on her desk.

"What is that?" she said suspiciously.

"Try it. A present. It's called a *sün torta*. It has rum buttercream and walnuts."

He had made it with Karoline, but he had never told her a word about Karoline. He didn't know why, but he wanted to see if he could get her to eat the pastry he had made with his lover. Dr. Kucher's eyes widened and filled the pink glasses frames. They shifted to the corner of the desk where the package stood. Somehow she knew this cake was a trap. Just thinking of it made her belly press harder into the waist-band. When doing doctoral work in Vienna, she had succumbed to pastry. Not that she had been thin before. But studying in the afternoon in cafés, especially one called Demel's, had rounded her even further, which always made her laugh—a little joke—because her professor at Columbia had told her that study in Vienna would "round her out."

"Where does it come from?"

"The best baker in my neighborhood—" He started to say "a German" but realized that she was tricking him into talking about her. He had said enough.

Dr. Kucher tried to imagine the significance of the cake—also the flavor and texture. Behind her desk, she pulled her blouse out of her skirt to relieve the pressure, reached under the shirttails and pulled at her skirt to give a little breathing room, momentarily exposing soft, pink rolls of flesh.

Is she doing this for me? Nathan wondered, catching a glimpse. He thought she might be cute, all pink and roly and naked. Then he realized he was being perverse. "I think too much about sex," he confessed.

"Are you thinking about it now?" she asked, still thinking about *sün torta*.

"Of course, I'm talking about it now." Nice save, he thought to himself.

Nice save, she thought to herself, and wrote on the pad, "Typical agility." For the rest of the hour, she refused to look at the package. When the hour was up, she said, "Tell me something, what causes a slump?"

"A slump?"

"A slump. Everything is working pretty well. The pitchers are in form. The batters are getting on base, and suddenly Darryl Strawberry can't hit a ball. Why?"

"Look, this is the Mets. What do you want? They may win, but they are going to make you sweat for it."

"Think about someone to help you."

"I will."

"And try to remember your dreams."

"Oh, let me tell you about the cheese."

"Next week."

"Okay."

As he was walking out the door, he looked back and saw her opening the wrapper and examining the light and dark layers from several angles. She picked it up and took a bite.

"Oh my," he heard her say involuntarily, and she took another bite. "Oh, my God." She tasted again. "Mmmm . . ."

The human mind is like a thicket. Many things blow by, and it is almost impossible to predict which ones will snag on a branch and remain. And so, while riding the 6 train, not to his wife but to Karoline, the phrase that had stuck in his conscious mind was "or other things." Dr. Kucher had said, "Go down in the subway, or other things, and he or she will be there to help you." He wanted Karoline to help him with the "other things." He was even a little excited about his idea, until the train changed rhythms, began to mark out a slower beat, and then slowly . . . stopped.

The hiss of the air conditioner, more silent than silence, was all Nathan heard. That feeling, which was becoming familiar, rose from so deep within him that he could not discern the location. The search, a physical inventory, for the location of the synapse from which this sickening, jellylike panic oozed—this search offered a distraction. Was it from his stomach? Or was it from his chest? Were his lungs still working? Could they bring him enough air? Was his head, being pounded as though by a steel hammer, about to give out?

"Ladies and gentlemen, we have a train in front of us. We should be moving shortly." A good announcement. It was comforting. Now if they would only start moving he would be all right. In the meantime, was it possible that he had forgotten how to inhale? He could not recall ever having learned the technique. Now the skill might have vanished from his repertoire and he would suffocate, drown in his seat on the number 6 train. He opened his mouth and attempted to suck in. His lungs filled. Everything was working.

He felt a sudden jerk. The train had lurched a few inches, but then it stopped again. Why were they playing with him like this? He wanted to seize a conductor—where were they, anyway?—and vent his wrath. "You think this is a game! *Move this fucking train now!*"

Then the train began slowly rolling—an easy, soothing kind of roll. He would be fine. This was not so bad. He had dealt with it. He was learning, just as Kucher said he would. He wished Kucher said more. She was a sly one. But she had eaten their pastry. He could tell that she liked his dreams, but she didn't say why. Nathan thought about his new program "with someone you trust." Not the subway, but "other things." Someone he trusted would not be Karoline. But wasn't that the point? He could risk anything with Sonia. After all, hadn't they already risked marriage? And parenthood? But what would he risk with Karoline?

By the time the train reached the Astor Place stop, Nathan was smiling. He almost forgot to get off the train.

Karoline seemed most excited when she baked Hungarian. Hungarians were the true hedonists. It showed in their cakes. If she was going to mix sex and pastry, the Hungarians made the best cakes. But she expressed all this to Nathan simply by saying, "Haven't you noticed we're at our best when we bake Hungarian?"

"Best baking or best sex?"

She smiled and said, "The total performance is what counts. And I have something perfect today," she added while grating chocolate. "You are lucky, because this is not something I would do in the summertime. But we had a special order."

They were going to make a Rigó Jancsi. "It's perfect for us. In fact, this should be our cake. Like other people have a song."

Nathan realized that this was as close as she had ever come to saying something sentimental about them.

Rigó Jancsi, she explained, had been a Gypsy violinist from the Hungarian town of Székesfehérvár. Once again, she had perfectly pronounced the unpronounceable. "He had unruly dark hair that fell in clumps, soft dark eyes that always looked a little confused, a lean and slightly hunched body." Nathan wondered if she was deliberately describing himself.

"He was the kind of man you just wanted to touch, to grab by the throat, and to take, that way that women weren't supposed to. Rigó Jancsi was trouble. And worse, he played the kind of violin that was so sweet a sound, your eyes would just start shining like puppy eyes. When he played, he could destroy all your resolve.

"He moved to Paris and played in one of those restaurants in the eighth arrondissement"—she pronounced that perfectly as well—"with mahogany dividers and etched glass and art nouveau fixtures giving off amber light."

That a great pastry maker would also be a great storyteller was the kind of thing that would seem obvious only to a true pastry lover. It was striking that her artfully composed words could sound perfectly conversational, as though she were the Brothers Grimm, just chitchatting. For Nathan, the way she could tell a story was another one of those things, like her baking, like her pronunciation, that she did so well that Nathan knew he had to have this woman—that it couldn't stop.

"And people would come to this restaurant to be seduced by this Gypsy—not literally seduced, but the combination, the perfect balance of being melted by his violin while being warmed by the dark game dishes for which the restaurant was famous—venison stewed with its own blood and chops of baby boar with earthy-tasting wild mushrooms and slightly sweet little chestnuts. Then they were sent into near sleep by their cellar of old and black Bordeaux—people came there to be put into this very delicate and lovely stupor.

"Among the people who went to this restaurant was an aristocrat—a very wealthy man, very well-known throughout Europe, the kind of man who was clandestinely photographed for the European magazines that poor people read to dream of another world. A little bit older, but not bad looking. He was tall and had a very strong jaw for an aristocrat."

Karoline stroked Nathan's jaw as she said this, leaving him to wonder exactly what kind of jaw he had and how she would rate it. All the time she was telling this story, she was grating enormous amounts of chocolate into a very large double boiler.

"The princess herself was considered extremely beautiful but of a different type. Her hair was the color of vanilla satin and her skin was even lighter, delicate looking, like tissue, and her eyes were a brilliant, pale blue. She looked so white next to the Gypsy, it looked as though if he touched her, he would leave dark marks on her skin. This is what most shocked people later. It was 1895. They were all bigots then.

"The prince with the jaw and the white princess started coming to the restaurant every night. Every night Rigó Jancsi spent a little more time playing at their table while they sipped their Haut-Brion 1878—the last good year before the vineyards were wiped out."

"Save the wine part for the cops," said Nathan.

"No, I just save the wine for them."

But Nathan couldn't help but wonder if the story had that wine detail because she had practiced it on Joey Parma. Had she had him over to make Rigó Jancsi, too?

"The blond princess, the Princess Chimay, stared at the Gypsy violinist as though she were looking at a chocolate torte. She sipped her wine and ate her bloodied deer, the dark sauce sometimes lingering on her shiny lower lip like a dark stain against her white, white skin.

"The prince with the nice jaw noticed his wife licking the Gypsy with her eyes, but he was an aristocrat and he could not let anyone see him noticing—you know, like a WASP. He looked perfectly content with his perfect profile seated in their booth, eating and sipping and watching. He would quietly bring up fabricated anecdotes about their two little children to try to remind her that she had two little children whom he had always thought she loved very much. But she did not even hear him.

"Start separating about eight eggs," Karoline ordered Nathan. "One night, with all of the restaurant's fashionable clients watching, including several novelists who were not likely to overlook this, the blond princess slipped a ring off her finger—it looked like one of her eyes, a brilliant, pale sapphire, surrounded by diamonds—and handed it to Rigó Jancsi, who slipped it onto the smallest finger of his bow hand, not missing a stroke as he played Brahms's Hungarian Rhapsody. The prince did not flinch. Not even his eyes betrayed the least concern. But he knew his home had been destroyed.

"Beat the eggs stiff in that mixer. Not stiff, but to a soft peak. A little stiff, but falling over. You can use a little sugar. . . . The Princess Chimay started having secret afternoon meetings with the Gypsy in his little studio where he practiced the violin. He would play the violin and then take off her clothes and make love to her, and then, both of them naked in the bed, he would play more until she wanted him again, over and over again. Neither of them could stop. Soon she didn't care about the prince anymore. She didn't care about her two beautiful boys with blond hair and handsome jaws. She and the Gypsy ran off together. Disappeared.

"Now take about ten ounces of butter and put it in the other mixer with the paddle attachment on medium speed until it's all soft and smooth.

"The Hungarians heard this story because a Hungarian writer had been in the restaurant the famous night when Princess Chimay gave Rigó Jancsi the ring. And the Hungarians loved the story. Hungarians love pork fat and goose cracklings and eating big piles of whipped cream in the afternoon. And they love stories like this. A famous pastry maker in Budapest made a new chocolate *torta*—this *torta*—and named it Rigó Jancsi, and it became one of the most famous cakes in Budapest, making the love story even more famous.

"When Hungarians are cooking, they have trouble knowing where to stop. But in storytelling, they always know the exact right spot. So the Hungarians went on eating Rigó Jancsi with coffee every afternoon and never heard the rest of the story."

"What is the rest of the story?" Nathan asked anxiously, unable to decide which he wanted more, the story, the storyteller, or the story's cake.

Karoline handed him a pot of chocolate and a ladle. "Three ladlefuls slowly added to the butter while the paddle is beating. They ended up hating each other. To the princess, he was the man who had robbed her of her babies. And he, he felt like a prisoner. He *owed* her because of what she had given up. And she didn't leave with the family jewels. There was the ring and not much else, and he had to keep playing the violin in provincial restaurants because he couldn't work in Paris anymore. Finally he left her and went off to seduce other women and get other jewelry, and she was completely alone.

"It happened again. It wasn't clear if it was him or another Gypsy violinist. One of them ran off with an Englishwoman. She was not married and did not have two beautiful children and she married him and they made spectacular children with dark skin and blue eyes and they were very happy. That's a better story, but when it got to Hungary they invented another cake, a Jancsi kiss *torta*, which is not a very good cake and no one makes it anymore. Happy stories do not inspire great cakes."

Nathan, with improving skills, folded the whites into the chocolate and dusted flour on the top, folded that slowly into the batter, and then spread the batter on a baking sheet. Then he turned to have his storyteller, but she pushed him away. "No, that only bakes about eighteen minutes and we have to start the filling.

"There are only four things in the filling, so they must be in perfect balance. There are always these things that have to be balanced. The flavor, the texture, the sweetness, the richness. This filling is chocolate, which is the flavor. Chocolate is so strong that you cannot bear it by itself—strong and dark and almost overwhelming. So you add sugar to weaken it to the point where we can taste it. But just enough to taste the chocolate, not the sugar. Then you melt this with the cream. The cream gives richness, smoothness. And also it holds the air. If you have too much cream, it dilutes the chocolate. It becomes boring."

She poured the syrup of melted chocolate and cream into a mixing bowl and put the mixer on a medium speed. Steam rose from the bowl as the chocolate was cooled and beaten. "It takes some time. But not too much time. The air gives lightness, but if it is too light, it has no character. It is just fluff."

She watched the filling getting beaten by the machine, and Nathan watched her, longing to open her apron and touch her skin. Finally, she nodded her approval and reached up to shut off the mixer. Dipping her arm so that it disappeared up to the elbow in the mixing bowl, she scooped up a small amount of thick, light-colored chocolate on her finger and tasted it. "The cake's done. Take it out."

And he obeyed.

"This is perfect. It's everything we lack. It has balance. You and I, we are all chocolate. Maybe a little sugar. No cream. No air. It's inedible. That is what this relationship is. Out of balance and inedible." She reached behind and untied the top of her apron, exposing her breasts. Then she dipped into the bowl with both hands and rubbed the mousse on her breasts. Her body heat immediately started to melt the composition, and chocolate rivulets ran slowly down. "Come here. Try to eat it."

Kneeling in front of her, Nathan tried to lick her breasts.

"No. No," said Karoline, holding out her long fingers. "Fingers first."

Nathan carefully, systematically, licked her fingers, index to pinky and then thumb, same order on both hands. Then she grabbed him by the hair with her freshly cleaned fingers and pulled him to her breasts, where the chocolate was indeed a perfect balance, the bittersweet chocolate coming alive with the salty, buttery taste of Karoline's skin. But when he was finished, she gently shoved him away. "We have to finish the Rigó Jancsi."

With a rubber spatula, she lavishly spread the thick filling on half the cake, then covered it with the other half and spread melted chocolate on the top, stroking the chocolate with the spatula until it lay perfectly flat, like polished wood.

While he felt this way, wanting her, thirsting for her, was the perfect moment for his experiment. He told her about his claustrophobia, about his airless panic at being trapped, about Dr. Kucher's idea of experimenting with a friend, someone he trusted, little by little. . . .

"You want me to take you to the subway?"

Nathan shook his head no with a slightly anxious smile.

"What?"

"I want you to tie me up."

Confusion melted into a wicked grin on Karoline's face. "This may open whole new worlds for us."

"But you have to do it slowly. Step by step. And if I start to panic, you have to untie me right away. You have to promise me that."

She promised nothing, yet he proceeded. If he trusted her, why did she have to promise? This he thought was in itself a good sign. He was not afraid. She told him to sit in the straight-backed chair by the table. Then she produced some clothesline and tied his ankles to the chair legs.

"Are you all right?"

"Yes. Fine."

"You are sure?"

Just as Nathan was thinking that Karoline was curiously well prepared, as though she had done this before with other men, just then— she dangled in her hands a shiny pair of handcuffs.

"Are you ready?"

Nathan shook his head uncertainly. Gently, she snapped a cuff on his left wrist and pulled it behind the chair and brought his other arm around and attached the other cuff.

"But you will stop if I say so?"

She smiled enigmatically as she, magicianlike, presented a long green silk scarf and tied his neck to the back of the chair. Nathan could not move at all. And he had no idea what she might do next.

And yet . . . he felt no panic, no anxiety whatsoever about his situation.

"Are you okay?" Karoline asked.

"Yes," said Nathan with a hint of surprise in his voice.

Karoline lightly slapped his cheek. "Are you sure?"

"Yes."

She slapped him harder. His cheek stung. "You still sure?"

"Yes," Nathan said incredulously.

Karoline touched him between his legs to see if he was aroused. He was.

"Well, I am in control, and you don't get what you want. You know what you get?"

Nathan shook his head from side to side as she felt him becoming more excited.

"You get more pastry lecture."

"What!?"

"Quiet."

She walked to the refrigerator and took out a tall cake, long, spongy ladyfingers forming a circular wall. Dark red raspberries, like a setting of garnets, studded the top. After placing a slender slice on a plate, Karoline walked over to her prisoner and started feeding him forkfuls. "You see the contrast of textures and balance? The cake is spongy, the filling is thick and creamy. The filling has five parts—raspberries for flavor, custard for richness, gelatin for stiffness, and cream to hold air and give lightness. Too much of any one of these will ruin it. It's the tension between them that makes it. And that is what I want in my life. You just offer me the raspberries. Pure flavor without texture or richness or lightness or stiffness is worthless. But I have a man who wants to marry me. He keeps saying he is in love with me."

"What's the matter, no raspberries?"

She held out her hand as though she were about to slap him. "Unfortunately, you are right. He is everything that you are not. He has the right touch of gelatin. You have a bit too much. He has a nice custard, of which you have none. And he has the whipped cream you lack. Maybe too much. But you don't have any. And he also doesn't have a wife."

Karoline slapped him playfully on the cheek. "What would you say if your wife walked in right now?"

"I'd say, Thank God you've come. This woman has kidnapped me."

"And suppose we were naked on the bed?"

"And stolen my clothes."

"And forced you to eat raspberry cream."

"What would you say if the boyfriend showed up?"

"Come back later, dear, I'm busy."

"What's his name?"

"Dickie. It's a silly name. He's a silly man. All cream. No flavor. But he has money, and he wants to save me. And I need to be saved. I have to know that he could save me. You couldn't save me."

"From what?" Nathan said, though he understood exactly.

She took the key and opened the handcuffs. "From this place, this neighborhood, and you." But as though there were not a contradiction, she untied him and led him to the bed, where they made love in the weighty, sticky air of a New York July afternoon.

When it was time for him to leave—past time, he realized—he opened the door cautiously. "I have to be careful. I ran into your mother the other day."

Her cobalt eyes turned the color of steel. "She saw you leaving here?"

"She was in the stairway."

"You let her see you? What did you say?"

"I think I said, 'Excuse me.'"

"Oh, 'Excuse me.' That's very good! Someday I am

going to go to your apartment while your family is eating dinner and knock on the door, and when they answer, I'll just say, 'Excuse me'!"

There was her temper. There was her body and making love and the way she baked and used her hands. The way she told a story. The way she could pronounce any word in any language. But then there was her terrible temper, which was how it always seemed to end. Yet he had let himself get tied up by a bad-tempered woman. He was not doing that badly. He was still in control, he reasoned.

CHAPTER SEVENTEEN

A Ratlike Cunning

NATHAN HAD NOT CALLED Sonia all day, and now he was coming home late and carrying the scent of chocolate and butter and Karoline. Had she left any marks on him? He examined his wrists.

In the summer, when it was warm at night but felt cool in contrast to the day, the streets were full of people and the bounce of Dominican merengues and the throb of Puerto Rican *plenas* and the beat of rhythm and blues. On evenings like this, most people in the neighborhood were irresistibly drawn to the summer air, compelled to wander the streets purposelessly, like freewheeling sleepwalkers. In spite of himself, Nathan could not bring himself to hurry home.

Someone had put flyers on the walls and streetlamp posts. There were more of them along Avenue A than DUKAKIS FOR PRESIDENT signs:

DEPRESSED?
Homeless?
Worthless?
Medication treatment is available
AT NO COST as a part of a research study.
To see if you qualify, call
555-1848

An easy number to remember, Nathan thought almost subconsciously, assuming as he turned onto Tenth Street that almost everyone would recall the European revolutions of 1848.

There was a time when the drug trade operated at night on Tenth Street in discreet darkness. In the summers, buyers would wait until late evening for it to be dark enough to buy drugs there. Then, in the 1970s, every street in Manhattan got ultrabright streetlights that gave the night an unworldly orange tint. Still, you could feel anonymous in the orange sodium light of night: Everyone was orange. Tenth Street was a relatively dark street because there were few stores or restaurants; most of the storefronts had closed steel gates like the Meshugaloo Copy Center. But now, with a new Japanese restaurant and the new grocery store, which suspiciously remained open after dark, and a few other lit windows, the street had become bright at night. Instead of that driving the drug trade later into the night, it was starting earlier, since it was no longer dark after nightfall anyway.

During his drug-dealing days, Felix had liked standing on the street on these warm and active summer nights. It almost felt like Santiago or Santo Domingo or San Juan. He always thought of them in that order—the progression of cities that had led him to the Loisaida. Now he was a shop owner. He had changed the name of the store to East Village Gourmet. The owner of a gourmet shop did not stand on the street and did not have his shop open in the evening. Gourmet shops were for people who were free to do their shopping during daytime hours.

He knew staying open made him suspicious—more suspicious. But he did not want to stand there with the store closed. That would be worse. It was his store that showed that he was a shopkeeper and not a drug dealer. So he sat in front of his lit and nearly empty shop, massaging an egg with one hand, until it was late enough to go to the casita and play congas.

This was a hot summer, and in such summers the rats, like the tomatoes, grew to enormous size. They scurried up the trash cans and sifted through the contents, making slight rubbing sounds. Passersby could hear the rubbing sounds and, if they were local, would look for a tail. It was not unusual to see a slightly curved pink tail sticking out on top. Felix thought the rats were smarter than the cops, because the rats always found the grass.

Felix hated rats. Most people could barely hear the rubbing sound. But Felix could hear it from his shop with the door closed. Sometimes one of the Jews going to the deli would run over a rat while trying to park a long, black Cadillac. Felix admired the Jews, the way they would drive into the neighborhood, looking rich, looking as if their pockets were stuffed with cash, but secure in the understanding that the dealers would protect them. There was more money in dealing than mugging, so the dealers wouldn't allow anyone to be robbed on their block. Even these Jews from the suburbs knew they didn't have to be afraid here. Felix liked Jews. He felt bad about giving Seltzer's name to Joey Parma. But he shouldn't have been taking out Rosita. He had no pride anyway . . . the way he wore no socks. Felix congratulated himself on the Puerto Ricanness of this judgment. Besides, Felix was being squeezed, and no one would care about giving up Seltzer. Why was someone always squeezing him?

In fairness, the cops were as smart as the rats. They knew where the drugs were kept just as well as the rats did. But if they arrested a pusher and the drugs were not on him, he could not be charged with possession. Some of the dealers, preferring to face possession charges rather than rats, would not use the trash cans. Some put their stash under a corner of loose sidewalk concrete by a tree. But in time, the rats would find that, too. These rats were crazy for marijuana.

The amount of metal on some of the people he was seeing in the neighborhood this summer, including the drug dealers, horrified Nathan. Little silver rings were piercing their ears and eyebrows and belly buttons and nipples. To Nathan, the nipples were the most disturbing. You were out there on the street like that. Suppose you got into a fight? Dealers got into fights. Wouldn't someone tear those things right out of your nipples?

Nathan wondered if the girls who coyly displayed silver rings through their navels had rings in their nipples, too. He would see dark circles pressing the thin cotton of their tight sleeveless shirts and hope there was not a silver ring underneath. They had them in their noses and their eyebrows and sometimes tongues. And tattoos had made their bodies resemble the graffiti-covered walls.

Nathan saw a white delivery truck and he smiled. Everyone smiled at these delivery trucks. It was almost seven o'clock in the evening, a time when no one made deliveries. The truck was completely white with a hand-painted sign saying "Tom's Grocery Delivery Service." It was the FBI or DEA or, as the dealers like to say, the DUM, the local police. If they had the budget for the trucks, why didn't they have the money to hire real sign painters? This was one of the mysteries of East Village law enforcement.

Two men were inside, dressed in white aprons. One was Joey Parma.

"Joey," Nathan called out.

"Can't talk to you now."

"But this is silly. Everybody knows you."

"Get away from the truck. Better check up on your brother."

"Mordy? What's wrong with Mordy?"

"Get away from the truck. I'm not going to tell you again."

Nathan at last started to hurry—almost run. He was worried about Mordy, but also he realized that Sonia must have been trying to call him all afternoon to tell him whatever it was about Mordy.

Did the chocolate leave traces? Did Karoline? He tried to examine himself as he ran and almost stumbled on top of Arnie's pallet. He had forgotten about its new location.

"Hey, Nathan. Where you going?"

Arnie's usual weathered skin had an odd matte finish. "Are you all right?" Nathan asked him.

"I'm fine. I'm a little bit cold."

"It's ninety-five degrees."

"I know, but it gets cold for sleeping at night. The other block was warmer."

To people who didn't know the neighborhood, this might have seemed strange. But Nathan understood. The temperature in the neighborhood varied from block to block—something about alignment with the rivers or the angle of the sea breezes. New Yorkers never think about sea breezes, but they live by them. The coolest spot was the corner of Tenth and Second Avenue. A summer vegetable market set up in the Atlantic gusts of that intersection, but in the wintertime that was the intersection to avoid because of its bone-stabbing cold wind. Arnie's new block probably was a lot cooler than his old location. It would be bad in the winter.

"Do you need any blankets?"

Arnie pointed at the pile of wool that was his home.

"Okay. Take care." Nathan handed him $2 or $3, not exactly sure which.

"*Viva la huelga,* man."

"*Viva.*"

Three prospective tomato customers came to Felix's store. A quick glance at them made Felix regret he had stayed at the shop. They were uptowners and didn't fit in. Puerto Ricans recognized them as Dominicanos. Dominicans recognized them as trouble. It was a curious thing about uptown street criminals: Like undercover cops, they wore uniforms that made them easily identifiable. They had calf-length baggy shorts and tank tops and wore gold chains and gold rings, and in case anyone missed all this, they walked with the ghetto saunter. Chow Mein Vega once said it was a Jamaican drop beat, a reggae beat.

Everyone in the neighborhood watched the three reggae down First Avenue—dup-beep, beep—and across Tenth Street, to no one's surprise, straight to Felix's tomato store, the East Village Gourmet. Felix knew the smallest one, the one with the most gold, a man named Limon from a village near his. Limon used to operate in the neighborhood out of Bob's Greasy Hands. But the police had closed down the ribs store—no one saw them do it—and Bob was in prison, which made taking over his arrangement particularly unappealing.

"*Es acabado,* finished for this neighborhood, Limon," Felix argued while rolling a hard-boiled egg in his right hand.

"It doesn't look that way to me," Limon answered in Spanish, looking out the shop window at the commerce on Tenth Street.

"Not much longer," Felix said in Spanish. "It is not the way the neighborhood is going. There is more of a future in tomatoes than drugs."

"Tomatoes? You are worried about your fucking tomato business, Mamao?" Limon said menacingly, using the name Felix was known by before he left home. It was Limon's way of reminding him that he knew his family, knew where they lived, knew they were waiting for money from him, which he had stopped sending. The other two smiled nervously, because they were not sure they were supposed to really laugh at this.

"We are coming back with the shit, Mamao. And you're taking it."

They left.

Mamao had a gun. A good gun. Not a Saturday night special. A .38 like the cops had. Or .32, anyway. He had never fired it. He was trying to be a grocer. He flipped the egg in the air and caught it, rolled it between his hands to break the shell, peeled it, and ate it.

Harry was walking up Avenue A, not singing. He was worried about Mordy. At the end of the block he saw Nathan hurrying in his direction, and he was about to call out to him when he heard, "Hello, Harry Seltzer."

He didn't have to turn—didn't want to turn. It was Florence. "I can make you feel good again."

"No. Look. It was . . ."

"A mistake? Was it a mistake, Harry Seltzer?" Florence laughed, but it was easy for Harry to see desperation on her face and something else. She looked tired. It was, after all, a hard job. But Harry had his own desperation because family was walking toward him.

"Can't you leave me alone?"

"Couldn't you just give me a few dollars? Twenty dollars. Just give me a twenty."

"Here's ten," said Harry, but when he looked in his wallet, he had only twenties, one of which she grabbed.

"I'll bring you change."

Nathan was getting closer. "Keep it," he said, not looking at her and quickly walking away.

Nice man, Harry Seltzer, Florence thought.

Nathan, feeling fragrant in sweat, chocolate, and Karoline, greeted his father and was about to explain why he looked so disheveled, but his father said, "I was just out for a walk. Just enjoying the night air," and did not even seem to notice Nathan's appearance.

"What's happened to Mordy?" asked Nathan.

"He's not in jail," said Harry.

"Where is he?" said Nathan.

"I don't know. The cops had some kind of tip that they were dealing drugs out of his building and they raided it. But they only found one used bag of marijuana. They didn't take him."

Cabezucha stumbled past them, wild-eyed, his hair looking as if it had been charged with electricity, his head ready to explode.

"So they didn't press charges," Harry continued. "But the landlord, that son of a bitch Dubinsky who has been trying to get them out for years—this was his perfect excuse to get the police to throw them all out because they are squatters. He had another building of squatters that he set on fire. He is the criminal. He gives Jews a bad name. He plays right into the hands of the anti-Semites. Of course, the cops are anti-Semitic...."

When Nathan arrived at his building, he took the elevator to the fifth floor and unlocked his door, full of questions, explanations, and digressions. He had run into Harry. Mordy was all right....

But the apartment was quiet. Was no one home? Was he alone? He felt a familiar panic creeping up his chest, not the panic of a philanderer caught, but that of being trapped in a subway. His chest heaved as he exhaled the fear and resuscitated. Sarah was asleep in her bed, completely happy, certain of her safety. Sonia was sitting at her writing desk, stiffly, he thought, maybe angrily. This stirred the philanderer's breed of panic, but for a man who knew what true panic felt like, this seemed a minor attack.

Nathan entered the room armed with news of Harry and Mordy, but before he could say anything, Sonia said in a hoarse voice, "Is she attractive?"

"What?" said Nathan, stalling for an answer.

"Is she attractive?" Sonia repeated. Then he realized she was looking at something in her hand, a photograph. It was the broad, rough face of Emma Goldman. "Do you think she was attractive?"

"Not... no, I don't." He was trying to be careful because he still detected something stiff in her posture.

"She thought she was. And that's all you need. When she was young, she went places a woman alone didn't—unless they were prostitutes. So men were continually propositioning her because they thought she was a prostitute. But being continually propositioned, for whatever reason, started giving her the notion that men were attracted to her. And I guess it was true, because she always had lovers. Several at a time...."

Sonia was wearing a white shirt, and Nathan noticed dark spots on her back.

"Ménage à trois and all."

"You're bleeding!"

She turned around to face him or to hide her back. "It just goes to show that if you think you are attractive, you are."

Nathan turned her around. "Why are you bleeding?"

"It's nothing," she said, turning around again.

"What happened?"

"No. Nothing."

"Was it a customer?"

"It's nothing."

"What happened? Did somebody do something?"

"It's nothing! It's just stupid." She looked at him, and it was clear he would not be satisfied with this. "It's a butterfly."

"What?"

"It's a goddamn fucking butterfly. A monarch butterfly."

"A monarch butterfly."

"Yes. A stupid fucking monarch butterfly. It was all I could think of. Once when I was little, my parents took me to this valley that was completely covered with these orange butterflies. They were on the branches like blossoms. An orange lawn of them covered the ground."

"You mean it's a tattoo?"

Relieved, he started to smile.

"Yes, it's a fucking tattoo. Don't you dare laugh, you fucking gringo *pendejo*. You're the one who said they were sexy."

"A butterfly?"

"It was all I could think of."

"Let me see it."

"Leave it alone. It's bleeding and it hurts like hell. For a few days. Then it will be nice. Is it stupid?"

"I don't know."

"Don't tell your parents, okay?"

Nathan nodded. "Harry probably thinks monarch butterflies are anti-Semites." Then he thought of another tattoo. A spoon, dripping its contents.... Then he was jolted by a sudden revelation. Karoline must have gotten those handcuffs from Joey Parma!

CHAPTER EIGHTEEN

Stimulants

Nathan at last understood that a tiny window, not much more than a peephole, was located under his hair near his right temple. When Karoline came very close to him, as she often did before making love or sometimes even when they were lying together afterward, it was not so much to whisper in his ear, not so much because her warm, erotic breath against the side of his face made him want to have her again—though of course she was aware of this effect, also—it was that by being close to him, she could look in the little window and see all his thoughts.

This discovery made everything clear to Nathan. She knew how much he wanted her, how having her made him want her more, knew everything he was thinking. If he didn't want her to see a thought, he had to avoid thinking it. This kind of thing takes a great deal of discipline. The more you try not to think something, the bigger the thought becomes, the more visible it becomes in the little window.

He was dreaming about the moist, chocolatey afternoon they made three Sacher tortes. The awkward truth was that at the moment what he most wanted was for Karoline to reach down and undo his zipper and reach inside and hold his penis in her hand. He tried not to think this, which made him think about it more. Or did it make him want it more? Perhaps this wasn't a thought at all. Perhaps all these yearnings for Karoline were feelings that did not involve thinking and therefore could not be seen in the window. Still, deciding whether or not it was a thought was thinking, and Karoline would be able to see that. She saw the thought and so she did it.

And as the zipper was going down, Nathan suddenly remembered that his penis was made of chocolate. At least it was dark chocolate: 70 percent pure cacao, it had said on the label.

"Chocolate is never disappointing," she said, clearly able to see that he was thinking she would be disappointed. "It just lacks balance."

There was some music in the distance, and she stopped laughing and moved close again and lightly wet her lips and said, "I hold you." But she said it in German—"*Umschlungen.*" Why did he always have perfect German when he was asleep?

"Because you just make it up," she said, answering the thought she had just read. She held him very tightly and started to administer a very engaged kiss, first whispering in a husky voice, "*Diesen Kuss der ganzen Welt!*"—This kiss is for all the world! Now he was in the last movement of Beethoven's Ninth:

> *Seid umschlungen, Millionen.*
> *Diesen Kuss der ganzen Welt!*

Nathan woke up and his feet were flailing, or maybe goose-stepping. It was 9:15. Sarah never woke him up when he wanted her to.

Sonia was at her desk, writing.

"Sonia?" Nathan said as he quickly got dressed. "Do you think I would be stupid not to take Ira Katz's offer? Is it stupid for us to pass up the money? For Sarah?"

Sonia did not look up. "Emma would tell you that you would be stupid to do it. Surrender property to capitalist robber barons. Even Margarita—what would she say? She thought property should be nationalized. But certainly not sold to corporations."

"I see," Nathan said flatly as he left for his appointment. Emma, Nathan thought, would probably think that *we* were capitalist robber barons. Does the fact that we aren't any good at it entitle us to moral superiority?

He opened up the shop late. Carmela started to lean down toward him, and for a second he slipped back into his dream and thought she was leaning down to spy in the little window to his brain. "*Cómo 'tá',*" was all she said.

He opened the store so late that he soon had to close it, taking the little bag of pastry he had set aside, and run for the subway. "Getting something fixed?" he heard Carmela shout after him. The way he had been feeling, he should have taken a bus. But there was no time. Dr. Kucher started running her clock on the hour whether he was there or not.

The subway ride did not cause an attack, and he arrived at Kucher's on time, presenting her with "something from the neighborhood. It's called Rigó Jancsi and it's pure chocolate."

"You shouldn't be bringing me things," said the fluff of hair and pink glasses frames on the other side of the desk. "And you shouldn't eat chocolate."

"No, it's for you."

Judging from her furious note taking, it seemed Kucher was getting more from the sessions than Nathan. And his condition was clearly becoming worse. His problem was no longer subways. At any moment, anywhere, he might be overcome with this unapproachable, irreconcilable fear or be gripped with a desire to flee. He had felt it in his own apartment the night before when he first walked in and it seemed empty. "Why shouldn't I eat chocolate?"

"Stay away from alcohol, coffee, or chocolate. They can aggravate the condition," said the hair and glasses.

"And apricot preserves?"

"Apricots? Why apricots?"

Nathan noticed that Kucher answered every question with another question. He could do that, too. "Why chocolate?"

"Chocolate is a stimulant. Avoid stimulants. Why do you think of apricots?"

"They go well with chocolate, don't you think? I was just thinking about Sacher torte."

"Oh, my God, yes! I love real Sacher torte. When I was a student in Vienna I sometimes had it at Sacher's."

"Really? And did they do the preserves under the chocolate or split the cake in layers and fill the center?"

"Well, Sacher's split it, but Demel's used to . . ." She tugged at her blouse at the belly. Karoline had left the cake unsplit and had spread the preserves under the chocolate coating. She had said it was more "elegant." She thought Demel's did it right and Sacher's was wrong about their own namesake.

"We are getting a little off course here," Kucher asserted, trying to change her own direction. And she thought, This one has secrets that he isn't sharing. She told Nathan at the end of the session that he should take the cake.

"I can't," he said. "It's chocolate."

. . .

After he left, she decided to throw it away. Or give it away to the building staff or to the doorman at home. No, that would mean taking it home. First she wanted to look at it. She questioned her motives but argued to herself that it might contain some clue. Why was he bringing these cakes? She needed to know what kind of cake he was offering. She unwrapped it to look at. He was right. It was all chocolate. Very bad for claustrophobics. Great for everyone else, though. It was a layered square—a chocolate rainbow. A quarter-inch layer of a dark taupe color, then a rosy brown one, then another dark one, then the blackish top, which looked like solid chocolate. Yes, it was like a good, dark chocolate bar.

Dr. Kucher believed that she had concealed her irritation with Nathan. Even the patient who was trying to be "cool" was a better patient than Nathan. She wanted to point out to Nathan that therapy was futile with the kind of attitude he had. I know this neurotic, passive-aggressive, tied to mom's apron strings, have a cookie wise-ass is holding out on me, Kucher thought. He knows I'm dieting, for one thing. But she did not want to send him away, because he was interesting. Why had he brought up apricots? What did this mean? Cyanide in the pits? Or was it arsenic? She couldn't remember. Had he brought her something with apricots?

The cake would probably be best in a vertical bite. Oh yes. That was the way it was meant to be eaten. Oh my, yes. Mmmmmm. In one minute the Rigó Jancsi was gone. Dr. Kucher was tugging impatiently at the waistband of her skirt, lost in dreams of student days at Sacher's and Demel's with little layered confections that pressed against great white tides of whipped cream in the fast-darkening Viennese afternoon.

When Nathan got back to the neighborhood, he had that odd feeling that something had happened. The streets held a tension, almost an excitement. Someone had reached into the wrong garbage can, someone had come into the neighborhood who was not supposed to, it wasn't clear.

When he saw the three chalk outlines on Tenth Street, one on the sidewalk, two on the street, he knew. Carmela offered more details. Last night, in the cooling breeze down where huge rats scurried from gutter to trash can, where children played on the stoops and, Nathan always feared, would one day be bitten, someone had produced a small handgun and fired about six shots that scattered children and rodents. At first, most people, accustomed to firecrackers, did not react. But there were three men dead, two on the sidewalk and one in the street. By the time everyone realized what had happened, it was too late. No one saw who had fired the gun. The chubby boy with curly black hair, the Fat Finkelstein of his generation, had come back out and to the envy of his friends found one of the shells.

Nathan knew this about the boy because when he walked onto Tenth Street, instead of immediately running, the pudgy boy came up to him with a closed fist, which he opened briefly to show Nathan the shell. Then he closed his fist again and ran away. Self-preservation had been subordinate, only for an instant, to uncontrollable vanity.

At home, Nathan was confronted with a bored and restless Sarah. He sniffed the air dramatically. "Sarah. What's that?"

She stuck her small, turned-up snout in the air and worked it like a spaniel.

"*Sfogliatella!*" he declared, and thought of the delicate pastry crushed under his teeth, making the sound of a minuscule earthquake in his mouth and revealing what is at the center of culture and civilization— warm ricotta cheese. He loved *sfogliatella* hot out of the oven.

"From the cookie man?"

"No," said Nathan with as much energy as he could pump into his answer. "From Sal Eleven."

"I want to see the cookie man."

"No *sfogliatella*?"

"No. The cookie man." She liked visiting Moellen.

"Get your mother's apple strudel while you're there," shouted Sonia from the next room.

"Yes!" said Sarah, jumping out of her chair and half running, half stumbling, like a merry drunkard, to the door.

They walked to the Edelweiss, along Nathan's block of Tenth Street, where everyone was still talking about the shooting. Considerable curiosity had been stirred up because a police officer had gone into the East Village Gourmet. Most people on the block, including Nathan, thought the man running that store, Felix El Cuquemango, had something to do with the shooting, though the white outlines marking where the body had fallen were not in front of his shop. Nathan did not want Sarah around this. Surprisingly, she had not asked him about the outlines, and he wanted to get her off the block as quickly as possible, even though that meant going directly to the place where he most did not want to be.

As he walked into the Edelweiss, the only one behind the counter was Karoline's sad-eyed, soft-spoken mother. She nodded politely and said, "Just a minute," and walked noiselessly to the kitchen door. Nathan wanted to leave before she brought out Karoline, but what explanation could he give Sarah? Sarah always required good explanations. He had to be careful, because he thought Sonia was suspicious, and he did not want to do anything that would tell her where to direct her suspicions. And Karoline had threatened to approach his family— knock on the door during dinner. Nathan shuddered like a dog shaking off water. He was never sure what Karoline might do.

From the kitchen, Nathan could hear the blunt staccato of northern German. Even when awake, he could understand some German from his school studies and because of its similarity to Yiddish, which he also only sometimes understood. Mrs. Moellen seemed to be arguing for her husband to come out and talk to him. He was apparently reluctant, but she argued that he had been wanting to talk to Nathan and this was his opportunity.

"But you know who he looks like, don't you, Bernsie?" she whispered hoarsely.

"No, he doesn't, nothing like Viktor."

"He could be Viktor Stein to look at him!"

Nathan took Sarah's hand. "Let's come back later," he said. But Sarah sat on the floor, a human anchor to prevent his moving.

"Hello," came an enthusiastic voice from the kitchen. Too late.

"Vell, *meine kleine Gretel,* fresh from da forest. We have been baking your friends."

Sarah squealed with delight. "Who have you baked?"

"Vell, let me see," said Moellen the cookie man, placing a baking sheet on the counter. "Do you have a cat?"

Sarah earnestly nodded her head. "Pepe Le Moko."

"Oh, dat's a nice name. Vat kind a cat is dis?"

On the tray was an assortment of cookies shaped like reclining, sitting, or running cats. Some were frosted white, some were glazed in chocolate, others were chocolate and white. There were even a few calicos made with the addition of a caramel spot. All of them had emerald green eyes.

"Pepe is a black cat."

Moellen handed her a chocolate cat. "Here you go, you bad little girl, you can eat Pepe."

Sarah giggled as she reached up for the cookie. She looked at Nathan for permission and, taking advantage of a momentary lack of response, shouted, "Look out, Pepe," and started eating the cookie.

Moellen extended a long, artful hand, a hand, Nathan thought, not unlike Karoline's, and said, "Bernhardt Moellen."

He didn't click his heels. He did not even start to click his heels. But it was there in his stiff, proper manners. Nathan could feel it as he said, "Nathan Seltzer. I think I have known you all of my life."

"Yes, but we have never been properly introduced."

Why, Nathan worried, were they introducing now? "Yes, I always used to think of you as Mr. Edelweiss."

Moellen patted Nathan on the back and doubled over in a big wheezing laugh. "Edelweiss. Mr. Edelweiss. That would be such a silly name."

Mrs. Moellen, with her tear-scarred cheek, stared at them silently.

"I wanted to talk to you about something."

"I could come back later, without my daughter."

"Ach!" He shoved the idea aside with his large hand. "Dat does not matter, Mr. Seltzer. Dat is my point. You have a child."

"I don't think—"

"Und I am told you have a shop in the neighborhood?"

"Yes. A copy shop."

"So vhy do you never come to our meetings with the police where we try to convince them to clean the neighborhood so that drug dealers are not shooting people on da street and sings like dat, which are very bad for business?"

"You are right," said Nathan, suddenly gregarious. "I should come. When is the next meeting?"

"At three o'clock at the Boys Club." His face, voice, even posture, shifted as he looked toward the door. "Ah!"

The moment Nathan dreaded was now here. Karoline was standing in the doorway with a tray of pastry that glittered. The gems were little squares of Rigó Jancsi, the Rigó Jancsi they had made. Their Rigó Jancsi. Nathan felt as though she might as well be showing Sarah their bedsheets.

"Mr. Seltzer, do you know my daughter, Karoline?"

"Yes, I think so," said Nathan, and in trying not to look at her, he accidentally collided with her mother's sad stare.

"And this is his daughter, the *Kuchenschmecker.* She is trying to eat the neighborhood."

Sarah smiled what was intended to be seductively and said, "*Ihk been ayn Cookiescmecker.*"

"*Also!*" exclaimed the delighted Moellen in German. "And you are a *Leckermaul.* Do you know vat ist a *Leckermaul,* a sweet-mouth!"

"Tooth," his wife corrected.

Moellen smacked his forehead. "*Jah.*"

Sarah repeated, "*Leckermaul,*" and smiled a chocolate-smudged grin as she finished her cat cookie. "*Ihk been ayn Leckermaul, zout bedottin ik schone . . .*" Her German quickly broke into a combination of Yiddish and made-up syllables, a made-up language, though she seemed nonetheless convinced that she was speaking German. Soon she was singing, "*Bay dem schtetl schteyt a schtibl.*"

"Vat is she singing?" asked Moellen.

"Nothing, a song," said Nathan. He did not want his daughter being cute in front of Karoline. It showed how stupid he was for sleeping with her. Couldn't all this familial merriment stop? thought the increasingly desperate Nathan.

But Moellen was merry. "I remember you were a *Leckermaul* in your day, too."

"You have a good memory."

"That's my business." He pointed to his head with its thinning straight hair. "I have a very good memory."

"Yes, you do."

"Maybe Mr. Seltzer is still a *Leckermaul,*" Karoline teased with a perfect Prussian accent while Nathan cringed as though just smacked across the face. "Mr. Seltzer," said Karoline with laughter hidden so deep in her voice that only Nathan could hear it, "would you like to try a Rigó Jancsi?"

"It's Hungarian," said Moellen.

"No, thank you," said Nathan. "I'm not supposed to eat chocolate."

"How unfortunate," said Karoline. "And do you do what you are supposed to?"

"He can't eat chocolate," Sarah confided to Karoline with an earnest face, "because he's having a midwife crisis."

For a very long moment, the three Moellens studied Nathan. "Ah," said Karoline. "But you're not."

"No," said Sarah, breaking into a smile across most of her face as she quickly grasped the implication. Then she reached up and took a small square. As Sarah ate, Nathan was remembering the taste, and even while he felt desire firing from synapse to synapse across his body, he was resolving to end this before it was too late. End it now. He thought he saw a smile of approval from Mrs. Moellen.

Leaving the Edelweiss, Nathan looked troubled and Sarah looked very happy. "Look," she said, pointing her little finger across Avenue A. "There's Uncle Mordy, back from vacation!"

It was a squatters' demonstration, and Mordy was leading the other tenants who had been removed from his building, marching down the street with an inappropriate smile and his loose shoelaces flopping around his ankles. The others were all at least fifteen years younger than Mordy, who looked like the bizarre leader of a Boy Scout troop for misfits.

"Mordy, do you have a place to stay?" Nathan asked.

"I want to be in the parade," said Sarah.

"No, they threw me out on the street."

Sarah reflected on the image of being thrown in the street.

"So come stay with us."

"Thanks. I'm all right."

The police were gathering and watching the squatters, but most of the people on Tenth Street were more interested in the ongoing police investigation inside the East Village Gourmet. The policeman had not yet come out. Joey Parma was interrogating Felix.

"What species of tomato is this?"

"They are from Jersey. Rutgers. That is where they developed them. They are like beefsteak tomatoes but rounder. I lay down straw so that they don't touch the soil, and I grow them straight up on strings, cutting off all the side shoots. I pinch off the top, too."

"This is so delicious. It's too good for my mother's sauces. I heard that at Jean Jacques . . . You know?"

Felix tried to look as though he knew something about Jean Jacques.

"He does some kind of a reduction of tomatoes with sugar."

"A ketchup."

"No, not a ketchup. It's a reduction over maybe five hours and the sugar and maybe some vinegar. . . ."

"That's ketchup," Felix insisted, but he saw that he was irritating this slightly unpredictable cop. "Yes, these would be very good for that kind of thing."

"Yes, the intensity of the flavor. And they are all grown in Manhattan?"

"The originals were from right here in the neighborhood. But now I am getting them from casitas all over the barrio and the South Bronx. At home we grow them in between onion rows, which is better for the tomatoes. But here there is no room." Felix realized that he had just made a mistake, referring to "home," but this was of no interest to Joey Parma.

"It would be interesting to see if the Bronx or Manhattan has better soil."

"What you need for tomatoes is spring rain and summer sun."

"Just like wine grapes!"

"It's a vine. They are related."

"Still, soil has to make a difference. It does with wine. They had farms in all of the boroughs at one time. Probably farmers knew the difference in soil. Maybe you people do. Does it grow better in Manhattan or the Bronx?"

"We have a tradition of growing anywhere. San Juan is full of crops," said Felix. He had almost slipped, had almost given himself away by saying "Santo Domingo."

· · ·

His mother dragged the Fat Finkelstein of his generation into the Boys Club for the neighborhood association meeting—truly dragged him by the arm, shouting at him in Spanish as they struggled. Nathan had not realized that this Fat Finkelstein was Latino. The boy's recalcitrance turned to fear once he realized that Nathan was in the room. Did he think he was going to be forced to confess that he had been sticking out his tongue? Was that what he imagined to be the purpose of this meeting? Had Nathan Seltzer called the meeting to discuss his tongue wagging? His bright little dark eyes stayed on Nathan while his mother shouted at him.

Attendance, provoked by the three recent chalk outlines in the street, was considerably better than at the previous meeting. One indication of the new seriousness of the issue was that Sal Eleven had come. Before the meeting started, he made his way to Nathan and, standing to one side so that his words would go directly in Nathan's ear, explained, "The way I see it . . . ," waving his hand in the same gesture he used to dismiss everything in life.

Nathan waited politely for more, and when nothing came, he said, "What do you mean?"

"I mean, they can't shoot. You know what I mean? They are never going to hit anything but a window, and even that would be blind luck. They buy these cheap guns and they can't aim." He leaned closer to Nathan's ear and whispered, "I got insurance for my window."

When Nathan stepped back and looked at him, he nodded his head emphatically. He meant what he said. His window really was insured. It was a particularly curious attitude, because Sal Eleven spent the entire day behind his counter directly in front of his insured window.

"But three men are dead on the next block."

Sal gave a big dramatic shrug.

"You mean someone in the neighborhood did it? To get rid of the dealers?"

Sal would only shrug and say, "I think they were shot by someone who knows how to shoot." Then Nathan realized what he was saying. Sal thought the Mafia had killed the drug dealers. But why would they leave the bodies? A warning?

Once the meeting began, Sal became silent. He had said everything he had to say, and it was for Nathan's ears alone. Why had he come?

People were sitting in tan metal folding chairs. At the front of the room was Joey Parma and a uniformed officer, a broad-shouldered giant of a man with close-cut blond hair and the suggestion of a pot-belly on the front of his huge frame. His name was Lipinski. A man was talking whom Nathan always thought of as Doberman, a wiry man with thick, smudgy lenses on wire-framed glasses mended at one stem with tape, a man Nathan never talked to because he kept two, possibly three ferocious-looking black Dobermans who pranced down the street with chain-link collars, looking primed and ready to kill. It was always ru-mored that he beat those dogs to make them mean.

Doberman insisted, "You cannot deal with the problem unless you attack it at its roots." Quite a number of people agreed with this, and he felt encouraged to talk on. "If you are not willing to take on the causes, you ain't gonna solve nothing."

Even more people agreed with this.

"The truth is, there are too many foreigners in the neighborhood—"

Bedlam erupted. The Puerto Rican women started shouting at the Dominican women. Spanish Fat Finkelstein's mother was trying to ges-ticulate with the same arm that imprisoned her son, the boy shaking as she made her points.

"I have said before," Moellen began, standing near the slouching police in his customary erect posture that made it seem, by comparison, that he was the one wearing a uniform. "This kind of thing is very ugly and not at all helpful. I don't know vhy you come here to say dese sings. I think you should leave, Mr. Hansen." He fixed his eyes on Doberman as though they were lethal weapons.

So Doberman was Hansen. Edelweiss was Moellen. The Fat Finkelstein of the new generation was Latino.

"Foreigners," Doberman insisted. "When I say foreigners I don't mean foreigners. I don't mean people like you. I mean these other peo-ple. People who don't have American values. Who don't want to work."

Shouting erupted again and was broken by a quivering voice, a voice that silenced with frailty rather than strength. It was Jackie, the performance artist, in his or her long wig and violet-and-yellow or-gandy dress.

"Oh, perfect," scoffed Hansen. "Look what country we hear from now."

Sal Eleven looked at Nathan and shook his head and dismissed it all with a hand gesture.

Jackie raised his or her eyebrows in a mock glare. "I wish to say something!"

"Yes, let her speak," said Moellen, though most of the others were saying let *him* speak. Then there was some laughing. Hansen sat down.

"Officer Lipinski," he or she began. Lipinski nodded. "It certainly is hot today. Do you know this entire week has been a record? They are advising everyone to stay home. But you can't stay home in my building. Do you know why?"

Lipinski shook his head cooperatively.

"There is no air-conditioning. The wiring in our building is so bad—so old that you cannot use air-conditioning. It is probably a fire hazard. It's against city regulations."

"I'm sorry, but this is for the housing authority."

"All you have is excuses."

"This isn't a police matter."

"Drugs are supposed to be a police matter," someone shouted.

"How about guns?" someone shouted.

Sal turned to Nathan and shook his head sadly. "They've got to get proper assurance."

"Insurance," Nathan offered.

"All kinds of surance."

The Puerto Ricans were shouting in Spanish. Suddenly Moellen said, "Why don't we listen to these people." He turned to them and started speaking Spanish. It didn't sound like their Spanish. It sounded like a combination of Italian, Spanish, and German.

Slowly, from the gut, a sense of panic began to overtake Nathan. He had to get out of this room. No, he had to try to master this. He had to try to stay.

Moellen was translating for the mother of the Spanish Fat Finkelstein, who was still directing his trapped and terrified gaze at Nathan. The mother said she had "evidence" and demanded that the boy produce the shell, but the boy insisted he had lost it. With an open hand she swatted him on the head. He began to cry but still insisted he had no shell.

"It's not important," said Lipinski. "We are not looking for evidence."

"Exactly," said one of the Puerto Rican women in suddenly discovered excellent English. "You are not looking for evidence. You are not making arrests."

"I meant at this meeting we are not looking for evidence. We could make arrests. But it wouldn't help you. The only thing that would help you is if I could place a few officers on the block twenty-four hours a day. The plain truth is that I don't have the men."

"All the men are in richer precincts."

"Maybe. I don't know. I have to work with what I have. I'll tell you something else. There is no judge in Manhattan that is going to send a pusher to prison for retail trade. You know, small amounts. They want the wholesalers. We can arrest them and hold them a couple of days until a judge gets to them, we can make it pretty ugly for them in the bullpen those two days, but all the judge is going to give them is an impressive-sounding suspended sentence. They know it. All they have to do is not get caught with a big quantity. If we could find some big stash, that would be different. But really big. So we watch them."

"What about that Gourmet?" someone shouted.

Lipinski looked at Joey Parma with confusion. Joey whispered to him, "Puerto Rican vegetable shop on Tenth Street. The best tomatoes in New York. I'm trying to get him to grow baby vegetables. You know, these little tiny zucchini and—"

"What do these people want with him?" Lipinski whispered back.

"Don't know. Some kind of prejudice, I guess. Don't worry about it."

Nathan was watching the two policemen and wondering why Karoline had Joey Parma's handcuffs. He was so focused on this thought that his feeling of panic had subsided, though it was being replaced by anger.

Doberman was saying, "What does she care? When we didn't have these people, when we just had working people in the neighborhood, we didn't have this."

Fury showed in the woman's eyes. Her son was restless and wanted to roam, and she held his one arm as though he were tethered. "I am a working person."

"Don't let's get excited," said Lipinski. The woman turned and said something in Spanish to her friends, who hurled wild gestures and a deluge of undeciphered words with trilled r's at Doberman.

"Stop this," Moellen said with a quiet authority. "What good does this do?" He turned to the man behind him. "I know you are implying that this woman cannot be trusted because she is Spanish."

"Oh, give me a break."

"No. That is what you are saying. But we are all living here. We are all raising children here. I raised them here. This is a good place."

Then Moellen raised his voice. "I'm sorry to say this, Officer Lipinski, but we are here because we want the police to do more. You should be doing more. We know that the police can do many things when they want to stop something. There are dangerous criminals in the open on our streets. You don't like the people in the park. But it is the ones on the street that have guns. You see them there."

"We are trying, Mr. Moellen. . . ."

But Nathan was having two other conversations in his mind. One was about ending his relationship with Karoline—before it is too late, he kept telling himself. The second was about Karoline with Joey Parma's handcuffs.

"You know what they do?" said the Puerto Rican woman. "They don't arrest them. They just watch them to see what they can find out. Who they work for. As long as they stay out of nice neighborhoods, they don't touch them. That's how they get their information to protect the rich people in the good neighborhoods."

"You know," said Moellen, "that sounds very reasonable. Maybe you do do that, Officer Lipinski. But I want to tell you that this is a very nice neighborhood also and we need your help."

"Well," said Lipinski, "the first thing you have to understand is that I and the other officers in this precinct do care about this neighborhood. But we don't run the department."

The meeting went on a little longer, but it didn't seem to resolve anything. It didn't even appear that anybody expected anything to be resolved. As they were walking out, Moellen extended his long, bony hand and arm, which was sinewy from a lifetime of kneading dough, to Nathan.

"I like this country," Moellen declared again as they walked down the sidewalk. "Everyone comes from everywhere and it doesn't matter. That's why I had to stop that man who was talking that way to the Spanish woman. You cannot let that kind of thing start. Believe me, I know."

"From Germany."

"*Jah*. Terrible times. Terrible. People who didn't live it will never know."

"Yes. Other people have told me that, too."

"Oh, it's true. Un-i-ma-gin-a-ble." He stretched out the word as though each syllable had a special meaning. The two barely noticed the cacophony surrounding them. "Smoke, smoke?" Everyone was being asked but them. They glided down Tenth Street invisible and untouchable.

"Where were you during the war?" Nathan at last had the opportunity to ask.

"In the German army." He sighed. "Like everyone else." There was a small polite smile. Nathan remembered that Nusan had predicted that line. "You had to go. There was no choice. Terrible time. Well, I wish we could talk more, but my wife is not feeling well and I better look in on her. I'm very glad you came. With your little girl, you need to be concerned."

Nathan had to see Karoline. He had to end it now. This afternoon. But he could not walk there with her father, so he said good-bye and headed to his shop. The Spanish Fat Finkelstein suddenly ran up to him, gave him a defiant stare, and stuck out his fist. In his hand was a small copper bullet shell. The fist closed over it again and he ran into his building.

CHAPTER NINETEEN

A Plucked, Ripe Fruit

THIS WAS THE SUMMER of tomatoes. Everybody had them. Perfect ripe fruit—crisp, with deep cavities of juice and flavor so rich that you could smell it the second the fruit was cut into. The people at the casita sold them to Felix and still had extras to give away. Felix had few customers, because everyone continued to believe that he was involved in drugs. This belief was oddly unshaken by the fact that Felix's best customer was a policeman. Joey Parma had made it his mission to distinguish between Manhattan, Bronx, and Brooklyn tomatoes. He thought the "local crop," the tomatoes grown in the East Village, were the best. Felix was hoping he could interest others and so labeled these "Loisaida Jugosos." He also sold Barrio Rojos and Bronx Grandes, of which there were several subspecies, including Kratona Park Beefsteaks and Prospect Avenidas and Kelly Street Plums.

Upstate and New Jersey tomatoes were cheap at the Tuesday market in front of St. Mark's Church—with its breezes, the coolest spot in the neighborhood. But casitas all over New York were getting repaired and painted with the money Felix was paying for tomatoes. He barely made a profit selling them, but he was certain that in time he would become established as a grocer. The Casita Meshugaloo put its tomato earnings into a good tin roof and new speakers for the music and a fresh coat of turquoise and red paint.

Many people got free tomatoes at the casita. Those that Felix didn't buy, Chow Mein gave out to the many single mothers of the neighborhood. Palo always silently delivered a box along with a tall bunch of white, pink, and yellow snapdragons to Dolores, the mother of the Spanish Fat Finkelstein of his generation. A box held far more than she and her chubby little son could eat, and a few would go bad and end up in the garbage, where her son found them. He liked to throw them against walls and watch them splatter. One day he barely missed Jackie, the woman who might be a man, who was fanning him- or herself on the brownstone stoop. He or she became very angry and frightened the boy away but later termed Spanish Finkelstein's attack an act of protest. True theater. A dramatic visual representation of rage. He or she designed a poster to that effect with a close-up, black-and-white photo of a smashed tomato and took it to Nathan's shop to have several hundred printed, which would then be posted on walls throughout the neighborhood. "Really," he or she explained to passersby, "we should all be out here throwing tomatoes." Then Jackie fanned him- or herself feverishly with a stack of flyers as though overheated by the very idea. Jackie often referred to the heat, and though it was more than ninety degrees, and though most people guessed that Jackie probably was male, he insisted that the problem was that he was menopausal.

The three Sals grew tomatoes in gardens in Brooklyn and said they had not made such good sauce since they left Palermo or, in Sal A's case, Catania. They also sold them fresh. "Listen, you want some tomato?" Sal Eleven would say in the same way he pushed mozzarella the rest of the year. Another change to his shop was the mounted head of an American bison that was now hanging above the cash register. "Twenty times a day I got some smart popping in here wanting to know if my mozzarell' is made from buffalos," he explained to Nathan.

"Isn't that the wrong kind of buffalo?" Nathan suggested gingerly.

Sal made an upward gesture with his thick right hand. "What are you, another smart? That guy over on Avenue A isn't even Sicilian and they buy his mozzarell'."

"I thought he was from Catania."

"Whatever. Catania, that's a place to be from?"

On Avenue A, Sal A announced, "The tomatoes are in. Vine-ripened. Real Italian tomatoes, from my garden in Brooklyn." There was this widely accepted notion in New York that Italy was located somewhere in Brooklyn.

The summer was moving on. Dukakis, at last, was officially nominated at the Democratic convention and was still comfortably ahead in the polls. The Mets were also comfortably ahead in the Eastern Division, despite occasional two- and three-game slumps or, as Dr. Kucher insisted, "neurotic episodes" when it seemed that no one could hit the ball.

Nathan and Karoline's plans to give each other up remained elusively in the near future. Their hunger was insatiable and, worse, it was addictive. The more they had each other, the more they wanted each other, beyond reason, beyond any sense. That irrationality felt as good as sex. Maybe it was the best part of sex. They could make love for hours, get up, get dressed, and then at the doorway decide to do one more. If they were dangerously short on time, that made it even better.

The summer air, sluggish and chewy as caramel, had the sweet-bitter smell of things rotting and things cooking—of last night's chicken bones and fish heads, and frying *cuchifrito* and potato knishes, of Greek and Italian and Israeli sandwiches, and decomposing mango and orange peels.

Sonia was walking down Avenue A in the white heat with its odors, passing lightly clad women and shirtless men with lean, hard bodies that she liked to look at. Nathan was right. Tattoos could be sexy. But Nathan wouldn't get one. It is always the woman who makes the sacrifices. And it really hurt. She remembered how much that little butterfly had stung her back, but she was trying to imagine what Emma could say to Margarita after Margarita announced that she had come from the nineteenth century and intended to live in her house. Sonia had a pen and pad in her hand in case the missing line came to her. After that, the play would fall into place. Alongside her was Sarah, struggling to keep up with her mother's pace, holding the one free hand and also her own notebook and purple pencil.

Sonia saw a couple walking toward her. Both had identical black jeans and black T-shirts and close-cropped hair dyed an acrylic white. But she could tell from the difference in size and shape that the black silhouettes moving toward her were a man and woman. They were holding hands—but not quite. No, they were swinging their arms in unison. No . . . it almost appeared that . . . they were handcuffed together. Just an illusion, Sonia thought. Yet there were reasons why she would see such a mirage. After all, isn't that what marriage is? Consenting to be handcuffed together for life? It wasn't necessarily a bad thing. People could be happy that way. Her parents were. Margarita had been.

Or had she? She had been seventeen when she married Juárez, who was thirty-seven. . . . Thirty-seven. Nathan's age. Emma would have never let herself be handcuffed.

By now the matching couple was close enough that she could see it was not a hallucination, they really were wearing handcuffs. And both had leather, chrome-studded dog collars on their necks and large silver rings piercing the septums of each of their noses. Was all this the naked reality of marriage—or only the handcuffs?—and the dog collar. . . .

"Hello, Daddy!" said a delighted Sarah.

Sonia turned from the shackled couple and saw Nathan standing in front of her with a look of fear.

"Hi! Where did *you* come from?" asked Sonia.

"I was looking for linzer tortes," Nathan said, buttoning his thin cotton shirt.

She looked at him uncertainly. "Those dark little pies with the raspberry jam?"

"Yes!" Nathan answered with an odd overdose of enthusiasm.

Then she realized that they were in front of the Edelweiss.

"Let's get some from the cookie man," Sarah said cheerfully. "Look, there they are." And she pointed in the window, where sitting in a neat row were three five-inch crusty pies—thin, with latticed crusts and dark, jammy holes that in places had bubbled reddish on the pastry.

"My God, she knows everything about pastry," Sonia muttered.

Nathan looked guilty.

"She's going to end up with tellas like you," Sonia added, poking him in his side, but there was nothing there. "Where did they go? Have you been working out in secret?"

Sarah and Sonia were both staring at him. Sarah started writing something in her notebook.

"No," said Nathan with disdain. "These are all wrong. The pastry should be dark with cinnamon."

"Let's get some, Daddy. Shall we?"

Cabezucha ambled by slowly, looking almost like a sleepwalker.

"*Buenos tardes, Sr. Badígo,*" Sonia greeted him.

He didn't answer.

"You know him?" Nathan asked with surprise.

"Why don't we get a few?" said Sarah.

"You think too much about pastry," Sonia said to Nathan. "I wonder why you aren't getting fat."

"Protein!" Nathan announced a bit too earnestly.

"What?" answered a perplexed Sonia.

Too late. He had to finish it, so he halfheartedly explained as they walked past the pastry shop, not daring to turn his head to her on the left or to the shop on the right. "I eat a lot of protein, and it has amino acids that break down fat."

"Really. Where did you learn that?"

"I don't know. I . . ." Nathan paused to look back at Cabezucha in his slow, somnambulist's stagger. "You know him?"

"I gave him a massage. What did you say to Katz?"

"Katz?"

"Daddy, let's have linzer tortes," Sarah whined, beginning to realize that she was not getting her father's attention.

"You said you were going to talk to Katz about the shop," said Sonia. Going to see Katz had become a standard explanation.

"*I want linzer tortes!*" Sarah shouted. And then over and over again, the chant of her militant action, the slighted Sarah protested, "I want linzer tortes, I want linzer tortes . . ." Nathan was sure that she could be heard inside the shop by Karoline's parents.

"We are not getting any linzer tortes!" he shouted at his daughter, who retaliated by wailing loudly.

Sonia stared at her husband. "You didn't have to shout at her like that, Nathan."

"Miss Moellen?" said the muffled voice in the plastic box on the wall.

Karoline's instincts, which seldom failed her, told her not to answer. But curiosity overruled fear. "Yes?"

"Can I come up? I want to talk to you."

"I'm sorry, who are you?"

"I want to talk to you about my husband."

Karoline pushed the button and heard the door open downstairs. So he finally did tell his wife. And now she was going to have to endure this. Why couldn't she have just married Dickie? She could have started her pastry shop. It would have been written up in the *Times* by now instead of her having to endure this conversation she was about to have. Holding open the door she let in a well-dressed woman who chimed with jewelry. Attractive, Karoline thought. She had a nice body, and it looked good in her expensive linen suit, though she was not at all what she had expected of Nathan's wife.

The woman looked around the apartment judgmentally. Karoline guessed that she didn't think much of it. She probably didn't bake. Of course, that was part of her own appeal. Nathan was married to a woman who couldn't bake.

"I want you to leave my husband alone."

"Fine, tell him to leave me alone." Karoline had thought she would be nicer. But she was angry. Why did they always have to tell their wives?

Billows of water like lenses covered both eyes. The woman tried not to blink, because she knew that if she did, tears would spill down her cheeks. "So it's true."

"I'm sorry."

"Are you?" The woman turned around and opened the door. "You can tell Joey not to bother coming home." And she ran down the stairs.

Joey? "Wait!" Karoline called after her. "Are you Joey Parma's wife? I thought you were someone else."

Mrs. Parma almost laughed at the preposterousness of that line. "Original, though," came her involuntarily pronounced judgment.

Fridays were particularly difficult for Nathan that summer. It seemed to be the busiest day in the shop, he was almost always needed for the minyan on Sixth Street, and there was pastry to be made.

Nathan's family found that he had mysteriously discovered a talent for making pastry to correspond with his passion for eating it. From his point of view, if he made the Friday night dessert, he was not required to go to the Edelweiss to buy one. And he liked making pastry. He thought of selling his shop and opening a bakery. What would Karoline think of that? In truth, Ruth and Harry were both a little disappointed with their son's new hobby, because they liked the Edelweiss's apple strudel. But they tried to resist complaining, since there was a long-standing accusation that Harry belittled Nathan's creativity. Nathan had tried to get Karoline to teach him strudel, but she didn't make it. The strudel was always made by Mr. Moellen, the dough stretched over his long, bony arms where hundreds of strudel leaves had been stretched to translucent thinness before, by a gentle pounding motion from underneath that he had not taught his daughter. Nathan preferred making pastries that he did not make with Karoline. He did not want to share her with his family. She was his own private folly.

Every day there was news of the heat wave, of temperatures higher than a hundred degrees. But it didn't matter. In New York, once it got over ninety-five everything hurt. The heat crashed down from above, ribbons of searing white light that silhouetted the tops of the buildings, sparkled on the pavement, and bounced back up. Everybody who could stayed off the streets. Even the drug dealers did not come out until evening.

Casualties were reported—usually elderly people who died of strokes or heart attacks. People like Nusan. Nathan would check on him, though he hated doing this on a Friday because it meant that he would have to escort him to the synagogue on Sixth Street and then he would be forced to stay for the service. Nathan hoped that if he went by early enough in the day, he could leave before it was time for services. So he hurried through his morning work, closed the shop early, finished off the *kugelhopf* he was baking in spite of himself, and scrambled into a taxi.

The driver, with the name of Am Islam, drove as though his taxi were a wide-bowed ship with a loose rudder—steering far to the right, then overcompensating to the left. The one advantage of Am Islam was that he got Nathan to Rivington Street very quickly. Nathan had him stop a block away from Nusan's building. Though Nusan had no view of the street from his apartment, he did sometimes rest on the front stoop in hot weather, and Nathan wanted to avoid the lecture about not walking like everyone else, which was certain to lead to a reference to a death march, which he never explained.

Nusan was not on the stoop, but in his apartment with his hat and scarf on. He seemed in a good mood. When Nusan was in a good mood, he did not smile or seem happy. He was simply more energetic than when in a bad mood.

"So, ready for lunch?" Nusan asked.

Nathan, who had not counted on lunch, ignored the question and made his way over the papers and other rubble that filled Nusan's apartment, to the window, which he opened. Although Nusan had an air conditioner, it was on the floor by the window, covered with piles of papers and making it that much more difficult to open the window. Harry had bought the air conditioner for Nusan, thinking that even though Nusan refused anything that he perceived as a luxury, if Nathan delivered it, there was a chance that Nusan would use it. Nathan believed that he would be no more effective than a deliveryman, that Nusan would argue, "When you have experienced real cold, you don't mind a little heat."

But Nathan had been wrong. Actually what Nusan said was, "Who am I to be spared a heat wave? Millions of people all over New York are suffering. I hear it on the news. It is in the newspaper. But now Nusan Seltzer is so special, he stays cool. Too good to sweat. This is from your father. I know. Your father thinks he is too good to sweat. Because he is an American, because he is safe, he should not sweat like everybody else."

"It's really hot out," said Nathan.

"So, kreplach or pirogi?" Nusan answered.

Any of Nusan's places would be unbearable today. "Look, Nusan, how about ravioli?"

"Ravioli? Who are you with the ravioli?"

"It's okay to have ravioli, Nusan. In Italy the poorest people eat ravioli. Really miserable people eat ravioli in Italy."

"What's with Italy?"

"Come on. You'll like it. It's little pieces of dough with cheese inside."

Nusan shrugged. "So what's not to like?" It always surprised Nathan when Nusan was agreeable. He couldn't help suspecting that Nusan chose to be agreeable every now and then just to throw people off balance. The real clue to Nusan's moods was his sleeve, and on this hot day he was keeping his tattoo covered.

But on the way out he shoved up the sleeves of his jacket. Then he tapped the right doorpost. That tap always irritated Nathan. If he wanted a mezuzah, why didn't he put one up?

They went to DiFalco's, a dark little place with tile floors and auto-graphed pictures on the wall. It was certain without looking that one of the signed pictures would be Vic Damone, another would be Frank Sinatra, and that several of the records in the jukebox would be versions of "My Way." Nathan ordered himself a salad and Nusan ravioli in butter. Nusan seemed happy. He liked the way they kept filling the bread basket. Each time, Nusan would take a roll and shove it in his jacket.

"So, I have good news for you."

When Nusan said this, it was never good news. "The Mets have lost two in a row," Nathan argued.

"Dave Johnson," said Nusan, referring to the Mets manager, "said the team has an affliction. An *affliction.*"

"But they're still in first place."

"For now. Clark's not hitting. Strawberry's not hitting." Nusan pushed up his jacket sleeve, not to expose his tattooed number, not to cover up the little label that said "100% pure wool," but as his way of saying, "Now to business." He leaned forward so that he could be heard in a whisper. "There was never an SS Standartenführer Bernhardt Moellen."

Nusan had surprised Nathan again. It actually was good news. "You are sure?"

"Absolutely." Then he smiled. When Nusan smiled . . . "There was a Reinhardt Müller, as I told you."

Nusan clearly enjoyed the look of dismay on Nathan's face.

"But he was never a *Standartenführer,* either." He deliberately gave Nathan a moment of relief before adding, "He was only an *Obersturm-führer,* a lieutenant."

"In the SS?"

"Yes," said Nusan, feeding a breadstick into his mouth like a carrot into a juicer.

"Could be somebody different."

"Could be. Could be the camps were only a dream. I think that sometimes. I think that I am glad they tattooed me, because now I can look at my arm and say, 'Look at this number.'" He turned his arm over and looked at it. "'Look at this. I wasn't dreaming. It really happened.' That's like the Germans. You know what I think? I think they did the tattoo so they could prove it. They want the documentary proof for everything. Germans understand that nothing exists without documentation. They preserve their facts even when they are things that anyone else would hide. I am one of their artifacts. But your pastry maker? He could just be an illusion. A mistake. Tell me, did he ever say anything about Argentina?"

"Argentina?"

"Yes. Reinhardt Müller was last seen in Argentina."

Was that why Moellen spoke that lilting Spanish? "No," said Nathan, "he has never said anything about Argentina. It's probably not him."

There was no more heat, no more temperature, that day. Nathan wandered the streets with Nusan lost in a world that ended before he was born. Yet it was a world he sometimes lived in. Nusan made him feel that they all wore blank spots on their arm where the tattoo was missing.

Why did the Nazis tattoo? Was it as proof, or was it just to mark them? Was it because they understood that tattoos were against Jewish law? Leviticus: "You shall not make gashes in your flesh or incise any marks on yourself." It was the same passage that forbade trimming sideburns. It also outlawed rings in your nipples. Tattoos were no more against the law than trimmed sideburns, than not wearing *payess.* There was a time when you could rebel by trimming your sideburns. Mordy thought *not* trimming his sideburns was rebellious. If he had lived back then, he would have shaved them off. Today, you had to wear tattoos and a ring in your nose or, better yet, three or half a dozen on your lip or one through the nipple just to do what you once could do by a little sideburn trim.

Nathan had found a forgotten law in Leviticus near the one about marking flesh: "Reprove your kinsman but incur no guilt because of him." Incur no guilt because of him. As though you could be commanded not to incur guilt. Even God cannot control guilt.

But as he wandered with Nusan and these thoughts, Nathan did find the time to buy a challah. He was even early enough to get one of the kosher ones. Tomorrow, he and Sonia would eat their *traif.* But it wouldn't be ribs. With Bob's Greasy Hands in prison, the neighborhood was getting a new French Asian fusion restaurant with—and this was the part that had everyone laughing—a "smoking room" upstairs. When the restaurant had first advertised the smoking room, some of the people in the neighborhood had thought it was a place for curing your own fish. But once they saw the restaurant, they knew they were wrong. A smoking room turned out to be a place for twenty-four-year-olds to smoke large, contraband Cuban cigars that had returned to fashion on the mistaken belief that they were less deadly than cigarettes.

Reluctantly, Nathan pointed out to Nusan that it was almost time for services, but Nusan did not want to hurry. It was clear to Nathan that he wanted to maintain his tradition of arriving at the last minute. There in fact was no last minute. Services did not start at sunset, they started when the tenth man got there. When they arrived they were still a little early, being numbers eight and nine. They lacked one man, even with the two tourists from the Upper West Side who seemed both excited and uncomfortable in the circumstances in which they had found themselves. They had probably planned a different kind of evening in the East Village.

"Nusan, you could get your brother, Harry," said Chaim Litvak. "Or your brother, Nathan."

"My granddaughter's *shagetz* is converting. He's almost there. We could use him," said Yonah Kirchbaum.

"Who is doing the conversion?" Chaim Litvak wanted to know.

"It's an Orthodox rabbi in SoHo."

"In SoHo?" Chaim Litvak said suspiciously.

Yankel Fink said, "It will be havdalah before you settle this one. I'm going to the corner and taking the first Jew that comes by." And he did, returning only five minutes later with another young man whose evening in the East Village was deferred an hour.

During most of the service, while Nathan was reflecting on how he had to break off his relationship with Karoline, the others were engaged in the subject of Chaim Litvak and Yankel Fink's imminent trip to Israel. The men would chant in Hebrew with gravelly, off-key voices, nodding their heads vigorously, and then from time to time someone would say, "I'll take three minutes."

It was a moment of reckoning in the neighborhood. After years of joking about the unusual weight and density of Yankel Fink's knishes, Chaim and Yankel had decided to take with them the two heaviest, the kasha and the potato, and set them afloat in the Dead Sea, a body of water where humans and reportedly horses and camels would float indefinitely. They were taking bets on how long it would take the knishes to sink. Yonah Kirchbaum said they would never sink. Nusan said they would be out of sight in one minute. The other bets were in between.

"The kasha or the potato?"

Kirchbaum insisted this was a mistake—that the fastest-sinking knish would be the cheese—but he was the kid of the group, and they were not interested in the opinions of people only in their sixties. Jack Bialy, also too young to know, drew patterns with his finger in the flour on the toe of his shoe and whispered to Kirchbaum, "I've been in dough all my life and I am telling you, you're right. But I'm not going to argue."

While the bets were being placed, Nathan, wrapped in a prayer shawl but thinking about Karoline and her father, was overtaken by a feeling that if he did not leave the dark synagogue, he would suffocate and die. He tried to look casual as he sauntered toward the door. When he was almost there, his body throbbing, his shirt soaked through with sweat, his nostrils flared wide looking for air, his eyes met the stern glance of Rabbi Litvak, who was slowly shaking his head from left to right. Nathan could not leave. Without him, there was no minyan. He signaled to Litvak that he was going out for only a minute, but Litvak walked over and, with his arm around him, led Nathan back in. Dark blotches of sweat were appearing on the vanilla-colored cloth of his prayer shawl. Nathan marveled that no one could see what was happening to him.

By the time the service was over and the other men were wishing him a "good *Shabbas*," Nathan was back in control. The three outsiders escaped before the *mofongo* and herring, but Nathan could not because Nusan wanted to eat. Nathan made the argument he always made, that dinner was waiting for them, but Nusan pulled back his head to pour down a shot of vodka, then took a slow breath, ate another herring, and once again pointed out, "It is foolish to starve yourself because you might have food later."

Chaim Litvak also poured down a shot of vodka, shaking his head so vigorously that it gave his hat a jaunty tilt—almost like Charles Boyer as Pepe Le Moko, who could not escape. He handed a small plate with *mofongo* and herring to Nathan and confirmed that even Hillel agreed that "it is an insult to good fortune to walk away from food."

Nathan found it hard to believe that Hillel had really said that. The men ate more herring and, with breath like harp seals, pondered ancient teachings, the meaning of life, and the specific gravity of Yankel Fink's potato and kasha knishes.

Nathan realized that he had to do something. His condition was getting worse. He now felt that at any moment, anywhere, without warning, he could have an attack. One day he would die from it. And he had to stay away from Karoline and her SS father. Why was that so hard to do? The SS daughter. The ultimate *traif*. Better than Saturday night ribs.

During the part of the Seltzers' Friday night known as "waiting for Nusan," Nathan slipped down to his own apartment and called Dr. Kucher to tell her it was getting worse and something had to be done quickly. She might still be in her office.

"Hello, is Dr. Kucher there?"

"I'm sorry, she is gone for the day."

"This is Nathan Seltzer. I am a patient and I am having an emergency. Couldn't you find her for one minute?"

"As a matter of fact, she is walking out now. Let me see if I can grab her. Oh, Dr. Kucher! Dr. Kucher?"

"Njaw, njaw, njaw, njaw, njaw . . ." she shouted with her hands over her ears.

When Nathan returned upstairs, Nusan had arrived. Nathan noted with pleasure that they had made a minyan without him. Mordy was there with a woman named Priscilla, who was the oldest woman Nathan had ever seen his brother with. She seemed to be in her late thirties, a lean, athletically built woman. Everything about her seemed utilitarian. Her straight blond hair was cut short so that it wouldn't be in the way, but not so short as to be self-consciously fashionable. She wore khaki pants and a cotton-knit, pale blue blouse—all drip-dry, perma-everything. A duck in flight on her shirt was the closest thing to ornament she had. Her brown shoes had leather ties and rubber soles. She looked as though she were dressed for sailing.

Ruth had already said the blessing and lit the candles, Harry did the wine, passing the goblet around the room in order of age, and Nathan did the bread, cutting two extra pieces for Nusan to slip in his pocket when no one was looking.

"I think that's the most beautiful grace I have ever heard," Priscilla said with great sincerity.

Oboy, Ruth thought. She is really trying to be nice. I should try to be nice back. Later, I am going to kill Mordy.

"So," Ruth began, serving the herring. "How did you two meet?"

"He was protesting for squatters' rights," said Priscilla. "And I noticed that his shoes were untied. So I told him, and do you know what he said?"

They all nodded their heads and droned, "Yes. . . ."

"Unbelievable," said Harry. "I have a son who meets girls by walking around with his shoes untied."

"You should rethink your whole footwear," said Mordy.

"Are you from the neighborhood?" asked Sonia, who knew that she was not.

"Now I am!" she said with too much enthusiasm.

"Priscilla bought my apartment," Mordy explained.

"That bastard Dubinsky has already sold them!" said Harry.

"Yes," said Priscilla. "He is completely redoing the building and breaking through walls. We are going to have a three-bedroom apartment. It won't be ready until the fall. But my family has a place on Cape Cod where we can stay until it's ready." She smiled pleasantly about all this good news, and Mordy attempted unsuccessfully to wear a matching smile. The rest of the room was silent.

Mordy has found a way to keep squatting, Nathan thought, smiling to himself.

"It's a *shanda*," said Harry. The Yiddish word for disgrace, in Harry's mouth, was always a prelude, and everyone turned, dreading what they thought he was about to say. "Jewish people are selling out these properties and having them rebuilt by anti-Semites so that Jews can't move back in."

"Really," Priscilla said with great concern. "I didn't know anything . . ."

Nathan patted her hand to tell her it was all right and then turned to his father for more of this story. "How do you know they are anti-Semites, Dad?"

"The doorways. They keep putting in steel door frames. So you can't nail up a mezuzah."

The room fell silent again, except for the soft muttering of Nusan, "*Tokhes oyfn tish.*" Nathan strained to understand what he was saying about the table, and then Priscilla ventured cheerfully:

"Why not put magnets on them? You know, like refrigerator magnets. In fact, that would be a great product. Refrigerator mezoozoos. Something Mordy might want to undertake."

They all turned to Mordy, unaware that he was looking for something to undertake.

"Well," began Mordy, "that's a market without much elasticity . . . to say the least. I actually have other plans."

"Really?" purred Priscilla.

"I have decided to get my MBA—master's in business administration."

The entire family unconsciously let slip a collective sigh. Mordy was not changing.

"First," Priscilla explained, "we are going to the Cape."

Sarah's eyes widened. "On vacation. Are you going on vacation?"

Mordy thought it over and looked at Priscilla. "Yes, I think I am."

"Will you take swimming lessons?"

"No, but I think I will float." Everyone laughed at Mordy floating, but Sarah didn't want to be laughed at.

"Do you know how to swim, Uncle Mordy?"

He didn't answer.

Priscilla looked at him. "You don't know how to swim? That's so sweet! I'll teach you how to swim."

"Everybody at the table who knows how to swim, raise your hand," Sarah commanded.

Priscilla, Sonia, Ruth, and Sarah raised their hands. Sarah looked triumphant. "Girls win!"

"She's started swimming lessons this summer," Nathan said.

"Uncle Mordy, if you are going on vacation, you should take swimming lessons," Sarah insisted in a reprimanding voice. "And you should also buy stuff. We are going to start buying stuff."

At this moment, just as Ruth reentered carrying the unloved brisket on the large platter on which the brisket was always carried, the doorbell rang—a loud, intrusive, drilling noise.

The second Nathan heard the bell, he knew who it was. He had seen the anger in Karoline's eyes when she found him talking to her father. He remembered her threat to one day come here. Now, at last, the disaster with which he had been toying was at the door. He was ten feet from the door and his life would unravel if he did not get there first.

He leapt to his feet so quickly that he knocked his chair over backward. Unfortunately, Harry had also gotten up and, because of the chair, had a head start to the door.

Sonia was laughing at the two of them fleeing the brisket.

When Nathan got to the door, Harry was already there with his hand on the knob. Father and son looked at each other with oddly matching glares of desperation.

The harsh, intruding buzzer sounded again.

"Why doesn't someone open it?" said Ruth.

"Sit down, I'll get it," said Harry, resurrecting the old-time voice of parental authority. Nathan sadly returned to his chair to await his destruction.

But Harry, to Nathan's amazement and admiration, stepped discreetly into the hallway and closed the door behind him.

"Hello, Harry Seltzer," said Florence.

Harry looked at her as though he were considering pretending he did not know her.

"It's me," said Florence. And she pointed to the spot on the side of her head and grimaced in pain to remind him of their one tryst. Then she burst into laughter.

"Shhh!"

"It was funny."

"What are you doing here? I thought prostitutes didn't do this. I thought you could keep secrets."

"I don't want to tell any secrets, Harry Seltzer. I just need some help. I'm in trouble. I need some money."

Harry looked at her. She was in trouble. The reds and purples of her heavy outer layer of makeup were gone, and Harry could now see that she was much older than he had thought, not much younger than him. And she was losing her plumpness, acquiring a drawn look. She was not well. Sweat was beading on her forehead. Harry reached into his wallet and took out the $15 that he had. The two bills quickly vanished into her shiny blue dress that was not as tight on her as it was meant to be.

"I need more than that. I need at least forty. I'll do what you want." She seemed to start to drop to her knees and, panic-stricken, Harry grabbed her to stop her—grabbed her a little too hard, and suddenly they were in an embrace. Florence started to laugh. Harry stepped away. "Never mind. I'll get you forty," he whispered, having already forgotten about the fifteen. "Just wait for me out on the street."

Matching his hoarse whisper, she said, "You will come down, won't you?" and then added in a full voice, "You won't leave me there?"

"I promise! Just go downstairs." He waited for her to disappear behind the elevator door, which closed slowly, seeming to erase her. Then he went back in the apartment and said, "I have a building problem. I'll be right back." No one seemed particularly curious. Nathan, his face flushed and his soul suddenly joyous, started talking with great enthusiasm about Sonia's play. Deliberately affecting a casual saunter, Harry made his way out the door, closed it slowly, smacked the mezuzah almost as a rebuke, and ran down the stairs.

But by the third floor he had to stop. He was out of breath and his chest hurt. While standing in the hallway gathering his strength, Birdie Nagel suddenly pounced.

"I can't help you with the birds right now, Mrs. Nagel."

"It's not birds," she pleaded. "The dog is going to die!"

"What dog?"

Mrs. Nagel touched the center of her chest as she tried to gather herself, seemingly more out of breath than Harry. "Three C is away for a week. Boca Raton. Why? What is it with Boca Raton?"

"I don't know." Harry started to walk toward the next set of stairs. If he did not appear soon, Florence would take the elevator back up and sound his door buzzer.

"Wait!" shouted Birdie Nagel in such a commanding voice that it stopped him. "The dog! I said I would feed the dog. The keys don't work!"

Harry looked longingly down the staircase and then took the keys from her hand and walked to 3C and opened the door. "You just have to jiggle the key a little."

"It needs a new lock. This dog could have died." The front hallway to the apartment had little piles of droppings, and an anxious little white fluffy animal was trying to climb Harry's leg.

"It's not the lock," said Harry. "It's the key. Someone made a bad copy."

"Oh, thank God, thank God," said Birdie Nagel, embracing the dog. "Here, help me. Open my door. I am going to keep the dog with me."

Harry got the fluffy dog and Birdie Nagel back into her apartment. "God bless you, Mr. Seltzer. *Lang lebn,*" she said, wishing him a long life.

"That's all right," said Harry, anxious to leave.

"Wait a minute!" She disappeared into her apartment and returned with a twenty-pound sack of birdseed. "It's for the birds. I can't feed them with the dog. I asked my neighbor, that new boy you rented to. The *fardarter.* No, he's too busy. That's the best you could rent to? That *fardarter.* They bury better-looking people. . . ."

Harry saw the elevator coming back up and grabbed the birdseed and ran to push the button. When the elevator door opened, he stepped in without even acknowledging the impatient Florence, apparently en route to destroy his life. "Bye, Mrs. Nagel," he said as the doors closed.

When the door opened on the second floor, the new tenant, the *fardarter* himself in seersucker, stepped in.

"Hello, Mr. Seltzer, I have a problem," said the new tenant. Harry couldn't help thinking that Birdie Nagel was right about him, he was a *fardarter,* a withered, dull young man. "I am having trouble getting cable TV. The cable company said that the building has never been wired. No one has ever had cable TV here? How is that possible?"

"I don't know. It never came up. There is a very nice theater on Second Avenue, a multiplex. They chopped up a beautiful old theater and now you have a choice of six movies." The elevator opened to the ground floor and Harry fled to the door and would have made it if it hadn't been for Mrs. Kleinman.

"Mrs. Kleinman, I know nothing about the postal service. There is nothing I can do."

"I am not talking about the postal service," she said indignantly. "I am talking about my gas line."

"I'm sorry. What is wrong with your gas line?"

"I am charged five dollars a month for gas and I never use my stove."

"But that doesn't have anything to do with me either."

"I know. It's the man who reads the meter. But don't you see?"

"What?"

"He's the one who's been stealing my mail!"

"I've got to go." He started to walk out of the building with Florence following behind.

"Please, Mr. Seltzer. I have to get my mail."

"I'm sorry, Mrs. Kleinman, I will try to figure this out for you."

"You promise, Mr. Seltzer?" Somehow the order had gotten mixed up and Mrs. Kleinman found herself behind Florence, shouting at her instead of Harry. Florence smiled politely and backed away.

"I promise, Mrs. Kleinman, I will work on the postal problem. But not right now."

"May you live to a hundred, Mr. Seltzer," Mrs. Kleinman shouted at him as he scurried down Avenue A, Florence at a discreet distance struggling to match his pace.

He was almost at the cash machine at First Avenue when a tough-looking, dark-skinned man with no shirt and several rings in his right ear stopped him. "Are you Harry Seltzer?"

"I can't believe it."

"Believe what?"

"I am Harry Seltzer."

"So why is that hard to believe?"

"What do you want?" said Harry, his manners at last fraying.

"I am Wilson Morelos," the young man declared with great drama. Harry could not find a response.

"The merengue trumpet player."

"Ohh, wonderful. Where are you playing?"

"That's just it. I was told you could find me a booking."

"Who do you play with?"

"I thought you could help me."

Harry looked back at Florence, resting against a brick building like a tired but determined hunter. Even from a distance, he could see the sweaty shine of her face and skin. But she was determined to follow. "Talk to Chow Mein Vega."

"He doesn't do merengue. He said to talk to you."

"Do you have a phone number?"

"I'll write it down for you. Do you have a piece of paper and a pen?" Harry found a scrap of paper, the back of someone else's card in his wallet. But he had no pen. He was standing by a newsstand. "Can I borrow a pen a minute?" he asked the vendor.

"Are you buying a newspaper?"

Harry started to reach into his wallet and realized he was still carrying twenty pounds of birdseed. Then he remembered that he had given Florence all his money. He looked at the young man, who reached fatalistically into the low-slung empty pockets of his baggy pants. "Florence," he called after her, and she started to back off nervously. He coaxed her like a deer, and when she was finally near him he said, "I just need some money for a newspaper."

"You know I don't have any money."

"The fifteen dollars."

"What fifteen dollars?"

"Oh, God. Listen, Wilson." No one ever had to give their name more than once to Harry. "Wilson, I am going to a cash machine. Come with me. I'll get some money and buy a paper and use his pen and you can give me your phone number."

"*Gracias,* man."

"Yeah."

So Harry continued toward the cash machine, birdseed in hand, with the lean and shirtless horn player Wilson behind him, and Florence behind Wilson, and, Harry thought, maybe Mrs. Kleinman behind her. The wide avenues of bright lights giving off orange haze as they refracted in the humidity were crowded with people in the warm summer night, but the narrow side streets were dark and silent and their footsteps clopped loud as horse hooves.

About to round the corner to the cash machine, he nearly ran into Cabezucha, who suddenly appeared, looking very large, his eyes barely fitting in his head, bloated and tense like a tire with too much air. Harry did not notice this, did not notice the wild-eyed way this large man looked at him, like a hungry animal eyeing prey, almost licking his chops. Harry only remembered his previous encounter with the man, because Harry prided himself on remembering previous encounters.

"You see, you didn't listen to me," Harry scolded in a friendly way. "The cash machine doesn't give change. Now here I am without a dime to give you."

Cabezucha stared at Harry helplessly.

"I am going to get cash, but it will all be twenties. And I can't give you a twenty." He reached up, patted the giant on his back, and walked past him. Wilson followed uneasily. Florence did not dare.

Harry got the money, all twenties. Wilson was waiting for him outside, but he could not find Florence when he came out, and in any event, he did not want Wilson to see him giving Florence money. He decided to walk back to the newsstand with Wilson, buy a paper, and borrow a pen, but on the way back he found Florence in her blue dress hunched over the sidewalk in the position of a Muslim praying.

"Florence, are you all right?!"

"Yes, I am all right, Harry Seltzer." She smiled and struggled to stand up.

"She's a junkie, man," said young Wilson Morelos.

"Here, let me give you some money," said Harry, not at all interested in Wilson's assessment. "Here, take sixty. Will sixty be okay?"

Florence nodded her head yes but then said, "I'll never get home with it unless you walk me. Cabezucha will get me."

"Who is Cabbage Suit Ya?"

"It's that guy," said Wilson. "He saw her get the money from the corner. He'll get her. Too easy to pass up."

"I know him from the neighborhood," Harry protested. "He's wearing a Dukakis button. Look!"

"Shit, look at that!" said Wilson, and Harry thought he was referring to the campaign button on Cabezucha's T-shirt. But Wilson reached down to the sidewalk near where Florence had fallen and picked up a silvery ballpoint pen. "Here, let me write my number."

But juggling the birdseed, his wallet, and his banking card, Harry had somehow misplaced the business card where he was going to write Wilson's telephone number.

"Here, man, give me your arm," said Wilson, and he wrote the seven figures on Harry's forearm and then seemed eager to be off to brighter parts of the neighborhood.

Harry did not want to be seen walking Florence, but he had no choice. Crossing Seventh Street, Florence said, "It's all right, he's not following."

But Harry was not thinking about Cabezucha. He was watching a gaunt, angry-looking man with a craggy face, who was carrying a large, black plastic garbage bag. Harry noticed the fury in the man's eyes as he walked up to Harry with an almost violent deliberateness and shouted, "I pay my taxes!" He seemed frozen, waiting for Harry's response.

"I know what you mean. I pay mine. Florence pays hers, too. Don't you, Florence."

The man glared at Florence, waiting for a response.

"I'm pretty much off the books." She could see from the glowing eyes deep in his rough-hewn face that this was not the right answer. But he was willing to wait for it.

"I pay my taxes, too," Florence said weakly. The man nodded agreement and walked to the curb, where he stuck a long arm into the garbage and began groping around with a quick professional touch in search of retrievable items.

"Are you sure you're all right?" Harry asked Florence.

She ran her fingers lightly through Harry's thick white hair. "You are a nice man, Harry Seltzer."

Harry, not especially believing her pronouncement, looked at his watch and saw that he had been gone from dinner for forty-five minutes. He hurried down the street, nearly running, which was not easy to do with twenty pounds of birdseed.

Waiting in the lobby for the elevator, the seersucker *fardarter* seemed to be having a fight with his girlfriend.

"What's wrong with seersucker?" whined the *fardarter*.

"It's not exactly a power suit," she said.

The elevator arrived, and they and Harry stepped in.

"It's a way of saying 'Even if it's ninety degrees, I'm still here with my pinstripes.' "

"Yes, but at what price?" she said as they got off at their floor. As the elevator was closing, Harry heard him protest, "I got it at Syms!"

"That's not what I meant."

A full hour late, Harry burst through the door, exhausted. Dinner was finished, and Mordy and Priscilla had left. Sonia had fallen asleep on the couch. Sarah was playing with Nusan in the stuffed armchair.

While Nathan and Ruth looked on in horror, Sarah was insisting that "Nusey," as she sometimes called him, recite the numbers on his arm. And Nusan was playfully engaged in the game. It had started when she asked why he had the numbers and he had explained that it was a number he was trying to remember. And so she was testing him.

Suddenly she shouted, "Grandpa has one, too!" and pointed at Harry's arm. Not realizing that Nusan had used the same explanation, Harry said, "No, that's just a number I had to remember."

Ruth, seeing the birdseed, said, "Oh, you got stuck with Birdie Nagel!"

"Yes, she was complaining about the new tenant. You know what she called him? A seersucker *fardarter*."

"I don't care if he is a *fardarter*," Ruth said expressively. "As long as he is a rent-paying *fardarter*!"

The words suddenly woke Sonia. "What? What did you say?"

Ruth repeated, "I said I don't care if he is a *fardarter*, as long as he is a rent-paying *fardarter*."

"Yes!" Sonia said triumphantly, and she wrote something in her notebook.

"Is there any strudel left?" asked Harry.

"Nathan made *kugelhopf* tonight. It's very good. We saved you a piece." Ruth took a plate with a piece of yellow cake dusted with sugar and slid it across the table toward him.

"Why don't we get apple strudel anymore?" asked Harry. Then, without warning, he raised his hand over his head and slammed it on the table, making a loud thump that startled the half-asleep Sonia, spilled coffee into saucers, and overturned his piece of *kugelhopf*. He seemed to have thrown the cake on the floor in anger, which was not the way Harry acted. Everyone looked at him in silent shock. Sarah was motionless, studying the scene with fascination.

"God, I hate these things," Harry said as he picked up the remains of a water bug from the floor with a napkin.

"Oboy. That was on the table?" said Ruth in disgust.

"Right on the edge here. I'm sorry. I'm sorry. Just the same, why don't we go back to apple strudel?"

"Why is it," Nathan asked with uncharacteristic irritation, "that Moellen is the one man you never suspect of anti-Semitism?"

"Moellen," said Harry, curling his lower lip reflectively. "I know Moellen."

Nusan laughed quietly as he stood up, still wearing his hat and his maroon wool scarf and his dark wool suit jacket. Bundled against the cold, he said good-bye and stepped into the midsummer heat.

Sonia hurried to her manuscript.

(Emma walks into the room and finds a tall, thin woman with long fingers and curly hair.)

EMMA: Who are you?

MARGARITA: I am Margarita Maza Juárez. *(She waits for a moment but gets no response from Emma.)* Wife of Don Benito Juárez, the exiled president of Mexico.

EMMA: Boyoboy.

MARGARITA: This is absolutely true.

EMMA: The exiled pres . . . Exiled my *tokh* . . . You know, you can get pretty far with a lie. *(She raises an index finger and swings her hips for emphasis.)* But there is no getting back.

MARGARITA: But it is not a lie. I am Benito Juárez's wife.

EMMA: I don't care if you are an exiled *fardarter,* as long as you pay your share.

Yes! thought Sonia. And now a relationship begins.

CHAPTER TWENTY

Narrow Escapes

WHAT AM I DOING? Nathan demanded silently, but not in the least rhetorically, of Oggún, still elegantly swathed in *El Vocero* on his shelf, still as blank faced and silent as ever, although, Nathan thought, no more silent and no more blank faced than Dr. Kucher.

A narrow escape, like beauty, is in the eye of the beholder. But Nathan always believed he was experiencing important brushes with disaster, such as the logic-defying near miss when Karoline "almost knocked on the door when the family was having Friday night dinner." The fact that Karoline, who loathed such confrontations, had never seriously considered doing this did not enter into Nathan's calculation. That could have been Karoline instead of just Birdie Nagel, and then where would he have been?

It was a busy day at the Meshugaloo Copy Center. Felix's East Village Gourmet was having a flyer printed announcing a sale—on tomatoes. Jackie, the woman who might be a man, was printing something up about "Tomato Street Theater." It was a complicated job involving reducing a picture of a tomato and superimposing it over the skull on a picture of Hamlet. The neighborhood association had an order for flyers, and so did a group of street poets, whose program included Gilberto Banza's latest work, "Fucked in the Loisaida." Harold Kaskowitz, the classical kazoo player who for years had failed to convince Nathan to perform chamber music with him on his harmonica, was giving a concert. There were several flyers to be done for different groups in defense of squatters' rights. And Sonia, to Nathan's complete amazement, was having *Emma and Margarita* produced by a small but famous East Village theater group and needed twenty scripts, which seemed a lot for a two-character drama or, as Sonia labeled it, "a feminist out-of-body dialogue in three acts."

Quietly, in a corner, on a small table Nathan had placed there, Sarah, whose mother was at rehearsals, was at work with crayon and paper, drawing what she said were depictions of herself having swimming lessons at the Jewish Community Center pool.

Sonia had decided that she did not want to give massages anymore. She was hoping to be a successful playwright. With *Emma and Margarita* still in rehearsal, Sonia had already been profiled in four publications. The *Forward* was featuring her as a new Jewish writer, another wrote of her as a new Latin writer, a third as a Latina feminist, and a fourth as a Mexican-Jewish feminist.

Money was not going to be a problem, because Nathan had decided to stop "gambling with Sarah's future." He was going to take Ira Katz's offer. He had also decided to finally confront his claustrophobia.

Ruth demanded to know.

Harry could not bear Ruth knowing. How did she find out? How did women find these things out? Florence certainly wouldn't have said anything. It must have been someone who saw them walking together. How much did Ruth know?

"It's a passive-aggressive thing, isn't it."

"A passie a . . . ?" Was she going to a psychiatrist? Did she find out that way? Scientifically?

"Maybe it's not even conscious. You resent my not cooking and so you go outside searching for the most unacceptable food."

He hadn't thought of prostitutes as a meal substitute. *This* was a diet that would sell.

"You are a grown man. You can do what you want," said Ruth. "But it makes me look ridiculous. It makes *us* look ridiculous. All the Puerto Ricans probably laugh at us."

"I don't think all the Puerto Ricans know. She wasn't even Spanish."

"Who?"

"Who?" replied Harry.

Ruth continued impatiently. "You think you can sit in that what do they call it, cookiefrito, eating all that pork without every Puerto Rican in the neighborhood laughing about the Jew and the *lechón*. Oboy. I know we are not kosher, but—"

Suddenly a piercing scream stabbed the stale air of the room. And then another one. "Noooo!!"

Harry and Ruth ran to open their door and heard the screams echoing through the hallway. As they rushed down the stairs to see what had caused the uproar, Birdie Nagel was coming up, her glasses askew and eyes wide with fury. "I was coming up to pay the rent," she declared with great and breathless indignation. "But this is the end. I am leaving! I don't care if I have to go to Boca Raton!"

And without handing Harry anything for the three months of back rent she owed, she turned around and stamped her way down four flights of stairs, leaving the rhythmic echo of her slapping shoes.

Underneath was a more gentle sound, the soft rhythms of a drum. Harry and Ruth continued down to the fifth floor, where they found Cristofina with a large green-and-black silk scarf extravagantly wrapped around her head. Next to her, seated on the floor, was Panista from the casita, playing a small drum he held sideways, tapping it in such intricate and lovely patterns that at last his restless fingertips seemed satiated.

In Cristofina's hand was a headless, milk-chocolate-colored pigeon out of which she was pouring blood in the doorway, humming like a nimble and contented seamstress fast at work. Puddles and splatters of dark, wine-colored blood filled the doorway like an abstract expressionist painting in progress. Like stoppers and empty bottles cast aside in a bout of drinking, bird heads and drained carcasses with crumpled feathers were scattered in the hallway. Nathan was seated on the floor dressed in white, strands of green and black beads around his neck, a grayish feather resting on the side of his head, a bashful smile on his face as he looked up and saw his parents.

Cristofina poured honey over the blood and then sprinkled feathers on the sticky, bleeding pools while singing in a gentle, happy voice in Yoruba.

Chow Mein Vega was hunched over the table in the dark, cool corner of the casita, tapping out page 611 of his autobiography, in which he was performing in the Catskills. On the porch, the other cool part of the house, Panista was leaning back on a metal folding chair, balancing himself against a post, his fingers tapping out a *plena* beat against a book called *A Taste of Japan*.

"Did you know that *kamaboko* was first made in the fourteenth century?"

"What do you mean, made?" said Palo, who, too tall for the casita, was seated in the garden on a wooden stool. "I thought *kamaboko* was a vegetable."

"No," scoffed Panista, "that's *takenoko.*"

"Bamboo shoots," said Panista, still tapping.

"Okay, *pendejito,* what is *kamaboko?*" Palo challenged.

"It's fish puree, asshole," said Panista. "They mold it so it is shaped like your head."

"Hello, Mr. Seltzer," said Palo, suddenly seeing Harry coming through the front gate.

"Hey, Mr. Seltzer," said Panista. "Know of any openings in Japanese restaurants? We can wait tables, cook, whatever. Ask me something, Seltzer-san."

"Well, Palo-san, I have no sushi work, but I do have a boogaloo gig."

"Sí, señor!"

"One night. A wedding."

"A wedding. Old people?"

"Afraid so. People in their fifties. Third marriage, no white dress, but they wanted boogaloo. Latin boogaloo. Where's Chow Mein?"

The three simultaneously pointed inside the house, where the typewriter could be heard. Felix had said that Chow Mein was the last person in New York to use a typewriter.

As Harry walked into the casita, Chow Mein looked up from his work, saved by an interruption. "Man, writing is hard. Who was it talked about the blank page, Hemingway or someone. I got too many pages."

"Anybody can write," Harry said. "A pencil or pen, some paper, and then you just sit down and write."

"Hemingway said that?"

"No. Irving Berlin."

Mrs. Kleinman kissed the mezuzah on her doorpost softly as she left for the third floor to Birdie Nagel's, where the door was open and Birdie really was packing. "You're getting out? Good for you! Good-bye to all the goddamn cockroaches and the stolen mail and the guy who pisses in the doorway every night. Where you going? Boca? God bless. You'll probably get an eat-in kitchen and a living room and closets big enough to dance in."

The seersucker *fardarter* leaving his apartment a floor below heard her and, for the first time, noticed the building's tile floors had dirt caked in the edges and the paint was peeling in large curls off the wall.

When Nathan asked Ruth where Harry was, she had said pointedly, "At the casita—eating *lechón!*" Nathan was not sure what significance Ruth was attaching to this, but he left to look for his father. Today was the day he would straighten out his life, and he was anxious to talk to Harry before settling things with Ira Katz.

On his brisk walk to the casita, it struck Nathan that Arnie was missing. He did not see him or his pallet, blanket, or books.

At the casita, Nathan was stopped by Palo. "Here's the man *que corta el bacalao.* Nathan, how do you make miso?"

"I don't have any idea. But it seems to me that miso is one of those things, like pizza and hot dogs, that you don't try to make. You just buy it. Ask José Fishman. He's Japanese now."

After Nathan walked into the casita, Palo whispered to Panista, "That's bullshit, man. He better get with the program or he's not going to make it in the neighborhood."

"Got that," said Panista. "Things are changing."

Harry was seated next to Chow Mein Vega but was not eating *lechón.* Chow Mein was hunched over his typewriter, stroking his stumpy ponytail, while Harry was explaining their strategy for the future of boogaloo. Nathan knew he would have to be patient, that Chow Mein would want to go to the *cuchifrito.* It seemed probable that the only meals Chow Mein ever had were when he could get someone to take him to lunch. That and the food available at weddings and receptions at which he performed. For a while he did well with bar mitzvahs. Chow Mein believed that more food was available at bar mitzvahs than any other type of event. He even wrote a "Bar Mitzvah Boogaloo." But it was the parents who wanted him, not the bar mitzvah boys. Besides, there were fewer and fewer bar mitzvahs in the neighborhood. Still, mysteriously, Chow Mein grew ever larger.

Just as the conversation seemed to be wearing down, Chow Mein clapped his hands together with sudden enthusiasm and said, "How about some *cuchifrito?*"

At the *cuchifrito,* which posted a "Free Ruben García" sign, Nathan noticed that as his mother had predicted, Harry ordered *lechón,* the suckling pig. But since almost everything at a *cuchifrito* is cooked in pork fat, Nathan could not see anything particularly galling in Harry's choice of *lechón.*

Finally, after Harry paid the inexpensive bill and Chow Mein left them, Nathan had a chance, as they walked home, to talk to his father.

"You don't sound very happy about this."

"I can get five hundred thousand dollars. Maybe more."

Harry did not react, so Nathan tried a different way of expressing it. "It's for the money." He wanted to say, "It's for the money, stupid." But money meant nothing to Harry. He wouldn't understand. "We have to send Sarah to school. Preschool, then school. And swimming lessons. There are a lot of things kids need now. The shop doesn't make money, Dad. It never did."

Nor was Harry moved by this revelation.

"Sometimes it broke even. Right now it is not even doing that."

"This company seems anxious to get it."

"They just want to put it out of business."

"Look, Nathan, I have to tell you something. We are rich. The family is rich." Nathan was either not understanding him or not believing him. "We're rich people. You don't have to sell your business. Mordy doesn't have to run off to Cape Cod with a shiksa. We have money. . . . Okay, we don't have any money. But we have property. Do you know how much property we have? It's better than money. I get offered millions all the time. They keep offering more and more. The more you say no, the more they offer. It makes me wonder why anyone would ever say yes."

"Because if you don't, you never have any money."

Harry stared at him with a look that was not approval, a look Nathan knew well.

"What would be wrong with taking the money?"

"It always means throwing somebody out of their home. Besides, I never like the people making the offer. A bunch of anti-Semites. I don't need to do business with them. Say, where's Arnie?"

It was true there was no trace of him on Avenue A.

"People get older. They die or go to Boca Raton, which is probably the same thing. Fly away, like Birdie Nagel. Someday we will sell something. Or maybe we will just let the properties earn money. Give Mordy a building to manage. We could make him a landlord."

"Free him from Priscilla."

"Who knows. I'll tell you a secret. When I was sixteen years old I met a woman—a woman, she was maybe eighteen—on a train to Warsaw. I can still remember her. Or maybe it is all wrong, but the way I remember her she had straight blond hair, real yellow stuff, like yellow silk. And that white skin that you can almost see through. And eyes so blue, they had no color at all. A real Pole. And she didn't see that I was Jewish."

Harry stopped walking.

"For some reason, I have never wanted anything in my life more than I wanted to sleep with this girl. And she wouldn't. Maybe she knew I was Jewish. If she had slept with me, she would have seen I was Jewish. Maybe I was afraid because of that. But I lied. Pretended I was a Pole. Even tried to sound a little anti-Semitic. I couldn't do it very well. But I could see that she didn't like it when I talked like that. Then I really had to have her. No excuse. She wasn't even an anti-Semite. Well, she was a Pole. Klara. And I couldn't have her. I still remember her. I still remember wanting her. Disgracing myself, pretending to be a goy. I always remember it—her and how I acted and how I wanted her. I think I would have done or said anything. So if Mordy wants to spend the summer on Cape Cod, I wish him God bless. If I could have had a summer on Cape Cod with Klara, I would have forgotten her by now. That would have been better."

They walked in silence. In his entire life, Nathan had never felt so close to his father. He thought that for the first time he might be able to understand who Harry was. He had to ask. "Why is Nusan angry with you?"

"Nusan is angry."

"There is more, though, isn't there?"

Harry shrugged. "He thinks I should have saved him. Saved the whole family."

"Why didn't you?"

"I didn't know that they needed saving. They never said anything. When I went to America, none of them wanted to come. None of them ever said they wanted to come. Then suddenly they were all gone."

"This woman, this Pole, you wanted her so much that you didn't care about anything. . . ."

"Nothing else. It wasn't love. I didn't even love her. I just craved her. A kind of sickness."

"You know . . ." Nathan began.

Suddenly the street was filled with a throbbing, pounding noise. It was Dolby and his speakers, pedaling his bicycle past. And on the back of the huge, throbbing boxes, almost obscured by the silver and blue duct tape that secured the speakers to the bicycle, was a bumper sticker—BUSH FOR PRESIDENT. There, at last, the neighborhood Republican had been identified. By the time Dolby was far enough away so that they could talk again, Harry had dressed himself in the kind of silence that meant he did not want to talk anymore.

CHAPTER TWENTY-ONE

Fresh Kills

DAYS PASSED in the cleansing but unexciting spirit of reform, yet Nathan had not taken the last critical step in his program—the visit to Karoline. As he said to his orisha, the *Vocero*-shrouded Oggún, he should have never started with her. He loved his wife and his daughter. Why did he have to get involved with this other person—this other who was so much other? He knew why, but sex was not something he wanted to discuss with an orisha.

By the time he went to Karoline's to tell her all this, Joey Parma had a bruise on his right cheek. This showed a number of things about Mrs. Parma, including the fact that she was left-handed, or else, like a professional, led with her left and had not delivered the finishing blow.

She did not hit him when he came home that night. She was too hurt. But then he infuriated her. He denied the entire affair. When asked to explain why the woman had confessed the whole thing, he did not have an answer. All he could say was, "Who knows why women do things?" That was when she started getting angry. Then he made it worse by telling a preposterous and elaborate story about storing wine at the woman's apartment.

"Don't lie to me, Joey. I could see this was a lot more than trading Zinfandellis."

"Zinfandels."

"What?"

Joey walked out and drove to the East Village, attaching the red dome light to his roof and turning on his siren to force his way through traffic jams. In Karoline's apartment, he grabbed the first three cases of his wine that he found, refused to talk to Karoline, who was trying to explain, and drove back to Queens.

He showed his wife the bottles, lovingly extracting a 1981 Chassagne-Montrachet, and read from the label the words "Morgeot premier cru."

Then, seeing that she was unmoved, he tried to impress her with a 1982 Bordeaux. "It was a big year for Médoc," he argued as he presented a bottle of Château d'Agassac, pointing to the lemon-colored label with the engraving of the castle. She simply turned away in disgust. So he made her go with him to a local wine merchant, who appraised the wines at over $3,000. She glared at him as he drove them home. "What did you think?" said Joey. "Remember that wine when we had the Feguccis over last weekend? You thought that was good, didn't you?" He mimicked her voice in falsetto Queens: " 'Vewy noice, Jowey.' Yeah, nice. Chassagne-Montrachet for seventy dollars a bottle!"

She said nothing, but when they got home she asked him how many more cases he had. Joey said, "Six."

"Six! So this is about ten thousand dollars you spent on wine!" She was a grocer's daughter and tabulated quickly.

"You miss the point. It's an investment. The value goes up. I probably only spent eight thousand." And that was when she hit him. He, holding the stinging side of his face, argued, "Ten years from now, you know what it'll be worth? You're looking at maybe twenty thousand in wine."

"Twenty thousand dollars. In *wine*! And you drink it! And with the Feguccis!" He was lucky she didn't hit him again. She wanted him to sell it. She wanted to see the money in a bank account or in "low-risk, medium-term Treasury bonds."

What kind of bond? Where had she learned to talk like that? Joey wondered. But he went to Karoline's to gather the rest of the wine. He asked her why she had told his wife they were having an affair.

"I didn't know who she was."

"So that's why you said you slept with her husband. When in doubt, confess adultery?"

"I thought she was somebody else."

"Somebody else?"

"Somebody else's wife."

"Ahh, so *you're* allowed to have secrets."

A loud buzzer intruded. She pushed the button. "Karoline," came Nathan's muffled voice from the white plastic box on the wall.

Joey and Karoline examined each other. "No, I don't get to have them either," said Karoline with a sad smile as she pushed the buzzer button. Then she opened the door wide and stepped back so that Nathan would see Joey.

"I think you know each other."

"Yes, how are you?"

"How you doin'?"

Nathan could not dismiss the impression that Joey Parma was— was *leering* at him. "You look like someone smacked you," Nathan observed.

"Naw. It was a door. A swinging door."

"They always say that," said Nathan, but he saw that no one was amused, so maybe he was right.

"Well," said Joey. "The last of it. Thanks, Karoline."

"Sure, Joey. Sorry it—"

"Forget about it," he said, picking up two cases of wine with surprising ease and walking out. "See ya, Nathan."

Nathan and Karoline did not move as they listened to Joey's footsteps, almost counting them. They both had the same thought: I am not going to start this speech I have been practicing until Joey is gone. Once the door downstairs was heard closing, Nathan began first.

"I have to talk to—"

"Don't you ever call first?"

"I'm sorry. Listen, I have to—" But the next words out of his mouth were not the ones he had been planning. "We were using his handcuffs, weren't we."

"What?"

"The handcuffs. They were Joey Parma's handcuffs. You had used them with him."

Karoline took her hand with the strong, skilled fingers and covered her mouth, attempting to conceal the fact that she was laughing.

"It's funny? It's funny? Why is it funny? Why do you always laugh at me? Am I that comic?" But it was a rhetorical question. Nathan knew the answer.

"There are three things you need to know here," said Karoline, extending three fine fingers in front of her face. "The first is for general release. Please tell the world. I am not now, nor have I ever been, involved with Joey Parma." Then she muttered, "Not my type. You're my type. I'm sick of my type." Then she resumed in full voice, "Number two: The handcuffs were given to me years ago as a joke, and you are the only one I ever used them with. And number three"—she walked over and opened the door—"number three is I'm getting married. I'm marrying Dickie, and I want you to go away and stop ruining my life. Good-bye, good luck, regards to the wife and kid."

Nathan looked at her in disbelief. How had she turned this around? Now she was sending him away? Why did she always have an advantage over him? He imagined the voice of Ira Katz: "Because you're married, stupid."

He walked to the door. Should he kiss her? Shake her hand? He could not look at her without aching to touch her. His nose filled his head with her buttery scent. Their noses filled with each other's scents. If they had been alone in a room with no God watching, they could have spent an hour just sniffing each other like dogs.

"Just one last time for good-bye?" Nathan suggested. With no more spoken, they were in her wide bed, the lumpy mattress on the wooden base of drawers full of pastry equipment.

He walked home hours later, still having said nothing but knowing that they had said good-bye. He told himself that he felt relieved and ignored the dryness in his throat, the aching in his face, the uneasy feeling in his stomach.

When he got back to the building, a new tenant was moving in. Birdie Nagel had left and Harry had run an ad in the *Voice,* and it was answered so quickly that he barely had time to clean and paint the apartment, which had been neither cleaned nor painted in decades, and Birdie had left behind stacks of twenty-pound bags of birdseed that had to be disposed of.

Most of the landlords in the neighborhood were trying to turn over apartments quickly. The apartments were rent stabilized, and only by changing hands frequently could the rents be brought up to the extravagant prices new tenants were ready to pay. The traditional alternative had been to set the building on fire. Fires usually broke out in buildings that were occupied by squatters. A fairly minor fire could get the building condemned and the squatters removed. Some buildings with paying tenants had rents so low that fire insurance was still the landlord's most lucrative choice. With people now willing to pay undreamed-of rents to live in the East Village, only the Seltzers were ever sorry to see a tenant leave.

So the cleaners and painters in the neighborhood had learned to work fast. And now the new tenant was moving in, a girl from Virginia with short, reddish blond hair and brown leather luggage. She had just graduated from somewhere and was very excited about her first job in New York. Nathan confessed to himself that most people he knew had yet to land their first job in New York.

"Hello, I'm Catherine."

"Hello, Catherine."

"Can I ask you a question? What's this?" She was pointing at a mezuzah on the doorpost, a simple tube buried in so many layers of paint that the Hebrew letter *shin,* the first letter of the prayer on the tiny scroll inside, a letter that looked like a *w,* was looking more like a *u.* It had been there even before Birdie Nagel. All the doorways in the building had them.

"It's a mezuzah. It's a Jewish ornament."

"What does it mean?" Catherine asked, wrinkling her nose.

"It means . . . It is a sign. It means that a Jewish family lives there."

"Oh! You mean it gives good luck!"

"Sometimes."

Arnie had run out of luck. With shops and restaurants opening all around him, the owner of the storefront by Arnie's new sidewalk spot realized that before he could rent the space, he had to get the homeless person off the sidewalk in front. The owner tried to talk to him but discovered him so sick that he could barely speak. He called the police and Arnie was taken away. Arnie regained consciousness only once. He found himself in a bed. A bed. He had decided some time before that he was to die on the street, and now for some reason he was in a bed. He never found out why.

People in the neighborhood went to his spot and lit candles and stood, some sat, and told stories remembering Arnie. Xabe, the former neighborhood graffiti felon and current mural artist, did a mural on the wall, the first nonpaid work he had done in years—a fuzzy likeness of Arnie in his beret with wings and his right hand clenched. In large orange letters across the top, as though written in a cloud, it said, "Viva la huelga, Arnie!"

Someone taped a sign to the wall saying: "On this spot died Arnie Johnson, killed by the landlords of New York." No one had known

Arnie's last name, and it was one of those landlords of New York, the one who had evicted him in the first place, who furnished the name. Nathan was surprised. Johnson. Everyone had always thought of Arnie as Jewish.

"*También,*" said Panista, tapping out an idea on a lamppost. "I guess it was just that he read a lot."

In the evening, neighborhood friends sat vigil on the spot, and Nathan, who had joined them, found his brother already positioned on the concrete.

"Mordy!"

Mordy patted the sidewalk next to him as though fluffing a pillow for his brother. "Have a seat, bro'."

Nathan sat on the sidewalk next to him. "Where's Priscilla?"

Mordy, in his best John Kennedy impression, said, "Ah, let me say this about that. Ah. I left her on Hyannis."

"What happened?"

"The ducks. I couldn't take the ducks. They had ducks everywhere. These painted wooden ducks like deities for some ceremony. And they had pictures of ducks on the walls. There were ducks painted on their mailbox. They wore duck ties. They had duck belt buckles. Now, here's the weird part. They hate ducks. They want to kill them all. They are spending all summer caressing this arsenal of weapons just so they can go out in the fall and kill every duck in Massachusetts. Even their dogs want to kill ducks. So one day I said to the father, 'What's with the ducks?' Just like that. 'What's with the ducks? If you hate them so much you want to kill them, why do you put their pictures up all over the place?' "

"And?"

"And they asked me to leave. I may be skipping some steps, but that's basically it. Priscilla said I thought I was better than them. I think that may be an anti-Semitic observation. We should ask Dad."

For more than a week, people sat vigil, remembering Arnie. The owner of the coming Mexican restaurant, a man from New Jersey who was not at all Mexican and did not know what *Viva la huelga* meant, was glad that the writing was in Spanish, because he feared being blamed for Arnie's death and he understood that in order to be accepted in the neighborhood, he was going to have to keep this mural as part of the design of the exterior of his Mexican restaurant. He felt that the Spanish message made it seem more authentic and was pleased to learn that it was actually a Mexican slogan or Mexican American or somehow Mexican. In fact, he decided, in a fit of public relations genius, to name the restaurant Viva la Huelga!

Palo, Panista, and some of the other Puerto Ricans thought this might be their chance for a job. The Japanese were certainly showing no interest. And this was a gringo. They started speaking Spanish in a slow, nasal singsong in the hopes of passing for Mexicans. But the gringo brought in his own Mexicans from his other restaurant on the Upper East Side. The joke to the Puerto Ricans was that his Mexicans weren't Mexican, either, but an assortment of Salvadorans and Guatemalans.

Nathan found the seersucker *fardarter* sitting on a curb in front of Arnie's memorial, clutching himself, his body heaving great sobs. Nathan was moved by the idea that even this *fardarter* smart mourned Arnie. He put his hand on the smart's seersucker shoulder, somehow conveying kinship.

"Oh God!" moaned the *fardarter*.

"Look," said Nathan, sitting next to him on the curb. "Look, Arnie was an original."

"Who? Oh God. Arnie? Is that the owner? I'm going to sue the son of a bitch." The face of the *fardarter* was the color of the blue stripes of his seersucker. He doubled over on the curb, the drainage gutter, an unsavory place littered with little green caps from crack vials, a used condom, and a dead pigeon that had probably died because Birdie Nagel wasn't here with her birdseed.

"Fucking sushi," groaned the *fardarter*.

"You've been eating sushi?"

The *fardarter* nodded in the affirmative.

"On Fourth Street?" Nathan got up, not waiting for his answer. "José."

"What?" groaned the *fardarter*.

"That's his name, José Fishman."

But where was Arnie? What had happened to his body? Neighborhood people wanted to know, because a disturbing rumor was in circulation. Nathan first heard it from Panista. "The city has all these homeless bodies. They just treat them as trash. Put them on the barges."

"What barges?"

"The trash barges for Staten Island. Arnie and a lot of other guys from the neighborhood are now landfill in Staten Island."

"Think about it," Mordy said. "Names are never meaningless. They are signals. Clues. Remember Bob's Greasy Hand? Someone was greasing it. You know what they call the place where the trash barges go in Staten Island? Fresh Kills. Arnie is going to Fresh Kills."

Nathan decided he would go to Bellevue Hospital and find out. Not only would he go, but he would ignore the First Avenue bus and go out of his way to take the Lexington Avenue subway, which arrived with a normal supply of oxygen. At the hospital he was sent to several different offices.

"What happens to the body of a homeless person if there is no name or friends or relatives?"

"Have you lost a relative?" a thin black woman demanded to know from an office so air-conditioned that she was clutching a green wool sweater.

"No. I am trying to find out about a friend. A homeless friend."

"Why didn't you give him a home?"

"He had a home. That's not the point."

"Homeless people do not necessarily come here. It is a myth. They are taken to the nearest hospital."

"And then what happens?"

"They are sent to the city morgue."

"And then?"

"I really don't know. Cremated, I suppose."

"Even if they are Jewish?"

"I don't know. If they are unknown, how would we know their religion?"

On the way back to the neighborhood, Nathan felt nothing in particular when the train slowed down in the dark tunnel just before Fourteenth Street. Even after the train stopped, he felt nothing more than the slight twinge of memory that may flicker across a scar. And when the train started filling up with smoke, he was one of the few to remain calm. In fact, he found that he helped the others deal with their panic.

"You have to breathe," he said. They did, though they then coughed from the smoke.

The train doors opened and transit police with large flashlights led them through the tunnel. "You're okay as long as you don't touch the third rail," said Nathan, recalling his childhood, to the woman walking with him as she buried her well-manicured nails into his arm. Tiny mice scurried out of their way as they walked toward the Union Square station.

There were mud holes, patches of water, that he could not detect until he stepped into them. He tried to walk in front of the woman who was clutching his arm, but it was difficult because she kept pulling him toward her. As a transit cop's flashlight shot a beam at their feet, Nathan could see that she was wearing open-toed, light summer shoes. They could hear but not see the scurrying of large, pink-toed black rats ahead of them. For a second he imagined that tough black rats might be waiting for him in the tunnel because they had heard of his record on killing mice. Was there rodent solidarity?

Everything cast huge shadows and looked larger in the beams of the flashlights. Nathan could clearly see one rat that was as big as his foot, a lumbering, black-furred animal with a bleeding sore on its back. Nathan stood ready to kick it away, but the rat knew to avoid him. As he trudged in the mushy, spongy, sometimes gravelly, and at other times slippery soil or muck that filled the floors of subway tunnels, the air seemed too hot and too still to breathe. The tunnel, dark and moist, looked as if it should have been cool. Nathan thought he had never been so hot in a dark, moist place. But he did not want to feel a sudden breeze, because the only thing that caused such breezes were oncoming trains. Well, they had radios. They had probably arranged for all oncoming trains to stop. Nathan felt in complete control of himself.

When they arrived at the Union Square station, he was not even sweating. The woman, still attached to his arm like a bat to a cave ceiling, was. She was younger than he had realized. Her black, wet hair clung to her shining forehead. The blurry smudges of makeup made her eyes look deep-set and wide, like those of a frightened nocturnal animal. Nathan, on the other hand, tall, dry, and calm, understood exactly how she felt. He sat her down on a bench and removed the talons from his arm. She was trying to express her gratitude in between epithets—

"I cannot believe this shit. Can you believe this happened? Thank you so much. Fucking assholes. I'm suing. I couldn't have made it without you. Fucking sons of bitches."

But Nathan knew that she could breathe again now and the sweat was drying and she would be all right. He would never get a chance to explain what helping her had done for him. He felt like singing as he climbed the stairs out of the station, rubbing his arms where a small amount of blood had pooled in the woman's fingernail marks. He was in control—unshakably in control. He was indestructible. A wound had healed without leaving a weakened spot. Cristofina's pigeons were well worth the $1,000—worth the sacrifice.

CHAPTER TWENTY-TWO

Calamity in Running Shoes

IT WAS THE SADDEST DAY of the year, the ninth day of Av, Tisha-b'Av. This was the day of Jewish calamity, the day of the destruction of David's Temple in Jerusalem in 586 B.C. Rebuilt, it was again destroyed by the Romans on the same day in A.D. 70, never to be rebuilt until the Messiah comes. It is also considered the date of the expulsion of Jews from Spain and the date of the beginning of the Holocaust. It is a bad day for Jews.

Nathan had been up most of the night before. Sonia had complained of nausea, she vomited, she still felt nauseated. At almost three in the morning, with only a distant siren and a few muffled voices outside, Nathan, who had been trying to comfort her, was overcome with happiness. Sonia saw the silly Raggedy Ann smile on Nathan's face and realized what he was thinking. Of course! He was right, and to her surprise she also felt very happy, though still very nauseated. She reassured him that she wanted it. Her play was in production, and now she really did want the child, though she thought she had been careful and didn't know how it had happened.

"But you're happy, right?" asked Nathan with his arms around her.

"Yes," she moaned as happily as someone can sound when they feel like vomiting.

It was hard to feel optimistic in the scalding August heat of Tisha-b'Av. There were some who said the Messiah would come on a Tisha-b'Av and the temple would be rebuilt on that date. But it didn't seem that the Messiah was coming this year, and most people in the neighborhood were reading signs for more short-term developments. For example, Dukakis, still in the lead, was on the defensive and had to release medical records to quiet the rumor that he was mentally unstable. While not articulating any ideas for the presidency, Bush had managed to shave away his sizable deficits in the polls by politely pointing out the risks of having a short, dark person in the White House. Such a bushy-eyebrowed dark person would be soft on crime and friendly to "criminal elements" sometimes known as black people. Hot Mediterranean blood would account for mental instability. And he could not be trusted with defense, a suspicion bolstered by the fact that he tried to ride in a tank and looked too short. It would have been hard for people in the neighborhood to have believed that Americans were weighing such things seriously, if experience had not already often demonstrated that people out in America thought about completely different things than did people in the East Village.

But on this ninth day of Av in the year 5749, Nusan, the cautious pessimist, saw reasons for optimism. The Mets were out of their slump. Darryl Strawberry's two-run homer had beaten the Pirates 2–1. In fact, the Pirates had been so destroyed in their series with the Mets that they had now slipped to third place behind Montreal. The Mets were comfortably in first place, and even Nusan allowed himself to imagine the unimaginable, the Mets back in a World Series.

José Fishman, who of course didn't know it was Tisha-b'Av, was setting off as usual with his shopping cart in the first summer light of morning, while Nathan and Sonia were still in nauseous joyous embrace, to get cash from the bank machine to go down to Fulton Street, to fight with the few remaining customers, mostly Chinese, over the few remaining fish from the night's market. It seemed no one in the neighborhood, and especially the smarts, could resist sushi at bargain prices. There had been some complaints of tainted fish, and he thought some might even have been true. By the time he got the leftover, sweaty fish back to his shop, they were a withered and rank catch. But what did they want for these prices?

He was beginning to get the feeling that someone was following him. At first he thought it had begun when he got the cash. But to his relief, when he looked in a window reflection, he could see that it was only one of those fucking Dominicano drug dealers. A real stereotype, he wore no socks and looked like he was just off a farm. It irritated him that after all his years in the neighborhood, they were still coming up to him and saying, "Smoke?" as though he were some stupid white guy down in the neighborhood for a weekend thrill. "*¿Qué quieres,* man? Why you follow me, you fucking *plátano* eater? I'm smoking nothing. *Nada!*" He spat.

The words were so angry that the man, more than twice his size, put up his arms defensively, like a boxer cornered against the ropes. The large Dominican was confused by this unexpected aggression and might have run away except that José kept jabbing his shins with the shopping cart, which hurt and angered him. The Dominican released a primordial roar as he grabbed the cart and flung it into the street, which did not yet have traffic. Now he became afraid that he had caused too much attention and, beginning to panic, he grabbed José by the collar and pulled him toward him.

"Fucking *Pandejo,*" José snapped and then seeing the gun at his chest, hissed his final curse, "*¡Hijueputa!*"

The Dominican fired his handgun three times into José Fishman's chest, the barrel held so tightly into his body that the shots made little noise. José's body began heaving and pumping great quantities of blackish blood so that it spilled onto the other man's T-shirt and blue jeans. The killer reached into the muck that had been José and managed to find the folded wad of $20 bills. Then, tearing off his own dark stained T-shirt, he ran east toward the river.

Tisha-b'Av had begun reasonably well for Nusan. Chaim Litvak had returned from Israel the day before with the news that Yankel Fink's knishes sank. The kasha went down in forty seconds, the potato in fifty-two seconds, and since Nusan's bet of one minute was the closest, he won the pot of $110. Kirchbaum, who had reluctantly taken kasha in two minutes, grudgingly pointed out that he had wanted cheese in forty seconds but they had refused to take cheese, saying it would go bad while traveling. "Go bad," Kirchbaum had countered. "There's no cheese. It's all potato, just like the kasha. They're all potato." But no one was going to listen to a sixty-five-year-old, barely retirement age.

Nusan spent his winnings on running shoes at the new store behind Arnie's former sidewalk home. On Tisha-b'Av, as on all days of fast and mourning, Jews are not supposed to wear leather. This was particularly directed toward shoes, it is always said, because leather shoes offer great comfort. It could be argued that the young men on Eighth Street wearing leather pants in the height of August were not especially comfort-able. And the assumption that leather made the most comfortable shoe predated the development of running shoes. Nevertheless, on Tisha-b'Av, or Yom Kippur, or in mourning, comfortable and expensive nylon running shoes were becoming the shoes of penitence.

Nusan, who spent his money on nothing, was pleased to be extrav-agant in mourning, with his crumpled hat and unpressed wool suit soiled on the edges but with the small "100% pure wool" label miracu-lously remaining white, particularly noticeable as a reprise of the white shoes. The shoes had swirling chartreuse and orange stripes intersect-ing in unexpected ways above the soles with clear tubing and spiraled cushioning. Nusan's mourning shoes positively glowed in the August sunlight.

What a perfect day, Nusan thought, to give Nathan the news. Herr Moellen had at last been exposed. During the war, he had been Ober-sturmführer Reinhardt Müller, an SS lieutenant. In 1942, stationed in Naples, he had carried out the execution of an entire family, parents, one grandmother, and three children, for hiding partisans in their house.

"What was the name of the family?" asked a disheartened Nathan.

"Scappi. Why?"

Nathan didn't know why he had asked. Moellen had killed Italians, not Jews. Did the Italians know? The Sals never liked Moellen. Had they known who he was all along? In search of something to say, Nathan asserted cheerlessly, "At least he didn't kill Jews."

Nusan smiled his hard grin. "He was a lieutenant in the SS. I'm sure he had opportunities to make it up. We know that in 1944, he was work-ing at a little concentration camp in Silesia called Gross-Rosen." He smiled gently. "Such a pretty name—Gross-Rosen. The Catholics got him out somehow. He disappeared, and a pastry maker named Bern-hardt Moellen turned up in Argentina applying for a visa to the U.S."

Nathan was silent. Just a week before, Sarah had insisted on going to "the cookie man." Moellen had shown Sarah chocolate men that had melted in the window in spite of the air-conditioning. Some were standing a little sideways. One had completely lost its head. One had lost a shoulder and one side of a face. One had dropped to its knees. Sarah ate two and wanted a third. Moellen cautioned, "Now you are full of chocolate. You will be like them. When you go outside you will start melting."

"No, I won't."

"I think your head will go first, but as you can see, it is hard to predict. Different people melt in different ways."

So it was true, this gruesome talk that fascinated children was his life, his past, it was the real man, and Sarah was fascinated because, unlike her father, she understood that it was in some way all true.

Sarah did not melt in the heat as Moellen had predicted. But she insisted for days that she was melting. Nathan, remembering an anecdote about Beethoven cooling himself off, told her that they could do what "old Ludwig used to do." He filled a pot with cold water, and after fluffing his hair out in a vain attempt to resemble Beethoven, he poured half of the water on her head and, while she was still shrieking with pleasure, poured the other half on his head. It did cool them off, and Sarah thought this was great fun and for the rest of the summer regularly asked for a "lug wig" so that she wouldn't melt.

This man who was part of the sweet and comic life of his little daughter, was he a mass murderer?

"And what about Viktor Stein? Did you run across someone named Viktor Stein?"

"Of Viktor Stein I know nothing."

"It's just a name. The name of somebody he knew—Viktor Stein."

"A Jew?"

"Maybe. I might look like him."

"Viktor . . . Viktor . . . Stein. I will look into this. But"—he held up his hand in a gesture like a traffic patrolman—"one more point," he said, studying a dog-eared piece of lined paper with a handwritten list. "Reinhardt Müller was from a small town north of Berlin. His family ran the local *Konditerei*."

"*Konditerei*," Nathan repeated, as though pretending he had never heard the word.

"They were pastry makers."

It was certain that Nusan would be relentless. With tremendous publicity, Moellen would be exposed, prosecuted, perhaps deported. Nathan had to warn them. He had to warn Karoline. She had never been in the SS or killed anyone.

"Hey, Nathan," said Harry. He seemed very happy. "Let's get some *cuchifrito*. We'll go get Chow Mein to come with us."

"I have to do a little work."

"Working on Tisha-b'Av?" Harry said with mock incrimination.

"Isn't this a fast day? And what did you want to eat?" Nathan was immediately sorry he had said this. He could see from his father's change in posture that he had taken it as an actual reprimand. "I was joking. I have something I have to do. I'll meet you at the casita in fifteen . . . twenty . . . in a half hour."

"Okay." Harry smiled, happy again.

Nathan watched Harry walking up Avenue A with that purposeful Jewish four-beat, singing:

> *If that's your idea of a wonderful time take me home*
> *Take me home*
> *I want you to know that I'm choking*
> *From that five-cent cigar that you're smoking.*
> *You came out with a one-dollar bill,*
> *You've got eighty cents of it still . . .*

Up Avenue A went Harry Seltzer.

And with an even more purposeful step, his son Nathan made his way west two blocks to the Edelweiss Pastry Shop. Bad idea, he realized, and tried three pay phones before going to his copy shop to use the phone.

"I have to talk to you."

"It's over."

"Yes, it is, but I still have to talk to you."

"I'm getting married."

Indifference was not going to be easy. "Congratulations."

"No. I am getting married today."

"Oh. Really? That's so fast!"

"We have been dating for seven years."

"Listen, I just need a few minutes."

"Then we are going on a honeymoon. Won't be back for weeks. Bermuda."

"Bermuda?"

"Dickie picked it. Who cares. Leave me alone."

"It's about your father."

Through the phone he could hear her breathing. "Okay, come over."

When he arrived at her apartment, he sat down in the chair by the small table and told her. She described Nusan's information as "nonsense."

"I don't know."

"I know!"

"I hope you are right, but you should warn him." Nathan was wondering if Nusan could be wrong. There was the similarity in names, the fact that he was a pastry maker, that he spoke Spanish, perhaps Argentine Spanish. These could all be coincidences.

"You believe it, don't you?"

"I don't know. Was his father a pastry maker?"

"Of course. So was my father. Does a pastry-making father make you a Nazi?"

"No," Nathan said apologetically. "From a town near Berlin?"

"From Berlin, Mitte, right in the center. Allied bombing leveled the shop."

"Am I supposed to feel bad about that?"

"Who are you to judge?"

"I don't know. I am just warning you. Who was Viktor Stein?"

In a whisper Karoline repeated, "Viktor Stein. How do you know about him?"

"I heard your father mention his name. Who is he?"

Karoline shook her head, looked confused, sat in a chair by the table. "I don't know. He is somebody I used to hear my parents fighting about when I was a child. I don't know."

"Is he some kind of key to this?"

"I don't know. I only know that my father is a kind and loving man who adores children and always tries to be a good, responsible citizen. You have known him all your life."

Nathan was becoming uncomfortable. He wanted to leave. He noted with pleasure that he didn't *have* to leave the apartment. Without panic, without anxiety, he just preferred to. But he did not know the exit line. "Have a nice wedding"? Or "Have a nice life"? Or "Best to your father the *Obersturmführer*"?

While he was sorting out these thoughts, Karoline began to smile. "I can see what you are thinking."

"You can?"

She cast a deliberate glance at her lumpy mattressed bed. "A little prenuptial."

Before either had completely decided what to do, they were in the bed, Nathan thinking that this was the most wonderfully perverse thing they had done yet—even Mordy might not have done this—and Karoline trying not to think at all, which was her favorite thing about sex.

The police were circulating, looking for anyone who had been on Allen near Stanton Street at about six A.M. that morning. Sonia had heard about it when she went out to the pharmacy. She was now staring at her pregnancy test, wondering why there was no blue line. She knew she was, and yet . . . She could hear the police loudspeaker outside. José Fishman!

How could she tell Nathan that it was only bad sushi? She never thought anything would make her sick. She grew up in Mexico without ever being sick. Three little pieces of tuna. How was she going to tell Nathan?

Harry waited for Nathan at the casita. But after an hour had gone by, he and Chow Mein decided to go to the *cuchifrito*. "I don't know what happened to him," Harry said. Then, brightening, he said, "I'll bet he got mixed up and he's waiting for us over there." But when they got to the little restaurant with the carryout counter and two tables, Nathan was not there. Harry ordered his usual *lechón*.

Afterward, he debated about walking home or going to the copy shop to find Nathan. But the weight of the August heat made him long for home. He sang Berlin back down Avenue A:

> *My wife's gone to the country, hurrah, hurrah!*
> *She thought it best, I need a rest, that's why she went away.*
> *She took the children with her, hurrah, hurrah! . . .*

He finally got to his building. It was cooling just to enter the lobby. He felt tired and decided to relax on the couch in the lobby before going up the elevator. He whistled and sang: "We may never, never meet again, on the bumpy road to love." He loved that little slide. "But I'll always keep—"

Suddenly the seersucker *fardarter* appeared. "I love that song. Cole Porter, right?"

Harry said nothing as he stiffened, got up from the couch, and went out the door back into the clench of summer. "Cole Porter. Cole Porter," he muttered. "Where do these people come from with this Cole Porter meshuggas? *Genug,*" he said, throwing out his hands. Enough. "Settle this once and for all." Despite the heat, he was soon at the bookstore all the way over by Broadway.

On the way back, he struggled to accept the news that the song had been written by the Gershwins. At least it wasn't Cole Porter. He still had plenty of Berlin:

> *Don't do that dance,*
> *That's not a business for a lady*
> *I tell you Sadie,*
> *'Most everybody knows*
> *That I'm your loving Mose,*
> *Oy, oy, oy, oy*
> *Where is your clothes?*

His song was stopped by a sharp blow to the solar plexus. "Oy, oy . . ." He struggled to continue. He couldn't breathe. He gasped. His arm hurt so badly, he thought he must have broken it. He collapsed to the sidewalk, his cheek scraping along the concrete as he tried to find air. Oh God, *lechón,* he thought. Jews aren't made to eat *lechón.* Then he realized that he might be dying and he had never found the magazine. *Big Black Booty* would be found among his possessions. He groaned out, "Magazine." He could not die with it in his file.

"Magazine" was the last word Harry Seltzer ever spoke.

CHAPTER TWENTY-THREE

Tears

Nusan was sitting on the floor, his clothes torn. "I have had . . ." He tried to count on his fingers and gave up. "Nobody knows how many heart attacks I have had. But the *tokhes oyfn tish* is—I never die. No matter what I do, I never die. My brother, my *younger* brother, dies from his first heart attack. And I am still here. For what?"

Ruth didn't want him there. She had never wanted him there. But he had a right to be there. He was Harry's brother. She had learned that lesson.

Nusan's shirt was torn in vertical tears, showing his skin underneath whiter than his yellowed shirt. He had cut deliberate slashes in the lapels of his suit jacket, clean cuts made with scissors. Yet he still did not think to touch the label on his sleeve announcing the purity of the wool. He even cut the brim of his gray hat. A slash in his pant leg exposed a white bony knee. The only clothing spared was the maroon wool scarf—and his bright new running shoes that were for mourning.

The first day of the shiva, Yankel Fink brought what he called egg knishes, eggs—though Felix thought they were life—being for Jews traditional at the meal after a funeral. Fink's egg knishes were mostly potato and weighed more than gold.

By the second day, Ruth, wishing to spare everyone the knishes, had made brisket for eighty people. During the course of the day, more than eighty people visited the Seltzers, but only a few of the uninitiated sampled her brisket. There was also herring. She wanted apple strudel, but when she went to the Edelweiss it was closed—out of business. She had asked Nathan to bake something, but he pointed out that Harry hadn't liked his baking. Or his harmonica playing, Nathan thought to himself.

Nathan was told of his father's death by Mordy, who found him while he was walking down First Avenue biting into a *sfogliatella*. His first thought on hearing the news was that he should stop eating the pastry out of respect. His next thought was how he was supposed to have met his father for lunch and instead was "*schtupping* a Nazi"—surely that was how Harry would have put it. This led briefly to thoughts of physical pleasure—and before Nathan realized it, the *sfogliatella* had been eaten. It was a good one, too.

Nathan was a fortunate man who had reached his late thirties having had little familiarity with death. When Nusan had been Nathan's age, most people he had ever known were dead. Nathan's experiences had been few—that one moment witnessing the violent struggle for life that incongruously preceded Sarah's arrival and now this, this sense that his father was gone, never to return, and he had not said good-bye. When he was in school, he had become close to a student from Minneapolis, Madison, Milwaukee? He could never remember. After they graduated, she was going back there. And she just left without saying good-bye. Nathan understood. It would have been unbearable for them to have said good-bye to each other. But maybe if they had, he would have forgotten her. Instead he still thought about her, wondered about her, because they had not had an ending. Like Harry and the Polish woman Klara. Now he felt that way about his father. He had left without saying anything.

Nathan was not sure what he wanted to say to his father or what Harry might have said to him, but he was certain that there was more to be said. How could he be gone with so much unsaid? He never even told him how much he liked his stupid Irving Berlin songs that no one else remembered. But he had always had the feeling that if his father had known what he was thinking, knew who he really was, he would not have approved. Just before the end, that day walking down the street talking about Klara, he realized for the first time that his father was a friend he could have confided in. He could have told him about Karoline. He would have understood. Here he was now at Harry's shiva. And he was thinking of Karoline. That was the real reason that he couldn't bake something. He couldn't bear baking because it reminded him of *her.*

He had been so desperate for a confidant, he had told Mordy. But his brother only laughed at the gravity he attached to it. "People do this because they enjoy it," Mordy had said. "Look, I'm sure Sonia has done the same thing."

"That's what you don't understand," Nathan had argued. "That's why it is so terrible—so unforgivable. Sonia would never do something like this."

"Well, then you better not tell her," was Mordy's only answer.

Would Harry have understood that his son was in mourning not for him, but for a relationship with the daughter of an SS officer who didn't want him and had just married someone named Dickie? Would Harry have understood that? Nathan didn't know. He didn't know Harry. He hadn't known Harry, and now he never would.

It is always the simplest of remarks that are most regretted. Why hadn't he just eaten *cuchifrito* with his father instead of lecturing him about Tisha-b'Av? Who cared about Tisha-b'Av, anyway? It was just a joke. But Harry had just wanted him along. Karoline—he couldn't go because of Karoline. Would Harry have really understood? *Not now, Dad, I have to go see this woman I've been sleeping with to warn her that Nusan is going to have her father deported because he was an SS officer.*

Three times a day, Litvak and Fink would bring over the group from the shul so the Seltzer sons would have a minyan to say kaddish. Nusan would answer the door and Litvak would say, "May the Almighty comfort you among the mourners of Zion and Jerusalem." And Mordy, for reasons known only to himself, would shake his head and show the beginning of a smile. Nusan let them in and showed them into the dining room just off the living room where everyone was seated, and they said the prayer for the dead, the rhythmic, rhyming Hebrew chant. *"Yisgadal, yisgadosh . . ."* And when finished, the men would mill around the living room, determining that all of the food was *traif* and should not be eaten except for Fink's knishes, which they could no longer bring themselves to eat—not even Fink. Then they would pour shots of bourbon into plastic cups, the bourbon they had provided, throw down the whiskey, place the plastic cups back on the table, say a few words to Ruth, and leave. All of which did nothing for Ruth.

Ruth did not worry about how to get through the day, or the seven days of shiva. But what would she do after that? How could she live in this apartment, in this neighborhood, without Harry? How could she ever walk down Second Avenue again? She would move to another part of town. Maybe up to the Bronx with her friend Esther. No, it was too late for that. Nobody moved to the Bronx anymore. And her sons were here and little Sarah, who had so many important things on her mind and did not allow other people to be unhappy. Sarah had a bit of her father, a questioner. She would not remember Harry. Strange, he had been there every day of her little life, but she wouldn't remember him—except through Ruth. Ruth could not be far from Sarah. But maybe in a different apartment in a different building.

Throughout the day, for days, there were never fewer than twenty visitors in the apartment. Musicians of all kinds came. Nathan never realized how many musicians Harry knew. Harry would have loved having them all in the same room. Mordy found a dark-haired, fleshy woman with a music scale tattooed around her round and soft upper left arm. He had spotted her immediately.

"Hey, Nathan," he had whispered, "she's a *saxophone player*! Alto. Have you ever made it with a saxophone player?"

Nathan had to admit that the best he had ever done was a violinist.

"Cellist would be better."

"I guess," said Nathan. "You mean the leg thing."

Mordy laughed and sauntered over to the saxophonist.

"He never saw my play," said Sonia.

"No. He was excited about it," Nathan said. "We've never had anyone in the family who actually did anything before. He told everyone about his daughter-in-law's play."

"Yeah. He always added, 'She's Mexican, you know.' "

"He could never get over that. Jewish, but she's Mexican."

"I should have made him enchiladas."

"Yeah."

"How do you make them?"

"Don't know. They have to be better than this brisket, though," said Nathan, looking at an untouched platter of gray brown meat.

Chow Mein Vega came over with the tall and lean Palo, and they helped themselves to large platefuls. Nathan thought of warning them, but then he heard Palo say, "This is good *carne,* bro'."

Chow Mein agreed, scraping his plate with a fork. "I wonder if it's kosher. Jews make good *carne.*"

"It reminds me of my mother's *ropa vieja.*"

"Better."

"When did you have my mother's *ropa vieja?*"

"Your mother made it every Sunday and everyone in the barrio used to hide."

Palo smiled. "Me too. It was terrible. I forgot about that. I used to try to eat over at Ramito Sanchez's so that I could get out of the *ropa vieja*. It was like *ropa vieja,* like somebody's old clothes. But this stuff is good," he said as he refilled his plate.

When Chaim Litvak and Yankel Fink came, they were careful not to eat anything. Fink brought another aluminum foil platter of knishes—spinach, mushroom, kasha—all mostly potato, of course, and no one ate them but Chow Mein and Palo. Then Saul Grossman came over with his celebrated *pasteles.*

"Now that's a knish," said Palo.

Ruth explained to Leo Sussman, their lawyer, who liked the herring and the knishes, that she was trying to sort out Harry's papers. "I think we are broke," she said with a distracted smile.

"How can you be broke?"

"I don't know. I can't find any bank accounts with money in them. We have lots of property, but no money. I think we will have to sell something. But it's hard to sort out the property, too."

She had tried. In the room she had rarely entered, she sat in his worn wooden office chair, which he had proudly carried home after finding it on Tenth Street with "only one broken arm" that he had repaired with glue. She ran an index finger over the crack. "It will hold," Harry had correctly predicted thirty years earlier. She fondled a small brass bust of Irving Berlin that she had given him, half in jest, on their twenty-third wedding anniversary. Or twenty-fourth? She opened up the first gray metal filing cabinet. On top was a *Time* magazine from 1962 and a theater program, a not very funny Yiddish comedy by Kornblith that they had seen on her birthday one year. There were other playbills, other magazines. Some deeds, some bills. A Giants program from the Polo Grounds with the scorecard filled out in pencil. Had he taken the boys? She tried to remember. She tried not to remember. There were tax records and crayon drawings by Mordy and Nathan. No signature required. Nathan was a realist, with demanding detail in a young but skilled hand. Mordy had stubbornly remained abstract, with wild strokes and an almost sophisticated sense of color.

Old copies of the *Forvitz* and menus from restaurants and flyers from forgotten concerts, some of which had never happened. In time, Ruth could recognize the financial folders so that she could separate them. She wanted to have a pile to hand to her lawyer. Why did he keep so many magazines? She filled an entire large black plastic garbage bag with old magazines. Should she save the program from the *Broadway Concert for Peace* in January 1968, where they had seen Leonard Bernstein and Barbra Streisand? "And Harry Belafonte," she could hear Harry's voice over her shoulder, sounding so real that it made her jump.

Sal A arrived with a tray of freshly baked *sfogliatella,* whose warm ricotta fragrance seemed to chase away years of brisket and herring. But now Nathan felt guilty about *sfogliatellas,* maybe because he had eaten one instead of mourning at that first moment, or was it that he was not feeling good about pastry anymore? Oh, Karoline, are you in Bermuda doing the same wondrous bad things with Dickie? Dickie.

"I don't know what to do," Nathan confided to Chow Mein. "I didn't want to sell the shop. My father told me not to sell. But now we really need the money."

"So sell it if you need the money."

"I don't like these guys. I don't want them taking over the neighborhood."

"That's what everybody says. But they are taking over the neighborhood, because everybody is selling. They all say, 'I don't want to.' Then they sell. If you don't want them to take over, don't sell to them. Stand up, man. It's time to put your *tokhes sobre la mesa.* Just say no."

"What did you say?" asked Nathan.

"Say no."

"No. About *tokhes sobre la mesa?*"

"Yeah. Put it on the table. Stand up and be counted. Put up or shut up."

"*That's* what it means! Where's Mordy?" He looked around, but his brother and the saxophonist were both gone. "Where did you learn that?"

"Put your *tokhes* on the table? I learned it in the Catskills."

· · ·

When Nathan noticed Mordy missing, an inappropriate thought slipped into his consciousness. Without his brother, there would not be a minyan for the evening kaddish. According to Jewish law, kaddish for your father was one of the primary obligations, but there were too many obligations. He gave his daughter swimming lessons. *Genug,* as Harry used to say when an argument went on too long. Enough. Harry had never been one for davening. Though he had gone to synagogue once a year to say kaddish on the anniversary of his own father's death. Standing with these men, repeating in rhythmic Hebrew the words about God's greatness, was not helping Nathan. And he could see that it didn't help his mother, either. It was for Nusan. Nathan too was doing it not so much for Harry as for Nusan. Or because he couldn't not say it in front of Nusan.

The evening knock on the door. The greeting, "May the Almighty comfort you among the mourners of Zion and Jerusalem." The parade of elderly men into the dining room. And Nathan waiting coyly for the discovery that a tenth man was missing. He looked around the room. At the moment, there were no other Jewish men there. And then Mordy walked in, looking dazed and slightly silly, the way he usually looked.

"On time for the kaddish," he whispered to Nathan.

"I thought you wouldn't make it," said Nathan.

"That's what Harry would have thought. That's why I'm here," Mordy declared.

After the last kaddish, Nathan walked Nusan home. "I have lost my only living relative," Nusan said on the way back to Rivington Street.

Nathan never bothered to correct him. "Are you sleeping, Uncle Nusan? You look like you are not sleeping."

"Sleep? I never sleep. Harry is sleeping."

Nathan inhaled deeply—one last chance—blocked his nasal passages, and opened the door. Nusan took off his slashed jacket and hat and his glowing running shoes. His socks had holes also, but this was probably not for mourning.

Stretching out on the couch in his shredded clothes, Nusan gently laid his head down where there should have been a pillow. Instead it was a brick—not even a new brick, a blackened used brick from the street.

"What are you doing?" said Nathan.

"It's supposed to be a rock. I couldn't find a rock . . . for mourning."

"But you can't sleep like that."

"How do you know? Have you ever tried to sleep like that? Don't say you can't until you have tried it!"

Nathan didn't argue with Nusan. No one did. An hour after Nathan left, Nusan realized, rubbing his head where the brick had been, that he couldn't sleep once again, and he put on his jacket and hat and scarf and went for a walk in the summer night.

In the dark silence of Third Street, almost unconsciously, Nusan checked his jacket pocket on the left side to see that the two pieces of bread he had taken from his brother's shiva were still there, as though he had gotten away with the sleight of hand.

From the corner, Cabezucha, in darkly soiled blue jeans and a new white T-shirt with a picture of Jamaican singer Bob Marley on the front, had seen the old man checking nervously on what was probably a wad of money in his pocket. He walked directly up to Nusan, pulled out his revolver, and lowered it two feet until it was pointed at Nusan's head. Nusan looked up at him with his ice cold dark eyes and began to laugh. "You want to kill me? Kill me! Do you think you are the first? Kill me! Here I am." He stretched out his arms and closed his eyes.

Cabezucha held the pistol barrel to Nusan's white forehead and pulled back the hammer, but he did not fire.

"What! You don't want to kill me? Why does nobody want to kill me?" Nusan, trying to clear his path, pushed upward at Cabezucha's chest with a stiff arm. The arm could barely reach the larger man's chest but still managed to deliver a hard thump. Cabezucha, caught off balance, clawed at Nusan and ended up grabbing on to his maroon scarf.

"Not that!" shouted Nusan as he struggled furiously to wrest the scarf from Cabezucha's slow but powerful grip. With his other hand, Cabezucha fired the pistol point-blank at Nusan, slowly squeezing the trigger six times, firing six shots—all of which missed.

Cabezucha released the scarf and ran down the street in the opposite direction from a police patrol car that suddenly lit up the buildings' dark windows, carnival-like, with flashing colored lights.

Nusan roared with laughter as he straightened his scarf. The laughter exploded out of his mouth as tears ran down his cheeks. "Not me. Can't kill me. Can't be done." And he laughed some more as salt water flowed like a new rain from his eyes, a long-dammed flood. There Nusan stood on the littered Third Street sidewalk, bathed in the pleasure of at last releasing his tears.

CHAPTER TWENTY-FOUR

The Millionaires of the Loisaida

Rᴜᴛʜ ꜰᴇʟᴛ ᴛʜᴇ ᴋɪᴄᴋ, that intrusive stab, that was Harry's foot. She did not have to look at a clock. With eyes closed, she knew that it was between three-thirty and four, the time of night when Harry turned over. He didn't snore. Early in their marriage, that had surprised her. "You look like a snorer," she had said.

"Close," Harry had quipped, and she knew he meant schnorrer, a con artist, which in reality he also wasn't, though he liked to think of himself that way—the slick operator, the impresario.

She would not reach down and remove his leg, the way she always did, because she knew that Harry was gone. She would just go back to sleep, though in the morning he would still be gone. He would not show up on Houston Street. She could never again tell him anything. He no longer existed. And she had not even been able to say good-bye. What would she have said? Something. Something lovely. Something funny. Then she realized that she did not want to say good-bye. She just wanted another chance to talk to him. She fell asleep, though she already knew what her first thought would be when she woke in the morning.

For now, Harry was walking on Second Avenue, looking so real, so lifelike, how could he be gone? And he was singing. It was his voice, un-mistakably. Singing Irving Berlin.

> *I'm going on a long vacation,*
> *Oh, you railroad station . . .*

After the arrest, everyone but Nusan imagined close calls. That large man they called Cabezucha, who was now suspected in eight neighborhood killings and had already confessed to shooting Eli Rabbinowitz, had gotten a massage from Sonia.

"The most disturbing part to me," Sonia had said, "is my judgment. I thought I could tell who to trust. If you can't tell, this business is much too dangerous. But you know, he was really nice."

"Really?" Nathan had always thought of him as a dangerous drug dealer.

Sonia whispered, "He was nicer to me than Eli Rabbinowitz."

Nathan smiled. "Really?"

Most of the neighborhood was relieved when he was caught, though not Mrs. Skolnik, who came into Nathan's shop dressed in a red-and-white sundress with little scenes of Paris in the pattern, a large-brimmed straw hat with a red-and-white cloth band, and a string of beads, also red and white, around her neck. The beads gave her away. Mrs. Skolnik was always color-coordinated, so only a few with experience like Nathan recognized Cristofina's beads. She may have gotten the entire outfit from her. Red and white were the colors of Changó, the powerful light-ning orisha. So powerful, Nathan recalled, that Cristofina charged more for this spirit. Mrs. Skolnik's earrings, red lightning bolts, must have been sold to her by Cristofina as well. Nathan strained over the counter to see if she was wearing red-and-white shoes. She was—red-and-white patent-leather polka-dot high heels.

Mrs. Skolnik stared urgently at Nathan through her pearl pixie glasses and fumbled with her beads, as though invoking extra protec-tion as she spoke. "I need twenty copies. Could I post one of them here?"

Nathan looked at the page while he heard the clicking of plastic beads. "Sure. Are you selling all of your furniture?"

"I have to get out of here. That killer is out!"

"No, they caught him."

"They caught that one and they let out the other one. And he knows I identified him. He'll come after me."

"Ruben García?"

"Yes," she whispered, shaking her beads nervously.

"But he never killed anyone."

"Did you see his eyes?"

Cristofina was like a lawyer. She won no matter how the case went. She earned money making sweet-faced Ruben scary, and now she earned more protecting Mrs. Skolnik from her best work, his scary eyes.

Mrs. Skolnik, too, thought she was having narrow escapes. As she left, Nathan could hear Carmela above saying, *"A'ta 'uego, Changó."* See you.

Fearless, Nathan took the F train to Delancey Street and felt no anguish even when the train slowed to a near stop in the tunnel. At Delancey he got out and walked to Rivington Street to see Nusan, once again the survivor.

Nusan scoffed at the suggestion that he had narrowly escaped death. He had his own ideas about narrow escapes. "He tried. He shot at me six times. The police found all the bullet holes."

Nathan and everyone else in the neighborhood had already heard this. "Why do you think he didn't hit you?"

"Exactly. That shlemiel could hit nothing. It was the bystanders who barely survived. They are the survivors." They both laughed together, one of the few real laughs they had ever shared.

"Really, Nusan, how did he miss so many times right up close?"

The smile left Nusan. "I am not so easy to kill. You think this fellow was smarter than Hitler? Do you think he was tougher than the Gestapo? I have more to fear from your friend with the pastry." Then he grew silent and adjusted his scarf. "You know what?" he said in a quiet voice. "He probably would have killed me if it wasn't for the scarf." He pulled his maroon wool scarf tighter around his neck.

"The scarf?"

"Yes, this. He tried to take it and I went crazy, and that scared him. He didn't know what he had. Look, come here." Nusan beckoned Nathan with a conspiratorial gesture. "Feel this," he whispered, holding out his scarf.

Nathan felt the scarf. It felt like wool. But there were some very small, hard bumps. Nusan whispered three inaudible syllables.

"What?"

Nusan tried again, not much louder. "Diamonds."

"How many are in there?" Nathan whispered.

"Twenty-seven." Nusan smiled and continued whispering. "I have been living off of this scarf since 1948. I bought my trip to New York. I rented this apartment. This is how I live." Still whispering, he added with unconcealed glee, "Guess how many I have already used."

"How many?"

"Guess."

"Twenty."

"Only nine, since 1948. They are good stones."

"Where did you get them?"

Nusan laughed like someone who had just heard a very good joke, loudly, uncontrollably. He saw Nathan's surprise. Struggling to regain his voice, he said gravely, "This is really funny." Then he broke into a wheezy, shoulder-heaving laugh. Finally he managed to whisper, "I stole them—from a German—a Nazi. When I was in the DP camp waiting for my visa. He had hid them so carefully. Just like his war record. But I found both. I'll get your pastry maker, too."

"He's harmless. Leave him alone."

"Oh? You really think he is innocent?"

"Yes."

"I can tell that you don't. You are keeping something from me."

"I don't know a thing about him. Just that he is from Berlin and changed his name."

"No, there must be something else. If you think he is innocent, tell me. We can clear him."

"He is innocent. He is just a pastry maker who loves children."

"Tell me, then."

Nathan let the scarf drop on Nusan's belly.

"Remember," Nusan said in sudden earnestness, "if something happens to me, get the scarf."

"All right."

Nusan grabbed Nathan's wrist with a surprisingly powerful grip, the grip that must have surprised Cabezucha. "It's important."

"I'll remember."

But Nusan was wrong. Bernhardt Moellen was not Obersturm-führer Reinhardt Müller. He was Schütze Bernhardt Müllen, Private Müllen, a draftee in the Wehrmacht, the German army, just as he had always said. He and his wife did go to Argentina before immigrating to the United States. When he entered the United States, he changed his name to Moellen because he thought the umlaut would be too difficult.

Moellen had always tried to conceal his war record. But now he was forced to tell the truth. He had written it out years ago, so that if he ever had to tell the story, he would have all the facts before him. He used the third person so that it would sound like a document, not a confession—the truth in its proper absurdity.

The *Schütze* Shoots *Ein Geshütz*

Bernhardt Müllen had managed to stay in Berlin for most of the war, baking pastries for meetings of chubby mass murderers who plotted death with his powdered sugar still on their lips. He actually did once make a *kugelhopf* for Adolf Hitler, which was when he had learned that the cake was a favorite, though to his great relief, he did not have to actually meet the Führer. He never even heard if Hitler liked his *kugelhopf,* though he supposed it had gone reasonably well, since Müllen did not receive orders to report to the army for some time. And it was the Austrian cake, not at all the Alsatian brioche his daughter liked to make.

Then, in 1945, without having ever been inducted or trained, he was given *ein Geshütz,* a gun. He knew nothing more about the tool. It was a gun. He had no idea how to shoot a *Geshütz,* though to be honest he made no real effort to learn since he had no intention of using it. He was told that he was now a private, a *Schütze.* He was sent out of Berlin to the south along with hundreds of other *Schützen* with a variety of *Geshützen.* Though he was already in his forties, most of the others were about sixteen years old. For two days, he wandered with his *Geshütz* and several armed and terrified children through muddy Prussian fields and woods dampened in spring rain until, half-starving, he found himself behind a thick tree with someone in the distance shooting at him. Hearing the flat, hard *thwack* of bullets hitting the tree, he was afraid to look out, but he finally gained the courage for a quick peek. To his joy, they were Americans and not Russians. He had wandered too far and missed the Red Army, which was probably in Berlin by this time. He looked again. There were three Americans with *Geshützen* far bigger, it seemed, than his.

"Apple pie à la mode!" shouted the cornered, starving Private Müllen, suspecting that this would make little sense to the Americans. But it was the only American phrase he could think of. The shooting stopped, and Müllen threw away his gun and came out from behind the tree with his hands in the air. Suddenly he was rolling in the mud. An American had shot him! He had been shot in the leg. Then Müllen remembered something else. "Strawberry rhubarb! Strawberry rhubarb pie!"

One of the Americans shouted something back about strawberry rhubarb pie. Incredible, Müllen thought, and repeated it again. "Strawberry rhubarb pie!" It turned out the American loved strawberry rhubarb pie, and that was how Müllen convinced him to take him prisoner instead of killing him. And he still had a phrase in reserve, "*Boston cream pie,*" to say in the event he was interrogated. Private Müllen's military career was over.

Karoline was relieved to have the truth at last, yet when she had warned her parents of what was about to happen, they had acted as though they had been caught.

"We knew this day would come, Bernsie."

Moellen sighed. "Yes, we knew."

Karoline did not understand. Surely they could prove who they were. He could prove that he was not Reinhardt Müller.

"Yes," said Moellen, "but we will never be accepted in this neighborhood again. The Jews and the Italians and the others, they will never buy pastry from us. They will never let me play with and tease their children. But you will get married and live on the East Side with Dickie and open a better shop in midtown. And we will retire. It's funny, when we first came here, we didn't want to live on the Upper East Side because it was full of Germans. We wanted to get away from Germans and be here with the Jews and Italians and Poles."

And now the Edelweiss Pastry Shop was over, too. The Moellens waited for a visitor. One came in only a few days, someone from immigration. They hadn't expected that. They had thought at least FBI.

There were so many different kinds of federal agents in the neighborhood. They thought it would have been something rarer than the people who checked the papers on the dishwashers at the restaurants. It was not difficult for Moellen to prove who he was, though, and once that was cleared up, they quietly left the neighborhood.

Karoline had been trying for days not to think about the idea that if she had not become involved with Nathan Seltzer, this might not have happened. Maybe it would have. Her parents thought that it would have happened anyway. That it was predestined.

"But you are innocent," Karoline insisted.

Her father said, "No one is innocent. Babies are innocent."

"Viktor Stein," said her mother. And her father affirmed by repeating the name.

"Who is Viktor Stein?" Karoline shouted in exasperation.

"Shh!" both her parents responded.

"No one is listening," Karoline said.

"Viktor Stein was my oldest friend," said Moellen. "We grew up together. He and his wife and two children lived in our building. They took away his job. Then they made him leave our building. Then they took them all away."

"And killed them," said Karoline's mother.

"And killed them," Moellen confirmed.

"What does that have to do with you?" said Karoline.

"Exactly," said Moellen. "That is what I said, too. Why should I do anything? So my oldest friend and his family are robbed and murdered. What does this have to do with me?"

It was an ordinary summer afternoon at the Casita Meshugaloo. The tomatoes were still coming in. Felix estimated at least three more weeks and then he should have enough capital to buy produce from the Italians in the Bronx. The multieyebrowed Ruben was out, his face still tattooed, the Dominican flag around his head now concealed by dark, thick hair. He was free and futilely brushing up on his Japanese, even though Panista, who had talked to several Japanese restaurant owners, told him, "They are never going to hire a dude with two sets of eyebrows."

Then something happened there that had never happened before. For the first time, Ruth Seltzer came through the gate in the chain-link fence that still had the sign that said "Free Ruben García," through the garden, and into the casita. Was she now going to take Harry's place? Try to promote boogaloo? Eat *cuchifritos*?

No, Ruth had come to tell Chow Mein Vega that she was selling the lot that the casita was on. Probably a high-rise luxury apartment would be built there.

"Luxury? This is Alphabet City. Loisaida."

"That's their problem. They want to pay the money. I have to sell something, and boyoboy, this is the best deal and it displaces the fewest people. Nobody *lives* here."

Chow Mein could not answer. He had no other home. He would move back to the barrio where he was born, where it was still a neighborhood . . . for now. But if they were building luxury apartments off Avenue B, anything was possible. Someday they might even buy Spanish Harlem.

"I didn't even know that Harry owned the casita."

"We own the land. You knew somebody owned it."

"I didn't. It was just an abandoned lot. We worried about the city taking it. Harry never said anything. Maybe he didn't know that he owned it."

Ruth smiled. It was perfectly possible that Harry Seltzer owned property that he didn't know about. But he knew about this. "No, he knew," she said. "They had been offering him money for several years. Every time they offer a little more. I wish I could afford to hold out longer and let the price go up more."

"Harry never said a word."

Ruth knew what Chow Mein was thinking. This was how it always worked. Everyone loved Harry because Harry never charged anything. So now he left us without any money and I have to sell something. If he had collected a little rent now and then, I wouldn't be selling the lot. But I am the one left to do the bad thing, and Harry is loved. It's what Harry left me, she wanted to argue. "My soul isn't a raisin, if you know that expression." He did. "It's what I have to do." She did not tell him that she was thinking of moving into the new building. It was what she needed, a place in the neighborhood that had no connection, no reminder of the old neighborhood. But they would hate her for moving there, too. And now she realized that if her father had not failed, if he had realized his dream of developing the neighborhood, he would have been the most hated man on the Lower East Side.

"The funny thing is," said Chow Mein, "all the time I was feeling guilty getting Harry to pick up the tab on *cuchifritos,* and now it turns out he was the landlord."

"No," said Ruth. "He wasn't the landlord. Landlords charge rent."

Chow Mein smiled. "Yeah, that's true."

Then some words came out of Ruth's mouth that as far as anyone knew had never come out of her mouth before. "Oh, shit," she said.

She looked behind her to make sure no one was listening. "I can find an apartment for you."

"I have no money."

She looked around again. "We still have lots of people squatting," she whispered. Chow Mein smiled. "But you can't tell anyone. And if Harry comes back from the dead to laugh at me, don't tell him, either. Just don't tell anyone."

"No. I mean, thank you. Thank you. But this isn't going to be any place for me."

"Harry would want you to stay."

"But Harry's not here. The casita won't be here."

"I know that we are lucky because my father left all this property, but we have never earned any money on it. The best thing it's given us is free places to live. Can I tell you something?"

"What?"

"Have you ever had"—she hesitated to pronounce the word—"a vacation?"

"Oh man, when boogaloo was hot, we had everything. Don't know where it went. I just drank it all up, I think."

"I have never been on a vacation. Have you ever been to Iceland?"

"Iceland?"

"All my life I have wanted to go to Iceland. It has glaciers, volcanoes, and towns half-covered in lava, and geysers and mineral springs so warm you can swim in the winter with the ice and snow all around. And the people are all Vikings."

"Vikings," said Chow Mein, indicating a horned helmet with his two hands.

"The Vikings never wore those. I think that was Germans. The Vikings wrote literature, sagas describing their adventures. It's all written down. How they came to America before anyone. I've read some of them. And today they still speak Viking and eat putrefied shark and whale blubber. When I told my son Mordy that I wanted to go to Iceland and eat whale, he was completely disgusted with me."

"Are there any Jews in Iceland?"

Ruth laughed. "What a question. You've become more Jewish than my sons."

"I've tried to teach them." They both laughed.

"Probably if there had been any Jewish Vikings, they would have moved to Israel by now. I think Jewish Vikings would definitely make aliyah."

Chow Mein laughed.

"I would love to go to Iceland. I would even go over a bridge to get to the airport if I could fly to Iceland for *vacation*." Her voice caressed the last word. "Is there any place you want to go that you haven't been?"

Chow Mein nodded.

"Where?"

"You won't tell anyone?"

"No. Of course not."

"Puerto Rico."

"You have never been there?!"

"Once for a concert, but it was in a club near the airport. I have never seen the part of the island where my parents were born. Cabo Rojo. You know, the people there make *pasteles* stuffed with crab and *mofongo* with *carrucha,* you know, *carrucha,* scungilli . . . You don't eat that stuff. Big sea snails and pepper sauce. When I finish my book, I'm out of here. I'm going to get a place in Cabo Rojo. That's why I don't need an apartment. I'm not even going to be here much longer."

Ruth took his thick right hand in her two small ones. "You made the neighborhood a better place."

Chow Mein looked at her. "That's because I thought it was my place, too."

．　．　．

It was Chow Mein Vega's idea, the perfect tribute to Harry Seltzer: a concert. On the program were a dozen musicians Harry had tried to help. Many young musicians offered to play, some out of respect for Harry, some because various club owners and music people who knew Harry, such as Tommy Drapper, would be in the audience, and some for both reasons. Nathan did not offer to play his harmonica because Harry had never liked it. The whole concert made Nathan sad, reminded him of the great distance that always stood between him and his father. Mordy was undeterred and installed equipment to perform his "Pentium Processor Concerto," a series of electronic bleeps and bongs. At several points the piece seemed to stop, and invariably a few people would make themselves foolish by starting to applaud just as it started up again, so that when it finally ended no one dared applaud.

Wilson Morelos had asked for a spot, saying that Harry had been very kind to him. Chow Mein let him play a short horn piece and was surprised to hear a restrained, cool, muted sound, not Dominican merengue.

Chow Mein Vega had to play the finale, even though Ruth and almost everyone else found it hard to imagine how boogaloo would fit in a memorial concert. The piece was listed on the program as "Un Boogaloo Mas," "One More Boogaloo." Chow Mein had asked Felix to play congas with him, as he often did, but there were no other musicians. It did not begin with "Ahhhh!" There was no singing, only a slowed-down boogaloo beat on congas while Chow Mein plucked an acoustic guitar, the two playing and thinking about loss. Felix, as he patted the skins of his congas, remembered the green Cibao and all the people waiting for the money he could no longer send since he had left the drug trade, while Chow Mein lost himself in memories of baseball championships in the barrio and the scream of crowds in the great years of boogaloo and his wife, who died in New York while he was touring—and of Harry Seltzer, who had always tried to help.

After the concert, Tommy Drapper was at the head of a phalanx of music people who headed for Chow Mein Vega and Felix with offers. Felix listened with excitement and then horror as Chow Mein turned them all down. "I am a boogaloo singer. We'll play boogaloo."

"Nobody wants boogaloo. They want what you just did," said Drapper.

"I'm just a boogaloo singer," Chow Mein kept saying. His only explanation to Felix: "Everybody has to have something that isn't for sale."

"Everyone who is rich. Poor people have everything for sale."

"If you are poor, it is even more important to keep something for yourself, to have something that is not for sale."

"Fine. We're the millionaires of the Loisaida. We are above making money!"

Chow Mein could see that Felix didn't understand. Harry would have understood. Harry was the old neighborhood.

Nathan took Sarah by the hand and walked to the copy center. He lifted the iron gate to let them in but kept it halfway down so that the shop remained closed.

"*Lamento mucho* about *tu padre*," said Carmela from the fire escape. Nathan waved up at her.

Nathan gave his own memorial concert with an audience of Sarah and Pepe Le Moko, who sat together in a corner in rapt attention as Nathan exhaled on his harmonica the soft, dark, pleading, slightly Middle Eastern notes of a Kol Nidre. The Kol Nidre is to remove guilt for unfulfilled vows. Harry did not particularly like the piece. Harry did not like Kol Nidre, he did not like classical music, and he most definitely did not like the harmonica. But it was Nathan's music. It was his harmonica variation of a Max Bruch cello piece that Nathan had played in synagogue for Yom Kippur when he was fourteen. Harry had gone up to him afterward and told his son that he thought it was beautiful. It was the only time Harry had ever praised his music. Then he turned to Ruth, saying, "I'd love to hear Nathan's music on a cello! On a cello, that would be something!" Even as Nathan played now, he could hear Harry saying, "That would be something!"

"Hey," said Ruben, sticking his head under the gate.

Nathan looked up.

"The guy who did this said to be sure to show it to you. Said you would appreciate it."

"Let's see it."

Ruben turned around and yanked up his T-shirt, revealing an American flag unfurled across his back flying from a tall red penis. Nathan tried to think of a way to distract Sarah. But Ruben protested, "It's art. You should see what I paid for this. It's art. *Tu sabe'*, your father bought me my first tattoo."

"I want to see it again!" said Sarah.

CHAPTER TWENTY-FIVE

The Bread of New York

THE SUMMER was over and so were the Mets, Michael Dukakis, and the Jewish year. George Bush was ahead in the polls 45 to 41 percent. Sixty percent to 27 said that Bush was "stronger on defense," though from the East Village point of view, who was there to defend against, except maybe George Bush?

The Mets clinched the Eastern Division, but Nusan saw what was coming. The Dodgers, a team people used to root for until it moved to Los Angeles, had a pitcher with the weird name of Orel Hershiser that no Met, not even Strawberry, could hit. "Orel?" said an angry Dr. Kucher. "Oral! They are shut down by a pitcher named Oral and you don't think there is something Freudian going on?"

Karoline married into what she called "a rational life," which meant a life without her destructive passions. She was glad that there had been a time when she had let herself indulge, that she had in a sense "gotten away with it"—done it and stopped before it destroyed her. Still, sometimes she caught herself wishing for one last time. In time, she hoped, she would not remember this summer.

Now, twenty years after the first Fat Finkelstein was killed in a place called Khe Sanh that Nathan had refused to fight for, Nathan walked by the Moellens' abandoned Edelweiss Pastry Shop and found that it too was now called Khe Sanh—a much-talked-about new Vietnamese restaurant.

Khe Sanh instantly became the most popular new place in the neighborhood. Nathan overheard the girlfriend of the seersucker *fardarter* discussing the restaurant situation. "Khe Sanh," she explained, "is a good place to be at the end of a long day. You can sit there and have some coconut milk. But it's not for a birthday!"

"Oh God, no," agreed the seersucker *fardarter*. "For a birthday you need something like Viva la Huelga!"

"I don't know. Mexican?"

"But it's *nueva cocina.* They have red snapper chimichangas."

Both restaurants were making money. In fact, it seemed almost everybody was making money. Most of the old neighborhood people complained about what was happening, but rather than put their *tokhes* on the table, they put their signature on the contract. And they made money. Worthless properties commanded fortunes. Failing businesses could be sold for profits. It was a time of moneymaking for New Yorkers. Even Dr. Kucher made money. When no academic press would publish her *Pathology of the Mets,* she sold it to a commercial publisher for a $500,000 advance under the title *The Mets: A Psychodrama.*

This was Nusan's explanation: "In Europe, all you can do is survive. But if you have the kind of luck to survive in Europe, chances are in America you will end up rich. Whether you want to be or not."

Even Nathan's shop was showing a profit—in part because of the higher prices he charged the new restaurants for their menus and flyers. A producer was investing in Sonia's play, and it would soon move to a larger theater. But also the Seltzers were about to get a great deal of money for selling their vacant lot, which would become the tallest apartment building in the neighborhood. Ruth had been offered the penthouse, but having never lived higher than the sixth floor, she didn't like the idea; it made her feel queasy, a feeling that was enhanced by the possibility of gazing from her living room out on the bridges of lower Manhattan.

Ruben and Palo had given up on the Japanese and found employment at a new "caviar bar." Panista and several others had also been promised jobs there. At the soon-to-be-closed casita, afternoons were passed arguing details.

"I love belugita."

"Fuck beluga, sevruga is where it's at."

"Beluga is like gold."

"No, *pendejo,* that's ossetra. I can get into ossetra. But beluga has those skins that just melt away on your tongue."

Chow Mein Vega was not yet making money, and like most of those who weren't, he would soon be out of the neighborhood.

Felix, observing that the Italians were making money and the Puerto Ricans were not, became Felice and pronounced it in the Sicilian way that rhymed with how Nusan said "knish." He renamed his store Felice's East Village Gourmet. He even made a point of dropping in on the Sals who had never noticed him as a Puerto Rican and showing off his Sicilian dialect. But the Sals were not interested in new Sicilians coming to the neighborhood and creating more competition. Sal Eleven didn't like his accent. After Felice left the store, Sal would make an expression as though he had just smelled something extremely unpleasant and dismiss the upstart with a wave of his hand. Then Sal would explain to whatever customer was there, "That guy thinks that because we are from Palermo we're supposed to be *fratèlli*. But I can tell that he's not from my *mandamento*. I'm from Kalsa, there's no way he's from Kalsa. Maybe Albergheria, but not Kalsa."

"How do you know?" the customer would ask.

"The accent," said Sal, brushing away the interloper with another dismissive sweep of his arm. "*Che accènto*. It's a different part of Palermo. We Sicilians are never fooled by accents."

Sal First went even further. "That guy says he's from Palermo, but I hear his accent—Catania." He whispered the word harshly, as though it were a curse capable of summoning up the forces of darkness. But when Sal A heard the new grocer was from Catania, he stopped by to visit him. Felice denied being from Catania and said he was from Palermo. Sal A could see the Arab in him and hear it in his voice, reasoning he was from Erice, Trapani, or even Favignana, "but more likely, he is a Tunisian here illegally. That's none of my business."

Felice's East Village Gourmet became one of the popular new stores. He no longer specialized in produce from the casitas—the tomato season was over. He had started buying produce from Italians in the Bronx and had even made some contacts with upstate farmers. When the plumbing supply store next to him went out of business, he rented that and expanded his store, putting a kitchen in the back. He hired Dominican women from the neighborhood and taught them how to make caponata, but he would never speak to them in Spanish, even the ones whose family knew his back in the green Cibao. They would speak Spanish and he would shout in Italian, not Italian but Sicilian dialect, as he rolled a hard-boiled egg in his right hand. He said *ova* instead of *uova* for egg, even though the Italian would have been easier for a Spanish-speaking person to understand. He believed that hard-boiled eggs, *ova duri,* should go in almost everything, and he found a good egg connection in Washington Heights. Tomatoes were never excluded. One of his specialties was hard-boiled eggs in tomato sauce, *ova duri ca sarsa.* He grated hard-boiled eggs on top of his caponata and added artichokes, octopus, shrimp, and squid, which the Sals, in a rare point of agreement, considered an atrocity. Even more infuriating, he put a label next to the platter: "*Capunata Palirmitana,*" Parlermo-Style Caponata.

"They do this in Palermo," said Sal A, "but it is an exaggeration. It is not in good taste."

But Sal Eleven leaned forward with a knowing nod that meant he had won the argument and said, "Catania."

At the new Felice's East Village Gourmet, everything, besides Felice and his staff, was Sicilian except for two dozen bialies that came in from Grand Street every week.

Felix had become so proud, so confident, about his new business that he invited Rosita to come look at his store, the kitchen, taste some of the specialties.

"This could be, you know, what they call a mom-and-pop business."

Rosita gently pushed away from him and walked aimlessly through the store, examining vegetables. She smiled almost shyly and said, "It's just not what I want."

"It's clean, Rosita. I know what everybody thought, but there is no drug money in this business. I built it on casita tomatoes."

"This neighborhood. It's changing. Everything's changing. New opportunities. You know what I think? I told this to my mother, I thought it would make her mad. But she said, Good for you, Rosita!"

"Good for you, Rosita, what?"

"I've decided—no Puerto Ricans. Everyone is going somewhere but us. I don't want a Puerto Rican."

"I'm going somewhere." But she didn't believe him—because he was Puerto Rican, which he wasn't. His next move had been planned, even studied for. "Rosita, I'm not Puerto Rican."

"What do you mean?"

"My name is not Felix."

"I know. It's El Cuquemango."

"No," he said with irritation. "It is Felix."

"I thought you said it's not Felix."

"It's not. There are different levels of not being, *tu sabe'*, and I am not El Cuquemango. But on a much deeper level I am not Felix, either."

Rosita stared at him the way she would have looked at a magician whose trick she had not yet figured out.

"I pretend to be Puerto Rican because Puerto Ricans are citizens. I'm not a citizen. I'm—I'm Italian, Siciliano, from Palermo." He started speaking in the Italian he had studied, Sicilian dialect, Palermo accent, with the final vowels swallowed. Rosita spoke to him in Nuyorican and he spoke to her in Siciliano, and they understood each other.

On the afternoon of Rosh Hashanah, the first afternoon of the Jewish New Year, the tradition is for Jews to walk to the water's edge and rid themselves of the sins of the past year by casting them in the form of pieces of bread into the water. For the Lower East Side, the nearest available repository of sins was the East River. The Seltzer family and many others would walk through the alphabet avenues. They walked past the baths, which were now jade green and called the Kyoto Baths, and past the casita, where it was written on the sidewalk, "Our home has been stolen by the Seltzers."

This had been written in the night and Chow Mein tried to wash it off the next morning, but the white paint had already set. The Seltzers and the other repentant Jews stepped over the words, walking past the projects and the Latin people who were used to seeing them over there every September.

Palo was standing in front of a brick wall where someone had written, "Jew landlords took our Casita." He was trying to block the words until Chow Mein got back with spray paint to cover it over. But Palo was not wide enough to block it completely. When Nathan walked by, Palo said, "Sorry, it wasn't us."

"I know that."

"We know who it is. We'll take care of it."

"Let it go."

"We clean up our own dirt."

Sarah, who was holding Nathan's hand, looked up at Palo and said, "Can you say '*Bay dem schtetl schteyt a schtibl*' really fast?"

Palo shook his head.

"Try! Really fast."

"We have to go, Sarah," said Nathan.

"By da stable sat a stebl," Palo said gamely. Sarah giggled.

The Jewish sinners could smell the smoke from the building Dubinski was burning down on Avenue C. The squatters would be out, the insurance would pay. Nathan could hear Harry say, "Burning them out on Rosh Hashanah, the anti-Semitic bastard."

Up the steps to the walkway over the speeding traffic of the FDR Drive they walked, down the other side through the park that was, for the first time in years, starting to be used again, so that the few remaining drug addicts, mainly old-fashioned heroin shooters, would stare in confusion as though caught with their pants down at the parade of Jewish sinners. Then they all walked to the railing by the river along the blacktop walkway, some with broad-brimmed black hats, some with colorful Israeli skullcaps so small only a hair clip would keep them on, others bareheaded, and all sharing the riverside walkway with panting joggers. The Seltzers chose their spot, under the massive steelworks of the Williamsburg Bridge, like standing between the stocky legs of a giant. Across the water were the sugar docks that landed Dominican cargo in Brooklyn.

As always happens in these matters, those with the fewest sins cast them off the most grandly. For three-year-olds sins are nearly weightless, pondered painfully but readily shed, so Sarah delighted in holding the loaf of bread Sonia had carried for her and breaking off pieces, huge chunks in rapid succession, and hurling them through the fence and into the green brown opaque and churning waters of the East River. Sarah talked of feeding the fish and strained her little body to see fish rush for the bread, but the only fish she saw had its white belly showing and was floating in the current along with what appeared to be a chair leg.

Poor Harry, afraid of rivers, never got rid of any sins. Nathan thought of how his father had carried to his death the sin of having lusted after a goy, a girl named Klara. When Harry was a child in Poland, where did he cast his sins, or was that how he learned to fear rivers?

Nathan noticed that his mother, deep in thought, occasionally dropped a piece of bread with a delicate flick of her thumb and forefinger. Ruth could not bring herself to look up at the bridge or even turn her head to the right or left, where waited the unbearable sight of more bridges. She concentrated on the water and the bread.

Nathan walked over to her, a piece of stale bread in his hand. "Mordy never comes," he said.

"Oboy, it's a gift," Ruth answered.

"What is?"

"Mordy doesn't have to come here for the New Year because he has the ability to cast off his sins wherever he finds them. He just tosses them off. The rest of us can't do that. You can't. You are like your father. Like Nusan."

Nathan thought about his father. Remembering not going to the *cuchifrito* with him, he tore off a piece of bread and threw it. He thought about Nusan. Did Nusan go to another part of the river, or did he just keep his sins to torture himself? In any event, Nathan could not imagine Nusan willfully throwing out bread.

"Why was Nusan so angry with Dad?"

Ruth shook her head as though trying to shake off the question. "He wasn't. He's angry with me. Everyone's angry with me. Now all the Puerto Ricans are angry, too."

"You just did what you had to do. Everyone understands that."

Ruth shrugged.

"You know what I sometimes think?" said Nathan, putting his arm around his mother's shoulder and staring at the troubled East River. "There are a lot of things men do and they are understood, but as soon as a woman does it . . . You are entitled to a living for your family, too."

"That's nice, Nathan," said Ruth, patting his cheek the way she did when he was a small and earnest boy. "But I'm not as innocent as you imagine. Boyoboy. You know what I did?"

"What?"

Ruth sighed. "We should all be more like Mordy." She threw more bread in the water. Then she turned to face her son. "I did something really terrible. Not everything can be cast off and forgiven."

Nathan stopped asking, and they stood there in silence. Ruth turned back toward the river. "Just before the war, Nusan wanted to come here. The whole family. They were desperate. I wouldn't help them."

Nathan looked at his mother.

"I didn't understand. We didn't understand. There were almost a dozen of them—brothers, sisters, parents, aunts and uncles, even one grandmother. We had to agree to take them all in, house them, feed them. They had no skills. They didn't even speak English. They were shtetl. They would have turned Avenue A back into a shtetl. They were everything Harry had escaped. Literally. He came here to get away from his family and their life. You hear of Jews fleeing the Cossacks, the pogroms. Harry fled the *mespuchah*. He was running away from his family. And happily for him, they didn't want to leave. But then they had to, and we didn't know what to do. You know this country was very anti-Semitic at the time. These people were like a provocation. We would have had a lot of trouble if this neighborhood had started filling up with them. And Harry would have been right back in the place that he had just escaped. But we had to do it. So, oboy, we talked and debated. And thought and agreed that it was what we had to do, and by then the Nazis had taken Poland and you couldn't get them out. Then Hitler killed them all. We didn't know that Hitler was going to kill them all. Who would have thought that? We heard that. We even read pamphlets that claimed it. But who would believe it?"

Nathan could see the tears gathering in his mother's eyes. He wanted to comfort her, but she pushed him away.

"I haven't told you the worst. And this was not your father, it was completely my stupid idea. We sent them money. Can you imagine? The Nazis got it all. It was like paying the Nazis to take them."

Nathan thought of how he struggled to live with his choices. Karoline. Not going to the *cuchifrito*. He put his arms around his mother and held her safe under the menacing bridges. But she pushed away again. "So now you know."

She started to walk away and then turned and came back to the rail. "Nathan," she said, "I've been talking to your father. He comes to me every night."

Nathan nodded with understanding.

"You too?"

Nathan nodded, not looking at her.

"It's so real. To tell you the truth, we haven't been getting along of late. Every night he's crabbing. The whitefish at Saul's isn't good anymore. It is better on Grand Street. I tell him that Saul Grossman is convenient. I don't want to walk to Grand Street. He says I can get them when I go for bialies. I say, What do you care, you're dead. That's no excuse, he says. And then he starts in on the seltzer delivery, which he says is a plot. By delivering seltzer, they are getting a list of where all the Jews live, like they did in Europe. Oh, and suspending alternate side of the street parking on Jewish holidays is philo-Semitism, he now says. Just anti-Semitism in disguise. This is the meshuggas I listen to every night. Boyoboy, he is a bigger nudnik dead. Do you think this is some way of telling us that his spirit is still alive, in us?"

"I don't know," said Nathan. "It just happened to me one time . . . twice."

"But if he's coming back as a spirit, why isn't he more—I don't know—more spiritual—and not such a nudge? And can I ask him things, like where is the title to number 425? But it's my dream he comes in, and I don't remember these things while I'm dreaming—which makes sense—I mean, I'm asleep. But what about him? He's dead and still he's remembering things like the whitefish at Saul Grossman's."

Not expecting an answer from Nathan, she quietly started walking back into the neighborhood. Sarah saw her leaving and took her hand. The two walked back holding hands, Ruth weighted to the ground, Sarah skipping, like a balloon tethered to Ruth by an outstretched arm. "*Feygele, feygele, pi-pi-pi,*" they chanted together.

"*Vu is der tate?*" Ruth sang gently.

"*Nisht ahie',*" Sarah shouted.

"*Vos t'er brengen?*"

"*A fesele bir.*"

Little bird, little bird, peep-peep-peep. Where is your daddy? He's not here. What will he bring? A mug of beer.

"You haven't thrown much bread," said Sonia, her curly blond hair vibrating in the swirling river winds at the edge of Manhattan. "No good sins this year?"

Nathan always suspected that Sonia knew about Karoline. But he would not confess. Karoline had insisted that he would, and he had sworn that he never would. He was not going to let her be right about that. Living with his lie was the only honor he had left. Like Karoline and, for that matter, the Democratic National Committee, he hoped that in time he too would forget this past summer.

"I'll tell you a good sin, if I'm not limited to last year," said Sonia.

She's bargaining, Nathan thought. Going back in the archives to get something really good so that I will match it. But no matter what it is, Nathan was resolved that he was not giving up Karoline.

"I slept with Mordy."

To his own surprise, Nathan's first reaction was to laugh. How did Mordy do it?

"Not now. Years ago. When we were first dating."

"A lot?" The pain was setting in.

"One time. I was panicking. I had come to New York to be a bohemian, a free spirit, an artist. And I was getting deep into this Jewish family with the photocopy guy."

"The photocopy guy? And what was Mordy?"

"I know. It was stupid. And every time I see the photocopy guy, if it's just been a few hours you were away, I feel that I love my life because you have come back."

Nathan reached over and took some bread from her hands and tossed it over the fence into the river. "Gone."

"Yeah," Sonia said, smiling. "Gone."

And they turned their back to the river, now filled with floating scraps of bread, the sins of New York rushing out to sea, swirling quickly down the thick and soupy East River, spinning in circles as though someone had pulled the plug in New York Harbor. Nathan and Sonia walked together, his arm around her shoulder.

"We should take a vacation sometime," Nathan said pensively.

"That would be nice."

"It's okay if I bring along my mother?"

Sonia started laughing.

"What?" Nathan said. "It would cheer her up. I asked her where she would like to go and you'll never guess what she said."

"Puerto Rico?"

"Iceland."

"You're kidding."

"Where would you want to go?" Nathan asked.

"Really? You won't laugh?"

"Where?"

"Yellowstone Park," she confessed.

"Yellowstone Pa . . . Why?"

"I want to see the geyser, and the bears. And I miss mountains."

"I always wanted to go to Carlsbad Caverns."

"What do they have?"

"Bats, I think—"

"Oh," said Sonia. "Sarah got into a preschool."

"With swimming lessons?"

"I don't know."

"Learning swimming is important. It says so in the Talmud."

Nathan knew that he would never again taste that dangerous
hunger. He would never dare, though it might occasionally visit him in
a dream, just as Klara had intruded on Harry's sleep unexpectedly all his
life. Nathan would have to live with his lie. That was Karoline's curse
on him. And he knew that it was not his dreams that he needed to
worry about. Someday, in a dark tunnel under Manhattan, a nameless
demon would once again, without warning, grab him by the throat and
cut off all the air.

CHAPTER TWENTY-SIX

The Kishka Good-Bye

Nathan awoke remembering his dream. The sidewalk was lined with palm trees that hissed in the breeze, and the sun was so bright that it hurt his eyes. He saw Birdie Nagel in a sundress with a green parrot perched on her shoulder. And Mrs. Skolnik in a red-and-white bathing suit with a red wraparound skirt and large red-and-white hoop earrings. Arnie was sitting on the sidewalk in a turquoise shirt with red parrots and green leaves. He was sitting under a hot pink parasol that was torn and a little faded, and he was still wearing his wool beret but had a pink flamingo pin stuck on it.

"I found it on the beach," Arnie explained, and Nathan knew he meant the umbrella.

"God, it's great to see you. I thought you were dead."

"You know, they ship you to Staten Island and then to Boca."

Suddenly he heard someone singing. Nathan recognized it. It was Irving Berlin.

> *I'm going on a long vacation,*
> *Oh, you railroad station,*
> *First in years, so give three cheers . . .*

"Dad?"

It was Harry. Nathan ran up to him, but on the way, still dressed in army fatigues, he saw Finkelstein, who had died at Khe Sanh.

"How could you be here?"

"How? What do you mean, how? I'm from the neighborhood. They offered me a package—car rental included, medium compact!"

When Nathan woke up and reviewed this dream, he remembered that neither Arnie nor his father was going to show up in Boca or anywhere else. Harry did not exist anymore. His existence had been canceled. Like Ruth, Nathan understood this but could not comprehend it.

. . .

"What's this about being Italian?" Chucho Vega wanted to know.

"There was no future in being a Puerto Rican grocer," said Felix. "The Italians are doing well. The Puerto Ricans are going out of business. Let's face it, the *Loísaida es casi acabado*. This neighborhood is finished."

"Yeah," Chow Mein said reflectively, stroking his stubby ponytail by the side of his neck. "*Fartík*. Finished. Like boogaloo."

"No," said Felix. "Boogaloo might come back. But this is *gastado, acabado, finito, se acabo*—it's over."

Twelve Recipes
from the Neighborhood

CAPONATA

SAL FIRST'S CAPONATA

This is my mother's recipe. Any other way of making caponata and they would just laugh at you in Palermo.

2 nice big eggplants
Sicilian sea salt from Trapani
Olive oil, cold-pressed, virgin Sicilian—don't use that stuff from Tuscany
*   and Italy, and if you use Spanish, you should shoot yourself*
1 large onion, sliced
3 ripe plum tomatoes, peeled, seeded, and chopped
1 cup Sicilian red wine vinegar—if you use French, you'll be sorry
2 tablespoons Sicilian salted capers, soaked and dried
1 cup of the big Sicilian green olives
Freshly ground black pepper

Cut the eggplant into small cubes. Let stand in salt for 2 hours.

Heat the olive oil in a skillet with 1 cube of eggplant. When the eggplant starts to sizzle, add the rest.

In a separate pan, sauté onions and tomatoes and then a bit of water. After 10 minutes, add the rest of the ingredients and cook for another 10 minutes. Nothing else! Leave it alone.

SAL A'S CAPONATA

2 nice big eggplants
Salt
Olive oil
1 large onion, sliced
4 ripe plum tomatoes, peeled, seeded, and chopped
2 teaspoons sugar
1 cup red wine vinegar
2 tablespoons Sicilian salted capers, soaked and dried
1 cup of the big Sicilian green olives
½ teaspoon unsweetened cocoa powder
Freshly ground black pepper
2 ounces blanched sliced almonds

Cut the eggplant into small cubes. Let stand in salt for 2 hours.

Heat the olive oil in a skillet with 1 cube of eggplant. When the eggplant starts to sizzle, add the rest.

In a separate pan, sauté onions, then add tomatoes and a bit of water. After 10 minutes, add the rest of the ingredients except the almonds and cook for another 10 minutes.

When finished, sprinkle top with sliced almonds.

SALT COD

ROSA'S FRIDAY *BACALA POMIDORA*

Buy only a nice, well-cured *bacala* that you can grab by the tail and the whole thing will stick straight out like a board of wood. Soak for 3 days. Keep changing the water. For the last 24 hours, pinch off a taste from time to time. It should taste not too salty, but a little. Be careful not to soak all the salt out, or the curing, the soaking, the whole thing was for nothing.

Fry the fish in virgin olive oil. Heat a tomato sauce that can be made only in the summertime from ripe summer tomatoes skinned, seeded, and simmered slowly with a pinch of salt and a pinch of sugar and fresh-picked oregano leaves. Pour the sauce over the fish. The sauce freezes well to use the rest of the year.

SAL FIRST'S SICILIAN *BACALA*

First of all, forget about this Neapolitano thing with all the tomatoes. You soak the *bacala* until it is soft, then you sauté it in Sicilian olive oil with 2 chopped tomatoes, 1 teaspoon of soaked salted capers, and a handful of fresh oregano leaves.

Then—this is the part I don't like to talk about—you get one of those little hot green peppers and chop up only half of it and sauté it with the tomatoes and capers.

CONSUELA'S *BACALAITOS*

I remember in Puerto Rico, *bacalaítos* were sometimes full of chopped vegetables, especially red and green peppers, which made them very colorful. But when making *bacalaítos,* it is essential to understand that a lot of people like *bacalao,* but *everybody* likes garlic.

Buy a 1-pound box of salt-cured boneless *bacalao.* Soak the cod in water until it is soft—anywhere from 15 minutes to a day. Take equal amounts of cold water and flour and mix into a batter. It is nice to soak the fish in advance and then use that water for the batter. Add 7 or 8 finely chopped garlic cloves, a pinch of hot pepper, a little finely chopped cilantro. Chop fish into small pieces and work it into the batter with a wooden spoon or potato masher until you have a smooth but still liquid batter. If it's not liquid, work more water into the batter.

Heat cooking oil, olive is good, in a skillet until very hot, and carefully drop dollops of batter in. If the batter is the right consistency, it will spread out flat. Turn after 1 minute, and after both sides are brown place on a paper towel, which will absorb excess grease.

PUERTO RICAN HOLIDAY SPECIALTIES

MRS. RODRIGUEZ'S NUYORICAN
CREAM *PASTELES*

I make several *pasteles,* but these are my best, the ones I make for Christmas Eve. If they do not make them this way exactly on the island-we-love-so-much-we-all-had-to-leave, it's because these are better, no matter what certain snobs like to say.

Before you can make *pasteles,* you have to make some chicken broth, though the people in Cabo Rojos who are so fine use only water. But here in America, where we don't have to live on bananas and snails, we sometimes like to take a big hen and cook it slowly in water with onions, oregano, cilantro, garlic, salt, pepper, and some saffron until the chicken is falling off the bones, and that leaves a very nice broth that can be used in many things, including *pasteles.*

To make a *sofrito,* take a pan and heat olive oil. Add achiote seeds, diced cured ham, sliced garlic, 1 chopped onion, 1 chopped green pepper, salt, and ground black pepper. Stir until well sautéed and then add 5 skinned, seeded, and chopped tomatoes, a few leaves of cilantro, some leaves of culantro, and some fresh chopped parsley. Stir until it becomes a tomato sauce.

To make the filling, take 1 pound of pork and dice it. Put it in a pan with 3 cups chicken broth and 2 or 3 chopped garlic cloves. When the liquid is about half gone, spoon off 1 cup to use later. Add a little less than 1 pound of cured ham cut into large chunks, 1 cup of *sofrito,* ½ cup soaked and cooked chickpeas, and ½ cup raisins. Cook slowly with cover for 20 minutes.

To make the *masa grate,* take 10 peeled green bananas, 2 pounds peeled taro root, and 2 pounds peeled potatoes. They should all be grated finely. Mix this thoroughly with your fingers and add the leftover stock and ½ cup warm heavy cream. It is this cream to which so many self-appointed guardians of *Boriquismo* object, but that is also why my *pasteles* are best! Stir with a wooden spoon until the batter is smooth as satin and does not stick to the spoon. If it is too thick, add more cream and stock.

To put together, take 12 banana leaves and cut into about 9-inch squares. Fill a baking dish about halfway with hot water. Take a leaf square and dip it in the hot water so that it becomes soft. Pat it dry with a paper towel. Do all the leaves. Lay out the leaves and spread each with a thick coating of masa. Put filling in the center and fold over the leaves into a packet. Tie them shut and place them in a shallow pan of water. Cook for 45 minutes.

This recipe makes 12 *pasteles*, but if you make it right, you will need at least twice that many.

CONSUELA'S SATURDAY *GANDULES*

When we first decided to leave Puerto Rico, the first English I learned was that *gandules* in English were called "pigeon peas." One of the first things I learned in New York is that no one has ever heard of a pigeon pea. They are just *gandules* or, to Jamaicans, peas. You can buy them here dried and soak them in water for 2 hours with a smoked and split ham hock, some garlic, bay leaf, salt, and black pepper. Simmer on low heat for another half hour. If you have prepared 1 pound of *gandules,* add 2 cups *sofrito* (my *sofrito* is made by sautéeing tomatoes, onions, garlic, green peppers, and little cubes of spanish-style ham in olive oil). Keep simmering another half hour, stirring occasionally.

DRINKS

TED'S PINK MARTINIS
AS MADE AT SAGITTARIUS

These are definitely the martini of the future. Pour vodka into an old shaker (I like the art deco ones). Use a 5:1 ratio of vodka to cranberry juice. Then add equal amounts of triple sec and lime juice, the same quantity as cranberry juice. Add cracked but not crushed ice and stir gently. DO NOT SHAKE!

CHAIM'S ORIGINAL EGG CREAM

Chaim left this recipe to his son in his will, which was fortuitous, even though his son hated the store and sold it to Koreans at the first opportunity. Were it not for the will, his son never would have thought to give the formula to the Koreans, who followed it scrupulously and kept egg creams in the neighborhood.

In a tapered—the tapering is indispensable—paper cup, give 3 good squirts of chocolate syrup, which should yield no more than 2 ounces in the cup. Add 3 ounces of milk that is nearly frozen. It should be the consistency of the slush that we are forced to step in at every intersection of Second Avenue while it is cleared away for nice folk in uptown neighborhoods. But maybe this lack of experience with slush is why no one uptown can make a good egg cream. Fill the cup with seltzer by holding a spoon over the milk so that the seltzer shoots in from the hose, spins off the spoon, and hits the slush with enough force to cause an explosion of bubbles.

ALMOND COOKIES

SAL FIRST ON HIS MOTHER'S
MINNI DI VIRGINI

This is my mother's recipe, so you know what I mean. She takes powdered almonds with a little flour and a lot of butter and works it together into a dough, then adds sugar until it is sweet and 1 egg for about every 4 cups of dough so that it holds together and is easy to work. Chill it awhile. Roll the dough out about ⅛-inch thick and cut it in circles with an upside-down old-fashioned glass. Put on the center of each a *zuccata*—you know, the long Sicilian squash, soaked in jasmine petals and water and then candied like a preserve.

Sometimes you can buy this already candied or you can take some American squash that doesn't have any taste and is gone to seed. Soak jasmine leaves in water for a day or two. My mother always says "a day," but then how come I see these pots of flower petals around for half a week? Cook the squash (you could even use gourds) until they are tender, and dry them for an hour. It is best to dry them in the sun; my mother dried them on a wall, which is why in New York this is a good thing to make in the summer. Then make a thick syrup with sugar and water and cook the squash slowly, adding about 1 cup of jasmine water and cooking it down slowly until it is thick and jamlike.

Each circle should have a big hump of the squash. Then you put another circle of dough on top and stick it together with beaten egg white on the edge. You also brush the egg white on top. Then you bake them in the oven until they are browned, and that's it. Eat them while they are still warm, and it's unbelievable. But don't put anything on the top unless you want people to think you are some jerk from Catania who knows nothing.

BERNHARDT MOELLEN'S *ISCHLER KRAPFERLN*

This is from Ischl in the part of Austria where they have lakes and salt mines and mineral baths for your health. Wealthy people went for the baths, including the Emperor Franz Josef, and where there are wealthy people there are famous pastry makers.

> *70 grams, which is 2½ ounces powdered almonds*
> *50 grams, which is 1¾ ounces sugar*
> *100 grams, which is 3½ ounces butter*
> *150 grams, which us 5½ ounces flour*

Place all 4 ingredients neatly on a board and work them together with your fingers until you have a workable dough. Leave it for 30 minutes and it will be better. Roll to 1 centimeter thick, very thin, and with a cookie cutter cut circles and bake them in a 180° Centigrade, which is 350° Fahrenheit, oven for 30 minutes. After they cool, take the circles and make little sandwiches with either apricot or raspberry preserves in the center and cover with melted dark chocolate.

PASTRY

KAROLINE'S *KUGELHOPF*

This is not like my father's Austrian *kugelhopf*, which is the eastern extreme of *kugelhopfs*. Mine is the western extreme, from Alsace, and it is much more buttery. It is all about how much butter a light pastry can hold. It is made in an earthenware mold, which if used regularly becomes infused with butter so that it doesn't have to be greased before using.

> ½ cup granulated sugar
> 1 cup amber rum
> 1 cup raisins
> 1 cup chopped almonds
> 2 teaspoons salt
> 2 tablespoons sugar
> 1½ tablespoons milk
> 3 tablespoons baker's yeast
> 2 teaspoons warm water
> 3¾ cups flour
> 6 eggs
> 1 pound butter
> 12 whole almonds
> Powdered sugar

Everything in this recipe must be done in this exact order.

The day before baking:

1. Heat the sugar with the rum until the sugar crystals dissolve. Add the raisins and chopped almonds and remove from the heat. Store until tomorrow.

2. In a mixer, dissolve the salt, sugar, and milk.

3. Dissolve the yeast in the warm water until it is creamy.

4. Add the flour to the mixing bowl and mix well with the salt, sugar, and milk.

5. Add the yeast.

6. Beat 2 minutes on a low speed.

7. Add 4 eggs and beat until homogeneous.

8. Add 2 more eggs.

9. Beat on medium speed for 10–15 minutes until it feels silky and no longer sticks to your fingers.

10. Cut up the butter into egg-size pieces and add them to the dough while beating. This must be done quickly and must take no more than 2 minutes.

11. Cover the bowl with a cloth and leave in a warm—not hot—place until the dough doubles in size. This could take as little as 90 minutes or as much as 2½ hours.

12. Slap it to let out the air and reshape into small bowl. Avoid too much handling. Place it in the bowl, cover with cloth, and place in the refrigerator.

13. After 2–3 hours, it will have doubled again. Slap it down once more and leave it to rise overnight in the refrigerator.

The next day:

Butter the mold if necessary. If you cannot find an earthenware one, there are many fluted, circular metal molds that provide a hole in the middle. At the bottom of each flute, place 1 whole almond. They will form a crown at the top once the cake is turned out. Roll the dough into a rectangle. Place the rum-soaked raisin-and-almond filling down the center. Roll the dough into a tube and wrap it around the center of the mold. Bake in a medium oven until the room is filled with the wonderful scent of butter. Take it out and turn it out. After it cools, dust it with powdered sugar.

MARK KURLANSKY is the James A. Beard Award–winning author of the *New York Times* bestseller *Salt: A World History*; *1968: The Year That Rocked the World*; *The Basque History of the World*; *Cod: A Biography of the Fish That Changed the World*; *A Chosen Few: The Resurrection of European Jewry*; *A Continent of Island: Searching for the Caribbean Destiny*; a collection of stories, *The White Man in the Tree*; and a children's book, *The Cod's Tale*, as well as the editor of *Choice Cuts: A Savory Selection of Food Writing from Around the World and Throughout History*. He lives in New York City.